To the b[...]
the world, [...]
for being the number
1 fangirl for my charac-
ters ♥

OF
LIARS
AND
THIEVES

Book One

Gabriela Lavarello

For Ginny. Thank you for helping me take the next step in making this book a reality. I am forever grateful.

And for thirteen year old me who wanted to tell stories for a living. We did it.

NOTE

A pronunciation guide is provided at the back of the book, after the acknowledgments.

Dragonkeep

Clelac Crag

DROLATIS

Creonid
Mountain

EONID

LAKE
LAGDRANULE

Steel Mountains

The Keep

CRUBIA

Notharis

i Citadel

RIA

Mitonir

Naldir

FARRADOR

OF

ARA

OF

LIARS

AND

THIEVES

PROLOGUE

Firelight flickered across the storyteller's silver eyes as he stared off into the distance, his mind far from the pub in which he was currently seated.

It was another peaceful night in a small village within Proveria, the fairy kingdom of Raymara. The moon was full, and the first day of fall would greet them with the rising sun. The smell of roasted lamb and old ale mixed with burning wood drifted through the storyteller's nose, acidity from the ale the only thing tethering a small corner of his mind to reality.

The rest of his mind was consumed by the heavy burden recently laid upon him. The storyteller knew his orders, and he was about to act against them. An image of his employer flashed through his mind, and sharp pain lashed through his insides, causing his hand to knock his mug and slosh ale across the table. The storyteller cursed, partially at the reek of alcohol that now clung to his tattered grey robes, but also at the spell that bound him to pain if he ever even whispered the name of his employer.

The storyteller shook his head, fully bringing himself back into the small pub. He was almost surprised by the roar of conversation and hearty laughter that rang through his ears, and he looked around to find the pub now full. He must have been seated in his thoughts for hours, for the small rickety room had been nearly empty the last time he remembered. Now was the time, then. There were enough people to listen to his tale. The storyteller's heart leaped into his throat as he wiped his ale-coated fingers along his ruined robes and opened his mouth to speak.

"I would like to tell a story of five beasts that existed before the war," the storyteller's low voice carried through the room. "They now only exist in books and nightmares."

A large man wearing a frayed cloak turned his head from his stew and frowned at the silver-eyed storyteller. The other occupants of the pub followed suit, shaking their heads and whispering to one another.

"Raymara is a peaceful realm, as it has been for a thousand years," the large man barked. "We are not interested in listening to your violent tales."

The man was right, but Raymara had not always been a realm of peace. It was once a place of bloodshed and endless darkness, the War of Seven Kingdoms the foundation from which the thousand-year peace was built. It was a time when the seven kingdoms were in turmoil, the king or queen of each kingdom claiming themselves fit to rule the entire realm as their own. Legend had it that the five goddesses that created Raymara came to the land and aided in ending the war, thus eradicating all creatures of violence and creating a peace law that ended all turmoil and lasted until this very night. For that peace was soon to end.

"I agree with you," a skeletal fairy woman slurred from a different table near the fire. "Why fill your head with such nonsense? Your terrible stories will only bring darkness to the realm once more."

"It is not only a tale of terror and darkness," the storyteller

2

spat. "It is the future, and if you do not hear what I have to say, you will not be prepared for what is to come."

The entire pub erupted with laughter, and anger boiled inside of the storyteller. He knew these foolish common folk in this unnamed village wouldn't care to listen to him. The laughter continued, and soon mocking boos and sniggers began to intertwine with the noise. The storyteller clenched his pale hands and stood abruptly from his seat, not caring when his chair clattered to the floor.

He raised his voice and yelled over the racket, "You will all regret making a fool of me by the end of this night. Mark my words!"

The storyteller pushed through the sea of fairies and rushed toward a rickety flight of wooden stairs near the back of the room. He passed by the bar, where the rotund pub keeper was attempting to hold back a smile as he wiped down the gleaming mahogany.

The storyteller fumbled through his cloak pockets and fished out the single rusted key that the pub keeper had given him when he arrived earlier in the day. He muttered under his breath, not caring about his loud stomping or the questionable give of the steps under his feet. Once he reached the landing, he started blindly down the hall, barely stopping before he shoved the key into the keyhole of the last door of the walkway and turned his hand. The door did not budge. His roar echoed through the narrow hall as he slammed against the door with a bony shoulder.

The door burst open loudly and the storyteller stumbled into the room. He shut the door behind him with a bang and looked around his musty accomodations. It was mostly bare apart from a small cot in one corner, a desk against the wall to his left, and a small dirty window looking out over the small forested street of the village below.

The storyteller walked to the window and pushed it open

3

with a creak. He was able to make out the figures of people milling about, preparing themselves for sleep as the sky darkened from navy to black. An eerie white glow was beginning to spill over the tall pines, the full moon nearly visible from the storyteller's room.

Everything was calm, for now. The storyteller sighed and turned from the window, untying the leather buckle of his traveling cloak, which was thankfully saved from his spilled ale. He hadn't eaten this night, yet he had to admit that was partially his fault for being lost in his thoughts for only the goddesses knew how long. He would have to sleep hungry.

The rough feeling of parchment grazed his fingers as he began to fold his cloak. He paused. His story had not been told, but that didn't mean that he had failed at his mission. He could still carry out his task with charcoal and parchment.

Each stroke bit angrily into the parchment and yellow light sparked and glowed from the storyteller's hand as he made long strokes and shaded in his creations. He knew the fate that was to fall upon Raymara. He was responsible for it. There would be five, and it would hopefully be enough. It would be the downfall of the realm, as well as the only way he could ensure a way out of the terrible things to come.

With one last flourish of charcoal, the storyteller leaned back in his chair and examined his work. A satisfied smile played at his lips as he looked at the drawings, each beast different and terrifying in its own way. He knew that once they were let out, the realm would never be the same. It would cause great fear amongst the people of every kingdom, yet he had sworn to let them out, sworn it with his own blood. Only not yet. He knew that his employer would be less than pleased to find out about his wrongdoings, but it was the only way. A shiver ran down his spine, followed by a spasm of pain in his abdomen, and the storyteller shook himself back to reality.

He set down the charcoal and stood from the rickety chair

with a groan, the joints in his shoulders popping as he stretched his arms over the white mess of hair atop his head. His entire being begged for sleep and he realized just how much magic had drained from him as he staggered to the cot and sat, kicking off his worn boots.

The low burning candle upon the table winked and flickered as he settled into the thin mattress with a groan. It was not comfortable in the slightest, but it was much better than the forest floor that he had made his bed for the past few weeks.

"With the swift approach of midnight, the meager wax candle atop the old oak table went out with a puff of smoke."

At the sound of the storyteller's words, the candle extinguished with a small puff of smoke, leaving the room dark spare a long beam of silver light that filtered from the window. The storyteller closed his eyes, the last remnants of the beasts galloping, roaring, and slashing through his mind before sleep overtook him.

Smoke.

His eyes flew open, the sounds of screams and roars coming from the street below grating his ears. He coughed and looked to the window, realizing that his scratchy throat was due to smoke streaming silently through the crack he had left open.

The storyteller leaped from the cot and tugged on his boots. He took two long strides to the window and stuck his head out to find a horrifyingly magnificent scene below. The thatched rooftops were ablaze and dark figures of people were running and screaming frantically through the street. A grotesque horned creature with dark red flesh chased after a young man, its ear-splitting scream sending a shiver down the storyteller's spine. A flash of something below the window caught his eye, and a curse flew from his lips at the sight of a scaly emerald green tail disappearing around the corner. The storyteller was barely able to register what he saw before a cacophonous, bone-chilling roar sounded from the sky.

The storyteller's blood went cold as he looked up to find an enormous black dragon silhouetted in the full moon, its giant membranous wings flapping as it circled the village. Two long ivory horns protruded from the top of its head and large spikes lined the length of its spine. Black dragons had been extinct for a thousand years, but the storyteller found that he wasn't surprised in the least to see the beast.

A sickening feeling went through his bones as he turned and lunged for the desk, already knowing what he would find. He muttered a few words and the candle sputtered to life, the weak flame giving him enough visibility to ruffle through the pages strewn across the desk. A shaky breath escaped from his parted lips as he took up one of the now blank pages of parchment, not even a mark of charcoal giving evidence to the beasts that had been carefully drawn upon them mere hours ago.

As if in confirmation, a loud crash, followed by the sounds of what seemed like hundreds of small men chattering to each other, echoed on the other side of his closed door. He held his breath and listened as the voices stopped and the stomp of dozens of little feet made their way down the hall and out of earshot.

A nervous laugh escaped the storyteller's mouth, and he threw the pages back onto the desk. It had worked. His creations had come to life by the powerful magic of his dreams. His stomach dropped, and he knew that the prophecy had now been set into motion. The storyteller was supposed to be glad of the chaos, for it meant he was one step closer to getting what he wanted, but he found only fear and bile in his stomach. He needed to get out of this pub before the dragon he created set it on fire.

The storyteller flung on his cloak and reached down toward the pages, yet his fingers faltered. *Best to deliver these to the fairies,* he thought. He would make sure the other three pages would be sent to the right hands.

With a shaky curse, the storyteller folded three empty pages into one pocket and two in the other before moving toward the door. He needed to leave before the fairy guards found him. They would likely arrive shortly, so he needed to be swift and careful as he left. With a final spell, the candle was blown out, and only the echoes of screams and a whisper of smoke remained as the storyteller closed the door behind him with a soft click.

❧ I ❧

LORIAN

The stench of death and other ungodly smells clung to Lorian Grey's nose, and his stomach threatened to empty the small amount of stale bread and cold soup he'd been given that day.

He'd forgotten what day it was, or how many days he'd been locked in the damp dungeon of Crimson Castle, the king's home within Crimson City, Keadora's capital.

Lorian had waltzed into the witch kingdom knowing very well that the mission he'd been given was a fool's errand, and yet he found himself surprised to still be in a cell. No one had ever tried to steal the bloodstone before, a witch relic from the days during the War of Seven Kingdoms. Lorian had never cared for history or fairytales, but he knew the legend of the bloodstone. It was said to have been gifted to the first Red King by Adustio, the sun goddess and creator of witches and humans. For thousands of years, the bloodstone had been passed down from one Red King to another, never to leave the possession of the most ancient witch bloodline and dynasty in the realm.

Everyone knew that stealing the bloodstone could never be done, but what was a little danger to Lorian? A chuckle rumbled through his emaciated body. He knew that he was fearless, but accepting this mission from the nameless bandit lord had erred on the side of foolishness.

Lorian looked down and clenched his dirt-encrusted hands with a shiver of frustration. He needed to get out, and he needed to get out soon. The cramped cell that he had been thrown into was dim and dirty, with only a pile of damp straw in a corner that he used as a bed. A small crack in the far wall was his only source of natural light and fresh air.

The floor under his filthy boots vibrated, and Lorian rolled his eyes at what he now knew was the opening and closing of the dungeon entrance. The stomp of heavy boots against stone soon echoed through the walls, but there was something different. Lorian shot his head up and leaned toward the cell bars. He careened his head toward the hall to his right, carefully avoiding the sight of the cell directly across from his. That cell was home to a rotting corpse that had been there since he'd arrived, which partially gave credit to the terrible stench holding thick in the air.

Lorian narrowed his attention to find the shadowy figures of three men approaching. One guard would have been normal, for it was the typical sign that his tasteless meals were coming for him. Three men meant something entirely different, yet he wasn't quite sure what. Lorian stood to his feet, gripping the cold metal bars for support and forcing himself to remain upright.

Their faces came into view and Lorian nearly cried out in relief. It was the fair-haired commander of the Ten, the Red King's most uniquely skilled and trained warriors. The Ten had been the ones to capture Lorian, so he wasn't surprised when the commander flashed him a humorless grin of recognition. Two stony-faced guards flanked him on either side, and a loop of gleaming keys jangled between the commander's gloved fingers.

"Ah," Lorian began, his low voice cracking from lack of use, "I must say, it is a delight to see your terribly handsome face again."

The commander's grin widened a fraction as he approached the cell, his tall muscular frame towering over Lorian's own frail body even though they were nearly the same height. The man's black armor made his wide chest and arms all the more intimidating, and he looked Lorian up and down before shoving a key into the cell's large padlock.

"I think you look much better since I found you falling from the Red King's throne," the commander replied, and jerked his chin at the guards.

They entered the now open cell and an especially sour-faced guard shoved Lorian forward. He stumbled and let out an involuntary wheeze, inwardly cursing at his body's protest to the sudden movement. The guards took their places at either side of Lorian, each grabbing one of his shoulders tightly.

Lorian found that the smell of death slowly faded as they made their way through hallways faintly lit by witchlight, the click of the guard's shining boots echoing through the stone walls. Every joint in his body groaned in protest with each step they took through the nearly deserted dungeons. Every few cell doors, a grime-streaked hand reached out through the bars toward them. Most of the poor souls locked in the cells were likely even more innocent than Lorian was, which wasn't very hard to achieve. Raymara was a peaceful land, after all, and being a thief was one of the most dangerous and illegal professions that existed.

"May I ask why you have come to set me free after I nearly stole your kingdom's most precious rock?" Lorian asked, his fingers itching toward his now too loose belt where his dagger should have been, but it was now sheathed at the commander's side.

"You aren't going to be set free, I can assure you that much," the commander replied confidently.

Lorian's spirits dropped slightly, but he continued forward. It wasn't like he had much choice in the matter, as the guards were nearly dragging his emaciated body toward whatever fate he was to face. They turned a corner, and the whisper of fresh air danced across Lorian's face as they came to a tall flight of stairs that ended in a heavy iron door. His legs trembled at the thought of walking all the way to the top in his current physical state. The guard to his left shoved him forward and Lorian stumbled his way up the first steps.

Hot frustration burned Lorian's cheeks. He was so frail, so weak. This was not the body of a master thief, this was the body of a dead man. Lorian was strong, and he was smarter and faster than these three men put together.

"If I'm not being freed, then why have you come for me?" Lorian panted as they reached the top landing.

The fair-haired commander did not answer, but instead withdrew the same ring of keys from his belt and promptly unlocked the iron door. The door swung open with a groan, and Lorian had to stifle a gasp as bright sunlight and cool air flooded over him, colors bursting across his vision.

"Don't just stand there like a blundering idiot, move," the guard on his left barked, and shoved him forward again.

"You don't need to shove me, I'm perfectly capable of walking without an assisted start," Lorian made himself reply, though he had to admit that he was still out of breath and terribly tired from the flight of stairs they had just finished climbing.

Lorian gaped at the floor-to-ceiling windows and bright marble hallway that he had not seen during his descent to the dungeons, as he had been quite preoccupied with a blindfold over his eyes at the time. The marble floors were spotless, and he brought his attention back to the windows to find an immaculate garden of hedges and white roses below. Indeed, the air smelled of roses, and Lorian felt sick from the strength of the perfume-like scent in the castle. It was nearly as overwhelming as the smell that Lorian's unfortunate corpse of a neighbor had given off in the dungeons.

The commander pulled once on the thick iron handle of the dungeon door with a gloved hand and nodded to the guards, who tightened their grip on Lorian once more and began down the hallway. Lorian kept himself occupied by watching the commander's short hair bounce with each step he took, which helped him ignore the countless paintings of previous Red Kings glaring down upon him with their identical black eyes. They rounded one corner and Lorian glanced at a painting of the current Red King, the oldest ruler in Raymarian history.

Rough cloth swept over Lorian's head, obscuring his view of the endless portrait-lined hallways. The blind itched his skin, and he let out an involuntary grunt as a hand pushed him forward.

"Again with the blindfold?" Lorian sighed.

"Let's go," growled the sour-tempered guard in reply.

"I must ask, why can't you Keadorans ever give a clear answer to my questions?" Lorian asked. "You have always been the most difficult lot to work with in my ten years of thievery."

"Perhaps it's because we are smarter than most and know better than to give clear answers to men like you," the commander replied, and Lorian could hear the hint of warning in his tone.

Lorian raised a brow under his hood and shrugged in response. It wasn't that the commander was wrong, in fact, it was the answer that Lorian expected to come from an arrogant ass like him.

They continued winding through the castle, and Lorian's head soon began to swim with both exhaustion and the permeating scent of roses in the air. He needed to figure out what was going on, and then he needed to escape somewhere far away from this terrible kingdom. Perhaps he would attempt a return to Farrador, the elf kingdom, as well as his birthplace. The mere thought made him stifle a snort and shake his head. No, he would much rather test stepping into Crubia's cursed lands than attempt a second chance of life in Farrador.

A shiver went through Lorian's body at the memory of endless seas of grey sand and hot air that blew against his face from across the shimmering kingdom border. Crubia, the death kingdom, as people called it, had been the first cursed kingdom that Lorian had ever seen in his life, and had been his only sliver of evidence that the stories of the Red King's curse was true. Lorian had found himself curious as to what would have happened if he'd stepped across the border from the elf kingdom into Crubia. Would he have been stuck and never able to step back into Farrador, as the legends said? Or would he find that he could simply walk back to the warmth of tall trees and lush grasses? Lorian had never been foolish enough to try, yet he found himself curious whenever his journeys brought him close to the death kingdom.

A hand ripped the bag from Lorian's head and he was blinded by brilliant light once more. He blinked the kaleidoscope of colors from his vision to find that they were approaching a flight of steps lined with slanted windows at either side. Lorian craned his neck to look out of the windows and his heart leaped—not at the sight of a perfectly groomed garden, but of a hill with browning grass that led to the expanse of Crimson City. Lorian could not see people through the tall buildings and thatched roofs, but he was sure that if he were outside he would hear voices and smell the faint waft of fresh bread and baked goods. His mouth watered at the thought of fresh bread, and he quickly put it at the top of his list of things to do once he escaped the castle.

He let his attention drift closer to find tall trees lining the white castle walls, the very tops brushing softly against the bottom of the windows. Delicate deep orange vines wound along the marble walls like a spider web, and Lorian tore his attention from the windows with a shudder as flame and caramel-colored eyes flashed across his memory. A pang of regret shot through his heart at the thought of the girl he would never see again.

The steps opened to a hall that was wider than the previous, a pair of ceiling-high oak doors waiting at the far end. Two guards were stationed at either side of the door, their eyes staring unblinkingly ahead with no acknowledgment of Lorian or the commander's approach. The guards turned stiffly and stepped forward, each taking a brass handle and pulling the doors open.

"Thank you, gentlemen." Lorian inclined his head toward the guards, who didn't even blink. "Perhaps a few lessons in hospitality would suit you well."

The commander of the Ten kept walking without a remark and turned abruptly to stand in line with nine other armor-clad men to Lorian's right. Lorian continued until he glanced up and staggered to a stop at the sight of the man seated upon the throne before him.

The Red King gazed down upon him, and Lorian shrank from the power that radiated from the ancient yet ageless ruler. His crimson robes and white hair were stark against the black iron throne upon which he was seated. The Red King was over one thousand years old, and it was said that the four remaining goddesses had granted him something close to immortality as a gift for aiding the end of the war. Lorian hadn't believed the tales until now. Now there was no way of doubting the Red King's eternal power and age, as it nearly radiated from him. His skin was smooth and white, his black eyes watching Lorian stumble forward before the guards released his shoulders and took two steps back to stand behind him.

"Welcome, Lorian Grey." The Red King's calm and yet spine-tingling voice echoed through the room.

Lorian gulped and bowed his head, now only mere feet from the throne. He focused on the plush crimson rug under his grimy boots, searching for anything to keep him from looking up at the Red King and the stone embedded into the throne above his head. The bloodstone.

"You must be wondering why I have invited you to stand before me." The king smiled.

Lorian dared to look up, giving the king a half-smile in return. "I must say yes, however I am not surprised that you wanted to get one last glance at my dashing good looks before you sentenced me to the Nether."

The Nether was the underworld, the realm where beings crossed to when their time in Raymara was over. It was a place of both demons and angels, goddesses and devils. Legend had it that the Red King seated before Lorian was the reason for its creation. During his final battle with Lux one thousand years ago, the Red King placed a curse upon the goddess and her kingdoms, turning her into Nex, goddess of death and destruction. Once the curse spread to Naebatis and Crubia, she fled to the underworld, turning the Nether into her new kingdom.

"Is it true that you were the one to curse Nex so that she couldn't take over Raymara? I have always been curious," Lorian added with a widening grin.

The Red King did not smile, but simply turned his head and motioned for Lorian's new commander friend to step forward.

"You," the king began, "can you swear upon your life and the honorable position which you uphold that this thief can be trusted?"

"I'd like to call myself more of a professional borrower of possessions," Lorian interjected.

It wasn't that he hated the term "thief", in fact, it granted him respect from even the most frightening of men. Lorian only wished for the current bounty upon his head from many years of unfinished jobs to be terminated, and to perhaps have the ability to make thievery a side occupation instead of his main identity.

Neither the king nor the commander acknowledged Lorian's words before the commander bowed low and answered, "Yes, my king. I can assure you that with right motivation and company, this man can help."

Lorian glanced at the commander with raised brows. He was trying to help set Lorian free? If so, what had the commander's words meant when they were leaving the dungeons? Lorian turned his attention back to the king, who tapped a long finger against the arm of his throne in contemplation.

"May I ask exactly what I am supposed to help with?" Lorian asked in confusion. "I am not being picky, I am simply curious."

The Red King's dark eyes sharpened back to Lorian. After a moment, the king seemed to decide that it was appropriate to divulge the mystery, and his expression turned grave.

"About one moon ago, three very dangerous beasts were unleashed by a storyteller's drawings. They destroyed a village in Proveria and are now running rampant and causing unrest throughout the five inhabited kingdoms."

A shudder went through Lorian's body. Storytellers were beings of immense power, born from books during the War of Seven Kingdoms to join the witch ranks. They did not belong to any single kingdom, as they were not truly born from bones and blood. Storytellers were both human and not, their magic contained within the stories they wove. Depending on the stories they told, creatures and events of either great beauty or horror would result from their weavings.

"That is truly awful. I apologize that I wasn't aware of this event, but I was slightly preoccupied with trying to stay alive in your dungeons," Lorian answered in a tone edged like a sharp blade.

The Red King chuckled, showing perfectly straight white teeth. "You attempted to steal the bloodstone," he replied. "You should count your blessings. You would have been sent to the Nether right away if my commander had not told me of your skills."

Lorian did not respond. He would not have been caught trying to steal the bloodstone if he had any real skill. Though he had not truly attempted to steal it. The bandit lord who had given him the mission was an idiot, and Lorian had taken the job simply to get out of Fortula, the only human-ruled city in Keadora. The risk of actually stealing the stone had been too high and he was not foolish enough to complete the task for only fifty pieces of gold.

"Bring in the witch," the Red King ordered after a moment of silence.

The large oak doors groaned as the guards opened them once more. Faint footsteps approached, and Lorian made an effort to remain facing the king instead of turning to see their new visitor. And then she was at his side. All breath was knocked out of Lorian's body and his vision blurred as his eyes landed on the witch.

She was as beautiful as he remembered, but older. Her healthy frame was clad in a simple grey healer's gown, and a weathered leather belt empty of any weapons was tied around her waist. Her long chocolate brown hair was fashioned into a long braid down her back, and her olive-toned skin was flushed with anger.

"Finriel?" The name felt foreign against Lorian's lips as he sputtered her name in surprise.

She turned her head to look at him, and he was sure that it was her by her eyes. They were the color of deep caramel, save for the dark orange veins winding around her pupils that set her apart from anyone he had ever met. A look of horrified surprise washed over her striking face. She cursed and looked away from him, her hands clenched into fists.

"What are you doing here?" Finriel hissed under her breath.

"What am I doing here? I thought you were dead," Lorian blurted. He couldn't breathe. The familiar sensation of guilt and regret that he had long since buried within reared its ugly head once more.

"Ah," the Red King said with a wry smile. "I see you two already know each other. I suppose I do not need to make introductions, then. Commander Tedric Drazak, please step forward."

The fair-haired commander of the Ten strode forward, his expression a mask of mild surprise.

So that was his name. Lorian didn't have to imagine the man as Stuck-Up Bastard or Fabulous-Haired Sissy. The Red King spoke again and Lorian broke from his thoughts, the tightness in his chest spasming like a fish out of water.

"The mission you must complete is very simple," the king began. "The three of you will embark on a quest at the rise of the new sun. With the aid of one of our kingdom's enchanted maps, you will take the blank pages we recovered and find these terrible monsters. Once they are all safely in your possession, you will find the storyteller and return both him and the drawings to me."

"Why choose us?" Finriel snapped. "And what do we get in return?"

The king studied the witch, and something strange flashed across his eyes that sent unease through Lorian. It was gone in a heartbeat, and Lorian began to question if he'd imagined the Red King's look.

"I have chosen each of you because of your unique skills, which I am confident can do great things when combined. Finriel Caligari, I have seen your work in the city and neighboring villages. Your healing magic is nearly unmatched even by the most experienced witches, which is surprising since you are only just over twenty years of age. Your skills and able physical state will be necessary on a journey as dangerous as the one you are to face."

Finriel's face turned a deep shade of pink and she looked away from the king.

"And you, Lorian Grey." The king slid his steely gaze to the thief. "I have been informed that you are the most skilled thief and trickster in the realm. If your skills are used correctly, I am confident that you will be able to find the monsters quickly and find a way of recovering them into the pages without much difficulty."

Lorian dipped his head in a small bow and winked at the king. "You flatter me, though I am not surprised in the least to have been picked. As you said, I am the best."

The Red King ignored his words and faced Tedric. "As for you, Commander Drazak, you are my most loyal and fierce warrior. I know that you will keep these two fools on task and ensure that the pages are returned to me safely."

"I would be interested in knowing what our reward will be if we say yes to this quest," Lorian said.

"Your reward is your head staying on your shoulders," the Red King snapped. "And if you return to Keadora alive with all three drawings and the storyteller in your company, I will wipe all of your wrongdoings clean. You could start a new life with that privilege."

Silence filled the room. Lorian didn't know what to say. The thought of never again having to sneak through cities because the bounty on his head was larger than the size of his purse sounded very good. He hated constantly having to look over his shoulder to make sure he didn't see a familiar face. He bowed his head in gratitude, the fear of being sent to the Nether at the hands of the Red King fading.

"I will also ensure that each of you receive five thousand gold pieces for your time and success, if that suits you," the Red King finished.

"Why do you want us to return the drawings to you instead of simply destroying them?" Finriel asked, completely ignoring the offer of more money than Lorian had ever seen in his life.

"We will take the money, if you needed a confirmation," Lorian interjected, and Finriel shot him a look of pure disgust.

The Red King nodded to Lorian and straightened in his seat. Power radiated from the king's body, and Lorian and Finriel shrank back from the throne. "I am not required to tell a simple witch girl the reasons behind my decisions, but if it is the only way to keep you satisfied enough to hold your tongue, so be it."

Lorian bristled at the harshness of the Red King's words, but forced himself to remain silent as the king opened his mouth and spoke again.

"I would like you to bring me back the pages and the story-teller so that I may question him and force him to destroy the drawings. You must understand that storytellers are wicked and mischievous. It is highly unlikely that the storyteller created the pages without enchanting them in some way to prevent destruction. Does that answer satisfy you?"

Finriel dropped the king's gaze and nodded curtly in response.

"I am also sure you are curious about your mother's where-abouts, are you not?" the Red King asked with the trace of a smile.

Finriel tensed and shot the king a look of both hope and terror. "How do you know of my mother?"

The Red King sighed. "I ordered her banishment, of course. No witch is allowed to practice battle magic in the middle of my city, nor in any part of Raymara. I do apologize that the ordeal occurred mere hours after your birth."

Finriel grimaced. "Where is she?"

"She is safe in the Witch Isles, where I sent her," the Red King replied calmly.

"How do I know that you are telling the truth?" Finriel asked, her voice nearly a hiss.

"It was only common sense to send her to the birthplace of our kind, where she could live the rest of her days with the priestesses and learn from them. She is of course banned from ever stepping foot off the isle, but she is safe."

"Will I be able to see her once the mission is completed?"

"Of course," the king replied. "I will have a ship with safe passage ready for you the day you arrive with the pages and their creator."

Lorian watched Finriel sort through the king's words in her mind, his breath catching at her terrifying beauty, as well as her proximity.

Finriel huffed, "Fine, I'll do it."

The Red King clapped his hands together and leaned back into his throne. "Well then, now that this matter is settled, we can move on. You will travel by foot, as horseback is quicker yet more dangerous. I expect for the three of you to depart Keadora at dawn, so I have arranged for you three to stay the night in the castle for promptness sake."

The king motioned toward a door near the back corner of the room that Lorian had not seen before. It opened silently, and a very unfortunate looking creature scuffled through it and headed toward Lorian and Finriel. The creature's skin was grey and gnarled, and heavy dark brown robes were wrapped around its hunched body. Two grey horns protruded from the top of its head and small pointed ears flicked back and forth directly below them. The being was not a human, but a gargoyle.

"Ah yes, Agonur," the king muttered. "Can you please lead these three ... companions to their temporary rooms?"

The gargoyle bent its already hunched body into a low bow, and an odd guttural sound uttered from its mouth. The creature then straightened and extended a dark clawed hand, indicating for Lorian, Finriel, and Tedric to follow it out of the room. Tedric bowed low to the king and Lorian simply gave a bright smile and a nod, which was frankly all he felt like his body could muster at the moment. Finriel merely glared at the king for a split second longer before she dipped her gaze and turned, brushing past Lorian and following Agonur. She paused after a few steps and faced the Red King once more.

"I need to go back to my cottage and gather my things."

Lorian looked between Finriel and the Red King, who sighed and shook his head.

"I am afraid that will not be possible. All of the supplies you will each need for the journey will be waiting for you in your rooms, and your mogwa will also be there when you arrive."

Finriel bristled and barely managed a nod toward the king before she spun on her heel and stalked out the door. Lorian offered one last tilt of his head toward the king before he made his way behind the gargoyle and Finriel, who were already leaving him behind.

Fresh air flowed through the now open windows that lined the halls, giving Lorian some relief from the insufferable rose scent. Lorian shivered at the foreign brush of cool air on his skin and sighed with pleasure at the faint birdsong in the distance, along with the idle chatter and city noises beyond. Lorian had almost forgotten what fresh air smelled or felt like. His chest expanded with a lightness he hadn't felt in a very long time and a smile began to play at his cracked lips.

Tedric strode calmly at Lorian's side and a grin spread across his chiseled face at the apparent look of elation coming from Lorian. He gestured at the window and his chocolate brown eyes flicked toward the city.

"All of the windows disappear at sunset and appear at night-fall so that fresh air can flow through the castle."

Lorian cocked his head to the side and glanced at Finriel's stiff and obviously livid figure, but quickly looked away again after his empty stomach gave an uncomfortable flop.

"That's how I entered your precious castle, you know," Lorian replied casually. "Your system makes it far too easy for unwanted visitors to infiltrate."

The commander stiffened but continued to look out of the open windows. The enormous expanse of grassy hills was now browning, the rows of cottages and buildings in orderly clusters near the castle blending into the changing terrain. Lorian supposed that fall had approached swiftly during his time in incarceration.

"I am aware of that," Tedric said. "But not many people are as foolish as you were to enter the Crimson Castle without proper invitation."

Lorian chuckled, thinking that perhaps he would grow to like Tedric Drazak. The new companions followed Agonur around a corner and the circulation of air dulled considerably. After a few moments, they found themselves in a dimly lit hallway bare of windows. Dozens of dark wooden doors lined either wall, and the gargoyle's loud breath bounced uncomfortably off the narrow space.

"This one on the right is yours, good warrior, sir," Agonur said in a raspy voice as he gestured toward the first door on their right.

Tedric stepped forward and nodded at both Finriel and Lorian before he grasped the brass door handle. "I will meet you two at first light in the stables." With that, Tedric opened the door and disappeared into his room with a soft click.

Both Finriel and Lorian remained in tense silence as the gargoyle shuffled forward, and moments later, he indicated a door a few feet to the left that was meant for the witch. Finriel grabbed the door and yanked it open, stepping through and slamming it behind her with a loud bang.

"She frightens me," the gargoyle said with a timid smile, and angled his head to look at Lorian.

Lorian nodded in silent agreement and the creature simply indicated the door directly across from Finriel's. "Your room, young thief, sir."

Lorian thanked the gargoyle before he strode to the door and stepped inside his room. He wondered if he could ever remove the title of thief from his name after this mission and shook his head with a chuckle as he closed the door. No, even with his bad history removed, he would still retain the name. It had been his partially unwanted badge of honor since he was eleven years old.

Lorian turned and his heart stopped at the simple splendor of the room around him. The light marble walls arched into gloriously carved designs on the ceiling and an extravagant chandelier hung at the center of the room, the orange and red crystals bathing the room in a warm kaleidoscope of color.

Lorian brought his attention to the plush rug before him, which was the same color as the rubies hanging from the chandelier. A large oak dresser was pressed against the far wall, presumably void of any clothing. Yet it wasn't the dresser or the carpet, or even the chandelier and carved ceiling, that made Lorian's already weak knees wobble. It was the bed.

The bed was large enough to hold five grown men with room to spare. Cream-colored sheets and stuffed pillows beckoned, and Lorian staggered over to it, kicking off his torn boots carelessly as he went. Lorian reached out to touch the silk covers, but paused and retracted his filth-encrusted hands. He would need a bath before even considering lying upon those sheets. A shiver ran down his spine at the thought of using water to bathe himself instead of simply drinking or splashing it upon his face.

Lorian turned and spotted an archway that led to another dark room. He moved toward it and a warm light glowed to life from an unknown source. A simple metal tub was placed in the center of the room and a stone basin full of water stood in the far corner. A small window overlooked the city, the nearly set sun bathing the room in more glowing light.

Lorian strode to the bathtub and blinked in amazement as steaming hot water began to fill it. He looked around, but there was no logical source for the flowing water. It was magic. Lorian shook his head and began to peel off his disgusting rags.

"Witches," he grumbled with a small smile.

He padded over to the tub once he had successfully ripped off his threadbare clothes and left them strewn upon the cold white floor. The water was scalding against his skin as Lorian gently lowered himself into a seated position with a gasp. The water swirled and surged around him, the soft ripples raising goose-flesh along his arms and neck.

As Lorian began to scrub at the dirt on his arms, a bar of hard soap and a small block of pumice appeared on the edge of the tub with a faint *pop*. He grabbed the soap and pumice without a second thought and began to scrub roughly at his skin. He needed to get the stench and grime of those dungeons off his body.

The soap smelled of lavender and pine as it cleansed Lorian's skin, and any dirt that swirled into the water quickly disappeared, keeping the bath clean. Lorian scrubbed everywhere, including his hair. A dark curl brushed the top of his shoulder and he looked down in surprise. His hair had gotten long since he'd been locked away. The dusty coating that had kept his hair brown for some time finally washed away into the natural raven black that it was meant to be. His fingers scrubbed against his itchy scalp, and brushed against the tips of his slightly pointed ears.

The water was still warm by the time Lorian struggled out of the tub, the sun already set for the night and his fingers wrinkled from being submerged for so long. He looked down upon his now clean body and sighed, realizing he would have to crawl back into the tattered clothes he had been wearing for only the Nether knew how long.

Maybe they'll be miraculously mended and cleaned, he thought. But when Lorian approached the spot where he had left his clothes, they were nowhere in sight.

"What in the Nether?" he muttered under his breath, and spun around in search of them.

His clothing had simply disappeared. Lorian shook his head, water droplets spraying across the room with soft splattering sounds wherever they hit the walls and floor. A thought then entered his mind and he moved out of the bathing chamber and into the main bedroom. Perhaps the dresser against the far wall actually did contain clothes for his use.

Lorian didn't even have to search the dresser. A bundle of cloth was sitting neatly on the bed before him, and Lorian approached to find soft grey cotton pants and a tan-colored tunic folded beside each other. He glanced around the room, wondering who had brought him the new clothes. He then shrugged and grabbed the tunic and pants, quickly dressing despite the dampness of his skin. An almost maniacal grin spread across his face as the soft fabric settled over his emaciated body. The pants hung low on his hips, and the tunic was nearly three sizes too big. He tilted toward the bed, a sudden weariness sweeping over him like a blanket.

And yet the growling and sharp pain that lanced through Lorian's stomach made him realize how hungry he truly was. The image of roasted potatoes, mushrooms, and a large chunk of steaming bread drifted through his mind, and Lorian closed his eyes as his stomach growled painfully again. He couldn't remember the last time he had eaten a proper meal.

Seconds later, the smell of garlic and butter wafted into Lorian's nose and he flung his eyes open. Lying atop the dresser was a plate filled with steaming food. Lorian turned and nearly ran toward it. He didn't have time to think about what he was shoving into his mouth until he had already eaten nearly half of the plate's contents. To his surprise, there were steaming baby potatoes and mushrooms lathered in butter and garlic sauce, along with a steaming loaf of bread. Lorian swallowed a large mouthful of potato, and then gingerly took up the plate in his hand and walked to the plush rug in front of the bed.

Lorian ate the rest of his food in silent reverie, relishing every last bite of the first warm meal he had eaten in a long time. His stomach was full by the time he set the empty plate down onto the rug with a satisfied smile. It disappeared with a *pop* the second his fingers let go of it.

Lorian sighed and looked around the room, his eyes suddenly drooping with sleepiness. It would be first light before Lorian knew it, and he would not get to sleep in an actual bed for only the goddesses knew how long. He got up with a groan and staggered over to the bed with exhaustion.

Lorian pulled the silken covers back and slipped onto the plush mattress, a moan escaping his lips as he rested his damp head on the pillows. It felt like heaven. And to think that only that morning he had been stuck in a rotting dungeon thinking about all the ways he was going to die. He owed that commander his life. He had done this. And the girl— Lorian dared not think of her. His stomach lurched, and Lorian shook the thought of her full lips and angry eyes from his head. He would not sleep if he began to think about her. That could wait until the next day.

The lights of the ruby chandelier began to dim, and Lorian swirled into a dreamless sleep.

TEDRIC

Tedric awoke with a start, his body lurching upwards as the dream of his father's anger-twisted face faded from his mind. He blinked as the chandelier in the center of the ceiling glowed to life.

First light wouldn't approach for another hour, but Tedric felt electric energy running through his veins nonetheless. Sleep would not be returning to him now, but he did not mind. He was used to waking up far before the sun rose. It had become a part of his daily life since he had been appointed commander of the Ten.

Tedric shook the dream from his mind and climbed out of the large bed, padding toward a chair coated in red silk that he had laid his armor on before he went to bed. Yet when he approached, the skillfully made armor was gone and a simple dark leather breastplate waited in its place. He attempted to ignore the flutter of frustration in his abdomen as he picked up the armor and inspected it.

The material was very light, and that made him nervous. There was no way that this simple scrap of leather would stand a chance against the beasts they were to face on this mission, though perhaps it was better to remain inconspicuous when traveling through other kingdoms, especially ones that were not friends of Keadora despite the peace law.

Not even Tedric had attacked another living being without good reason, as the consequences of killing someone, thereby breaking the peace law, was not something that he wished to face. He shuddered at the words that had been nailed into his memory since he was a child. *Break the law and you will be broken. No food shall satisfy you, nor will any liquid replenish your thirst. Any home you set foot into shall crumble, and love will be nothing but a distant memory. You will feel nothing but pain from the dissatisfaction of every day that you may live.*

Tedric fought off a shiver as he turned and opened the top drawer of the dresser he had placed his clothing in for the night, only to find that it too had been replaced by a fresh set. The tunic he pulled out was a forest green color and the pants a dull dark brown. He took them out with a shrug and pulled them on before turning back toward the silk chair that held his new armor.

Tedric jolted in surprise as a water skin, an apparently empty leather satchel, his sword in a new scabbard, and a thick dark green cloak popped into existence. A smile played on his lips and he reached down to collect his new belongings. Even as a human, which was considered inferior to witches and treated as such, he loved magic.

The castle was deathly quiet as Tedric strode down the windowless hallway, his booted steps echoing off the marble walls. The smell of roses drifted through the air and witchlight lined the upper walls, illuminating his way in a warm glow.

Tedric paused as he approached a side door he typically went through to go to the main square. He huffed, the dream of his father entering his mind once more. He clenched his fists, turning toward a separate door on the wall across from him. He needed to see his father before he left to make sure the man was alive, and that, if he was, he wouldn't drink himself to death from worry about Tedric's absence.

The cool predawn air kissed his cheeks as Tedric stepped out into a gravel courtyard. His heart lurched with longing at the sight of nine horses lined up a few yards ahead, the dark figures of men shifting in and out of sight as they prepared themselves for the morning watch. He strode toward them and smiled at the whispered jokes and conversation that passed through the men.

"Gentlemen." Tedric addressed the nine men and what would remain of the Ten while he was away on the mission.

"Commander Drazak, how kind of you to see us off," the man closest to him replied.

He instantly recognized him as Bordin, the best archer in all of Keadora as far as Tedric was concerned. Bordin, who was ten years Tedric's elder, had been the one who discovered Tedric hiding in the shadows and watching the Ten train eleven years ago. He quickly became one of Tedric's mentors and closest friends as the years passed, as well as the one who had suggested Tedric as the best candidate for commander when Eldron perished.

"I just wanted to make sure you would all be able to complete your daily tasks without me," Tedric replied with a grin.

Bordin grinned back, his green eyes barely visible in the coming light of morning. Tedric would need to be at the stables soon, but he still needed to make sure that his father knew he would be gone.

"Is it your father?" Bordin asked quietly, so that the eight men behind them could not hear. "You won't have time to see him, it's nearly sunrise."

Tedric nodded. "I know."

"Listen, I can go to him after morning watch and tell him. Better that you are not late for your first day of saving the realm."

Tedric chuckled and clapped Bordin on the shoulder. The rest of Tedric's men approached and nodded to their commander.

"Do us a favor and stay alive. We need you back in one piece," a man near the back said gruffly.

Tedric recognized Griffin's raspy voice, their scout and one of the newer members of the Ten. Tedric smiled, knowing that the scout's words were as close to a goodbye as he would get from the man.

"I will return as soon as I possibly can. Don't do anything too foolish while I'm away," Tedric said to his men.

They all laughed, and Tedric gave one last glance at Bordin, who nodded in confirmation and gave him a wink. Tedric nodded back and turned on his heel, heading toward the large arched gates that would lead to the main street and take him to the stables. Bordin was a good man, and one of the only people he could truly call a friend. Brisk dawn air blew across his face and ruffled his shortly cropped hair as he stepped out onto the deserted cobbled street. Fall had finally come to Raymara. It was Tedric's favorite season of all, spring and winter too cold or windy for his taste, and summer too hot.

The transition from fall to winter was one of the most spiritual times of year in Raymara, as the moon would turn blood red on the winter equinox. In Proveria, the event had been turned into a festival named Clamidas, or the blood festival. Legend had it that the blood moon birthed all fairies, and that Noctiluca, goddess of the moon, was their mother, though Tedric didn't know how much he truly believed in that tale.

Tedric breathed in the smell of baked bread and cinnamon, the telltale sign that Crimson City was slowly beginning to stir. Early morning vendors were setting up stands full of fresh apples and vegetables, and guards were taking over their watch positions by street corners and on rooftops. It was a peaceful city, and a smile came to Tedric's lips as pride for his kingdom filled his chest.

Tedric rounded a corner and headed toward the great stone building that held Keadora's best horses. Tedric had worked in those stables when he was a young boy, right before Bordin had found him and convinced Eldron, the late commander, to take him in to train with the Ten. Tedric had enjoyed working in the stables, the smell of fresh straw and horses always comforted him when only a drunk father for company had become too much to bare.

Tedric forced away the returning image of his dream and entered the stables. He stopped and blinked in surprise at the sight of Lorian's thin figure already standing in the dimly lit barn. The thief was clean now and already appeared healthier, his thick black hair curling just above his shoulders. Tedric snorted, having thought the thief's hair was brown from the copious amounts of dirt and grime that had encrusted it since the day he'd arrested him in the Red King's throne room.

Lorian wore a similar garb as Tedric, though his tunic was navy blue and the thick cloak covering his shoulders was as black as the night sky. Lorian gently stroked the muzzle of Dario, Tedric's grey stallion, which he had won in a sword tournament a few years ago. Dario rested his head upon the stall door, eyes closed as he relished in Lorian's calming strokes.

"I see you've met my horse," Tedric commented, a grin growing on his face as Lorian jumped and turned to face him.

The stallion bopped his head up with a start and snorted, disappearing back into the dimly lit stall.

"How did you know your way to the stables?" Tedric asked curiously, making his way down the long dark stone aisle toward Lorian.

Lorian shrugged. "I know how to find even the most hidden things."

"You have a point." Tedric nodded.

"I have to thank you for what you—" Lorian stopped mid-sentence, face paling as his eyes slid to something at the barn entrance.

Tedric turned to see what Lorian was so petrified of, and spotted the cloaked outline of the third and final member of their mission. Tedric's stomach leaped into his throat when he spotted the catlike creature slinking by the young witch's side, a mogwa, as they were called. Mogwas were native to Naebatis, one of the cursed kingdoms. It was the coldest kingdom of all, all thanks to the curse that the Red King set upon Naebatis, forcing the lands into a permanent winter. Mogwas were incredibly rare, and Tedric wondered how the woman had come across the beast.

The mogwa was larger than he imagined they would be, its back brushing against the woman's hip. Long silky grey fur speckled with white coated the creature, and its heart-shaped pink nose and knowing amber eyes were nearly identical to those of a house cat, if in fact a house cat had somehow grown to be the size of a pony and sprouted three extra toes in the process.

"Good morning, Finriel Caligari," Tedric greeted in a smooth voice, nodding his head toward the girl as she approached.

Her black tunic fit becomingly against her curvy yet strong frame, along with a sturdy pair of black pants that were covered to the knee by long black boots. Her hair was braided over one shoulder, and the handle of a dagger was just visible at her side, partially covered by the thick black cloak that brushed against the ground. She gave Tedric a sidelong glare and rolled her eyes. Her gaze then fell upon Lorian, and Tedric felt the strain in the air between them.

"Good morning," Lorian muttered sheepishly, his eyes darting to the ground before he forced his gaze back to meet her furious stare.

Tedric cleared his throat and stepped between the thief and the witch. "We should get a move on."

Finriel jerked her attention back to Tedric and nodded, withdrawing a rolled up piece of parchment from the folds of her cloak.

"I was given the enchanted map that we're meant to use to find the creatures and the storyteller. I was given a note that said the map could transport us to a specific location, but we can only use it once."

Tedric nodded, but then a terrible realization crossed his mind and he cursed under his breath. "I don't have the pages meant to capture the beasts."

Lorian glanced at Tedric and raised his hand. "I have them."

"Good," Finriel replied sharply, not looking at either of them. "The note also said that we must touch our hands onto the map and it will transport us to the beast nearest to us. If it is in a separate kingdom from this one, we will be transported about a day's walk away from the next kingdom so that we have time to plan and decide how we get in."

"That sounds simple enough," Tedric replied confidently. "Where is the nearest beast?"

Finriel shrugged and quickly unrolled the map to hold it out for both Lorian and Tedric to see. The map was exquisitely made, the mountains of Creonid, the gnome kingdom, drawn so realistically that they looked like a black and white image copied directly onto the parchment. The rivers, trees, plains, snow, and deserts all looked so real.

Almost too real, Tedric thought. He searched the map for a sign or marker indicating where the first creature was located, and his stomach dropped with a mix of adrenaline and fear. It did not say what the beast was, but a circular red smudge was located in the center of Millris Forest, the largest forest within Proveria.

"We have to go to the beast without knowing what it is. That's just wonderful," Lorian grumbled.

"And it has to be in Proveria of all kingdoms," Tedric replied with a surge of hatred for the fairies. He had never trusted them, and the countless meetings and gatherings Tedric had attended with the pompous creatures were always stuffy and exhausting.

"I don't understand how fairies are so terrible," Finriel said tartly.

Lorian raised his brows at the witch and the corner of his mouth quirked upward. "Oh, you will, trust me."

Finriel's lips tightened and she opened her mouth, blurting, "Well, as you said, we should get a move on."

Without a second glance at either Tedric or Lorian, Finriel placed a hand on the intricate map. When neither Lorian nor Tedric placed a hand on the page, she rolled her eyes and growled, "Oh, please."

Tedric puffed his chest out slightly and placed his hand on the map, not liking the diminishing tone that Finriel had used. Lorian finally shrugged and placed his hand on the map. As if someone had turned on an invisible faucet, dark fog began to spill into the barn, swirling and twisting as it formed a moving circle around the three companions. The fog began to spin faster and faster, and Tedric shut his eyes with a jolt as the fog crashed inwards from all sides and pushed the three of them together.

Tedric kept his eyes tightly shut, a sick feeling beginning to rise in his throat, the sensation in his body something like being crushed by an unbearable weight. The ground seemed to disappear below them, and Tedric yelled as he plummeted into the darkness, his stomach lurching into his throat. Something hard collided with his backside and his legs smashed against hard ground with a jolt of pain. The smell of fresh air and rich soil drifted through his nose, and he realized that he had just teleported. He blinked his eyes open and cursed at the mild pain that shot through his legs, then looked around to find his companions also cursing and wiping dead grass and dirt from their cloaks a few paces away. Finriel's mogwa was perched upon a fallen log a few feet away from her master, her amber eyes scrutinizing the three of them.

Tedric struggled to his feet and forced his legs to stay upright though they wobbled and threatened to give out. He had never teleported in his twenty-two years of life, and he found that he never wanted to do it again.

"Where are we?" Finriel asked as she, too, got shakily up to her feet and looked around.

Her long braid swayed against her back and now had clumps of dirt and grass clinging to it. She surveyed their surroundings with a scrutinizing expression, and Tedric quickly looked away. He found her incredibly unnerving, and by the way that Lorian watched her with wariness in his eyes, Tedric was sure that the thief felt the same way.

"We're at the edge of the night watch post," Tedric answered promptly as he surveyed their surroundings. "It's about a day's march east to get to the Proverian border."

Rolling hills scattered with trees expanded across the horizon, and Tedric squinted against the rising sun to find the small speck of Crimson City in the distance. The white marble of the castle glinted in the sun and Tedric was surprised to find that they hadn't traveled that far after all.

"Well, let's get going then," Finriel replied curtly, and turned on her heel in the direction Tedric pointed.

Tedric's stomach began to grumble after a few short minutes of walking through the tall grasses and open meadows of Keadora. The sun had now risen fully, setting the browning flower-dusted meadows in a soft glow. Blue birds chirped and flew overhead, and the mogwa's ears twitched with attention as a large dusty brown hare bounded across their path.

"I'm starving," Lorian said finally, voicing Tedric's exact thoughts. "Which one of us got the food?"

Tedric looked to Finriel, who shook her head. Lorian would not have asked if he had been given their meal supply. He looked down at the satchel at his side and frowned. It felt much too light to contain any food, but then again, Tedric hadn't checked what was inside of it and the bag had likely been crafted by witches.

He halted and reached down into the bag. His eyes widened in surprise when his hand immediately made contact with something large and warm. He pulled out a steaming loaf of dark bread, and Lorian lurched forward and snatched it in one swift movement, his eyes set with hunger. Tedric raised his brows and looked between the loaf of bread Lorian had ripped from his hands and the thief's ravenous expression. Lorian met Tedric's stare and hugged the bread closer. When Tedric didn't move or reply, Lorian took another step toward the commander and gestured at the satchel with a nod of his head.

"Go on, see what else is in there."

Tedric quirked his lips into a half-smile and obliged, pulling out a block of cheese near the size of his head, along with three gleaming red apples. Tedric tossed one of the apples to Finriel, who caught it with one hand and a glare.

"Is that enough food for you?" Finriel asked with an edge to her voice as she and Tedric both watched Lorian wolf down bread and large chunks of cheese that Tedric had sliced for him with the very dagger he had taken from the thief upon his arrest.

What amazed Tedric the most was how Lorian was able to walk and shove the large armful of food into his mouth without dropping a single scrap. Tedric already knew that he would be surprised many times over by the peculiar man. Lorian glanced at their amused gazes and gave a defensive look, swallowing a giant mouthful of bread before speaking.

"When either of you two get out of a dungeon after months of only having cold soup made out of discarded scraps and stale bread, then you can give me those looks. I personally think that I deserve to have a little bit of a feast. And Tedric, I know that I have impeccable taste in weaponry, but I would love it if you gave my dagger back."

Tedric certainly knew what it was like to go hungry for days, but he kept his mouth shut, allowing the thief to savor the moment. He looked down at the thin blade at his side and considered Lorian's statement. Perhaps it was the right thing to return the dagger, since the thief had no weapons at all.

"You probably deserved to be locked up in that dungeon," Finriel muttered, ignoring Lorian's words. Though her tone was casual, an edge of venom licked across the witch's tongue as she spoke.

Lorian stared at her, his eyes blank in surprise. Tedric looked between the two of them in confusion, and the question finally bubbled over.

"I'm sorry," Tedric sighed, "but do you two know each other from some previous incident?"

Finriel snorted in response and Lorian merely gave a cowardly shrug before shoving more cheese into his mouth.

"I don't know this thief," Finriel answered after a few moments of tense silence. "I stopped wanting to know him ten years ago."

Tedric remained silent at this. Their past was clearly not an enjoyable one, and certainly not one very high on the discussion list. Even so, he was curious about how they knew each other, as well as their pasts. He was confident that Lorian would not be difficult to crack, but he wasn't so sure about Finriel. She was clearly wounded, and Tedric knew how thick those scars could run.

Tedric remained ahead of his other two companions during the day, with Finriel one step behind him and Lorian lagging slightly behind her. Tedric found himself feeling bad for the thief while they traveled, as he was sure it was difficult to walk all day with barely any meat on ones bones or muscles to help. The companions walked in tense silence for the remainder of their journey to Proveria's border. The sounds of their footsteps and the mogwa's heavy panting were the only noises around them and the only things keeping Tedric's mind from running wild. They only stopped twice for short moments of rest and water from the water skin Tedric carried, which seemed to have had a spell put on it to make its contents magically replenish whenever it emptied.

The sun was beginning to set by the time they reached the crest of a hill that overlooked the tall looming pines and shimmering blue wall of light that indicated Proveria's border. Tedric's stomach churned at the sight of the enormous shimmering border and strange forest beyond. They were going to leave Keadora. He wasn't even sure when they would return, *if* they returned. He did not want to think about that. The beasts couldn't be so dangerous as to kill one of the companions, could they?

"We should spend the night on the Keadoran border and enter the forest at daybreak," Lorian suggested, the first words that were spoken since Tedric's misstep in conversation.

Finriel nodded in silent agreement and narrowed her eyes as she inspected the horizon. Tedric did the same, and moments later spotted a small patch of large jagged grey rocks only a few meters away from the Proverian border.

"There, we can make camp by those rocks," Tedric said, pointing to them.

Lorian and Finriel followed Tedric as they made their way down the hill, Tedric's legs groaning with fatigue with every step that brought them closer to the forest. They all staggered to a stop once they reached their destination, and Tedric looked at the shimmering border and tree line before him. The trees towered high above them, the tops extending past Tedric's vision. He'd only crossed into Millris Forest once, and was already dreading his untimely return into its mysterious depths.

"I wish we could make a fire," Lorian muttered, and scanned the ground in search of any stray wood or kindling.

Tedric knew he would find none. This area of Keadora did

not have trees, and therefore they would not be successful in creating a fire unless they ventured into the forest ahead.

"It's no use," Tedric replied. "Not unless you want to chance entering Proveria."

Finriel gave a humph and sat with her back against one of the large grey stones, her orange and caramel eyes set upon the ground. Tedric considered the girl, who, like Lorian, was no more than two years younger than he was.

"Have you ever shown signs of battle magic?" Tedric found himself asking Finriel.

"You're asking if I have the capability of producing fire magic?" she replied. "I do not, and even if I ever did, I wouldn't risk any sort of battle magic just to make a silly fire."

Tedric remembered the other half of his lessons about the peace law as a child. Any type of potentially violent magic was prohibited since the beginning of the thousand-year peace, and Adustio, goddess and creator of the witches, had long since cast a spell upon all witches living within Keadora that made battle magic dormant. That magic included creating fire and manipulating another's body against their will.

There were still some born with battle magic, however. The few unfortunately gifted souls were either given the same suppression enchantment, drowned by a bed of stones strapped to their backs, or sent to the Witch Isles for proper training and permanent isolation from the rest of the realm. The Witch Isles were an island in the Sandrial Waters, off the west of Keadora, and said to be the birthplace of all witches.

Lorian coughed, and Tedric glanced at the thief. Curiosity swam through Tedric as the thief watched Finriel with an expression mingled with both fear and frustration. Finriel shot him a glare and reached a hand out to stroke the mogwa now lying at her side.

"It's likely a good thing that you don't have battle magic

anyway," Tedric said, and Finriel's gaze narrowed upon him further.

"Why do you say that?"

Tedric shrugged. "Well, I thought that any witch or wizard born without the dormancy spell and not sent to the Witch Isles was drowned."

It was the dark side to Keadora's beauty, and Tedric shivered at the thought of whatever cursed souls were forced to commit such acts.

Finriel's face twisted at his words and she turned toward Lorian with murder in her eyes. "I was nearly drowned even though I don't possess battle magic, but I survived."

Lorian grimaced and his faced washed over with a sick green hue. He pivoted and moved away from the camp, his movements rigid and uneven as he made his way back up the hill.

"I have to take a piss."

3

LORIAN

A loud snore tore through Lorian's dreams, bringing him to the waking world with a jolt. He shut his eyes and blinked quickly, groaning as another snore rattled out of Nora, Finriel's mogwa.

His muscles groaned in protest as he brought himself into a seated position and surveyed the still dim light of the morning. The sun was just beginning to peak over a large hill, making its slow ascent and bathing the grass in warm light. Lorian took in a deep breath of crisp fall air and turned his head toward the dark thicket of looming pines and shimmering border of Proveria, a shiver running down his spine.

Lorian had never ventured very far into the fairy kingdom, as he knew that the creatures that dwelled inside the many forests and strange lakes were not to be trusted. One could only be so good at keeping their head on their shoulders even with the peace law in place, and Lorian was confident that he would have surely lost his if he'd taken a job within the Proverian borders. Yet, now he had taken on a mission that was leading him straight into the heart of Millris Forest, as well as only the goddesses knew which other kingdoms. Excitement coursed through Lorian's veins despite the fact that his mission was riddled with danger, and the part of him that reveled in mischief swelled with satisfaction.

Another rattling snore brought Lorian out of his thoughts, and he scrambled to his aching feet. Thank the goddesses neither Finriel nor Tedric snored, only the extra large cat did. He let his gaze wander over Finriel and Nora's sleeping forms with a strangled sigh. The witch was curled against Nora, her head resting upon the mogwa's side. The knot that had formed in Lorian's chest the day before tightened uncomfortably, and a curse flew from his mouth as he looked to the ground.

"I would be careful with that one if I were you," a low voice made Lorian jump and swivel toward the voice.

Tedric was still seated against a large stone that he had stationed himself against the night before. His watchful brown eyes met Lorian's own icy blue ones as he braced his hands on his knees and rose smoothly to his feet.

"I don't know what you mean," Lorian managed to reply, a defensive edge laced within his words.

Tedric raised his hands. "I know that you two have history. I don't know what happened, but you could be the spawn of Nex as far as she is concerned. You've got to set whatever bad blood is between you two right before she kills you, peace law be damned."

Pain lanced through Lorian's chest, and he found himself glaring at the fair-haired warrior. "I'm not charming and kind all of the time, especially not with this matter."

Tedric shrugged in turn and bent down to tap Finriel on the shoulder. She woke with a start, eyes darting to Lorian before she looked up at Tedric and rose to a seated position. Nora stretched and yawned, two rows of razor sharp teeth glinting as her mouth opened wide. Tedric handed Finriel a large chunk of bread from his satchel, which he strung around his shoulder with a swift motion. He turned on his heel and brushed past Lorian, clapping him on the back as he passed.

"Is it time to leave now?" Finriel's sleep-tinged voice called, her eyes set like pinpoints on Tedric's back.

Mood thoroughly dampened by Tedric, Lorian closed his eyes and willed himself not to answer as he grabbed the crumpled cloak he'd used as a blanket during the night.

"Nearly," Tedric began, "but it would be best to finish our meal before venturing into Millris Forest."

Lorian swept the cloak over his shoulders before he sat as far away from either of his companions as he could manage. He suddenly wished that he could have taken this mission for himself instead of having to share it with a witch who wanted him dead and a self-righteous bastard of a commander. Lorian knew he would be more efficient, more hidden, if he could gather the creatures himself.

An apple flew toward Lorian's head, and he caught it deftly with one hand. He shot Tedric a glare and the warrior shrugged.

"Just wanted to make sure you were still with us."

"I was thinking," Lorian snapped. "Perhaps it's something you would be interested in trying sometime."

To Lorian's surprise, Tedric simply smiled and popped a slice of cheese into his mouth. "I don't have much interest in thinking. It fogs the brain, and besides, it appears to be making you miserable."

Lorian gave Tedric a rude hand gesture, but found a small smile growing on his lips. The commander had more wit than Lorian gave him credit for, that was clear enough to see. He snuck a glance at Finriel, who watched him silently, her expression sharp as a dagger. The knot in his chest reared its ugly head once more, making the apple taste bitter in his mouth. Nora got to her feet with one last yawn, then turned and slunk out of sight.

"Where has she gone off to?" Tedric asked curiously, his words muffled by a mouthful of cheese.

Finriel shrugged and bit into the bread in her hand. "Hunting," was her response.

Tedric nodded silently and glanced at Lorian with a raised brow. Lorian did not engage, however. The overwhelming guilt was making him sick, and he wanted nothing more than to leave. He wanted to get as far away from Finriel as he could and never look back. It was escape or try to fix whatever pieces between them were left, if there were any pieces left at all.

Tedric shrugged and turned to Finriel once again, asking, "How close are we to the nearest beast?"

Finriel rustled around in her cloak for the map and withdrew it. The ink swirled and spread over the map to give a closer view of their position within the realm. The dense forest beside them was drawn in incredible detail, and a small name bloomed underneath the illustrations of looming pines. *Millris Forest.* Tedric let out a humph at the name, but Lorian leaned in, blood pounding in his ears as he looked for an indication of the nearest beast. Disappointment sank in his stomach after a few moments of searching and finding nothing.

"That's strange," he muttered. "Shouldn't the nearest beast appear when we open the map?"

Tedric ran a hand through his golden locks and shook his head. "Maybe we simply aren't close enough."

Finriel didn't reply to either of their comments as she rolled up the map and continued to eat her bread, only a shadow of disappointment crossing her face. They finished their meal in silence and packed up the rest of their small camp. Lorian considered the fact that they couldn't find a marker for their first beast on the map. Perhaps Tedric was right and they did simply have to cross into Proveria in order for it to be visible. Or perhaps something had gone wrong. Lorian shook his head and shivered against the chilly morning and mission that awaited.

"We should go, we've wasted good time already," Tedric announced, glancing at the sun that was now fully risen in the sky.

"Yes, sir," Lorian replied mockingly, bowing low before the commander, who simply shook his head in return.

Finriel ignored their exchange and started toward the shimmering border and forest before them, then paused.

"What is it?" Tedric asked with a sigh.

"Don't we want to come up with a plan before we enter?" Finriel replied, and Lorian raised his brows at the first sign of nerves he'd ever seen from her. "I mean, you are the Commander of the Ten, or whatever it is you call yourself. Don't you think it would be slightly stupid to just stroll into Proveria without welcome?" she finished.

Tedric smiled. "I'm flattered, but there is nothing else we can really do. Fairies are wicked and resourceful creatures. They'll know we've entered their lands even if we try to hide from them."

Finriel shrugged and the uncertainty instantaneously disappeared from her fierce features. Lorian shook his head in disbelief as she turned toward the forest. Lorian and Tedric exchanged a quizzical glance and Lorian shrugged, starting after the witch. Finriel stopped once more and turned in the direction Nora had disappeared, opening her mouth. An earsplitting whistle made Lorian cover his ears with his hands, and moments later Nora came bounding across the field, her large face splattered with something crimson and brown that Lorian assumed was the unfortunate animal she had just made her meal. A gag tore through his throat as the stench of death filtered through the breeze, and a muffled choke from Tedric alerted Lorian that the commander had smelled it too.

The mogwa padded up happily to Finriel, who scratched her lovingly behind her ear then tilted her head to examine her face and chest. She indicated for Nora to stay still and brought a hand down, sweeping across the blood-soaked areas of Nora's body. The blood and bits of flesh disappeared as her hand passed over them, and in seconds it appeared as if Nora had just bathed in a river, not killed an animal and eaten it whole.

"Unbelievable," Tedric marveled, shaking his head as he watched Finriel finish cleaning Nora.

"Let's see if these fairies are as terrible as you two say," Finriel said with the flash of a grin, and started toward the forest once more, Nora now slinking by her hip.

"I wish your oh so thoughtful king had provided me with a weapon," Lorian grumbled under his breath, eyes darting to his dagger, still strapped to Tedric's belt. Tedric met his gaze and Lorian forced himself to hold it, not daring to back down. Surprise expanded through his chest as Tedric sighed and withdrew the sheathed weapon from his belt, offering it to Lorian.

"Here, now you have one. I was just keeping it safe for you anyway," Tedric said with a grin.

Lorian smiled back with a wink and took the dagger from Tedric. The weight felt familiar and comforting to him, and he couldn't stop a chuckle from bubbling out of his throat at the sight of his worn, trusty blade held in his own hands.

"Welcome back, old friend." Lorian grinned and looked at the warrior. "Consider your insults from this morning forgotten."

Tedric shrugged. "What makes that thing so special?"

"It was the first item I ever stole for myself. I was twelve years old and it's been with me since. It's almost something of a good luck charm if you will," Lorian replied.

Tedric smiled and shook his head, and Lorian clapped the warrior on the shoulder in thanks. They both turned to find that Finriel had nearly reached the border and was about to leave them behind.

"Time to follow the angry witch into fairyland," Lorian sighed, and with a surge of excitement and renewed confidence from the return of his dagger, they started walking.

Lorian settled into step behind Finriel, his heart beginning to beat faster as her cloaked figure rippled through the shimmering kingdom barrier. Lorian took in a deep breath and stepped forward, a familiar shudder running through his body as the magical wall passed through him. He stopped and turned to watch Tedric, whose face was screwed up in something like distaste as he too stepped through the shimmering border and gave a shudder.

Weak sunlight filtered through the forest branches, casting odd shadows upon the thick grass and moss-covered ground below. Cold air swept over them, unnervingly different from the slight warmth in Keadora. Lorian wrapped his cloak tighter around himself as he inspected their new surroundings. The forest was beautiful, though it had a certain otherworldliness that made Lorian uneasy. The air was clean, though oddly perfumed with flowers and herbs that, with some distaste, reminded Lorian of the Crimson Castle.

Butterflies of different shapes, sizes, and colors fluttered and swooped amongst the trees, and birds called and chirped softly to each other in the looming branches above. The grass below their feet was a luscious vibrant green, quite different from the dry fields they had walked through in Keadora only a few minutes ago. The soft trickle of a nearby stream echoed somewhere in the distance, calming Lorian's nerves slightly as they walked. Exotic and unfamiliar creatures revealed themselves to the companions the deeper they got into the forest, some Lorian had never even seen within the book of beasts he had loved as a child. Lorian let out a grunt of surprise as wildflowers sprang from the earth and bloomed into a kaleidoscope of reds, blues, pinks, and yellows.

More animals and strange creatures peered out from behind the thick tree trunks and began to go about their business once more, uttering odd squeaks and barks as they moved. Small furry rodents with long snouts and tails scurried and hopped amongst the trees, a few jumping from branch to branch, keeping pace with the companions as they went farther into the forest.

Nora sniffed and narrowed her eyes at the small creatures

with a mingled expression of hunger and temptation as they passed over her head and chattered loudly. Lorian had known the mogwa for as long as he'd known Finriel, and was surprised at how much self-restraint Nora was demonstrating at the current moment. The Nora he had known would have ripped the creatures to shreds at first sight.

"It's beautiful," Finriel breathed, in awe at their surroundings, making Lorian look away from Nora.

"Don't be fooled," Tedric answered darkly. "Proveria may seem beautiful at first, but fairies themselves are not to be trusted."

"Why is that?" Finriel asked.

Lorian watched Tedric, who, though also looking around, maintained an expression of stony mistrust in place of Finriel's awe.

"Because they are tricksters and terrible at telling the truth, so bad that it can get you killed," he answered with a sneer.

"And how do you know this?" Finriel retorted. She became momentarily distracted as a small white tailed deer strode past her, pausing for a second as it sniffed at Finriel curiously and blinked its four black eyes. Nora licked her lips attentively and the deer set off again with haste.

"Because I have met plenty of fairy nobles who have come to Keadora to meet with the king," Tedric replied, and scowled at her. "They speak of peace but I can see the hunger for disunity and war in their eyes."

"That is a large assumption to make about people whose kingdom looks like the setting of a children's bedtime story."

"It's not an assumption," Tedric spat. "The previous commander of the Ten died fighting a band of fairies near Nocturn Lake, though they told the Red King that they had nothing to do with it. They are secretive and conniving, and I will be surprised the day that I meet a fairy worth liking."

Lorian gave Tedric an apologetic smile, his spirits dropping.

Tedric seemed to have more secrets than Lorian was aware of, but he still knew what it was like to lose someone close. Or so he thought.

"Usually the ones hiding the most terrible secrets have the prettiest masks to cover them up," Finriel answered coolly, breaking up the silence.

A jab of pain sliced through Lorian's chest at her words. *At least she thinks I'm pretty.* Lorian focused on the blooming flowers and springy grass to try to take his mind off the sudden pain crawling through his heart. He needed to speak to her privately.

Tedric cleared his throat and they all stopped, the momentary silence hanging thick in the air. The warrior scuffed his boot on the moss that had replaced the grass below them and bit his lip. "So, in which direction do we go now?"

"Preferably in a direction that doesn't smell like the Red King spilled his perfume everywhere," Lorian grumbled, receiving a glare from Tedric.

Finriel unrolled the map and pointed directly ahead of them after a moment of gazing upon the magical parchment. They began to walk once more, and Lorian made sure to follow a few paces behind his companions. He had clearly crossed too many lines within a painfully short amount of time, and was sure they could both bite his head off within seconds if he opened his mouth wrongly again.

Moments later, something odd caught Lorian's eye. Dense dark blue mist rolled slowly and silently toward them in a large wave, and Lorian called for Tedric and Finriel to stop.

"Do you have any suggestions as to what that may be?" he asked.

Tedric and Finriel both considered the approaching mist, the looks of confusion on both of their faces making it evident that in fact, they did not know what it was. Nora sniffed and backed up a few steps, growling as the mist swept around them. It smelled of ripe berries and smoke as it swirled around them, and Lorian blinked as his head began to swim delightfully.

"Well, that's a peculiar feeling," Lorian slurred with a smile, and Finriel shot him a look that he could have sworn was concern.

"It's the fairies," Tedric declared importantly, stepping one foot out in front of himself for stability as he staggered.

It took everything in Lorian's will not to laugh at the commander, whose brown eyes were now glassed over as he inspected the mist as if it were a criminal.

"Let's keep moving," Finriel cautioned, and they started walking, Lorian's steps feeling lighter than they had in ages.

❦ 4 ❧

FINRIEL

Midnight blue smoke swirled around the companions as they drew deeper into Millris Forest, the smell of berries and smoke growing stronger each step they took. Nora swayed slightly and shook her large grey head, as if attempting to clear a bug from her ears. Finriel reached down to stroke the mogwa's neck with slight concern, though the feeling was nearly swallowed by the inferno of anger that swelled in her abdomen.

She didn't want to be on this mission, and certainly not with the company she had been given. Finriel only wished to see her mother after twenty years of confusion surrounding the story of her disappearance. She knew that her mother was one of the best healers to have ever lived in Keadora, but there had been a mysterious accident when Finriel was born and her mother was forced to perform acts that most people were hesitant to recount. Some said that her mother had perished that night in the fight and others said she simply disappeared in a flash of light. Now Finriel knew that she was alive and she would be able to finally meet her once this mission was over.

"Finriel, I must say ..." Finriel swirled around as Tedric's slurred words continued from behind. "I never thought of you to wear your hair green."

Finriel grabbed her braid and furrowed her brow. It was the same chocolate brown as it had been since the day she was born. She stared at the commander in confusion, then found that both he and Lorian were swaying slightly and their eyes were glazed over as they regarded their surroundings in awe.

"My hair is *not* green," Finriel shot back. She wasn't sure why that remark bothered her. Perhaps it was the strange, sickly sweet mist that now enveloped them.

"You look like you need a hug."

Lorian lurched forward with his arms outstretched, and Finriel leaped back in alarm, barely avoiding the brush of his fingertips. Lorian stumbled and tripped, giggling as he collided upon the mossy ground and pressed up on his hands and knees. Tedric began to laugh alongside Lorian, and he too bent over to place his hands on the ground and flop over onto his back. The blue mist swirled and thickened, settling around them and obscuring Finriel's vision of anything but Nora and her companions.

"What's wrong with you two?" Finriel snapped, annoyance beginning to ebb at the ever-present hole inside her chest.

Lorian gazed up at Finriel from his seat on the ground and smiled softly. She pressed her lips together and fought against the lurch in her stomach that occurred every time their eyes met.

He left you to die. He doesn't care about you. He never cared about you and never will. Finriel forced herself to look away and watch Tedric as he rolled over and stretched out halfway over Lorian, who now appeared to be falling asleep.

"Get up!" Finriel hissed, glancing around in frustration. "You two are acting like idiots."

"They can't hear you. The mist has already overtaken their senses," said a silky and almost snakelike voice.

She whirled around to find who had spoken. Her pulse quickened in alarm as her eyes landed on the person, or rather the thing, that spoke. The creature was tall and willowy, its milky white skin shining unnaturally from an unknown light. Soft white hair sprouted from the creature's head and fell around two very long pointed ears. Finriel knew what it was. It was a shapeshifter.

"You silly girl," the shapeshifter crooned in a mocking tone that dripped with venom.

Nora growled at Finriel's side, the thick fur of her hackles rising in alarm. Finriel took a step back and placed a comforting hand on Nora's back, glancing quickly to where Tedric and Lorian were now facing each other, sitting cross-legged and giggling silently.

Something deep within Finriel's gut clenched, and her skin felt hot with charged magic, the chill fall air of the forest fading from her awareness. She silently brought up her energetic shields and drew her dagger, praying to the goddesses that the shapeshifter hadn't noticed her magic. The shapeshifter laughed, tossing its head back to reveal three rows of razor sharp teeth glinting in its mouth.

"Please, there is no point in trying to hide your powers from me, witch."

Finriel gulped and gripped her dagger tightly as she continued to draw up her magical shields. Nora began to circle Lorian and Tedric, her amber gaze set intently upon the shapeshifter.

"How do you know what I am?" Finriel asked, forcing her voice to come out evenly. She cursed when her voice cracked, and the shapeshifter laughed again. Finriel's stomach gave an uneasy flop at the black forked tongue that flicked out of the shapeshifter's mouth.

"There are a few key points that gave the fact that you are a witch away. Would you like me to name them?"

Finriel didn't answer, but kept her gaze steady, forcing the rising panic in her chest to fade into an emotionless haze.

"No answer? Well, I will tell you anyway. For one ..." It took a step forward and Finriel took a step back, her breath catching as razor sharp claws sprouted from the shapeshifter's delicate fingers. "My mist only works on those of powerless blood, since any amount of magic blocks my drug from entering one's bloodstream. You are not affected by the mist, whilst your two tasty-looking friends were knocked senseless the moment I freed it into the forest."

It took another step, and Finriel took another step back, careful not to tread over her drugged companions.

"Second, I feel your magic oozing from you as if you were a freshly killed beast still bleeding from its wound."

Finriel let the emotionless haze go and replaced it with the familiar, comforting blanket of anger. Her anger was her safe place, her armor. She supposed she could thank the now useless thief grabbing at her ankles for that. Finriel forced a wicked smile to her lips and she glared straight into the shapeshifter's pearly eyes.

"If you like my magic so much, then why don't you come and get it?" Finriel dared, tightening her grip on her dagger.

"Careful now, or you might be cursed for breaking the peace law," the shapeshifter crooned.

A harsh bark of laughter escaped from Finriel's mouth. "I have never felt peace, nor has anything I have ever done brought me satisfaction or happiness. I could be cursed already for all that matters."

The shapeshifter's colorless eyes widened and its black tongue slithered hungrily across its lower lip once more.

"So be it. You've chosen to become my little snack."

The creature took another step forward, its claws reaching for Finriel's face. Nora growled and began to leave her station by Tedric and Lorian to stand at Finriel's side.

"It's okay," Finriel whispered. "I have it under control."

Another growl emanated from Nora's large body as she

ignored her master's words and stepped closer. Finriel cursed under her breath and shot the mogwa a look that promised consequences if she didn't listen. The mogwa growled again and returned to her post by the two men, and Finriel nodded in approval.

"Now, what are you waiting for?" Finriel snapped at the shapeshifter. "Just kill me if you're so keen."

The shapeshifter retracted its tongue from its lips and smiled. "With pleasure."

The shapeshifter lunged forward with unnatural speed, and Finriel barely had time to scream before it was upon her, a razor sharp claw raking against the bust of her armor. A pained gasp tore from Finriel's throat as she lowered her head to find a faint trickle of blood dripping from the wound, but there was no time to feel pain. She staggered backwards and heard a grunt as her foot collided with one of her companion's appendages.

"Men are so useless," she hissed under her breath, allowing the anger to rise in her chest, and her magic along with it. Quick as an arrow, Finriel raised her hand and threw the weapon, not even bothering to hide her quick words that magically bound the blade to find its target. She knew that the blow would not kill the shapeshifter, only slow it down. She had no intention of killing the shapeshifter, for the thought of being cursed for the rest of her life was more frightening than the now hissing creature before her.

A sickening *thunk* reverberated through the cold air as the worn dagger sunk deep into the shapeshifter's abdomen, a sharp hiss escaping from its lips.

"You stupid *bitch*."

The shapeshifter wrenched the dagger from its stomach, inky black blood oozing steadily out of the wound. The dagger fell to the mossy forest floor, and Finriel stood in silent shock as a smile returned to the creature's lips. The shapeshifter quickly began to transform, and Finriel watched in horrified fascination as the luminous white skin on the creature's body began to simply fall off. She grimaced in disgust as the skin fell onto the mossy ground with soft thuds. What was once a terrifyingly beautiful being was now something out of Finriel's nightmares. Muscle and flesh held together by nothing but a slimy black-boned skeleton hovered in the mist. In another split second, a new body began to form and the skeleton dissipated into the same dark blue mist that bathed the forest.

A *pop* rang through the air and the mist disappeared. Finriel's mouth fell open and she had to look down at her own hands to make sure she was still there before she looked back up. Her exact mirror image stood a few feet away, smiling evilly at her. Yet instead of Finriel's own exotic eyes, this Finriel's eyes were the same dead pearly white color as the body the shapeshifter had been moments ago. The shapeshifter wearing Finriel's skin smiled broader and gave a spin, its dark brown hair swinging lazily behind what looked like her own back as it did so.

"Now you can have a fair fight, you filthy witch."

Finriel clenched her fists and glanced at her dagger, wishing that she knew a spell that could force it back into her grasp. A sudden wave of dizziness swept over her and Finriel shook her head, her vision coming in and out of focus. She took a step forward and growled, forcing down a wave of magic that swept through her body. She could not use it, not after suppressing the wild beast within that craved to be free for so long. Finriel blinked her vision into focus and glared at the grinning shapeshifter that wore her face.

"Give me your worst," Finriel spat.

Razor sharp claws protruded from Finriel's—no—the shapeshifter's hands and it widened its stance. Before Finriel could move, a blur of grey fur and a scream echoed through the forest. Nora bounded away from the shapeshifter, revealing a deep crimson gash along the mirror image of Finriel's own smooth neck. Tan skin fell from the shapeshifter's body, and the blackened skeleton dissipated into dark blue mist once more. Finriel gasped in shock. At once, her vision began to fade and she blinked quickly in an attempt to focus on the blurry figure of a girl and a small man who now stood in place of the shapeshifter.

"Have you been hurt?" the melodic voice sounded from the girl, and Finriel blinked again, still trying to focus her blurred vision.

Long violet hair was draped across her shoulder, Finriel was sure of that. Dark leather armor clung to her delicate form, accentuating the girl's athletic figure. A plain black cloak was secured at her throat, and Finriel could barely make out the hilt of a thin sword hanging at her belt. She opened her mouth to speak, but it seemed as if her tongue had lost the ability to form words.

Red hot pain stabbed through Finriel's lungs and she looked down at her chest again. She felt something hot and sticky under her fingers as she touched her wound. She gasped as she brought her hand up to find it coated in crimson, and quickly brought it down again, pressing harder against the wound. Suddenly, colorful splotches darted across her vision and her knees buckled, though Finriel didn't feel a thing as her body hit the mossy ground and her mind swirled into darkness.

5

LORIAN

Lorian opened his eyes to the sensation of something wet pressing against his forehead. He jerked back with a start, eyes focusing upon Nora, who was seated by his side, a loud meow reverberating through her body as she retracted her nose from his face. Lorian coughed and sputtered, glancing away from Nora to find himself lying upon the ground, engaged with Tedric in a tight embrace.

"What in the goddesses—" Lorian faltered and quickly untangled himself from the warrior before he scrambled to his feet.

The world spun slightly as he straightened, and he took a bracing step forward to find his balance. His head felt surprisingly clear, though he knew that the mist had been the culprit for his strange nap with Tedric. The blue mist was gone and Millris Forest was alight with birdsong and animal chatter once more. The sweet scent of flowers had returned, and Lorian found that he did not mind it as much now. His ears prickled at the sound of the nearby stream and wildlife around him, and he heaved a sigh of relief. Yet the relief was washed away when he looked down to find black and red blood spattered across the mossy floor, as well as a crumpled body feet away.

"Finriel."

Lorian ran to the witch and crouched by her fallen form. Nora's light footsteps approached and she stopped by Finriel's head, meowing loudly in Lorian's ear before she placed a large paw on Finriel's side and gently rolled the witch onto her back. Lorian sucked in a breath at the torn flesh that marred her chest. Nora meowed again and began to pace a small circle around her unconscious master.

"Don't worry, I've given her a healing draught. She'll live."

Lorian jumped at the unfamiliar female voice and spun around to find a complete stranger crouched next to Tedric's slumbering form, her fingers pressed against his neck to check his pulse. Nora growled and prowled at the girl, and Lorian lurched forward to grab her by the scruff. The mogwa hissed and shot him an amber glare, but he didn't let go. Finally, she let out another dejected meow and turned back toward her master, obeying Lorian's silent command to stand down.

The girl's pale hand was stark against Tedric's slightly tanned skin, and her delicate features appeared almost unearthly as she turned to meet Lorian's stare. Her green almond-shaped eyes bore into his, her long dark lashes curling upward, giving her a sultry stare. Her full lips were curled slightly downward into a scowl as she turned her attention back to Tedric. Strands of dark violet hair escaped from the single long braid draped around her shoulder and swayed at her side as she exchanged her weight from one foot to the other. Lorian placed a protective hand on Finriel's still body as he spotted long pointed ears peaking from under the strange young woman's hair.

"You're a fairy," Lorian blurted.

"I appreciate your observation, but I already know what I am, thank you."

Lorian turned back to Finriel and brushed her cheek with a

shaking hand. Her skin was cold, but a faint warmth was slowly returning. Her dark hair was matted against her forehead with sweat, and her eyelids fluttered as she fought against the pain.

"It was the poison in the shapeshifter's claws. It makes one lose consciousness and eventually fade to the Nether if the correct healing draught is not administered in time. It's their way of killing without breaking the peace law."

"And you carry this healing draught with you at all times just waiting for a rogue shapeshifter to slash open your chest?" Lorian asked quizzically.

The girl smirked. "Shapeshifters breed like rabbits in this region of Proveria, so I've learned to always be prepared."

Lorian studied the fairy girl, fear and worry rising in his chest. She stepped back as Tedric groaned and blinked his eyes open, groggily surveying the forest around him before he squinted up at her in confusion. His eyes widened and he moved to stand, but the girl quickly placed a hand on his shoulder to keep him down.

"You'll be okay, you're just recovering from the effects of the mist."

"Who are you?" Tedric demanded, his low voice slightly raspy from misuse.

Lorian glanced between Tedric and the fairy, and raised a brow as they merely stared at each other. The girl shook her head slightly, her pale skin flushing.

"Really? One of you tells me what I am, and the other asks." She quickly regained her haughty composure and turned to face Lorian. "Why don't you tell your friend, since you seem to know so well?"

Lorian pressed his lips together and raised his arms to show he was not a willing contender in the conversation. The girl sighed in annoyance and brought her attention back to Tedric, who was now examining her with an expression of both lust and apprehension. It was a combination of emotions that Lorian would not have guessed suited each other, but his new companion seem utterly unaware of his enraptured state.

"I'm—"

"I've got it!" a high-pitched male voice called from a tight group of bushes a few meters away.

The bushes rustled and a small man emerged from them at full speed, a clump of what appeared to be moldy fruit clutched in his childlike hands. The man stopped as he noticed Tedric and Lorian both staring at him and gave a weak smile. His excited expression quickly molded into one of severe neutrality as the gnome strode toward them.

His short legs were clad in bright red pants, and his loose fitting brown tunic was covered partly by a worn leather vest decorated with dozens of pockets varying in size. A small grey hat was perched atop his head, and shaggy mouse brown hair hung around the tops of his shoulders, framing his round face and storm grey eyes.

"I see that you are all mostly awake," the gnome observed, and inclined his head in greeting to Lorian, who nodded back to the little man.

The gnome walked the last steps toward them and stopped next to the girl and Tedric. He offered her the odd plant and she took it with a slight grimace. She ripped off a small piece, a terrible squelching noise echoing through the air as it was torn apart. Her nose wrinkled as she handed a chunk of the plant to Lorian and nodded at Finriel.

"Chew it up and spread it over your friend's wound. It will extract the poison from her blood and heal the cut."

Lorian reluctantly took the fuzzy green plant and dropped his gaze to Finriel. She was deathly pale and shivering, beads of sweat streaming down her face. Lorian forced down the tightness in his chest and crouched at her side.

"If only you could be conscious to see the things I'm still willing to do for you," he whispered. With a final displeasing lurch of his stomach, Lorian shoved the plant into his mouth and began to chew. An explosion of rot and sourness filled his mouth and Lorian forced back a gag. He shoved the disgusting plant into the corner of his mouth and spat sickly green liquid to the mossy ground.

"What in Nex's name is this shit?"

An excited smile bloomed on the gnome's face at Lorian's question and he stepped forward.

"Well, it's actually quite an interesting fable. Legends say that the goddess Noctiluca created this root to aid the fairies' healing during the War of Seven Kingdoms. It can heal nearly any wound in half the time—"

"Not now, Krete," the fairy girl snapped.

The gnome closed his mouth after shooting a glare at the girl and she sighed.

"It's veloria root. It grows in the most fertile areas of Proveria, so, surprisingly, you would be correct that it is mostly shit," she answered, and began to help a still confused Tedric into a sitting position.

The warrior leaned away from her warily, and he jerked his head back when the fairy reached a hand out toward a gash on his forehead, the green poultice thick on her finger.

The girl rolled her eyes. "Do you want me to help you or not? I am glad to let that cut open even more and drip blood into your eyes."

Tedric curled his lip in contained frustration and slowly leaned his head toward the girl, but only enough for her to reach out her hand and place the poultice against the gash.

Lorian raised his brows at Tedric's silence and began to chew again, making sure to keep his tongue from touching the foul-tasting root as much as possible. Moments later, when he was at the point of gagging yet again, Lorian spat into his hand. He pressed the mushed root delicately against the long angry gash that sliced across Finriel's chest. Lorian glanced over to the fairy and the gnome now standing a few feet away, arguing in hushed voices. The events had happened too quickly for him to think. Why had they helped? And why had he placed the root on Finriel so hastily? It could be a deadly poison for all he knew, not a plant of healing. At least he had caught the gnome's name, Krete. To a thief, even the smallest amount of information was as valuable as a crown jewel.

The gnome turned his head to find Lorian watching them, and he started toward him. Nora gazed at the gnome, her fuzzy ears pricking forward as she walked up to greet him. The sight was almost comical as the large cat looked like a sufficient size for the small man to ride. The gnome reached out a tentative hand for Nora to sniff, her large muzzle nearly swallowing his hand as she bent down to inspect it. A loud purr emanated from her body and her eyes closed lazily as she leaned into Krete's touch. Lorian widened his eyes in surprise at the sight. Nora didn't truly like anyone besides Finriel. Well, and Lorian on rare occasions.

"Who are you two?" Tedric asked abruptly as he struggled to his feet.

He wiped hastily at the now dried root on his forehead before looking between Krete and the fairy. His eyes lingered on the girl for a second longer than Lorian thought necessary as he waited for an answer. He thought that the commander hated fairies and anything that had to do with them, but now he looked like he was already captivated by this strange creature.

"I'm afraid we can't say," the fairy girl answered, her face hardening as she stared back at Tedric.

"And why is that?" Lorian interjected, the stare between the two of them making him far more uneasy than even he understood. There was something about the girl that set him on edge.

The gnome appeared to have the same notion as Lorian, and he cleared his throat.

"Because our mission is one of direst importance and we

cannot tell anyone where we are going or why," he answered, still scratching behind Nora's ear.

"My question is," the fairy girl started, her gaze now directed toward Lorian, "what are a thief, a royal warrior, a mogwa, and a witch doing in Proveria?"

"I'm afraid we can't tell you why or where we are going either," Tedric retorted in a testing tone. "However, if you tell us, perhaps we'll tell you."

Finriel gasped, and Lorian jumped, looking down at her as her eyes fluttered open. She jerked into a sitting position, then winced and inhaled sharply as she looked down at the messily placed poultice on her chest. Lorian sighed in relief and leaned back on his heels, smiling as she looked around in confusion.

"The shapeshifter did this to me," Finriel groaned. "What happened—"

"The shapeshifter is dead," the fairy girl answered with a bland smile. "Your mogwa killed it."

"How is that possible?" Tedric asked, and Finriel shrugged.

"Mogwas were born from an already cursed kingdom. Killing has never seemed to affect Nora."

"Animals and beasts are not affected by the curse as we are," Krete replied with a knowledgeable gleam in his eyes. "They must hunt and kill in order to live. How could they be cursed for doing something that is in their nature?"

Finriel looked between the fairy and Krete with a scowl and then turned her face up toward Lorian. For a split second her face was soft and questioning, and Lorian's shoulders relaxed. As if remembering that she hated him, her expression quickly hardened and she looked away, Lorian's spirits dropping once more.

"This smells terrible," Finriel grumbled, placing a finger over her chest. She began to wipe the poultice away and it shed off into a powder, giving her leather armor light green speckles. Lorian took in a breath of surprise at the sight of healthy olive skin showing through the torn leather, not a large bloody gash. A faint scar appeared on her skin, but only just.

"Would you stop gawking at my breasts?" Finriel snapped.

Lorian blinked. He quickly masked his surprise with a lopsided grin and a wink. "Oh, you wish I was gawking at your breasts."

Finriel huffed and rolled her eyes, then proceeded to press her hand against the ripped fabric of her armor. She closed her eyes and slowly exhaled. A strange pulling and scratching sounded from under her hand, and the torn leather plating slowly began to stitch itself back together. Finriel took her hand away moments later with a tired gasp and leaned her head back. Her armor was completely intact once more, looking new as ever. Finriel glanced between the fairy and Krete, to find them both staring at her in shock at what she had just done.

"You have quite a gift with magic," Krete said. "I've only known a few very old witches with those sorts of powers."

"Stop petting my mogwa," Finriel snapped in reply, and braced her hands on the ground before struggling to her feet.

Lorian jumped toward her and offered a hand as she swayed, but her glare made him lower his hand without a word. Krete lowered his hand from Nora's ear, who in turn meowed loudly and shot Finriel a dejected look.

"What do you want with us?" Finriel asked the fairy none too warmly.

The fairy and Krete exchanged the same strange look once more before the fairy sighed and rolled her eyes.

"We've been sent on a mission by Sorren, King of Proveria, and we are here because we are meant to steal the pages you possess and wipe your memories."

Tedric and Finriel bristled at her words, Tedric's hand drifting casually toward the hilt of his sword.

"Sounds just like something that your king would order," Tedric spat, and the girl stiffened.

"How do you know of the pages?" Lorian asked, trying to keep his voice as neutral as possible. He gave both Finriel and Tedric a warning look to hold back, and they choked back the insults no doubt ready to fly out of their open mouths.

"The first attack occurred in Proveria. Besides, the whole realm likely knows of the drawings and pages by now, the grand council held a meeting about it four days ago," Krete replied with a shrug.

"Which is why we must take the pages that you possess and be on our way to recover the beasts," the fairy girl continued.

"Why, so that the fairies can take all of the glory of saving the realm for themselves? I don't think that's very fair." Lorian shook his head.

"That is not the reason we were sent," Krete said quickly, and Lorian raised his brows.

"Please do explain."

"We don't have time for this," Tedric interrupted, and set his angry glare on the fairy. "I have met enough of your kind to know who you are. Your king is selfish and has constantly attempted to undermine the Red King."

The fairy girl clenched her fists. "It might surprise you to know that I do not find my king to be a good ruler, but duty comes first, even if he is a tyrant."

Tedric opened his mouth and closed it again, apparently as surprised as Lorian about what the girl had said.

"We were going to offer that you come with us. If we join together, the mission could be completed quicker," Krete said, breaking the silence.

Lorian exchanged glances with Finriel and Tedric and lifted a hand to stop them from speaking again. "You would come with us to recover all three beasts?"

The girl raised her left arm and patted the outside of a pocket in her long black cloak. "All five beasts."

"What do you mean?" Finriel challenged, and the fairy girl smiled.

Krete replied, "A villager who survived the dragon attack came to King Sorren with two pages he found in the storyteller's room. The man was half mad but he was very clear that the pages had been used to create the beasts. I passed him upon my arrival at the castle, which aided in my decision to help with the retrieval of these beasts."

"It seems that a common villager did a better job of learning about the storyteller's actions than your precious Red King," the fairy girl jeered, and even Lorian tensed as he glanced at the cloaked girl.

Tedric bristled at this and wrapped his hand around the hilt of his longsword.

"I wouldn't be so quick to draw your weapon, soldier," the fairy chided with a confident smile. "Don't you want to at least listen to what we have to offer before you decide to run from us?"

"What exactly do you have to offer?" Finriel hissed, and bent down to retrieve a blood-encrusted dagger from the ground.

Lorian recognized it as Finriel's dagger and raised his brows in surprise. He knew that she could take care of herself, but he wasn't aware that the shapeshifter's dried black blood upon the ground had been her doing.

"We want to offer a traveling pact," Krete said simply, his eyes wide and trained on her dagger.

"A traveling pact?" Tedric echoed suspiciously.

Krete nodded. "We travel together and aid one another in the recovery of the beasts, or drawings, well, whatever they may be. Once they are all safely in our respective possessions, we take our two pages back to King Sorren, and you take yours back to the Red King. We can simply pretend that we never met each other."

The offer made no sense. Lorian exchanged glances with his

companions, each wearing the same blank expression that he was sure was on his own face.

"Didn't you say that you wanted to wipe our memories merely a few minutes ago?" Lorian asked with raised brows, wrapping his cloak tighter around himself with a shiver as a cold breeze filtered through the air.

"And how did you know of our mission in the first place?" Finriel asked venomously.

Lorian ached to walk to her and place a reassuring hand on her shoulder to help the anger ease, but he knew he couldn't.

"King Sorren and the Red King had a meeting about the pages right after the first attack. He learned that the Red King was planning to send out a few brave souls to find the beasts from the pages that had been discarded at Keadora's border. King Sorren sent out spies, waiting for the arrival of you three. We were promptly sent to dispatch of you and continue the mission ourselves as soon as you entered the kingdom."

"So then why haven't you dispatched of us?" Tedric snarled, the words sliding from his tongue in a venomous warning.

"We believe that the safety of Raymara and maintaining the thousand-year peace is more important than the pride of any king," the fairy girl answered. "Besides, if we did what we were told, it would surely create more tension between the fairies and witches than there already is."

Lorian turned to find that the dappled light of the sun was setting to the east, bathing the forest in a soft orange glow. The birdsong had faded and the activities of the small animals and other creatures had also ceased. They needed to continue. They were wasting time engaging in idle chit-chat.

"How can we know for sure if you are telling the truth or if you just want to take our mission as your own so that you can get all of the glory?" Tedric shot with a new severity in the tone of his voice.

The fairy scoffed and tossed her long violet hair behind her shoulder. Her green eyes returned Tedric's glare, and Lorian could almost see the tense energy between them as they stared each other down.

"Of course you would only think of bringing glory to your kingdom, soldier," she retorted, smiling sourly as Tedric's brow furrowed.

"I'm *not* a soldier, I'm a—"

"Yes, the Commander of the Ten and one of the Red King's best warriors, I know."

"But how—"

"Oh please, a mealworm would be able to sense the insufferable amount of arrogance and self-entitlement radiating off you. There's no doubt that you are a member of the Ten," the girl interrupted once more, her grin widening as Tedric's scowl deepened.

"Aeden, we need to find shelter soon," Krete said in a hushed tone.

"Aeden, is it?" Tedric interjected, taking a step forward. "Not a very common name, yet it sounds oddly familiar."

A harsh bark of laughter escaped from Aeden's mouth and her smile turned into a steely gaze. "Please, don't flatter yourself," she retorted, a slight pink flush growing on her cheeks. "I am nothing, and I come from nothing."

"I am Krete of Creonid Mountain, if anyone cares," Krete offered.

"No, not particularly, but thank you for the introduction," Finriel retorted coolly.

"We don't have time for introductions," Lorian interjected, breaking off Tedric before he could speak. "Krete is right. It's getting dark and we need to find a place to camp for the night."

"Thank you." Krete smiled and gave Lorian a nod.

Aeden glared narrowly at Lorian, who shrugged in return. "Are you saying that you're agreeing to let us accompany you on your mission?" she asked dubiously.

"Absolutely not," Finriel interjected, and at that moment, Lorian had two fiery women glaring at him.

He turned to Tedric for assistance, but the commander was staring at Aeden, his hands clenching and unclenching. It seemed that Lorian had to fend for himself this time.

"I say that more company is better than the amount we currently have. Besides, I'll have more people to talk to than a paranoid soldier and a witch who would rather see me burn in a fiery abyss than be part of this mission with her."

Tedric turned to Lorian in surprise, and Finriel opened her mouth to say something that surely would've sent Lorian to the Nether, but was cut off short.

"So, it's decided then," Krete said in a bright voice, clapping his hands together and rubbing them as if about to eat a scrumptious meal.

Finriel gave Lorian one last sharp look before sighing and throwing her hands up in defeat. The company of three had expanded to five.

6

TEDRIC

Discomfort coursed through every fiber of Tedric's body, and he took in a deep breath in attempts to calm himself. The presence of the fairy girl, Aeden, as she had called herself, was agonizing against his right shoulder as they walked side by side through the darkening forest. She was taller and thinner boned than Finriel, though that was likely due to her ethereal blood. All fairies he'd encountered were thin boned.

They walked in a tense silence, and Tedric could not say that he was pleased by the sudden change of events that as good as ruined his entire image of how the mission would unfold. He glanced at Lorian and the gnome, who walked at his other side, and feigned a growl of annoyance at Lorian's jovial smile. Finriel led the group with a stiff back, Nora slinking by her master's side. She had returned to her angry silence when they began their trek through the forest once more, though Tedric still had questions about her fight with the shapeshifter.

"How did such a small man like you come into the company of fairies?" Lorian tilted his head toward the gnome, breaking up the strangulating silence.

Krete jumped in surprise and smiled at the thief, completely nonplussed by the subtle insult Lorian had thrown at him.

"I am a messenger of the royal household of Creonid, you see," he began. "I had just arrived in Proveria to transmit a message about a black dragon causing terrible fires and annoyance across Drolatis and the border of Creonid."

"Haven't black dragons been extinct since the war?" Lorian asked.

Krete nodded. "Yes, which is why you would understand that this caused some confusion and disturbance across the twin kingdoms."

"Yes, I would say that was a logical reaction," Lorian agreed, and Tedric glowered at the thief's good mood.

Krete shrugged and continued, "When I arrived in Proveria, King Sorren informed me that the dragon was not real, but a storyteller's creation, so I insisted on helping to recover it."

"And why exactly is that?" Lorian asked with a tone of mild interest.

Krete broke from Lorian's gaze and began to wring his hands with either concern or nerves, Tedric didn't know.

"Well, to start, the dragon's presence in Drolatis has caused a great many fires to spread over the dragon kingdom border and into Creonid. I felt like if I had the opportunity to end the threat to our kingdom, then I would do everything in my power to do so. And besides, I have known Aeden since she was just a young girl and felt that it was my duty to aid and protect her on her mission."

"That's a very kind thing for you to do." Lorian smiled. "I don't think that I would want to risk my neck if it weren't for a large sum of gold in my pockets and the bounty on my head being released."

"Perhaps the Red King should have left you in the dungeons," Tedric grumbled, and Lorian glanced at him curiously.

"Has someone pissed in your ale or were you just in an abnormally good mood before?"

Anger roiled in Tedric's stomach. Never in his many years of serving his king had he been insulted so profusely by one man, let alone in such a short period of time.

"I would mind my tongue, if I were you, thief," Tedric warned, and Lorian's eyes drifted casually to where Tedric's hand rested on his sword hilt.

Nora froze in place, and Tedric barely avoided falling over her, cursing as he stumbled sideways and brushed against Aeden. She shot him a glare and was about to open her mouth when a low growl emanated through the darkening forest. Nora pricked her ears toward the trees to their right and let out a growl of her own.

"What was that?" Krete asked in a whisper.

Aeden brought up her hand in a quick demand to remain silent, her pointed ears flicking and listening for the sound. Tedric heard nothing and yet Aeden's face paled as she listened.

"We need to go," she hissed, and turned in the opposite direction from where the sound had come.

"Wait a moment," Tedric interjected, placing a hand on her surprisingly muscled shoulder. "Shouldn't we investigate the sound? It could be a beast."

Aeden swiveled to face him again, bristled and ready for an argument. She gave Tedric a venomous glare and shrugged off his hand before she spoke. "Listen here, warrior. These are my woods, so I'll decide if we will or will not wait for a creature that may very well be the beast we are meant to capture."

"Don't we want to find it if it is the beast?" Tedric retorted, his cheeks growing hot.

"No."

"What do you mean, no?"

Aeden sighed in obvious annoyance but didn't answer. She had frozen again, her eyes half closed as she listened to the sounds of the forest. Tedric silently damned her and her heightened hearing abilities. A few moments passed in still silence as they waited for Aeden to move. Tedric tightened his grip around his sword hilt. It was all he could do to keep down the frustration and anger at being undermined by a thief and a common fairy. His grip of controlling missions and giving out orders had disappeared since coming into companionship with this strange group of individuals, and he suddenly missed the nine familiar faces of his men, his trusted warriors who followed his commands without a question.

"It's gone," she said finally, and Krete let out a short breath of relief.

Aeden brought her attention back to Tedric and placed her hands on her hips. "To answer your question, I said no because it is getting dark and creatures more sinister than even the shapeshifter come out to play at these hours. We have better chances of fighting and capturing the beast when daylight comes."

Tedric didn't answer, but nodded instead. He had barely known this woman for an hour and she was already driving him mad. He should not have let his eyes overrule his brain in agreeing to let her and the gnome come on the mission. His brain was now screaming at him to tell her they had changed their minds and the agreement was broken.

"Where is she taking us?" Lorian whispered as quietly as he could, nodding toward Aeden's cloak-clad back.

Tedric kept his eyes trained on her and shook his head. They had been walking again for some time, and the silence had consumed them in a bitter glove. The pit of anger toward Lorian had subsided enough, and Tedric found that he could finally speak to the thief without wanting to hurt him.

"I'm not sure," Tedric began, "but joining our missions together is going against everything I have learned in training."

Lorian shrugged. "We would have crossed paths no matter

what. She and Krete are on the exact same mission as we are, no matter how odd that may be."

"I suppose you're right."

"I'm right about most things," Lorian replied, and Tedric snorted.

They continued onward, the small furry creatures that scuttled through the forest now beginning to settle into their homes upon the trees and within the ground for the night. The birdsong and other animal calls had dulled down into a tranquil silence. The sun, or whatever amount of it that was able to penetrate through the dense forest, had completely faded now. Tedric was beginning to wonder if they would have to create torches to light their path when the mossy areas of the forest floor suddenly lit up with a soft yellow glow.

Lorian cursed under his breath as he stepped on one of the moss patches and it changed into a bright orange, no doubt blinding him. Aeden turned and smirked at Lorian's surprise, her angular face illuminated in the soft glow of the moss.

The forest had changed into a glowing oasis, with every patch of moss that Tedric could see now lit up in different shades of yellow and orange. The trees were now nothing but shadows as far as he could see, the ancient giants looming over their heads. The forest looked like something out of a dream, and even against everything he believed, Tedric found himself watching the softly lit forest in awe.

"It's meridiem," Aeden said quietly. "You don't have it in your realm?"

"No," Finriel called scathingly from across the clearing, "we have witchlight in our realm, not glow in the dark moss."

Tedric cocked his head to the side as he considered the witch. She'd been too far away to be able to hear Aeden, and yet she had heard her. Tedric wondered if she too had heightened hearing abilities along with her healing powers. Aeden looked over her shoulder and gestured for them to follow her toward a thick patch of bushes a few yards away.

"Here," she said, and waved her hand at the companions again as she squeezed her way through the bushes.

Tedric glanced toward Finriel, Lorian, and Krete's approaching forms and shrugged before pushing his way through the tight bushes. Tedric blinked in surprise as he emerged into a small clearing of soft grass within the clustered brambles, the sounds of the forest somehow muted. In fact, there were no sounds at all, save the soft song of crickets within the bushes.

"This will do," Aeden said, and made her way to the middle of the clearing, reaching into a pocket within her cloak.

Once their other three companions had stumbled into the clearing, Finriel and Aeden made a fire from a few dead branches they'd found in the bushes, while Tedric pulled out the bread, cheese, and apples that seemed to never diminish in quantity and handed everyone a portion.

He sat down next to Aeden, and a loud crunch filled the clearing as she bit into her apple. Every fiber along the side of his body that was closest to the fairy bristled from her radiating warmth and soft jasmine scent. Krete sat farther off, nestled up next to an already dozing Nora.

"So, which creatures do you have to capture?" Krete asked after they had finished their food in silence.

Tedric looked at Lorian and Finriel, and he suddenly felt foolish for not having asked that question the very second the Red King had handed them their mission. Krete seemed to notice their blank looks and smiled faintly.

"You don't know, do you?" he asked in amusement, and Aeden smirked as she picked at the piece of bread she had not quite finished.

Tedric shook his head. "There was no time. We were only told that we had to recover the beasts and take them back to Keadora."

"Are you serious?" Aeden snorted. "Your mighty Red King didn't tell you everything you needed to know before throwing you out into the wild?"

"How dare you question my king. He gave the amount of information he believed was important for us to know," Tedric snapped, though a strange feeling of shame washed over him even through his retort.

The Red King truly hadn't given them much information about what they had to do at all, only that they were meant to capture the beasts and the storyteller. Tedric pondered this with growing frustration. He'd never been given such vague instructions in his years as a member of the Ten, especially not for a dangerous quest such as this one.

"No, he didn't," Finriel continued, breaking through Tedric's thoughts. "Though he did bring us to the Crimson Castle and hand us the quest barely a day before we left."

"King Sorren did that as well," Aeden grumbled, glancing away from Tedric.

"Besides," Tedric said with renewed strength, "how could King Sorren have possibly known which beasts you were meant to capture if the pages given by the villager were blank?"

Aeden turned to look into his eyes, and he tensed as she replied sweetly, "The villager claimed that he watched the beasts exit the pages with his own eyes."

"Likely story," Tedric grumbled.

Krete and Aeden exchanged a look that Tedric could not quite discern, and Krete spoke quickly when he noticed Tedric watching them. "Did your king at least give you a map? King Sorren did not supply us with one of those."

"Of course we got a map," Tedric muttered. At least the Red King had given them that much.

"Could we see it?" Krete smiled.

"How would you know where to go if you didn't get a map?"

Lorian asked as they all leaned forward and watched as Finriel opened the map and the ink bloomed before their eyes.

"We were sent to find you first, remember?" Aeden replied, and Tedric fought off a shiver at the intonation in her words, but Lorian simply grinned in response.

The warm fire Finriel and Aeden had made gave enough light for them to see the lines of mountains and forests. Tedric scanned the map, half expecting for the illustration of a dangerous creature to jump out of the parchment and lunge for them, but nothing happened. Tedric raised a brow and kept searching, waiting for anything to happen at all.

"Ah," Krete said with an excited smile, the skin around the corners of his grey eyes wrinkling. "I haven't seen one of these maps in many years."

Tedric blinked at the gnome in surprise. "You've seen this kind of map before?"

"Oh yes," Krete replied enthusiastically, "they were quite a common gift to gnome royalty from the Red King a very long time ago."

"So ... how exactly can we discover where and what the creatures are?" Lorian asked quizzically as he gazed at the map, bearing an expression Tedric was sure mirrored his own.

Krete reached into a larger pocket within his vest and pulled out two rolls of parchment. "Here," he began. "These are the pages we were given by the fairy king."

He gestured for Finriel to place the map on the grassy ground. After she gently laid it down, Krete unrolled the pages and placed them next to the parchment so that the corners of each page just barely touched the map.

"If what I'm thinking is true, the location and illustration of our creatures will appear at any moment."

As if Krete's words were a spell, two simply drawn images swirled into existence at two different locations on the map. They all leaned forward to get a better look, and Tedric nearly laughed as he read the small description under each image. One was a drawing of the dragon that Krete had spoken about earlier. That was not the funny thing. No, facing the dragon would be perilous indeed. It was the drawing near the border of Proveria and Farrador, the elf kingdom, that made Tedric attempt to hold in his amusement.

"An army of brownies?" Lorian voiced Tedric's thoughts with the ghost of laughter in his voice.

"You may laugh now, but the villager said that he watched these brownies pillage anything they came across," Aeden replied darkly, brushing a strand of violet hair behind her ear.

Finriel actually did bark a laugh at these words, and Tedric gaped at her in surprise. That was the first time he had ever seen her laugh, let alone smile at anything.

"That's ridiculous," Finriel replied. "Brownies are the kindest creatures that I could possibly think of. They live to serve and worship people, not terrorize them."

Aeden simply waved a dismissive hand in the air. "I have traveled to three villages in Proveria that could prove otherwise. Countless homes destroyed, many villagers dead, need I go on?"

Tedric fought away a shudder, and Aeden glanced at him with the ghost of a shrug. "Now do the same thing we just did with your pages."

Tedric tore away from her green gaze and watched as Lorian chuckled and withdrew the pages from his pocket. He unrolled them, placing them all slightly over the map, as Krete had done before.

Three different drawings bloomed across varying locations within the realm. There was no desire to laugh or surge of confidence now as Tedric leaned in closer and saw what they were to face. Not too far from their position, a chimera was drawn with unnerving precision. So that must have been the growling that Tedric and his companions had heard.

"I think we're going to have to face him before we face your brownie friends," Lorian commented, pointing a reluctant finger at the drawing of the chimera.

Tedric looked back down at the map, his eyes landing on a frightfully accurate drawing of a rakshasa, a demon bound to myths and legends. Fear coiled in his stomach, and Tedric let out a strangled sigh. This storyteller had really meant it. These creatures had ceased to exist thousands of years ago, before even the great war had begun. Tedric only knew the drawings they were to face from legends and folktales.

He shifted his gaze to the last creature drawn onto the map and frowned. He'd never heard of the scaled, catlike creature. As if the map had heard the silent question in his mind, a word bloomed underneath the illustration in slanted letters.

"What in the Nether's name is a nian?" Tedric asked as he squinted, making sure he was reading it correctly.

"I'm not sure, but it doesn't look like a very cuddly creature, if you ask me," Lorian replied.

Aeden shot him a look of exasperation and then took up the pages from the ground.

Finriel shot a hand out for her to stop, shaking her head quickly. "Put the pages back."

"Why?" Aeden retorted.

Finriel and Aeden locked into a battle of glares, yet after a moment, Aeden huffed and placed the pages back onto the map. With a grumbled thank you, Finriel extended her hands over the map and closed her eyes. The pages and parchment began to shimmer and Finriel scrunched her face in concentration.

"What are you doing?" Aeden asked in alarm.

Finriel sighed and withdrew her hands. "I put an enchantment on the map so that we don't need to touch the pages to it each time we want to discover where the creatures are."

"You can do that?" Tedric gaped, and Finriel raised her brows.

"I can do more than just healing magic, warrior."

"Good thinking." Krete nodded, interrupting Tedric right as he opened his mouth. "I do admire your skills, though you're quite intimidating."

"I have another thought," Lorian said.

"Yes?" Finriel asked bitterly, her eyes not quite meeting Lorian's.

"Why don't we each carry a page? It would be much easier if we were each responsible for one rather than two of us being responsible for all of the creatures."

Tedric nodded in agreement with Lorian's proposal. "That's a good idea. Finriel, if you will?"

Finriel shrugged in return and Aeden took up her pages without a word. The drawings disappeared from the map in an instant as she handed one of the pages back to Krete, tucking the other into her cloak.

Finriel took up the three pages and silently handed one to both Tedric and Lorian. Tedric brushed the thick parchment between his fingers, a new sense of unease sweeping over him. He didn't have even a clue how they would put the monstrous creations back into these flimsy pages. He folded it gently and tucked it away into his cloak, deciding that he would think about all of that later. Tedric grunted and shifted back against the soft grass, his head suddenly feeling heavy with fatigue.

7

FINRIEL

S *he couldn't breathe.*

A strong hand gripped her throat, pushing her face against sharp stones under freezing river water. The cold was blinding and her throat burned as she screamed and choked against the water filling her lungs. She thrashed her legs in panic, her arms pressed behind her back with another hand. Light began to dance and burst behind her closed eyes, and all consuming pain began to numb her limbs.

The hands yanked her head out of the water, and she choked and gasped in relief at the sensation of a warm breeze dancing across her face.

"Come on, little monster," the young man spat into her ear. "Show me your filthy magic. Make me fear you."

The boy laughed as she stilled, not responding to his jeers. But she wasn't paying attention to the elf boy who held her life precariously in his hands. Her impending doom was not on her mind, instead, it was on the icy blue eyes of her best friend staring back at her from behind a tree.

Please help. *She tried to send the plea through her gaze as she looked at him, the hissing taunts and strengthening grip around her neck fading away. She focused only on those eyes. The way that when he was angry, they would somehow become overgrown with silver veins, and when he was happy, it was as if sunlight glittered upon the clearest of water.*

His young angular face was drawn as he weighed his options. Stay where he was told and watch her be tortured and maybe even killed? Or ignore her perpetrator's warning and attempt to rescue her? But she knew as well as he did that he was no good when it came to fighting. She was always the one that got them in and out of trouble.

Her friend stood up slowly, resolution set on his face. The hand around her throat tightened sharply, causing a wheeze to escape from her mouth. The lack of air was making her light-headed, but she made herself focus on those eyes.

"Are you going to try to save your friend? You aren't any better, halfbreed," the boy spat. Her friend's shoulders tightened at the sound of halfbreed. She knew he hated when people called him that. He simply looked at her with a small smile, turned on his heel, and began to run. A sharp laugh escaped from the boy and vibrated against her back.

"It appears as if your little friend doesn't care about you enough to save you. What a pity."

Finriel bolted upright, cold sweat running down her back and hot tears streaming down her face. She wiped at her face furiously and glanced around at her sleeping companions. She breathed in a sigh of fresh forest air, relief washing through her to find four slumbering forms. Finriel never cried in front of others, and if she did, she made sure that anyone who saw her tears promptly forgot.

She surveyed her companions, the sight of them helping the dream fade slightly from her racing mind. Jealousy tickled at her stomach as she looked down at Nora. The mogwa was curled around Krete, the gnome's hat-covered head resting atop her paws. Finriel didn't understand why Nora had taken such a liking to him, as she was notorious for hating everyone, much like her master.

Finriel glanced down at Lorian, who had taken up a position near the edge of the group, as far away from her as he could be, she noticed. His dark wavy hair brushed over his closed eyes and his thick lashes fluttered as he took in a deep breath. Finriel quickly turned away and got to her feet, her steps forming a tight circle where she had slept. She shook away the flash of her dream from her mind, her teeth grinding together almost painfully. She couldn't shake the hands from her throat, nor the water and stones slicing her face. For it hadn't been a dream; it had happened ten years ago. Finriel had been inches from death before Nora had come and gravely injured the elf boy who had tormented and hurt her beyond reckoning. It had been terrifying indeed, though it hadn't been the only thing that caused Finriel countless sleepless nights. Of course, it kept her from being able to bathe for more than a few minutes before her throat began to clench, but it wasn't the thing that caused her countless sleepless nights. It had been the dark-haired boy with striking blue eyes, Finriel's best friend. It was the fact that he had simply left that made her insides churn. She was expendable to him, nothing more than someone whose life meant less than his.

Ten years had passed where Finriel was convinced that she would never see her best friend, or the person Finriel had believed to be her best friend, ever again. Until two days ago, when she had been taken from her quiet cottage in the city and sent to the Crimson Castle and given this quest. And now he was lying not even two yards away from her, black hair shrouded over his painfully beautiful face, sleeping peacefully as if nothing had ever happened. As if he didn't care about what he'd done to her.

Finriel couldn't breathe. She needed to get out and walk somewhere, anywhere. She turned and swooped down to grab the cloak she had used as a blanket during the night, clasping it around her shoulders as she squeezed out of the thick bushes that had sheltered them.

The air exploded with sounds of life as Finriel emerged from the enclosure of bushes, and the muscles in her shoulders loosened slightly. The furry rodents were out once more, along with the colorful birds that called to each other in an exotic song. She closed her eyes, taking in a deep breath of the sweet forest air. Right as she began to step forward, a soft male voice spoke behind her and made her spine go rigid.

"Finriel."

It was Lorian.

Finriel ignored him and began to walk away, not caring where she was going. She had the map, she could find her way back to camp. Lorian cursed and his footsteps grew louder. Maybe she would be able to lead him into whatever cave or nest the chimera was making its home.

"Finriel, we need to talk," Lorian called behind her.

Finriel tensed as a warm hand encapsulated her wrist to slow her down. She inhaled sharply and stopped, spinning and wrenching her wrist from his grip as she faced him.

"Talk about what exactly?" Finriel snapped.

She wasn't going to make it easy for him. His eyes pierced into hers, and she held back a shiver as they locked into a silent battle. After what felt like forever and yet no time at all, he looked away and took a step away from her.

"I'm sorry," he mumbled.

Finriel barked a laugh. "You're sorry? After ten years' worth of time to think of an apology, that was the best you could do?"

Lorian's expression suddenly changed from one of discomfort to frustration. He took a step forward and Finriel quickly stepped back.

"Okay, I know that wasn't a good way to start," he replied with an edge in his voice.

"I got used to what you did eventually." Finriel placed her

hands on her hips. "I thought you would come back and explain why you ran like a coward. But you didn't, and I satisfied myself by thinking you were dead."

"Please, just let me explain," Lorian insisted, returning her glare with a pleading stare.

The desire to say no was almost overwhelming. She wanted nothing more than to slap that look off his face and feed him to the dragon they would eventually have to face.

"I don't think there is much to explain," she replied simply. "Leaving your best friend to be drowned at only ten years old is quite clear to me."

Lorian winced, but she found that she didn't care about the blow she had dealt.

"That's not what happened," he insisted.

Finriel raised her brows and crossed her arms over her chest, anger rolling in fiery waves within her core. "Then what exactly happened for you to just leave me at the moment that I needed you more than anything?"

"I left because I was trying to find help," Lorian insisted. "You remember what Barrin said. If I tried to stop him, he would have let you drown before killing me afterwards. I couldn't take the chance."

Finriel winced as Lorian spoke the name of the elf boy she had desperately tried to forget. "I could have died while you were gone and you would have only found out after you returned. Barrin wouldn't have been able to kill me, even by accident, if you had stopped him."

"I know, and I feel all the more a fool for it." He sighed. "But when I went to get help, I was—"

"Lovebirds, it's time to go," Tedric's deep voice called from the bushes behind them.

Finriel inhaled sharply and clenched her fists, glancing over Lorian's shoulder to find Tedric's head sticking out of the green-ery. Finriel waved at him in acknowledgement and the warrior's head disappeared. Lorian took another step toward her, his eyes shrouded by guilt.

"This isn't over," he said softly.

Finriel ignored the squeeze in her chest and moved past him without a word of reply. It wasn't that she didn't want to say anything, because she did. Yet Finriel knew better than to let her tongue slice through cords that were already frayed. The sounds of wildlife around her molded into one buzzing sound as she fumbled through the thick brush and into the clearing. Aeden and Krete's backs were turned to her as they spoke in hushed tones, and a flutter of wariness went through her stomach.

"I'm here," Finriel huffed, and looked to Tedric, who was watching her, a strange expression skewing his slightly plain yet handsome features. "What?" she snapped, and Tedric shrugged.

Lorian slipped into the clearing moments later, his expression set into one of cool and stony indifference. Finriel glanced at Tedric again to find the commander's brown eyes dancing between her and Lorian with slight concern. He paused as their eyes met, and he gave a nod of feigned casualness.

After a few minutes of shuffling around and gathering their belongings, the companions scrambled out of the safe enclosure and headed out in the direction of the chimera, according to Finriel's map. Finriel still held the map between her hands, staring down at it in concentration. Hours had passed and she hadn't spoken to anyone since her conversation with Lorian, and she still felt no desire to speak at all. She glanced back at the thief, who was walking a few paces behind her, to find him looking straight ahead over her shoulder. She whirled back toward the map, her cheeks and temper burning.

The things he had told her didn't make the burning hatred she felt toward him lessen, in fact, they made things worse. She didn't know what to think, and her mind whirled as she tried to guess what he was about to say before Tedric had cut him off. No matter how much she tried to deny it, there had to be something more to the story. Perhaps he wasn't lying and truly was unable to come back to rescue her after he supposedly went to find help. But why hadn't anyone come to her aid aside from Nora? She winced as her jaw popped, and she realized she was grinding her teeth together in thought.

❧ 8 ❧

TEDRIC

S ilence enveloped the companions as they made their way through dense thickets of emerald brush and clearings of soft grass and wildflowers. Their surroundings felt blurred, and Tedric was beginning to think that Millris Forest was simply one large dream.

Tedric walked by Lorian's side, the thief's face molded into a mask of nonchalance, though Tedric could sense the tension radiating from him. Tedric glanced up at Finriel, who walked in front of him once again, and watched her usually fluid movements now jerky and stiff. She was clearly in a bad mood, and curiosity prickled at Tedric's insides. He couldn't seem to figure out what had happened between them, but it was now clear that they had past business that hadn't been resolved. He sighed and looked away from Finriel, forcing his mind back to the present moment. It was not his place to pry into their business, and he would not speak of their relationship unless one of them brought it up first. He was the Commander of the Ten, not a gossip.

"What made you decide to become a warrior?" Aeden asked from Tedric's side, making him jump.

He hadn't heard her approach, and he met a beautiful smile

that nearly shocked him as much as her silent arrival at his side. Her green eyes flashed as he attempted a half-smile in return, and he quickly looked forward again, his insides feeling oddly tight.

"I grew up in a very poor sector of Crimson City, and my father has been a raging drunk since I can remember. I worked as a stable hand in the main city and soon became the one providing for both me and my father. I was eleven years old when I discovered the training grounds of the Ten and began watching their sessions whenever I had a free moment. After a few months, the previous commander of the Ten took notice of me and I became his student. I trained and fought with them for four years before they accepted me into their ranks at fifteen, and the Ten briefly turned into the Eleven. When Commander Eldron died, the Red King appointed me as the new commander of the Ten, and I have tried to fill that role ever since."

Aeden remained silent through Tedric's story, and he felt her eyes on him again when he stopped.

"And what of your mother?"

Tedric shrugged. "My memory of her is faint. She died when I was four, which likely is the reason why my father turned to the bottle."

Aeden inclined her head. "My mother died when I was young as well, though part of me wishes that I had known her only briefly, as you knew yours."

"Why is that?" Tedric asked.

"Her death was an atrocious thing, and it changed my relationship with my father in an unfortunate way. He's become a terrible man."

Tedric raised his brows and looked at Aeden, her gentle face screwed up in anger.

"I'm sorry to hear that," he offered. "Loss can change one in strange ways."

Aeden chuckled and shook her head. "My father has done things that would make even the most evil man question his methods. Yet, I believe that he's always been this way and my mother's death only helped him realize it."

Tedric didn't know why, but he found himself placing a comforting hand on her shoulder. Aeden's eyes widened and she opened her mouth, yet no words were spoken. The tightness in Tedric's chest squeezed, and he withdrew his hand. He didn't understand it, but he felt like he knew her. He'd never felt so comfortable telling his story to anyone, let alone a stranger.

Lorian cursed and Tedric whipped his head around to find the thief behind a tree not more than five paces away. Lorian motioned for Tedric to stop, and Finriel pressed herself against a tree. Krete was at Aeden's other side in the blink of an eye, his expression filled with concern.

"What are you all afraid of?" Tedric asked in confusion.

Krete pointed directly ahead, and Tedric searched the thick trees for what his companions had seen. His mouth opened in awe as his eyes landed on the sight ahead. He wasn't sure how he hadn't noticed the four fairies dancing and chanting, their melodic voices now carrying through the still air.

"That's not good," Aeden hissed under her breath.

"Who are they?" Tedric asked, keeping his voice in a low whisper.

"They're Sythril. They have the ability to see into the future, as well as learn prophecies from the four goddesses. The dance they are doing is one of the methods they use to tap into their abilities. It is a morning ritual that allows them to see how future events will unfold."

"That's a good thing, isn't it?" Lorian whispered, and Aeden shot him a look.

"How could it be a good thing? Sythril aren't only fortune tellers, but also tricksters. They tell the future in riddles and puzzles, and it can be enough to send a man into madness trying to unravel what's been said."

"Sounds like company I would enjoy to be in," Lorian

replied, slightly more relaxed. "Those sorts of people are useful in my line of work."

Aeden froze, and Tedric brought his attention back to the Sythril, who had now stopped their dance and odd chanting. Tedric's mouth went dry as they simultaneously turned their heads toward the companions.

"This is not going to end well," Krete whispered under his breath.

"What can we do?" Finriel asked urgently, coming from behind the tree with Nora to join Krete's side.

The Sythril were almost upon the companions now, and Tedric's hand drifted instinctively to the hilt of his longsword.

"Don't," Aeden hissed, her eyes sliding to Tedric's hand with a sharp shake of her head. She lifted her eyes to meet his questioning gaze and whispered, "Sythril hate all violence, even the kind that is caused in order to create peace. If they see that you are threatening them in any way, they will magic our brains into pudding before we take our next breath."

Frustration coiled around Tedric's stomach, but he dropped his hand as the fairies finally reached them. The Sythril were beautiful, even the single male fairy standing among them was unnervingly good looking. Their features were round and soft, unlike Aeden's sharp angles. Their long thick lashes exaggerated identical almond-shaped eyes. They looked like perfect images of each other, all save the female fairy who stood at the front.

Her long, snow white tresses that tumbled in waves around her slim figure gave her a serene and godly glow. Tedric nearly reached for his sword again when he looked into her unnatural eyes. One was soft red, glowing as if from a fire within. The other, however, was a stark black, as if the pupil had swallowed up the rest of her iris. Tedric noticed that she was also the tallest of the group, and seemed to tower over even his tall frame.

The lead Sythril considered the five companions, examining

each of them until her gaze fell upon Aeden. Her head tilted to the side as she noticed who, or rather what, Aeden was.

"A fairy within the company of a witch, a gnome, a human, and a halfbreed. What a very odd sight indeed," the Sythril began. Her voice was soft and melodic as she continued, "If I had not already seen this would come to pass, I would have been shocked, alarmed even, at this sight."

The three Sythril behind her nodded in agreement and Tedric bristled, attempting to ignore the strange shiver that ran down his spine at the sudden cold breeze that enveloped them.

"What do you mean?" Tedric ordered. "We don't have a half-breed in our company."

The lead Sythril tilted her head back and laughed, the sound similar to wind chimes. Tedric did not laugh, and he did not understand either.

"Halfbreeds are incredibly rare," Tedric reasoned, attempting to keep his voice even. "Magic-bearing creatures like witches, fairies, and elves mixed with human blood is a terrible idea. Halfbreeds are typically half mad by the time they're full grown, and if they don't end their lives, they typi-cally become—" he broke off, realization suddenly dawning upon him. He turned to look at Lorian, who was staring at his worn boots as if they held the secret to how they would capture the beasts.

The lead Sythril smiled and inclined her head with another sweet laugh.

"It is common for your kind to trust and be completely igno-rant of the details of important people in your company," the Sythril said, "but since the topic has only now been breached, I will let the future weave its own path."

"You may find what I'm about to say as odd, but our business is none of your concern and we must be on our way," Aeden said with a hint of urgency in her voice.

"We know of your business," the Sythril replied, her expression turning solemn. "I am afraid that your quest is one of great peril."

Tedric stepped forward. "What do you mean?"

The four Sythril turned to him and, as one, closed their eyes. Tedric tensed as they took in a breath in unison and an explosion of small lights cascaded into the air as they exhaled. The small twinkling lights stilled in the air as Tedric watched, and the fairies began to speak as one body.

"Blood is coming. The age of peace has come to an end and the time of war has returned. A game has begun, and the lives of many are now held in the balance."

Tedric stood paralyzed as he listened to the fairies' words and watched, enraptured, as the lights began to swirl and move around them, pulsing and brushing across their faces, clothing, and hair as they went. The lights pulsed brighter, and Tedric suddenly realized that they were stars. Nora lifted her head toward the stars and sneezed as her large nose came into contact with one of the small glittering orbs.

"Some players of this game are not who they seem, and you will all feel the sharp pain of betrayal when the serpent is revealed." The Sythrils' voices died down into a whisper. "One of the key's deaths will be foretold by the Youl. This death will be made and unmade by the one who spun it to be true."

Lorian snorted and turned away. "This is ridiculous, we should go."

"Wait," Finriel hissed, grabbing his arm tightly. Her eyes were transfixed by the fairies and swirling stars, and Tedric watched Lorian's face pale as he looked upon her hand clasped around his arm.

"This is probably exactly what they want, Finriel," Lorian replied coolly. "They want to stall us so that the chimera can sneak up on us and rip us to shreds."

"The one with fire within her soul has unparalleled power," the fairies began to speak again. "The flame within will either become a key that unlocks the salvation of this realm, or it will be our downfall. One key may not live without the other, though it may at times seem as if one holds more power over the rest. Each key will play their part in the game, but not until they are reunited with their locks. If this is not done by the end of the second summer, the realm will be bathed in darkness, and the tyrant of death shall reign once more."

The stars swelled, and with a loud *pop*, they blinked out of sight. If it wasn't for the awed and frightened expressions of his companions, Tedric would have thought he had imagined them being there at all. The four Sythril opened their eyes, and as if they could no longer see the companions, they turned their backs and began to walk in the direction from which they had come and were soon swallowed into the misty thicket of trees.

"Well, that was an odd experience," Lorian said, his voice thick with forced amusement.

Tedric nodded in agreement, his mind whirling. He turned to find Aeden's face deathly pale, though her expression was unreadable.

"What is it?" Krete asked gently, apparently noticing her strange behavior at the same moment as Tedric.

The question seemed to shake Aeden out of her reverie, and she blinked multiple times as if to beat away a memory.

"It's nothing," she replied quickly. "We should go."

No one answered as she set off, and they began to walk closely behind. The Sythrils' words whirled and knotted in Tedric's mind as he walked, the prophecy sounding more like a riddle than a prediction. There were no keys involved in their quest, unless they had been speaking of figurative keys. He shook his head, unsure what they meant about the key with fire in their heart. None of it made sense. He looked up to find Lorian directly in front of him, and he lengthened his stride to walk beside the thief.

"So, halfbreed, is it?" Tedric asked.

Lorian glanced at Finriel's back and then down at the forest floor. "It's a long story."

"We have time," Tedric replied, and Lorian shook his head, eyes still on the grassy ground.

"I've had quite enough stories and predictions for today."

"Lorian—"

A growl rumbled in the distance, cutting Tedric off. The growl echoed through the trees, setting off a few brightly colored birds that flew from the branches overhead. The companions stilled and Finriel turned to face the direction of the sound. Tedric drew his sword in a flash, and Aeden's hand went down to the hilt of her own thin blade.

"Finriel, check the map," Tedric ordered, and Finriel stiffened. "Now," he barked, feeling no sense of fear of the witch as Lorian did.

Finriel paused for a second longer, but another distant growl set Nora's hackles on edge, and the mogwa hissed in the direction from which the sound came. Finriel glanced down at Nora and clenched her jaw, scrambling to retrieve the map from her cloak before she unrolled it.

Moments passed in agonizing silence, and Tedric felt as if he may crawl out of his skin when Finriel's eyes went wide and she quickly rolled up the map.

"It's coming."

❧ 9 ❧

FINRIEL

F inriel had been partly lying when she said that the chimera was near. It was near, if her companions thought of a league as near. She simply needed silence, and for Tedric to finally keep his mouth shut for more than a few minutes. He and Lorian were both proving to keep her nerves hanging by nothing more than a thread, and she was growing tired of it.

She remained at the lead of the group, Nora close by her side as they wound their way through endless thick pines. The map was held firmly in her grip, and she was intent on acting as if she was reading it until they reached the chimera as long as it guaranteed a long moment alone. She needed some time to think about everything that had happened in such a short time, with Lorian, their new companions, and now the prophecy all crowding inside of her mind.

Finriel was smart enough to know that the Sythril were not to be trusted, yet the words they spoke echoed through her thoughts nonetheless. *Blood is coming.* She fought away a tremor. She simply knew that the words within the prophecy needed to be understood.

Someone cleared their throat from beside Finriel and she

jumped, looking down slightly to find Krete smiling up at her. She fought back a glare and forced herself to smile, or at least quirk the corners of her mouth upward as best as she could manage.

"Has your spell remained strong?" Krete asked, tilting his head toward the map in her hands.

Finriel glanced down, and her stomach dropped to find that two of the beasts had disappeared. She forced her smile to grow wider, and she looked back to Krete with a nod before rolling up the map and tucking it away before he could see.

"Magic reliability can begin to fade with older maps. I'm surprised that old thing hasn't dropped a few of the beasts off its surface yet."

The map *had* dropped beasts off its surface, but she was not about to tell him. She also was not going to admit that Krete's nugget of information made her feel slightly better about the maps faultiness.

"You have quite impressive magic, it's more than I've seen a witch contain in nearly twenty years," Krete continued, and Finriel tensed.

"I know nothing other than healing and performing a few party tricks," Finriel replied coolly, but Krete shook his head.

"I wouldn't count what you did with that map as a party trick," he replied.

Finriel clenched her fists, forcing down the rising heat in her abdomen. "If I had any sort of magic that proved otherwise, I would be dead or at the Witch Isles."

Krete shrugged. "Of course. I have to admit that my travels to Keadora have lessened greatly, so I am not aware of the powers you witches are allowed to perform."

"It likely hasn't changed since the last time you stepped foot in my kingdom," Finriel said, the anger in her middle rearing its head a bit higher.

Krete seemed to sense her tension and took a step away from

her, lengthening the distance between them. Silence filled the air once more, and Finriel glanced around the forest. The landscape was beginning to change, shorter trees with bark the shade of parchment now interspersed with the pines. Their leaves were beginning to change from pale green to the color of the sun, and relief swept through her soul at the slight change of scenery.

Finriel reached into her cloak, certain that they had walked nearly to the location where she had seen the chimera. Before her fingers could graze the map, a strangled growl emanated through the air. Finriel stiffened and stopped, Krete and the other companions coming to a halt behind her. The strangled growl came once more, this time much closer than it had been the first time. A high-pitched whine made the hairs on Finriel's arms and neck rise, and she quickly gathered her magic in preparation for the chimera's approach. An almost reptilian guttural sound echoed through the trees, and Finriel cursed under her breath.

Thump.

Thump.

Thump.

Thunderous footsteps shook the ground under their feet, and Finriel felt a cold bead of sweat trickle down her back. She let a small current of magic flow to her fingertips and she withdrew her dagger, noting a few specks of dried shapeshifter blood still encrusting the blade.

"It's almost upon us, I can sense it," Aeden warned, and drew her blade in one fluid movement.

Movement to Finriel's left made her turn her head, and she blinked in surprise to find a small bow in Krete's hands, as well as a quiver of blue feathered arrows strapped to his back. She didn't have any time to consider how he might have been able to shrink or make the weapon magically disappear, but the gnome noticed her stare and gave her a curt nod. She turned her attention back to the oncoming beast and tried to ignore the tremble in her legs.

"Do you have your page?" Finriel asked Lorian through gritted teeth as another loud series of thumps shook the trees around them.

"It's ready," he answered promptly, and Finriel snuck a glance to find the yellowing parchment held tightly in his left hand.

She nodded and her mouth dried as what sounded like a chorus of both high- and low-pitched cries rang through her ears. The trees before them split and crashed to the ground, revealing the chimera as it stalked over the fallen branches and came to stand before them.

It was unlike any creature Finriel had ever seen. It was at least ten times her size and ungodly in sight, the heads of two different kinds of beasts protruding from the body of an enormous lion. The center head was about the size of Nora and indeed a lion. The lion head opened its mouth, revealing large pointed teeth dripping with saliva. Its hot stinking breath blanketed over them as it scrutinized the five companions and Nora with hungry yellow eyes. Though it wasn't this head that made Finriel struggle to keep herself from turning in the opposite direction and running for her life. It was the two dragon heads on either side of the lion head that swung their long necks and snapped enormous sharp-toothed jaws at them.

The dragon head on the left side was dark green, the other a vibrant blood red. Large scales glinted in the soft light and their monstrous jaws ground and gnashed in anticipation. A long green spiked tail waved back and forth from the end of the lion's body, crashing into the bushes behind. A loud whine gargled out of the red dragon's mouth and the chimera started forward, headed straight for Lorian.

The thief stumbled back a few paces, looking around wildly for any kind of weapon he could use against the beast, but all he had was a meager dagger at his side and the piece of parchment that would somehow swallow the chimera inside of it. Tedric and

Aeden ran forward, slashing and stabbing at the thickly furred legs that were about the size of Tedric himself. However it was as if their weapons were nothing more than blunt toys against the beast's skin. The green head of the chimera whirled around and growled at the two, and the entire body turned with it.

"Krete, take aim under one of its front legs!" Aeden yelled as she quickly dodged and rolled out of the way of a giant clawed paw.

Tedric skillfully sidestepped out of the way and spun so that he was underneath the chimera's stomach. He thrust his sword upwards with all of his strength. The razor sharp blade barely punctured the beast's flesh, yet was still deep enough for the chimera to feel it. The beast let out three pained screeches and one of its hind legs kicked under itself. The world went into slow motion, and Finriel watched as the talon pierced straight through Tedric's shoulder. The loud crack of bones snapping reverberated through her ears and she watched as Tedric grunted and was sent flying several feet into the air. He did not move when he hit the ground.

"We need to get it into that page!" Aeden yelled over the chimera's yowls and screeches.

Krete aimed and shot an arrow toward the chimera's lower chest, and the arrow struck true to its target. The chimera yowled again and Finriel cursed as she leaped back, narrowly avoiding the green dragon head as it twisted and writhed in pain. She closed her eyes and flung a protective shield around Tedric's heaped form, praying that it would suffice to keep him from being trampled by the enormous monster they faced. Krete knocked another arrow into his bow and Finriel took in a deep breath, knowing what she needed to do. She closed her eyes and prodded at the hot anger in her stomach, willing for it to come to attention. Another roar made Finriel fling her eyes open, and without another thought, she flicked her fingers toward the arrowhead. Flame engulfed it and Krete cursed in bewilderment, staggering backwards as bright flame licked toward him.

"Just shoot the damn thing!" Finriel yelled, and Krete brought his attention to the chimera and released the flaming arrow.

His aim was messy this time, but the arrow still glanced across the chimera's side, sending sparks skittering across its pelt. The chimera roared and turned toward Krete, all three heads locked directly upon him. Finriel yelled and made herself run toward the small man. She may have only met him yesterday, and he might have already proved to get on her last nerve, but Finriel was not going to let him die if she could help it.

"Stop!"

Finriel's stomach did a somersault as Lorian brushed against her and came to block Krete from the chimera, page outstretched in his trembling hand. The chimera seemed to notice Lorian's approach, and to Finriel's surprise, it stopped screeching all at once. All three heads focused their attention on him and it walked over slowly.

The chimera stopped barely two feet away from Lorian, and Finriel found herself fighting the worry that crawled through her stomach. She bashed the feeling aside, inwardly cursing her weakness. Lorian remained deathly still as the three heads examined him with their large yellow eyes, blinking and sniffing him all over his body. Confusion swathed over Finriel's frantic heartbeats as she watched the odd scene fold out.

The lion's eyes softened and it lowered its head, gently rubbing against Lorian's chest. He was sent stumbling back with the sheer force of it. The lion head stretched forward and rubbed against him once more, this time more gently than before. Krete darted out from behind the thief, coming to stand slightly behind Finriel. He inclined his head in acknowledgment, though his expression made it clear that she would have to explain herself once this was over.

Finriel stalked forward and let flames dance across her fingertips, throwing caution to the wind. She glanced at Aeden, who was inching toward Tedric's limp form, her eyes flicking between the chimera and Finriel's flame-engulfed hands with mingled horror. The two dragon heads spotted her movement and they growled threateningly, snapping her attention back to the beast. The chimera stepped in front of Lorian, as if to hide him from her sight, and all three heads bared their teeth menacingly.

"Stop," Lorian called from behind the chimera.

The heads stopped growling immediately and the chimera turned reluctantly to face him once more. To Finriel's shock, Lorian tentatively outstretched his free hand and placed it upon the lion's broad nose. The lion's eyes narrowed, but not out of anger, and Lorian began to stroke it softly. Three pairs of yellow eyes closed, and the chimera began to purr. At least, as close to a purr as a three-headed beast could get. The noise was guttural and reptilian, ricocheting and clashing with the sounds of the lion's feline purr.

"It likes you," Krete said in wonder, his eyes wide as he watched the chimera lean into Lorian's touch.

Finriel let the fire surrounding her hand extinguish in a puff of smoke and she shook her head in amazement. A surprised bark of laughter broke from Lorian as he looked at the admiring creature.

"Put it back in the page while you still can," Aeden called from a distance.

Finriel found her kneeling next to Tedric's still form, and the worry slowly ebbed back into her stomach. Aeden's fair face was lined with concern as she looked back down at their companion, lifting a piece of torn leather from his shoulder. She gasped and looked back up at Lorian.

"Do it, now."

"But—" Lorian glanced at Aeden, his expression uncertain.

Finriel blinked in disbelief for what felt like the hundredth time. He liked the beast. Aeden shot him a warning glare and pointed her hand at the page he had tucked into his belt.

"Just show the chimera the parchment and make it come into contact with it."

Lorian stalled for a few moments, apparently considering his options. The chimera continued to purr, all three heads gazing down at him happily. The green dragon flicked its eyes toward Krete and Finriel, who stood slightly behind Lorian, as if warning them to stay away.

Lorian reached down and withdrew the page with a grunt of resignation. The chimera whined in protest when it spotted the page, as if in recognition. The beast took a step back and shook all three heads, as if saying that it did not want to return to the depths of the parchment.

"Please, I need you back in this page," Lorian said softly to the chimera.

It shook its heads again, but took a reluctant step forward. Lorian gazed at the creature tenderly as he outstretched his hand, holding the page. A growl escaped both dragon mouths, and Finriel watched as Lorian tensed his muscles but stood firm.

"I need you to go back inside."

The chimera appeared to understand, and after a few moments, it bowed all three heads. The green dragon reached its nose out and Lorian kept his hand steady as the creature's nose brushed tentatively against the page. The red dragon head reached around and nuzzled Lorian softly on the shoulder before swiveling toward his outstretched hand. The green dragon stretched forward again, and the chimera's body began to glow as it pressed its nose firmly against the page. The chimera's body began to shrink rapidly as it sucked into the parchment. Lorian stepped one foot back to brace himself as the chimera's body shrank and shot into the page with a loud pop. And just as quickly as it had appeared, it was gone.

Finriel let out a breath she was not aware she had been

holding and trotted over to Tedric. She glanced up as Lorian turned the page and looked at it, no doubt stunned at what had just happened. She could just make out a grotesquely beautiful image of the enormous beast that had been standing before them only moments ago, now etched onto the parchment with black charcoal. The three heads were arched and fierce as their black eyes stared up at the thief. A pang shot through her chest as Lorian exhaled slowly, rolled up the page, and silently tucked it back into his cloak.

He didn't speak as he turned and met Finriel's gaze, his face drawn and pale. She held his stare for a short moment and nodded in silent affirmation before turning back to Tedric and Aeden. She knelt down and cursed, partly from the state of Tedric's mangled form, but also from the pull she felt to check if Lorian was all right. But she would not. She could not.

"It seems to me that you're quite capable of much more than healing and party tricks," Krete said, and Finriel met his storm grey gaze.

She sighed and knelt down by Aeden's side, the fairy eyeing her with slight wariness.

"I've kept it a secret my entire life," Finriel said softly, and something similar to sorrow flashed across Aeden's face and she looked down at her hands.

Finriel looked at Krete, and the gnome simply gave her a sad smile. She knew that he would keep her secret safe, they both would.

"I'll go check on Lorian," Krete said, and turned away.

His kind voice echoed across the small clearing of birch trees and pines, and she heard him asking Lorian if he was okay as she set her concentration upon the wounded commander.

❧ 10 ❧

FINRIEL

"**D**o you think he'll be all right?"

Aeden's question rattled the growing fear in Finriel's throat, but she only shrugged and peeled back the bloodied tunic sleeve of Tedric's right arm. She stifled a gasp at the sight of a large bleeding gash that ran from the base of his shoulder down to his wrist. The chimera's claw had torn through his flesh as if it were nothing more than gossamer and penetrated deep into the muscle and tissue.

Finriel grimaced and leaned in to get a better look at the wound. Tedric's arm had been all but shredded. Milky white tissue and muscle were torn and clearly exposed, while blood ran freely down his side and back, dripping onto the soft green moss. There was no time to find shelter. He would bleed out before they found the nearest village or city.

"I can try to stitch his muscles back together and clot the bleeding," Finriel grimaced, feeling through the torn flesh with her magic.

Aeden nodded and shifted her position so that she was kneeling by Tedric's head.

"I've used a simple spell to put him into a deep sleep. He shouldn't wake for at least an hour."

"That's probably best." Finriel nodded. "I certainly would not want to be conscious for what is about to happen." Stitching the tissue and muscles back together, let alone clotting the wound to stop the bleeding, would drain Finriel of most of her magic. She needed time, and then she would need rest.

"Setting the muscle and tissue will probably take quite a while," Finriel said, and looked up at Aeden.

Aeden held Finriel's gaze evenly, and dread fell like a lump of iron in Finriel's stomach as the fairy said, "I saw what you did with that arrow."

Finriel opened her mouth to argue, but Aeden shot her hand up. "Please, there's no use in defending yourself. I wanted to thank you for it, actually. The laws of magic are too strict, and I feel for anyone with that much power and no way to use it."

Finriel had no words as Aeden once more inspected Tedric's mangled arm, her worry-lined face drained of all color. Finriel furrowed her brow as she watched the fairy girl, the thought of what she had said quickly melting away and replaced by a strange revelation. She hadn't noticed that Aeden had truly connected with Tedric in such a small amount of time.

"How is he?" Lorian asked as he and Krete approached.

Krete's face paled and turned slightly green as he peered down at Tedric's wound. He clapped a hand over his mouth and turned away, walking briskly into a small patch of bushes. Lorian raised a brow and gave Aeden a questioning look. She sighed and got to her feet.

"Krete is ridiculously squeamish when it comes to blood," she explained, then walked to Tedric's feet and gestured for Lorian to stand at Tedric's head. "Help me move him somewhere comfortable."

When Lorian didn't move, Aeden placed her hands on her hips and sighed, then muttered a few words a language Finriel did not understand. Though she wasn't sure of what Aeden said, Finriel was certain that it had been either an insult or a curse toward the thief.

"I don't know what you just said, but thank you." Lorian smiled.

Aeden huffed. "Just shut up and help me."

After a moment, he shrugged and scooped Tedric up by his uninjured shoulder. He grunted with effort as he waited for Aeden to pick up the warrior's legs, and they began to carry him toward a plush bed of moss.

"Couldn't you put some kind of spell on him to make him any lighter?" Lorian asked with a gasp. "He weighs a ton."

"Finriel needs to conserve her magic to help him heal, not make your short job any easier," Aeden retorted, also grunting with effort as they shuffled Tedric to the patch of moss.

"How did you know how that touching the page to the beast would work?" Lorian asked after they set the warrior down.

Aeden shrugged and wiped her hands on her pants, not quite meeting the thief's gaze. "It was a lucky guess."

Krete emerged from the bushes and walked stiffly toward the patch of moss where they had set Tedric down, still looking slightly green and disgruntled. Finriel's eyes widened in surprise as Nora bounded into sight behind Krete, her chest splattered with drying blood from the meal she had no doubt just come back from devouring.

"I will never be rid of blood, will I?" the gnome groaned, and hastily looked away from Nora before he jogged to Finriel.

"You lied about your powers," he said, "and you almost lit me on fire."

Finriel clenched her fists and glared at the gnome, who met her with a calm gaze.

"I was simply trying to help," she retorted, "and I am wasting my time with you right now. Tedric needs my help." Finriel didn't wait for an answer and spun away, stalking to her fallen companion, who Aeden arranged in a position that would allow Finriel to work freely. The stench of death hit Finriel's nose and she tilted forward as Nora pressed her head against her waist. Finriel held back a gag as the smell of blood and decaying flesh rolled off the mogwa in waves.

"Go clean up," she whispered softly to Nora. "I need to use my magic to help the pompous commander."

Nora regarded Finriel with a dejected expression and shot off into the darkening woods, hopefully to do as she had commanded. Finriel took in a deep breath and turned to Aeden. She prayed that they would be safe tonight out in the open, especially with whatever dangers in the forest Aeden had mentioned the previous day.

"Do you still have that root you used to heal us from the shapeshifter attack?" Finriel asked, taking her mind from the looming shadows that were beginning to close in.

Aeden nodded once. "Veloria root, yes. The forest is full of it."

"Good," Finriel replied. "I'm going to need a lot of that. Get extra if you can, we'll likely need some of it in the future if the men keep trying to play the hero."

"Do you need me to do anything?" Lorian asked from behind her shoulder.

Finriel angled her head toward him and considered. The cold mistrust and anger from their unfinished conversation seeped into her skin once more, overpowering the strange desire to like him again. She shook her head.

"Just stay out of the way."

Lorian's expression turned into stony coldness and he nodded once before walking over to a still slightly pale Krete and clapping him on the shoulder. They both walked away and settled by a small group of trees, muttering to each other about making camp. Finriel focused her slightly heightened hearing on their conversation, cursing herself silently for wanting to know what they were saying.

"You know, through all my years of being a messenger, I don't think I've ever met a witch with powers such as Finriel's."

Lorian grunted. "She's certainly a fiery one. I wasn't surprised in the least the first time she used battle magic."

"You knew of her abilities?" Krete wondered. "Why didn't you say anything when we questioned it?"

"I've done enough to put her life in danger," was all Lorian replied, and Finriel's stomach clenched.

The gnome sighed and Finriel heard them mumble something about making a fire for the night. Finriel could not see Lorian's expression, but she could feel his eyes upon her as she brought her attention back to Tedric's wound with another whispered curse.

Aeden had already disappeared in search of more veloria root, and Finriel took in a deep breath as she settled into a more comfortable position by Tedric's arm. She closed her eyes, allowing for her magic to flow and gather at her core. The flames came at once, eager and hungry to be unleashed from her fingertips. Finriel grunted and began to mold the flames into something softer, something kinder. Through her four years as a healer in Crimson City, she had always known this part to be difficult. Her body yearned for the flames, and pushing them away felt wrong. And yet she found the dampening switch within herself in seconds, and the flames were gone.

Finriel opened her eyes and placed her hands over his arm so that they were hovering just above the bloody, oozing wound. Finriel looked down and noticed that he was still bleeding too much for her to be able to fix the internal damage. She would have to clot the blood first so that he would not bleed out before she could even begin to stitch his mangled arm back together.

She steadied herself and closed her eyes again. She focused on directing the soft healing magic toward the dripping blood.

She pictured the crimson river stopping completely and the minor scrapes healing. A sucking noise sounded from beneath her hands, and Finriel opened her eyes to gaze down approvingly at her work. The arm had stopped bleeding and the thick crimson slowly began to disappear from the exposed skin of his arm. At least there was one good sign.

Finriel screwed her face up as she readied to move on to the tissue. This would be the difficult part. Her hands were already shaking slightly as she placed them over the wound once more. She had not exerted much energy at all on clotting the blood, so perhaps it would not be so difficult to fix the muscle.

Finriel reached out with her magic again to feel and examine the inside of his wound. A few cleanly severed muscles passed through her magic, and a surge of confidence went through her. Those would be easier to fix. The feeling of confidence plummeted when she landed on a shard of bone near his shoulder. She hadn't realized the chimera's claw had done that much damage. The bone was shattered, to say the least, with small pieces of bone scattered throughout the shoulder and bicep.

Finriel had never tried to fix a bone this broken before and had no idea how to even begin. Doubt seeped into her chest as she continued to feel around, multiple ideas of the best way to fix the bone forming in her mind. She nodded to herself with resolve. First she would force the small bones back into their places and close the wound, then set the larger bone that had been dislocated back into the socket.

She moved her hands up to his shoulders and slowly clenched her fingers, the larger shards of bone moving easily to their rightful place. The smaller pieces were finicky and slipped through her magic, and she cursed under her breath as she willed them to mend.

Finriel gasped as her magic stumbled across a piece of bone lodged into a spot next to his shoulder. It was inserted directly into a section of Tedric's arm mere centimeters from the brachial artery. If her magic slipped, he would be dead in minutes. She didn't want to focus on that for now, at least not until Aeden returned with the veloria root. Perhaps that would help repair some of the less severe injuries in his arm. Yes, she would leave that bit for later. She instead set her magic on a long tendon near his elbow that had almost been severed cleanly in two. She began to move her hands slowly, allowing for the ends of the muscle to bend and move toward each other. A small breath escaped Finriel's mouth as they touched, and she willed for them to slowly stitch back together.

The sounds coming from Tedric's arm were not pleasant, popping and sucking being the most prominent noises that filled the forest clearing around her. Finriel continued to force his tendons back together, moving painstakingly slow through blood and flesh. The meridiem lit up the forest after a good while of her work, making Finriel jump when a bright yellow light flashed behind her closed eyelids.

She had successfully stitched a good amount of Tedric's arm back together by the time she heard Aeden's quick footfalls coming toward her. Finriel retracted her magic and opened her eyes, allowing herself a short break as she watched the meridiem change colors with each step Aeden took. She would need all the energy she could possibly muster in order to complete the task that was to come.

"How is he doing?" Aeden asked worriedly as she came to sit by Tedric's head, her hands and cloak pockets full of veloria root.

"I've managed to piece most of the major tendons and muscle back together, but the chimera broke his arm in a place —" Finriel broke off, unable to finish the sentence. The act of speaking it out loud would surely make the pressure of performing the intricate task ahead too much to bear.

"In a place where?" Aeden pressed, her eyes wide.

Finriel wiped her brow and sighed. She was sweating, and as she looked down, she found her hands shaking harder than before. She was already beginning to tire, but she couldn't stop now. She had to get that bone out of there and put it back into place, hopefully without killing Tedric in the process.

"It's a hairsbreadth away from an artery," Finriel said finally.

Aeden gasped and placed her hand on Tedric's uninjured shoulder, her lips set into a determined line. She stretched her other arm forward and offered the foul-smelling root to Finriel.

"I will help you in any way that I can, but you need to get that bone out of there."

Finriel nodded and gently reached out to nudge Aeden's hand back. "If you can make a poultice with the veloria root and place it along the bottom half of his wound, that would be a great help in itself. The root will most likely continue to heal any smaller lacerations that need to be repaired."

Aeden nodded and lightly squeezed Tedric's uninjured shoulder before standing. Finriel stood and winced as her knees groaned from being in one position for so long. She and Aeden switched places so that that the fairy was closer to the lower half of his arm. Finriel settled herself by Tedric's shoulder and the crucial task before her. The wound did not look as daunting as it had before, but Finriel knew the worst was yet to come.

"This better work." Aeden shuddered between mouthfuls of the foul-smelling root.

Finriel looked at her and scowled, then returned her focus to the mangled shoulder.

"Just make sure he doesn't wake up," Finriel replied curtly. "The pain that he is about to experience would be best to endure unconscious."

Aeden did not answer, but Finriel was sure that her command had been heard. Finriel allowed for the magic to flow through her core and out of her hands, overtaking her body as she placed them over the hole in Tedric's arm and began to feel for the shard of bone. It was not hard to find, and Finriel began to feel around for the best way to extract it without pressing too close to Tedric's certain death.

It was so close to the artery, almost too close. Tedric had been damn lucky that the bone had not hit it directly, or that the chimera's claw did not stab right into it. He would have been as good as dead in minutes.

Krete and Lorian's whispered conversation carried to Finriel's ears, and she stopped her work with gritted teeth. She tried to drown out their voices and focus on the task at hand, but it was no use. She was tiring quickly and found her magic drifting slowly back into her core.

"Will you two kindly shut your mouths while I am doing this?" Finriel hissed through still gritted teeth, and she jumped as soft fur and a strong body rubbed against her back. "Not now, Nora," she snapped.

Her nerve was beginning to break, but she needed to concentrate and push on. Nora growled from behind Finriel's back, but she listened and moved away toward Lorian and Krete. Finriel couldn't afford to have stupid conversations and a damn cat make her accidentally kill their companion. But he was more than that, Finriel realized, almost surprising herself. He was becoming their friend, her friend. Finriel didn't have any friends in Keadora, or any other kingdom. Her secluded life in her cottage with only sick and injured patients filtering in and out never gave her much opportunity to meet others, though she had never truly wanted to. She enjoyed her life alone with Nora, spending her days helping others and studying whatever magic she could.

The thought of her new kindling friendship made a block of fear land in Finriel's stomach. She wiped her sweaty hands over her pants and got into position over Tedric's injury. The bone was much easier to find this time, and Finriel's heart began to pound as she wrapped a strand of her magic around it. She took in a deep breath and slowly, very slowly, began to pull. A thought entered her mind and she paused, sending another tendril of magic down to feel the size of the bone shard. The slightest wrong move and it would penetrate the artery. Finriel gasped and clenched her hands involuntarily, the bone wobbling in her magical grip from the movement. This piece was the largest out of the bone shards she had encountered. She ground her teeth and continued, willing it out slowly with her magic.

Sweat began to trickle down Finriel's spine and forehead, and she stopped in terror as Tedric stiffened and groaned beneath her. Finriel stopped pulling at once and flung her eyes open to watch Tedric writhe, his eyelids fluttering in pain. He was still under the effects of the sleeping spell Aeden had put on him, but it didn't mean that he couldn't feel the extraction.

"Can you do something?" Finriel asked Aeden breathlessly. The fear in her stomach hardened as she watched him, certain that the bone would shift back down if he kept squirming.

"I can try to ease the pain a little," Aeden said uncertainly, her face clouded with nerves and concern. She had finished applying the veloria root poultice, and to Finriel's relief, it seemed to be working. Aeden wiped her hands over her black breastplate, sending a smear of green across it before she stood and crouched at Tedric's head. His light hair was damp with sweat and pain, and his eyelids continued fluttering and fighting against the magical sleep Aeden had put him under.

"Hurry," Finriel urged Aeden, who crouched frozen in place, looking down upon his pale face as if he were a lost gem she had finally found and was suddenly being ripped away from her again.

Aeden placed her hands on either side of Tedric's temples. Tedric's taut body ceased fighting and relaxed instantly, and Finriel sighed with relief.

"Keep him under that spell," Finriel ordered, and reached her magic out once more.

The work was painfully slow and tedious, the bone moving

barely an inch at a time as Finriel maneuvered it through his flesh. She groaned as her magic faltered, and she sucked in a breath as the bone shifted and bumped closer to certain death. It would have to be pulled out right against the artery, unless she sent it in the opposite direction and extracted it from a different location. But that would take too long, and Finriel could already feel her magic starting to waver with each pull and shift she made. Finriel cursed as her hand slipped and dread made her freeze as the bone wobbled and stopped directly upon the artery. The slightest wrong move and it would be over.

"What is it?" Aeden hissed.

Finriel did not dare open her eyes, but instead focused her energy on holding the bone in place as best she could. Her entire body was beginning to feel like lead and she knew that her energy would soon be too depleted to finish extracting the bone.

"It's touching the artery," Finriel whispered. "I need you to keep him as still as you possibly can."

Aeden made a muffled noise in response, and Finriel pulled again. Her heart clenched painfully in her chest with every passing second. She willed her magic to stay as steady as possible, pouring every last ounce of her energy and power into making the bone bypass the artery without severing it.

Finriel's mind was beginning to fog with fatigue and she strained against it, shaking her head to force it away. She could not afford to be tired, not now. There was not much left to go now ...

The bone slid out from beside the artery and broke through skin with a sickening pop. Finriel stumbled onto her backside and blinked her eyes open to find the blood-spattered bone sticking out slightly from his shoulder.

Aeden let out a sigh of relief and a smile bloomed across her lips. "You did it," she gasped.

Finriel smiled weakly as she took in another gulp of air and let her head fall to the side. Her vision swam and her entire body screamed for rest, but she ignored her body's demand and pushed herself back up.

"Not quite yet," she answered.

She reached her hands out and, with a final surge, forced her magic out to maneuver the bone back into its rightful place. Her hands shook terribly but the bone obeyed and moved back into his arm with a sickening sound and found its place within the once shattered bone.

"Okay," Finriel croaked, "now I did it."

11

TEDRIC

The world slowly shifted back into focus as Tedric blinked his eyes open, finding himself in a clearing illuminated by meridiem and a crackling campfire. Stars peeked through thick branches overhead, and the slowly waning moon helped light the night sky. He closed his eyes in an attempt to remember what had happened, until a dull throb in his right arm made him look down and fall back into reality. They had fought the chimera.

Something brushed against his shoulder and Tedric flinched, only to realize that Aeden was kneeling at his side, a damp cloth held in her hand. He simply stared at her meridiem-lit face, shock and confusion swimming through his skull as she watched him with an unreadable expression. Her green eyes slid down his face as she leaned over and gently pressed the cloth against his arm, which was covered in green powder. A waft of familiar rot floated into his nose and he recognized it as the veloria root she had used on his forehead with the shapeshifter.

"Thank you," Tedric managed to rasp, still watching Aeden's angular features as she silently cleaned the veloria root from his arm.

The cloth against his skin stung slightly, but it was nothing compared to the pain he had felt during the sleep from which he hadn't been able to wake. He hoped the torn flesh underneath the compound was healing well. He couldn't remember what the wound had looked like when the chimera had first stabbed him, but he guessed that it hadn't been a pretty sight. Aeden simply got to her feet and glanced away as she dropped the damp cloth onto the ground by his head.

"I should get you some water," she replied in a monotone voice.

She turned abruptly and set off toward Lorian and Krete, who were huddled by the small fire only a few paces away. Sparks crackled from the flame and flew into the air, dancing upon the slight breeze with a swirl of smoke. Tedric watched Aeden bend down to speak to Lorian in a hushed voice and sighed. He shook his head and returned his attention to his arm. He had been so foolish to go underneath the beast like that. He was lucky to even be alive. Aeden returned moments later with Tedric's water skin clutched in her hand. She silently handed it to him, still not meeting his eyes. Tedric grunted with effort as he reached up with his uninjured arm and gave her a small nod of thanks before he began to drink. Tedric made an effort not to moan with relief as the water filled his mouth. His throat had felt like a dried up stream ever since he had woken, and the feeling of the cold liquid trickling down his throat felt like a gift from the goddesses themselves.

Aeden settled to her knees and reached down to grab the cloth from the ground before continuing to clean off the veloria. Her face was slightly paler than Tedric remembered, her violet hair messy as it escaped from her usual braid in large pieces. She was even more beautiful now that he could examine her closely. Tedric silently cursed himself as unruly thoughts of her full lips tempted to swirl through his mind. The pain from the wound must have messed with his brain for him to think those sorts of things.

"Thank you," Tedric said again, his voice sounding more even now that his throat was no longer an equivalent to the Crubian desert.

Aeden shook her head as she took a small wooden box from her cloak pocket and opened it, revealing an unfamiliar purple powder.

"Healing your arm was all Finriel's doing," she replied softly, and began to press the powder along his arm.

Tedric blinked in surprise and craned his neck to where Finriel's huddled form sat heavily against a tree by the fire, her body wrapped up tightly in her cloak as she stroked Nora, who was sprawled out beside her. The large hood of Finriel's cloak shrouded her caramel eyes, so Tedric could not tell if she was simply resting or if the procedure she had performed on him had taken a larger toll.

"She used up a lot of magic saving you," Aeden continued, and Tedric turned back to look at her. "Your arm was nearly in shreds and the chimera broke your arm in a spot—" She paused for a moment before continuing, "There was a shard of bone lodged very close to an artery. Extracting that bone and mending it without killing you took up most of her energy."

Tedric frowned. "Finriel must have more magic than most if she was able to manage that."

Aeden gulped and looked away, and he could tell that she was hiding something from him. He waited for her to speak, and after a moment, she said, "She has battle magic."

"How?" Tedric breathed in disbelief, and the ground tilted slightly from the sudden knowledge. "We could all be sent to the Nether for treason with that information."

Aeden shrugged. "She wielded fire against the chimera after you were injured. She will not speak any further about it though, Krete and I have tried."

Tedric glanced at the witch once more, and found that he felt no animosity toward her. She had saved him, and for that he owed her his life, even if knowledge of her abilities now put all of them in danger.

"How quickly will her magic recover?" Tedric asked.

"It depends on how strong she is." Aeden shrugged. "But from what I have seen, I think she will be fully recovered by late morning."

"I need to thank her," Tedric answered, "but you kept me from feeling most of the pain, and for that I really am grateful."

Aeden met his gaze, her piercing green eyes sending a shiver down his spine. "I should have done more, but my magic only goes so far as relieving pain and fear, as well as putting someone into a deep sleep."

She shrugged, and Tedric found himself placing his good hand on her knee. Aeden tensed at the touch, and Tedric quickly withdrew his hand.

"I likely would have died from the pain alone if you had not done what you did."

Aeden looked away without an answer and began to withdraw a tightly wrapped ball of cloth from her cloak. Tedric didn't know why his spirits dropped slightly when she began to wrap the cloth tightly around his arm and shoulder without a response.

"How are you doing, mighty commander?" Lorian asked with a grin as he approached Tedric and Aeden from their small camp.

Tedric managed to smile back and shrugged. Pain sliced through his shoulder and Aeden tightened her grip around the bandage. Tedric cursed loudly, the pain sweeping even through the various poultices and spells.

"I will take that as excellent," Lorian said, and stopped behind Aeden. "You look terrible."

"I'm sure that you wouldn't look much better if you'd been a handshake away from death," Tedric replied.

Lorian scoffed and took a step closer. "Look at me, I will be handsome even when the Nether greets me with open arms."

Aeden snorted and their eyes met again. Tedric was the first one to look away this time, the strange feeling in his chest overpowering the brief wave of pain.

"You need to get warm and rest. Can you walk?" Aeden asked.

Tedric nodded. "It's my shoulder that's injured, not my legs."

Lorian came around to help on his other side as Tedric sat up, and the thief and the fairy helped him to stand. The world tilted under his feet and Tedric stumbled backwards a step. Aeden and Lorian steadied him easily and he shook his head. They led him toward the crackling fire and helped him sit on a patch of moss across from Finriel. She didn't lift her head at their approach, and Tedric could now tell from the steady rise and fall of her chest that she had fallen asleep. Krete was lying beside Nora, his head resting upon her flank as he too slept, his small cap over his eyes.

Lorian settled down next to Tedric and took out a loaf of bread and cheese from the satchel, handing the food to him. "Do you still want to hear my story?"

Tedric ripped a chunk of bread with his teeth and nearly groaned in relief and gratitude for the food. He met Lorian's gaze and nodded once, a strange curiosity washing over him.

Lorian shrugged. "Once you hear everything, you may think of me differently."

Tedric snorted. "I'm not so quick to judge. I swear that even if I do think of you differently, I won't treat you as if I do."

"Lying is a thief's move." Lorian grinned. "I must be rubbing off on you already."

Tedric chuckled and took another bite of bread and cheese, wincing as his shoulder pinched at the movement. There was a moment of silence, and Tedric almost thought that Lorian might not speak again.

"My mother was an elf and the sister of some conceited elven duke. My father was a human from Notharis, a city near Mitonir."

"I know of the city." Tedric nodded. He had visited Notharis for a day after escorting the Red King to a council meeting in Mitonir, the capital of Farrador and home of Arbane, the queen of the elves.

"My parents met on a hunting trip and fell in love instantly," Lorian continued. "Elves don't respond well to interracial relationships, so when my mother's family heard the news that she was in love with a lowly human, she was disowned from the family and banished from Mitonir."

Tedric watched the emotions wash and wane from Lorian's face as he told his story, a strange feeling of brotherly protectiveness washing over him as Lorian spoke.

"My mother gave birth to me three years later, and we lived a poor but relatively good life. I met Finriel there and we became fast friends. We would spend every moment together and we thought that we were inseparable." Lorian paused and took in a deep breath before continuing, "Something terrible happened to her ten years ago, when she was ten and I was eleven. I couldn't help her, even though it was the only thing I ever wanted to do. I was captured by a band of thieves shortly after and never saw her again."

"Until now," Tedric murmured.

Lorian nodded. "Until now, and she thinks that I left her because I didn't care if she died. It's far from the truth, but it's the only story that she'll believe."

A lance of sorrow for the thief hit Tedric in the chest and he reached up his uninjured arm to pat Lorian on the shoulder.

"So you became the worst thief to ever exist and found yourself in the dungeons of Crimson City before being put on this mysterious journey," Tedric said in an attempt to lift Lorian's mood.

Lorian gave him a weak smile and nodded. There was a moment of silence, and Tedric jumped when Lorian spoke again. "Tell me, why did you suggest me to the Red King for this quest?"

Tedric raised his brows in surprise and answered easily. "I saw your expression when my men and I captured you in the throne room. You didn't want to carry out the job, and you certainly did not want to steal the bloodstone."

"No sane man would," Lorian replied with a grin, and Tedric returned the smile before continuing.

"I was brought to a private meeting when the outbreak of the beasts occurred in Proveria, as one of the riders from the night watch had come to the king with the three pages. The Red King immediately requested that I find two capable bodies for the quest, and my first thought was of you." Tedric paused and ran the hand of his uninjured arm through his sweat-dampened hair. "I knew that you had the face of a man who wanted to do better than what he was given, and I knew I had to give you the opportunity."

"How kind of you," Lorian replied, but Tedric could sense sincerity behind his sarcastic comment.

"I've been given very little in life," Tedric murmured, and flicked his eyes to Aeden's form upon the ground, but her closed eyes and even breathing made it clear she too was asleep. He sighed. "I will always pray for people to be presented with opportunities to help them become great, and so I tried to do that for you."

Silence filled the air and Tedric pondered Lorian's story. He was a halfbreed and a thief, and yet one of the best men that Tedric had ever met.

Tedric sighed and shook his head. "We all have our wounds and stories that shape us. It's not about forgetting those stories, but reshaping them into a lesson instead of a burden."

Lorian chuckled, "I never expected for such a wise man to be hidden beneath all of that muscle."

Tedric smiled. "You barely know me, but you will soon come to realize that I'm more than just a simple soldier."

12

FINRIEL

Nine days passed in a daze of walking slowly and resting frequently. Tedric's shoulder had healed considerably, but Finriel was adamant about him going easy on it. She didn't want her difficult work to be ruined by any foolish movements.

Sweat trickled down Finriel's neck as they maneuvered through a quick moving stream, the large black rocks giving her some stability as she led the way across. The water was surprisingly warm and she was able to bite back a surge of panic as the phantom grip of hands around her neck faded. Grunts and panting sounded behind her, and Finriel took a final step through the quick water before she was on dry land, the stream their marker of leaving Millris Forest. A large expanse of pale open land greeted them now, and a dry breeze blew strands of hair around her face.

Finriel turned and ignored the heavy weight of her wet boots as she watched Aeden deftly pick her way across the stream, followed by Tedric, Lorian, and Krete at the end of the line. Nora paced along the edge of the stream, a loud meow of indignation coming from her maw and making Finriel roll her eyes in exasperation.

"Come on, don't be a baby," Finriel called to Nora, who meowed once more.

Nora paused, resting her weight upon powerful hind legs before she sprang forward, leaping cleanly across the wide stream and landing with a puff of dust at Finriel's side.

"That wasn't so bad now, was it?" Finriel said, and scratched Nora behind the ear.

The mogwa closed her eyes at Finriel's touch and a loud purr emanated from her throat.

"She's as impressive as they say," Aeden commented as she stepped onto dry land, her boots squelching as she waddled to Finriel.

"They are creatures of hunt." Finriel shrugged.

"How did you find her?" Aeden asked, and Finriel met her eyes.

"I left Keadora to live in Farrador with my ward when I was six years old," Finriel began. "The day before we arrived in Notharis, we came across a small village. There were shouts and crashes coming from one of the homes and I went to see what was happening. After slipping out of my ward's grip and running into the stranger's home, I found a small grey creature darting around the house, destroying every last corner."

A smile found its way to Finriel's lips as she recounted the story, the image of Nora as a small kitten still vibrant in her mind. "I managed to use my magic to catch her attention, and within moments, Nora was sleeping upon my lap. She was barely three months old at the time, mind you, so she was about the size of a fully grown house cat."

"Did you steal her?" Aeden asked, her tone curious.

"No." Finriel laughed, and turned her attention to watch the three men scramble and curse their way across the remaining few steps of the stream. "The villager gave her to me within seconds of Nora calming. He explained that he had bought her from a traveler in Mitonir, but he hadn't realized that the traveler had brought her from Naebatis."

Aeden shivered. "Travelers have always made me uncomfortable."

"You've met a traveler?" Tedric asked from where he now stood at Aeden's side.

Aeden clenched her jaw and nodded. "Yes, in passing."

"Travelers are quite interesting people," Lorian said, panting, with one boot in his hand as he tipped river water from it. "Who doesn't enjoy someone who can portal without a portal stone, as well as conjure up a terrifying beast upon command?"

Finriel rolled her eyes. "They cannot conjure up just any beast, it's unique to each traveler."

Lorian shrugged. "I would love to have that ability myself. It would make breaking the law much easier."

"It's no wonder that they're strange, coming from a cursed kingdom and all," Krete added, his cap slightly skewed. "Let's pray that we do not have to encounter one on our journey."

Finriel nodded in silence, still scratching Nora's ear. The sun was beginning to peak in the sky, and Finriel closed her eyes in satisfaction. They hadn't seen the sun since entering Millris Forest, and it was a relief to finally feel the warm rays upon her skin.

"Do you smell that?" Aeden asked suddenly, and Finriel opened her eyes. She reached out her senses and took in a deep breath of crisp air, though something else mingled.

"Is that smoke?" Finriel asked, and Aeden nodded.

"I think so."

"There." Krete pointed. "Something is burning in the distance."

Finriel dropped her hand from Nora's back and turned to find that there was indeed a plume of black smoke rising into the cloudless sky. Her magic sparked and she quickly bit down against it.

Finriel had successfully avoided any questions about her magic thus far, but she knew that she was running out of time before it would be unavoidable, and now was certainly not the time for an interrogation.

"It's a village," Aeden announced, her heightened sight no doubt the reason for her knowing such a thing.

"We should go help," Tedric said. "It could be one of the beasts."

Finriel unrolled the map and searched it, her eyes landing upon their position in the realm. They were near the border of Proveria and Farrador, and an illustration of a small village sat at the edge of a small forest thicket by the shimmering kingdom wall.

"Do you see a beast?" Tedric asked, and Finriel glanced about the page before her eyes landed upon the image that had caused Finriel to laugh their first night in Millris Forest.

Finriel nodded. "It's the brownies."

The companions made good time trekking across the large open fields, each step accompanied by rising nerves. Finriel had ordered Nora to hunt in the forest thicket near the Farridian border, and the mogwa had set off at high speed, eager for her mission. The smell of smoke strengthened, and Finriel could soon make out three buildings reduced to nothing but ashes. Her stomach dropped at the sight, though she couldn't see any citizens of the village. The sight of wreckage was new to Finriel, and she couldn't help but feel a stab of fear.

The small village was deathly quiet as they walked through, inspecting their surroundings in confusion. Orange embers still popped and sizzled from the burned buildings, which, to Finriel's horror, appeared to be homes. She coughed against the smoke that held thick in the air, setting the sun in a red haze. Browning leaves cracked under their feet and dust puffed around them as they walked down the dirt street. Finriel scanned the area, spotting the shimmering wall marking Farrador's border near a thick line of ancient gnarled trees.

"We should knock on one of these doors to see if anyone is home," Lorian suggested as he peered through one of the small windows of a nearby cottage that was unharmed.

Finriel shook her head and shot him a glare. "Do you want to get us killed? It's too dangerous."

Tedric looked to Aeden, who was watching him closely. Finriel raised her brows in surprise as Tedric winked at the fairy before turning back to the wreckage and shrugging with his good shoulder.

"What's the worst that can happen? I am one of the most skilled fighters in Raymara, and you have untapped magic flowing through your veins. I think that we can fight a few untrained villagers."

"And what are we, bystanders?" Lorian asked, narrowing his eyes.

Finriel ignored Lorian and transferred her glare to Tedric with a shake of her head. "With your actions fighting the chimera and the state of your arm, I wouldn't be so confident about our chances."

Tedric opened his mouth to spew whatever commander nonsense he'd prepared for the day, but Finriel stalked off to continue investigating the deserted village, hoping to cut off any potential conversations about her magic. The village was desolate, and Finriel wondered if the inhabitants had fled from whatever, or whoever, had caused the fires. The hair on the back of her neck prickled as she remembered the illustration of the brownies.

"I think there are people in here," Finriel said, her mind focusing on the task at hand as she peered through the dust-heavy window of a small cottage. She walked around toward another window on the opposite side of the small door of the home. Shadows and dust obscured most of her view, but a flicker of movement within the barren cottage was clear enough to see.

Krete stepped forward and reached his hand out toward the

door. Before he could knock, Finriel put a hand on his arm to halt his advances. She looked out in the direction of the elf kingdom border, her face set with concentration as she listened to a distant rumble.

"Do you hear that?" She already knew that only Aeden would say yes as the fairy murmured in agreement. Finriel's hearing abilities were far from normal even in comparison to others of her kind. After a few moments, the sounds became clear, and Finriel cursed. It was the sound of hundreds of stomping feet, and it sounded as if those footsteps were coming right for them.

"It's the brownies," Aeden hissed, and she motioned for them to gather close and draw their weapons.

The companions gathered into a line across the main road, each drawing their respective weapon. Finriel yanked her dagger from its sheath, receiving strange looks from her companions.

"Appearances." Finriel shrugged, and they gave her a medley of forced smiles and feigned frowns in reply.

"Do you have the page?" Tedric asked, glancing at Aeden who stood at his side. She met his gaze and nodded, patting the pocket of her cloak.

The sound grew louder, and soon a distant puff of dust was visible at the outskirts of the village. Flame roared through Finriel's body, and a bead of sweat began to form on her forehead as she continued to shove down the endless inferno that roiled in her veins. She needed to keep her magic on a leash, especially now that it had gotten a taste of air after longer than she could remember.

"Ready?" Krete asked, the small bow in his hands held deathly still as he watched the hundreds of small creatures coming toward them at an alarming speed.

"I still don't think that we have anything to worry about," Lorian said casually. "I mean, they're brownies, for Nether's sake."

"Don't be so sure," Aeden answered quietly. "They're likely the reason for the burned homes."

High-pitched squeaks and excited chatter in an unfamiliar language became audible from the approaching dust cloud, and they were upon the companions in moments. Or rather, most of them began to swarm around Aeden, and the remaining furry creatures started toward the other four companions, fists raised to fight. They looked like very small furry men, even smaller than Krete, whose head reached Finriel's chest.

They all wore the same uniform of small plain leather vests and red hats that had holes on either side to accommodate long pointed ears. Their legs were covered in tufts of wiry brown hair instead of clothing, and their small feet were also covered in the same kind of hair in place of shoes. Finriel's eyes widened in alarm at the sight of Aeden standing defenseless as the brownies ripped her sword out of her hand and discarded it on the ground. She cursed and thrashed as they scrambled all around her, their excited chatter growing louder and louder. Less than half of them even seemed to notice the rest of her companions' existence.

Tedric surged toward the swarm of creatures, his sword raised. His face was set into grim determination, and a brownie soon noticed his attack. It growled, red eyes set on the warrior. It lunged and landed on Tedric's chest, and Finriel's stomach gave a flop as Tedric stumbled. Tedric grunted and spit wiry hair from his mouth and grabbed the creature by the side of its small vest, ripping its body from his face. Finriel whirled back to the swarm of brownies before her, but found that they were not keen on fighting her, nor Lorian or Krete for that matter. They growled as Lorian took a step forward, and the thief quickly retreated.

"Stop fighting the brownies!" Aeden yelled through the swarm around and on top of her.

"What do you mean? They are attacking you!" Tedric yelled, tossing his small assailant to the ground.

"No," Aeden gasped, and yanked a brownie from her shoulder, "they're not! Just lower your weapons and back away."

Finriel shoved her dagger back into its sheath and Krete lowered his bow. Tedric looked up and exchanged a glance with Lorian, and the thief nodded. Tedric lowered his sword and took a step away. For a few moments, Finriel thought they had made a mistake as she watched the brownies continue to crowd around Aeden. As if a torch had been extinguished, the brownies began to peel away and created a perfect circle surrounding her.

Tedric motioned for the four of them to step back as the brownies began to line up, and Finriel made her way to stand next to the panting warrior. The four companions stayed deathly still and watched the brownies all bow their heads and murmur in odd voices as they glanced amongst each other and toward Aeden who watched curiously. Her dark violet hair had come loose from its braid, and long strands hung wildly across her face and tumbled down her shoulders.

"They weren't trying to kill us," Aeden began in amazement. "They were trying to protect me from the four of you."

One of the brownies stepped forward and bowed before her, his small head nearly touching the ground. They all looked like children doting upon a loving mother, and Finriel blinked in surprise as the rest of the brownies bowed low as well.

"Get the page out," Lorian said, indicating Aeden's cloak pocket with his chin. One of the brownies turned and looked at Lorian with suspicion and distaste.

"You are a very dislikable person," the creature declared in a high-pitched voice.

Lorian snorted and gave the small furry man a grin. "Trust me, I agree with you fully."

The brownie humphed and turned again to Aeden with a bowed head.

"I don't understand why they are just standing there," Krete said from Finriel's other side. "They all but destroyed this poor village, and yet they do nothing to harm us?"

"Why are you all being so kind to me?" Aeden asked in a honey-sweet tone.

The brownie who appeared to be the leader of the small army stepped forward.

"We, the ones close to the ground, have been sent ready and armed to protect the maiden from a deadly prospect." The brownie smiled at Aeden, who glanced at her friends in question. Finriel raised her brows and looked pointedly at the page in her hand.

Aeden looked all the more confused but turned and smiled back at the brownie. "Thank you for your kindness," she began, "but for all of your safety, I need you to go back into your page, at least for a short while."

Aeden pulled out the page from her pocket and bit her lip as she bent down so that she was at eye level with the small creatures. She beckoned a brownie closer with a smile, and the creature shuffled forward with a sad expression skewing its furry features.

With one fleeting look at Aeden, the brownie stepped forward and disappeared into the blank page with a faint popping noise. One by one, the brownies began to line up behind one another and walk into the drawing. Aeden looked up to meet Tedric's gaze, and Finriel watched them exchange a strange moment of complete stillness, Aeden's eyes tinged with sadness.

After a few minutes, the last of the brownies had walked into the page with a faint pop. Aeden looked down at the scene they had been drawn into by the storyteller and then proceeded to fold it and place it back into her cloak.

She straightened and began to walk toward her companions' still frozen forms. Finriel was not quite sure how to react to what had happened, and judging by the still forms of her companions, they didn't know either.

"H-how was that so easy?" Krete stuttered, and shook himself slightly.

"I'm not sure," Aeden answered, a contemplative tone to her voice.

"It was as if they were waiting for you, and when we came to help, they were trying to protect you from us," Krete suggested.

Lorian nodded and sheathed his dagger at his side. "We should get—"

He was cut off by the sound of a door creaking open and a cry of gratitude. Aeden stilled, and in an instant, she was gone. Finriel watched the fairy dart behind a building, and her footsteps were quick as she headed toward the thicket of trees by the kingdom border.

She had no time to think further upon Aeden's strange behavior when an old voice exclaimed to them, "Oh thank the goddesses, you've saved our village!"

Finriel spun around to find a frail old woman standing in the doorway of the cottage Lorian had previously tried to check on. She was short and small boned in stature, covered nearly head to toe in a dark brown dress and matching shawl. Her grey hair was tied into a tight knot at the back of her head and her grey eyes pooled with tears as she looked at the four companions gratefully.

"Please, come in and rest. I have enough food and water for all of you."

The old woman stepped aside and beckoned them with a wrinkled hand. They looked at one another and shrugged before following the old woman into the cottage. The quaint home was mostly bare of furniture, with one large room containing a small table and cooking area. A small light wood door separated what Finriel assumed was the sleeping quarters from the rest of the space. She stopped abruptly at the sight of a young girl no more than fifteen standing in the corner of the cottage closest to the sleeping quarters door.

The girl looked at the four of them with wide eyes. Finriel snorted inwardly, though Finriel couldn't find that she blamed her for the look of alarm so plain on her face. Finriel thanked the goddesses that Nora was hunting and not with them at the moment if the girl was so surprised simply by their entrance. Though perhaps it would have been funny to watch the young girl collapse from fright at the addition of a mogwa in their company.

The girl's plain brown eyes seemed to take up a large portion of her face, making her button nose and thin lips seem as if they had just been placed on her face as an afterthought. She was very thin as well, and she looked at the old woman with concern as the woman huffed and sat heavily into a chair.

"My name is Naret, and this is my granddaughter Lola."

The girl gave them a nervous nod, her gaze not quite meeting their faces.

Naret sighed and waved the girl off. "Be a good girl and put the kettle on for tea, and find them some food once you've done that."

Lola bowed her head and shuffled toward the soot-smeared fireplace at the opposite end of the small cottage. Her hands shook visibly as she grabbed the flint and steel from the dirt floor, and after a few failed attempts to create a spark, Finriel walked forward.

"Here, let me help."

The girl looked at Finriel and gulped as she approached, coming to kneel by the girl on the dirt floor. Finriel closed her eyes and willed for a small spark to burst from her fingers the moment that she struck the flint, praying that her small spell would not be noticed by Lola. In the blink of an eye, the pieces of wood were alight with flame. Finriel turned and offered the flint and steel back to the girl, who looked simply terrified. Finriel's confidence faltered, but she was certain that the girl had not noticed her release a small amount of battle magic.

"Don't mind Lola," Naret said with a harsh sigh. "She's my son's daughter. He died a few moons back during a trip to meet with the elven scouts in Stenul."

Finriel nodded and stood as Lola sprang to her feet and busied herself filling their large rusty kettle with water from a bucket by the small pantry. The girl did not add to her grandmother's statement, but had clearly heard as her throat bobbed with the threat of tears. Stenul was the main training camp for elven scouts, and one of the most perilous areas of Farrador. Finriel only heard stories of danger and darkness from that place, and she scowled when she found Lorian looking at her knowingly. They had made a silly plan to sneak into Stenul when they were children, though it had never come to pass.

"Well, don't just stand there like a bunch of confused children, come and eat. You have had a trying day."

The old woman beckoned them forward with a gnarled hand and Lorian, Krete, and Tedric silently obliged. Tedric squished into the small chair with some difficulty. the chairs had obviously not been fashioned to accommodate large men. Finriel hid her smile and leaned against their wash basin, having no desire to sit with the strange woman and her uncomfortable male companions.

The food was simple, nothing more than a plain vegetable soup and bread, but Finriel ate it, thankful to have something warm in her stomach. It was a heavenly change from the food in Tedric's ridiculous magical satchel. Her companions ate their food in silence, their eyes wandering occasionally to the old woman seated at the head of the small table. Naret watched the four of them with curiosity and almost a hint of ambivalence as she waited for them to finish their meal.

Nothing but the soft clink of spoons against bowls and the occasional slurp filled the small cottage, giving Finriel time to ponder what had happened. The brownies clearly had not wanted to injure her, nor any of her companions for that matter. *So why would they have created the fires in the villages?* Finriel gently shook her head, deciding it best to speak to the others about the matter when they were free from the old woman.

After they had finished eating, Naret barked for the girl to clear the dishes out of the way and serve the tea. The girl scurried to the table and handed them each a steaming mug of tea before silently taking their bowls. Tedric gave her a warm smile as she took his bowl.

"Thank you for the meal. It was delicious."

Her cheeks went pink and she dropped Tedric's gaze like a hot coal, curtsying before she turned away. Finriel rolled her eyes at the warrior, who caught her gaze at the same moment and gave her a faint shrug. Finriel knew that he was the most respectable male she'd ever met, but that likely wouldn't stop poor Lola from getting any ideas from their small exchange.

"Now that you are all fed, you must tell me the reason for coming and saving us from those terrifying creatures," the old woman insisted.

Lorian glanced between Krete and Tedric questioningly. Tedric looked to him, and as if through a silent conversation in their minds, Krete and Tedric both shook their heads a fraction of an inch. Lorian noticed this small movement and his expression quickly molded into a withering smile as he turned to the woman.

"I think the correct thing to say to our coming here is thank you."

Finriel silently groaned at Lorian's words. *Can he ever think of saying something that isn't arrogant?* The woman's eyes widened and she smiled at him.

"Why, of course, the entire village is certainly grateful for your heroic act," she spluttered, and gestured toward the dirty window that looked out at the village. Finriel turned and looked out of the window to find people milling about once more, excited chatter and conversation muffled by the cottage's thick

walls. A group of villagers had congregated by the burned buildings, which had ceased smoking. Some pointed excitedly, while
others held each other and shook with anguish. Finriel ripped her
gaze away from the sight, her heart clenching at the destruction
and sorrow just outside.

"You are quite welcome," Lorian replied smoothly, and
bowed slightly in his chair. This time, Finriel actually did groan,
overwhelming annoyance and embarrassment making her cheeks
heat. The old woman simply looked at him, at a loss for words.

"What caused the fires in your village?" Krete asked, his
already high-pitched voice breaking slightly as he spoke.

Finriel kept her eyes trained toward the street outside as
Naret cleared her throat and said, "They came in the night, they
did."

"The creatures we captured?" Tedric asked, and Finriel
brought her attention to Naret, who closed her eyes as if in an
attempt to remember a lost fable.

"I could not be certain. It happened so quickly. They were
like shadows in the night, silent and moving in a way I had not
seen before. The brownies came at dawn, appearing to be
searching for something, or perhaps someone."

"We were all so terrified of the fires that no one dared go
outside." Lola quivered from behind Finriel. "The brownies were
banging on the doors when I woke, it was so loud."

Finriel considered for a moment. What Naret said sounded
strange, but it had to have been the brownies who started the
fires. She'd never heard of strange shadows creating fires before.

"Is everyone in your village safe?" Krete asked, and Naret
shook her head.

"We were too slow," she said softly. "Old Yerrow and his
wife were taken by the fires. Everyone else escaped in time."

Krete's face fell, and he looked down into his steaming mug.
"I am sorry for your loss."

Silence filled the small space, and Finriel pondered what had been said. She needed to speak with her companions in private, and soon.

"Are you lot on some sort of quest then?" Naret asked curiously, breaking the silence. "There has been an awful lot of hearsay of other strange creatures roaming about the realm ever since that storyteller lost his mind."

"We're merely passing through, but are glad to help in any way we can to keep your village as safe as possible," Krete answered kindly, the sad expression on his face changing into a wary smile.

The old woman humphed in response and scrutinized the four of them. She did not believe them for one second. The woman was smart, Finriel had to give her that, but they simply could not risk the chance of anyone knowing their quest. It was bad enough that they had agreed to travel with Krete and Aeden.

"Fine, don't tell me." The woman pursed her lips, and Finriel scowled at the sudden change in Naret's tone.

Naret surveyed Finriel's male companions before looking at Tedric's shoulder. Finriel's breath caught at a small dark stain on his tunic that no doubt was blood. She knew he should not have grappled with the brownies, and she would not be fixing any more snapped bones thank you very much.

"Are you injured, boy?" Naret asked.

Tedric looked down at the bloom of scarlet on his arm and smiled, barely able to hide the evident pain on his face. "It's nothing, I just had an accident not so long ago."

"Oh, please, you don't have to keep secrets about being hurt. I have a tincture that will make that wound heal ten times faster than it is right now."

Finriel met Tedric's questioning glance and shrugged. She didn't care if he wanted to take the tincture, as long as it wasn't poison. She refused to have expended that much magic to mend his arm just for him to be killed by a frail old woman.

"I'll go fetch it. It's just in the other room," the woman said quickly, taking Tedric's silence as an acceptance of her offer.

As soon as the old woman disappeared behind the small door, Lorian leaned forward to speak to Krete. Finriel strained her ears to hear what they were saying as they conversed in hushed tones.

"It was as if they were waiting for her," Lorian whispered. "Like they knew she was going to be there and they wanted to protect her from something, or someone."

Krete nodded slowly in agreement and began to speak, but the girl, Lola, returned through the small door at the back of the cottage and walked toward Finriel. Lola helped Finriel with the cleaning and smiled as they began to scrub at the bowls they had just eaten from.

"Here it is," the woman grunted, and she sat down heavily in the vacant chair. Lorian and Krete stopped conversing at once and both leaned back in their chairs bearing pleasant smiles. Tedric's face was slightly strained with pain, but he nodded in thanks and took the small vial from her outstretched hand.

"Place a single drop of this tincture on any wound internal or external and it will be cured within minutes."

"You are very kind, but I do not think my wound is so bad at the moment," he answered, and made to hand it back to the old woman. She lifted her hands in the air as if pushing the vial away from herself and smiled at Tedric.

"Please, you have done enough to help this village for me to give you ten more bottles of this medicine and a life supply of soup. Please, keep it."

"What is this medicine made out of exactly?" Finriel asked, allowing for a glimmer of her anger to shine through.

The woman examined Finriel, and her expression hardened from the warmth and kindness she'd been showing mere seconds ago.

"It's a compound of the ferendi flower and water from

Nocturn Lake. If you fear that the ferendi flower is one that is used to kill, you would be right."

Finriel bristled, and had to hold herself back from lunging forward and pouring the draught down the woman's throat.

The old woman seemed to notice Finriel's strain and chuckled. She raised a gnarled hand as if to wave the tension from the air, and then continued, "It has such strong medicinal purposes that it can be used to both heal and kill. The mixture of this flower's essence with Nocturn Lake's waters is a very powerful medicine that is sought out by many. Do not think that I am trying to poison you and your friends, girl. I could have done it a long while ago."

"And why isn't this tincture more well known if it works so well?" Finriel countered quickly.

The old woman simply looked at Lorian and shook her head. "Does she always argue like this?"

Lorian hid a smile as he looked at the woman and shrugged. Finriel turned back to the dishes before her, clenching her jaw. Tedric was foolish in accepting such a strange gift, especially one that she had never even heard of in her four years of healing practice.

"That man fancies you," Lola began shyly, and Finriel stumbled out of her angered thoughts to find that Lola was looking toward the table. Finriel turned her head to see who she was looking at, and forced down an irritated laugh as her eye caught who the girl was speaking about. It was Lorian. He seemed to notice their attention and looked up from the steaming mug in his hands. He held her gaze without fear, his high cheekbones smeared with dust from their scuffle with the brownies earlier. Finriel quickly turned her attention back and scrubbed at the simple wooden bowl in her hands with more strength than was needed.

"I don't think so," Finriel snorted.

Lola looked back at her own hands and giggled softly. The

sound irritated Finriel more, and she suddenly didn't care to help the girl at all. Lola could do all of the work herself as far as she cared.

"You may not see it, but he does," Lola answered sweetly, her shoulder bumping softly into Finriel's. "I've seen the way that he always has an eye on you ever since you came inside. He looks protective, or worried perhaps."

Finriel stiffened and forced herself not to lash out and burn the girl to a crisp right there and then. At least it would make this agonizing conversation go away much sooner than she feared it would.

"Well," Finriel began, trying to keep her voice as kind as possible, "even if he did fancy me, I fear any advances that he would try to make toward me would be in vain."

"Why is that?"

Finriel grimaced, not wanting to respond. Telling this girl of Lorian's and her past was one of the last things she wanted to do at the moment, or any moment, for that matter. The air suddenly felt restrictive, as if she couldn't take in enough air. Finriel clenched her fists, dropping her bowl into the washbasin with a clunk. The image of blue eyes and Lorian disappearing through the trees flashed through her mind, and Finriel took in a rattling breath.

"Thank you for the meal," Finriel said, her vision swimming and her breath suddenly feeling stuck in her chest.

Finriel turned and barged through shoddy wooden door, barely saying a brief thank you to the old woman and the young girl before she let it slam behind her. The streets were now bustling with the villagers who had been hiding, and soot swirled through the breeze as they took apart what remained of the burned homes. Their loud chatter about what Finriel and her companions had just done with the brownies rang through the air and clanged between her ears. She bowed her head and took off at a run toward the tree line that Aeden had disappeared into. She needed to get away from this decrepit village, now.

The air felt crisp and fresh against Finriel's face as she ran, and she took in a deep breath of relief when the shade of a lone oak tree brushed over her. The tightness in her chest lightened slightly as she slowed to a walk and continued down the road, almost at the thicket of trees that stood before the magical kingdom border wall. The faint sound of footsteps echoed in Finriel's ears, and she looked over to find Lorian following her. Finriel quickened her pace, but the sound of boots coming after her drew nearer still.

"I DON'T WANT TO TALK TO YOU," FINRIEL SNAPPED, AND Lorian approached her with the ghost of a grin. Finriel was standing by a small outcropping of rock in the center of the wood, her eyes closed as she listened to the sound of the village mixed with the chirping of birds around her and from the elven kingdom border beyond.

"I was just escorting your cat," Lorian answered calmly, and indeed Nora padded up softly and growled in greeting as she sat next to Finriel. Nora rubbed her head affectionately against her leg, and she stroked the mogwa's grey dappled fur. It was soft and clean, thankfully not crusted with blood and gore like it had been the recent times she had come back from hunting.

"Nora doesn't need to be escorted," Finriel grumbled, still not turning to look at him. She had had enough talking and being nice for a long while. She yearned for some peace and quiet. It had been too long since Finriel had friends and was required to speak to people every day, but she could not say that she enjoyed it at all now that she had it.

"I know," he said simply.

Aeden suddenly walked into view, looking fresh and clean. It seemed as if she'd just bathed, not rolled around in the dust, scratched and then worshipped by a group of brownies. Her long violet hair was back in its usual braid, water dripping from the ends and cascading down her cloak. Her eyes flashed as she glanced between Finriel and Lorian.

"I see you two finally made it out of the old woman's claws," Aeden commented. Finriel snorted and nodded in answer, continuing to stroke Nora's back. The mogwa was now purring loudly, the sound halfway between a growl and a low groan.

"You should be glad you left so quickly and were able to avoid it," Lorian snorted. "Krete and Tedric are still trying to leave without the old woman taking offense."

Aeden smiled and tossed her clean braid behind her back and took a few steps toward them. "I know the people of these lands well enough not to enter their homes when they offer it, even if they are only offering food. Most times they end up wanting to know exactly who you are and what your business is so that they can go off and sell it to someone else."

"That sounds about right," Finriel agreed, and pushed away from the rock. She looked down upon her cloak and pants, noticing how dusty and unkempt she must appear compared to the ethereal fairy standing a few feet from her.

"Where did you bathe?" Finriel asked, not caring that she had changed the subject so abruptly.

Aeden gestured toward the place from which she had emerged. "There is a small pond of fresh water a few paces back. If you're quick, you can clean up before Krete and Tedric get here."

"Thank you," Finriel replied, and began to head in that direction. Lorian started behind her, and she swirled around. She let a small flame light on her fingertips as she looked at him with her eyebrows raised. He stopped at once and returned the expression, though Aeden's face paled slightly at the appearance of Finriel's flame.

"What are you going to do, light my breeches on fire?" Lorian asked with a mischievous grin.

"You can wait your turn," Finriel said haughtily, ignoring his comment.

Lorian raised his hands in surrender and backed away. Finriel let the fire dancing around her fingers extinguish and started back toward the pond that Aeden had spoken of. Nora stood and trotted over to walk with her.

The trees were thick, but soon enough opened into a clearing where a crystalline pond about the length and width of a large food cart glinted in the sunlight. Soft grass sprang about Finriel's booted feet as she and Nora walked to the edge of the water.

Finriel looked around to ensure that Lorian hadn't changed his mind and was coming to join her. When she was sure that she was alone save for Nora, Finriel began to undress.

The clear water was cool and refreshing as Finriel waded into it. The bottom of the pond was covered in small stones and soft sand, her feet sinking in slightly with every step she took. The pond itself was only deep enough to cover her breasts, and Finriel bent her knees slightly so that her shoulders were immersed as well. She took her hair out of its messy braid and let it tumble down her back.

Dust clouded the crystalline water as Finriel scrubbed roughly at her skin. She hadn't realized just how dirty she truly was until the light layer of grime was gone and her skin returned to its dark caramel color. Nora stretched out at the edge of the water, her eyes half closed as she waited patiently for Finriel to finish bathing. It was true that she needed to hurry.

Finriel sucked in a deep breath and dunked her head under, the water covering her face and hair as she let herself sink down to the bottom of the shallow pool. Finriel reached her hands up and scrubbed at her face and her itching scalp. It would not clean her completely, but it had been many days since Finriel's skin had been remotely clean, and it felt pleasant enough.

The water turned blindingly cold and the shock of rough hands clasped around her neck. Finriel choked and thrashed, but the hands were clamped tight and unwilling to release. She screamed and allowed the fire to swell within her and around her until it was the only thing she knew. *It's not real. It's not real. It's. Not. Real.* Finriel forced her eyes open and looked around. The water was now a murky brown from her kicking and thrashing. Finriel blinked and pushed off the bottom of the pool, gasping for breath as she broke the surface. Nora's head shot up, and she meowed with concern as she looked at her master. The distant chirp of birds and a soft breeze caressed Finriel's face, bringing her back to reality.

"It's nothing, Nora. I'm okay," Finriel breathed, and settled herself back down so that her chest was submerged, letting out a sigh.

Tedric and Krete were standing with Aeden and Lorian by the time Finriel returned from the pool. Her friends were all gathered closely, conversing about the best routes to make during their journey. Finriel stood by the edge of an oak tree to watch the way Krete rubbed his chin contemplatively as he listened to Aeden speak. How every time Tedric looked down at Aeden, his eyes would soften in a way that sent shivers down Finriel's arms. And how Lorian was not a part of the conversation at all, but simply leaned against a tree some meters away from their other friends, his arms crossed in front of his chest. He bore a thoughtful and slightly worried expression as he stared down at the ground. It was the face he always made whenever he would think about an important decision when they were younger. Finriel's heart clenched at the memories, and at how the childhood friend she'd grown to hate had turned into this handsome man.

Finriel shook her head and then stepped out from behind the trees to walk toward her friends. Lorian's gaze shot up to meet Finriel's and he straightened. Aeden turned her head and smiled at Finriel, who offered her a slight upturn of her lips in reply.

"How was your bath?" she asked, smiling.

"It was adequate," Finriel answered smoothly.

She slid her gaze toward Lorian to find him staring at her, his eyes clouded with emotion. She gulped and quickly looked away, anger and curiosity mixing unpleasantly in her stomach.

"Did you take the old woman's vial?" Finriel asked Tedric, and the commander's brown eyes narrowed upon her.

"Yes. It would have been rude to refuse her gift," Tedric replied.

Finriel rolled her eyes. "I don't think it would have been rude, considering the fact that we saved their village."

"I'm not so sure that we did," Lorian interjected, and everyone looked at him curiously. "Naret said that shadows caused the fire," he explained, stepping toward them, though consciously moving away from Finriel, she noticed.

"It would be hard to see the brownies if it happened during the night," Aeden reasoned, but Lorian shook his head.

"The brownies were loud, if you remember. If it happened quickly and silently as she said, then I'm not so sure."

"It's getting too late to discuss these matters here," Tedric said, glancing toward the lowering sun. "We have the brownies secured, so the villagers are safe if it was the beasts' doing."

"But what if it wasn't?" Krete asked, and the clearing fell silent.

"There's no way of knowing for sure," Tedric said after a moment. "But we've done all we can."

"What's our next move?" Finriel asked, the conversation beginning to introduce a headache behind her eyes.

"We'll head into Farrador now," Tedric said. "I don't know if we will be able to capture and collect the rakshasa before nightfall, but even if we do not, it will be good to get as far as we can into elven territory."

"Why is that?" Finriel asked. She had a lot of experience with elves, and found herself dreading the thought of stepping across the shimmering kingdom boundary not so far away.

"Aeden and I both think that it is probably best to get through this part of the journey as quickly as possible."

When Finriel's look of confusion did not change, Krete stepped forward and added to Tedric's vague response, "Elves are quite regal and territorial creatures, and therefore do not like other breeds coming into their kingdom unannounced."

Finriel raised a brow and looked to Lorian. "Trust me, I know."

Lorian pressed his lips together and took a step forward, ignoring Finriel's snide comment. "You're right," he began. "We would be better off trying to get as far away from the castle before we even think about finding the rakshasa."

"Unless the rakshasa finds us first, in that case, we don't have much of a choice in where we meet it," Finriel muttered.

"I hope that I'm not interrupting this wonderful contemplation of our future, but we're going to run out of daylight soon and I would like to get to Farrador before nightfall," Krete interjected, and gave both Lorian and Finriel a pointed look.

Finriel's brow raised in surprise. "Did you just say something haughty?"

Krete gave her a mischievous smile in return and shrugged. "It's not too late for me to learn how to jibber and jabber like you witty folk."

Lorian laughed and shook his head as they began to move toward the shimmering kingdom border.

"Oh, Krete, I think I'm finally beginning to like you."

❧ 13 ❧

FINRIEL

"I don't know why I agreed to return to this dreadful place," Lorian grumbled under his breath, and Finriel looked over to find a rare scowl skewing his features.

They were walking side by side through a small forest on their seventh day in Farrador, and Finriel's feet ached with each step they took. She didn't answer Lorian, and it appeared as if none of their other companions had heard him. Finriel knew of his past in the elf kingdom, or at least the part before and during the time they had shared together in Notharis. She shook her head, dousing the question about what had happened to his mother before it reached her lips. A loud susurrus of wings sent Finriel's attention skyward, and she could just make out a large cloud of movement soaring above the tree line.

"That's strange," Tedric commented, voicing Finriel's thoughts.

"What is?" Aeden asked, her gaze following his toward the flock of small baby blue birds that passed overhead.

"Fisherbirds," Tedric replied. "I've never seen them fly outside of Keadora."

"I haven't, either," Finriel agreed.

Lorian shrugged. "Perhaps they decided on a change of scenery, though I'm not quite sure why they would choose to come here."

"They're headed west, back toward Keadora," Tedric said, and Finriel nodded and shrugged.

"They're birds, they'll fly where they wish."

"Perhaps they'll take a shit on the Red King upon their return to Keadora," Lorian snorted, and Finriel could almost feel Tedric's fury burning her back.

"He is the one who will take the bounty from your head," Tedric growled. "I would be careful where you place your words."

Lorian chuckled. "I can thank the man for saving me, but it doesn't mean that I need to dote on him like a dog."

"Enough," Aeden interjected. "We don't need to bring attention to ourselves just because of your bickering."

Lorian snorted. "And who are you to speak? I would rather kiss the Red King's boots than your precious King Sorren's."

Finriel slowed her pace, allowing for Tedric, Krete, and Aeden to pass her and take the conversation over. She was not one to take to politics, or to openly discuss her opinions. Her hatred for the Red King ran too deep for words, and she'd wished every day to blast him to bits for taking away her mother.

"I am not claiming my king to be a saint," Aeden spat. Finriel watched Aeden's confident walk grow stiff next to Lorian, though she still gave the appearance of walking upon a cloud with her fairy grace.

"Aeden," Krete reprimanded, looking up at his friend with concern in his stormy eyes.

"What?" she snapped, surprising Finriel. "Anyone with half a mind and some good education can see how stupid his laws are. He's selfish and puts his own desires before the people."

"I trust your opinion on his ruling more than anyone else

here," Lorian replied with an easy smile, "but I think all rules are a bit stupid."

"We're doing no good by speaking of kings and laws that cannot be changed right now," Krete interjected. "We should be trying to understand what happened to that poor village in Proveria."

Finriel sighed, and greeted Nora with a scratch behind the ear as she appeared from a group of bushes ahead and came to walk by her master's side. "We have no better understanding of what happened," she said, "and we've been over it many times. There is no other explanation than the brownies. The violence began at the same time that the storyteller released the beasts."

"It simply doesn't make sense." Krete shook his head. "Why would he bring such destruction to innocent people?"

"Most storytellers that I've met are mad," Lorian replied simply. "Though I would bargain half of the gold in my pocket that he was hired for the job."

"You have no gold in your pockets," Tedric countered, and Lorian tilted his head to wink at the commander.

"I just might have."

"You stole from the old woman," Finriel said in more of a statement than a question, and Lorian glanced at her from behind his shoulder.

"She gave Tedric a gift, so I took a gift of my own," he said with a shrug.

"I wonder why I like you sometimes," Tedric muttered, and Krete shook his head at the thief disapprovingly.

Silence followed, and Finriel let it wash away her worries. She brought her attention to their surroundings, the trees with massive gnarled and twisted branches and their slowly falling leaves. A lone rabbit hopped across their path, and Nora's attention narrowed upon it. The mogwa was off in a split second and she disappeared behind the rabbit into a patch of shrubs with a loud crash. The air smelled of nothing at all, or perhaps only of a bit of dust. It had been the thing that unnerved Finriel most of all upon arriving in Farrador as a child. Nothing but food and flesh gave off any scent in the kingdom, not even a blooming flower.

"Toss me an apple, would you?" Lorian asked Tedric. "I've got to do something so as not to bore myself to death with the silence."

Indeed, the silence was complete, with not even the whisper of a breeze, though the fall air was still pleasantly cool against Finriel's skin. The crunch of Lorian's teeth in the apple sang in tandem with a dead leaf crumbling underneath Finriel's boot, and she looked down at the browning grass at their feet. It was easy to feel lonely in this silent kingdom.

A long while passed, and Finriel came to walk at Lorian's left, with Krete still at his right. Aeden and Tedric walked a few paces behind them, conversing in hushed tones. The sky was beginning to change its color when Finriel decided to check the map for their next beast.

"We won't reach the rakshasa today," Finriel said as she inspected the map.

"How far away is it?" Lorian asked, peering over Finriel's shoulder.

She shied away from his warmth and rolled the map up quickly, throwing him a dirty look before answering, "Too far away to get to it today, at least not unless we want to try grappling it into the page after the moon has set and we're shrouded in darkness."

"We'll just have to stop and rest for the night before—" Aeden didn't get to finish her sentence before the sound of male voices made her go quiet and everyone stiffen. She raised a hand for the companions to stop, and they did. Finriel strained her ears to listen, and soon enough she heard the voices once more. The soft thump of footsteps walking through the forest belonged to three men, and they were headed in their direction.

"Elven scouts. We need to hide," Aeden hissed.

Finriel looked up at one of the trees, eyeing the gnarled trunk and wide branches. They were certainly wide and sturdy enough for someone to climb, and large enough for the five of them and the mogwa to fit upon. She hissed at the others and gestured up to the tree, not daring to speak as the voices drew near. Nora bounded through the shrubs and came back toward Finriel, and she stifled a cry of gratitude at her return.

Aeden nodded at the others and started toward the tree, but Krete crossed his arms and shook his head adamantly. Aeden stopped and turned to look at him, her expression one of urgency and desperation.

"Krete, we need to climb that tree," she whispered pleadingly.

He shook his head again. "I hate open heights. Gnomes were not built for scurrying up trees, we were built for burrowing inside of mountains."

Finriel rolled her eyes and strode forward, making to grab his arms. The voices of the elven scouts were almost so close that she could discern the conversation without reaching out with her extended hearing. She couldn't help herself, however, and let her hearing out enough to listen as one of the scouts spoke.

"Did you hear of the Red King's quest? I doubt those fools even made it outside of Keadora before one of the beasts killed them."

"Do you really think the beasts are that dangerous?" another scout asked in reply.

"Are you really that daft?" the first scout scoffed. "If what that pretty girl in the pub said was true about the demon, we should all be sleeping with one eye open at night."

The hair on her arms rose, and Finriel glanced at Tedric to make sure he wasn't listening to the conversation. She noticed that any mention of his precious Red King sent the commander in a spin, and now was not the time for that. But she found that Tedric wasn't listening at all, instead he was helping Aeden half-drag, half-carry a very unhappy and stiff Krete toward the tree.

"Go," Lorian whispered from behind, his voice urgent.

Finriel jumped and turned to him in surprise, finding his usually jovial features shrouded with worry.

"Please," he urged. "I'm not going to lose you to an elf again."

He brushed a hand against her shoulder, gently urging her toward the tree. Finriel gaped at him a moment longer, too surprised at what he had just said to move or retort. Lorian gave her another nod, and Finriel started toward the tree, gesturing for Nora to come with her. Nora bounded past Finriel and leaped up with ease, her giant claws digging into the trunk.

Aeden had reached the top and was now pulling up Krete, who was slightly green and shaking heavily as Tedric helped him up. The voices were getting closer, and Finriel hastily grabbed at a large knot in the trunk and made her way upward. She peered down and watched Lorian striding to the tree, looking over his shoulder as he neared. She bit down a pang of worry and paused, peering down at him.

"Lorian," Finriel whispered as she watched him feel his way for a good handhold.

She was able to see faint figures coming toward them now. There was no time to think about the fear that gripped at her stomach as she watched him slip from his handhold, scrambling and cursing as he fought to climb the tree.

Finriel also cursed and then turned to scramble all the way up to safety. She was now high up enough to see the branches curved out and upward in a cocoon around them. They were larger than she had thought, and the trunk of the tree was so large that it created a sort of platform that Tedric, Aeden, and Nora were seated upon, waiting for them. She looked around briefly before her eyes landed on Krete, who was huddled at the base of a thick branch.

Aeden ushered Finriel to come forward, her expression a mask of determination as she looked down between the large branches and leaves to watch Lorian's slow ascent. Finriel heaved herself up onto the top of the tree and then turned on her belly so that she looked down over the ledge.

Lorian had only made it three quarters of the way up, still cursing and grunting softly as he forced himself closer to safety. The shapes of the elven scouts were now discernible. They all had shortly cropped hair, their short pointed ears giving away what they were at once. They wore simple dark green pants and brown leather coats, most likely to help them blend in with the woods. They each carried a long bow made of white wood strapped to their backs, along with swords all of a similar fashion sheathed at their belts.

They're coming too close, Finriel thought. She looked down and cursed under her breath. Lorian was now in arm's reach, but he was climbing too slow. If she could just ...

His arm slipped and Finriel gasped. Without thinking, she lunged her hand, her magic, anything, down toward him to keep him from falling. Finriel's hand clasped his wrist. She grunted with the sudden weight of him and felt herself slip forward.

A strong hand wrapped around her ankle and began to drag her backward, pulling both Lorian and Finriel back up the tree. Finriel looked down into Lorian's icy blue eyes. They were stark with fear as he looked back up at her. She wanted to look away, but she couldn't. Fear and worry for him gnawed at her stomach with a surprising strength that Finriel hadn't thought she still felt for him. As Tedric pulled them up the rest of the way, Lorian scrambled his legs around to get a foothold and helped push his way up to their small hiding place.

Finriel fell onto her back with a relieved sigh when they were all safely on the tree, both her and Lorian panting from the stress and strain of holding onto one another. Finriel broke his gaze to look down right as the scouts walked directly underneath them.

She held her breath as she watched them, not daring to even move a muscle. Everyone seemed to do the same thing, and they watched and waited as the scouts continued silently underneath them.

"I've got to stop a moment, keep going without me," one of the scouts walking slightly behind the other two called. The scouts nodded to him and continued to walk. The elven scout looked around, and then down at the trampled ground below the tree. He shrugged and continued to take a step forward, when something caught Finriel's eye, causing her stomach to lurch. Tedric's satchel was hanging at the very edge of the trunk, just out of Finriel's grip. She moved to grab it, but it was too late. The satchel fell, landing with a thump directly in front of the scout's feet. Finriel felt like she might vomit as she watched the scout bend down and pick up the satchel, examining it closely.

The elf looked up, his gaze meeting Finriel's. Her heart stopped. The elven scout was handsome and almost familiar, his angular features still somehow soft with the magic of immortality. His dark blue almond-shaped eyes widened in surprise as he saw her, and then his gaze traveled to Lorian, who was lying next to Finriel, watching the scout with an expression of paralyzed horror.

When the elf's eyes landed on Lorian, his eyes widened, not only from surprise. He seemed to know the thief somehow. Finriel supposed she knew less about Lorian than she had thought. Lorian's body was taut at her side as he looked down upon the elf.

"Odonir, are you coming or have you stopped to smell the flowers once again?"

The elf's attention snapped toward the sniggering voice of what Finriel assumed was one of the other scouts and his face hardened.

"I'll be there in a moment, there are just some new tracks that I've found."

The elf looked back up at them, and to Finriel's utter astonishment, nodded in silent acknowledgement and then threw the small satchel up in the air toward them. Lorian reached out a hand and caught it without a noise. As if he had never even looked up and seen them at all, the elf straightened his back and began to walk calmly toward the other scouts.

Finriel let out a breath of relief and let her head fall. Lorian scrambled into a sitting position and moved to one of the enormous branches. Finriel brought her head up once more and pushed herself up so that she was facing her companions.

"That was incredibly close," Tedric sighed as he nervously ran a hand through his straw-colored hair.

Finriel shook her head and glared at Tedric in frustration. "Why did you drop the bag so close to the edge of the trunk?" Finriel snapped, then turned to Krete. "And you. You couldn't have been so scared of being in a goddamned tree to almost compromise this quest."

Krete simply shook his head, his face still pale and blotched with red around his cheeks. Being so high up seemed to have made him lose the ability to speak. Tedric's expression turned stony and he returned Finriel's glare with one of his own.

"I was quite preoccupied trying to get a rather stiff and heavy gnome all the way up the tree. It must have fallen." Krete shot Tedric a look of resentment that Tedric ignored, and Lorian handed the bag to him silently. "And it's not a bag, it's a satchel," Tedric muttered.

Finriel scoffed and shook her head, but Aeden interrupted the backhanded comment she was about to throw at the commander. "Calm down, we are all lucky that the elf didn't signal the alarm when he saw you two gawking down at him." She then looked at Lorian, who stared blankly down at his hands.

"Did you know that elven scout somehow?" Tedric asked, his brow raised.

Lorian met Tedric's stare and shrugged as nonchalantly as he could, but Finriel knew it was all a bluff. He was on edge; she could see it in his shoulders and in the way his jaw worked.

"I might have crossed paths with the man once or twice," he answered. At that, she knew he was not willing to say more about the matter.

Lorian looked at Finriel, and she dropped her gaze at the anguish in his stare. She busied herself with looking around the tree for a large enough branch to accommodate her without slipping off and falling to her death while she slept.

Aeden and Tedric appeared to catch on to what Finriel was doing and went to settle themselves upon one of the enormous branches. Finriel walked easily along a branch, Nora following close behind as she went. When Finriel reached the center of it, she settled into a comfortable position. The branch itself was as wide as a large cot and had enough space for Nora to walk around Finriel and settle her warm body behind Finriel's head.

In a few minutes, everyone had found a branch and was spread around the large trunk, all save for Krete, who had shimmied to the very center of the tree and curled into a tight ball with his arms wrapped around himself. A pang of guilt slashed through her stomach at the sight of the gnome's discomfort, but she said nothing as she adjusted her head to a more comfortable position on Nora's side. Finriel knew how it felt to be completely petrified and forced into being in a situation she hated.

Blinding cold water. Strong hands around her neck and hot breath against her ear. She blinked rapidly and shook the memory away as she turned on her side and closed her eyes. The fear she felt had worn off into a buzz, but her fuzzy thoughts were brought back into focus. She had felt worried for Lorian's safety, even if it was also fear for her own neck if the scouts had found them. Finriel gritted her teeth with the realization, but found that she was much too tired to hate herself for it. They needed to finish the discussion they had started before Finriel actually began to feel something other than hate for the man again.

It appeared that no one was in the mood for a chat, and Finriel wasn't either. Tedric's thoughtlessness about his bag had almost gotten them in terrible trouble, and Finriel wanted to let him feel his mistake, if even only for a little while. The tree was now quiet, and Finriel soon let the soundless forest and soft rise and fall of Nora's stomach against her head lull her into a fitful sleep.

❧ 14 ❦

KRETE

Krete blinked his eyes open, the rays of faint autumn sun filtering through the canopy of dying leaves above. A groan escaped from his lips and his muscles protested from being upon a hard surface during the entire night. He scanned the tree to find his companions still sleeping and silently cursed their slumbering forms for forcing him into this terrible situation.

Krete sat up, muscles straining and joints cracking as he stretched. He shimmied to the edge of the tree and peered toward the ground, his stomach lurching at the large drop.

"I don't know how in the goddesses' names I will get down from here," he whispered under his breath.

A sudden sorrow washed over him and Krete leaned back to rest his head upon the hard trunk. The pull within to return to the mountain was growing stronger with every passing day and every step closer to his home kingdom. He missed the smell of fresh snow melting upon the rocks with the first signs of spring, the sound of his fellow friends roaring with laughter around a crowded table. He missed his family and his wonderfully plush mattress. Yet, most of all, he missed the thick rock of Creonid

Mountain that sheltered him and his people, keeping them safe from any harm or threat.

His thoughts drifted to the poor village at the outskirts of Proveria, and his heart sank further. It worried him how little his companions had thought over the matter, as if blaming it on the brownies had solved the problem. Something didn't feel right about the fires, however, he could not pinpoint that something. Krete had interacted with the brownies, and it didn't seem to him that they would have been capable of creating such destruction for those innocent people. Krete shook his head, knowing that his companions would not believe him if he raised suspicions about an alternative to blame for the fires. There was a darkness spreading over the land, he could feel it in the earth and in his bones. Things simply didn't feel right, from the release of the beasts to the strange flock of birds that had passed over them the day before. He yearned for things to go back to the way they had been before this mess had begun.

The sound of Nora's loud yawn disrupted Krete from his thoughts, and his companions began to stir at the sudden break in the deafening silence. Krete was beginning to find that he hated Farrador most of all out of the seven kingdoms, and was glad that King Drohan had rarely sent him to relay messages to the elf queen. The barren trees and lack of wildlife confused him still, though he supposed that most animals that dwelled in the forest were readying to hibernate for the approaching winter.

Groans and hushed curses from his companions filled the tree branches, lifting Krete's sour mood ever so slightly. At least his friends now felt how terrible of an idea sleeping in a tree had been.

"I feel like death," Lorian groaned as he made his way down to the large center where Krete sat. "We shouldn't take any more sleeping suggestions from Aeden," he grumbled, and made toward Tedric's satchel, which was strewn at the warrior's feet.

Aeden gave Lorian a rude hand gesture and gracefully stood, making her way from her tree branch toward Krete and Lorian.

"I'm sorry that I made us all sacrifice one good night of sleep so that we wouldn't get captured and interrogated by elves," she retorted. "And besides, it was Finriel's idea originally."

Finriel shot Aeden a sour look from where she was still seated on her branch, and Aeden returned it with a raised brow despite her calm expression.

"I slept sufficiently enough," Tedric offered as he came toward them, trying to hide a wince as he rolled his shoulders, which cracked audibly.

Finriel snorted as she settled herself at Krete's side, eyeing the bread that Lorian had pulled out of Tedric's satchel with some reluctance. "Please," she said, "none of us slept sufficiently or comfortably. It was terrible."

Nora simply stood and arched her back with another loud yawn, then crouched and leaped off the tree branch. She landed on the ground with barely a sound, save the crunch of dead leaves under her feet as she padded off in search of food.

Krete reluctantly took the piece of dark bread and an apple from Lorian's outstretched hand, biting into the soft flesh.

"I don't think that I will ever want to look at an apple or dark bread again when this quest is over," Krete grumbled as he took another bite. No one argued with this as they ate in silence.

After a few minutes, Finriel looked over to Tedric and nodded toward his shoulder. "How is your injury?" she asked quietly.

Tedric smiled and moved his arm up over his head with ease. "Much better. I think the bleeding yesterday was more from stress than actual damage."

Finriel's lips quirked upward and she nodded, and Krete noticed a small look of triumph on her face. He didn't blame her, remembering, with a lurch of his stomach, the hours of terrible noises and magic she had used in mending Tedric's shoulder all those weeks ago. His curiosity about her magic nagged at him again, and he decided that he would try once more to ask her about her abilities.

After some time had passed, Finriel took out the map from her cloak and unrolled it. She set it down on the hard dark wood so that they could all see. Krete peered down at the intricate map and looked for the next beast they were to capture. He choked on a mouthful of bread as he saw that the creature was not hard to find at all.

"The rakshasa is coming toward us," Aeden announced.

"We need to move farther away from Mitonir," Tedric added, and pointed at the illustration of the elven capital not too far from them. "We wouldn't want to be caught grappling with a demon so close to the city."

The companions nodded in reply, except for Krete, whose stomach dropped at the idea of somehow getting down to the ground without simply dropping to his death. He looked at Aeden and raised his brows. She seemed to read Krete's expression the way she always could and rolled her eyes.

"You will get down this tree whether you like it or not. You agreed to go on this quest and therefore will have to do more things that a gnome typically does not do."

"Well, gnomes don't typically go on quests, so that is a start," Lorian added with a shrug.

"I have been going on quests my entire life," Krete snapped, "but perhaps I should have looked in the universal mission guide for gnomes to see how often I would be forced to climb up trees."

"We'll help you get down if we need to," Tedric said calmly. Krete took another angry bite from his apple and then discarded it off the edge of the tree. The taste had become sour in his mouth from eating the red-skinned fruit every damned day for over a moon.

"I could simply portal away and go back home," Krete grumbled, his mood growing worse with every passing moment. He knew he was not usually as foul tempered, in fact, he always prided himself on being friendly and high spirited at most times. Lorian scrutinized him, and Krete's thinning temper threatened to snap entirely. "What is it?"

Lorian raised a brow. "You said you could portal. I've never heard of gnomes possessing that sort of power."

Krete shrugged. "Only messengers are given a portal stone upon commencement of each journey. We are required to return the stone after each trip as a means to not have so much power or use the portal stone out of ill intent."

Lorian blinked in surprise and leaned forward curiously. "How are all messengers given portal stones? They're incredibly rare."

"Not in Creonid," Krete snorted. "They are as bountiful as a common weed grows in Keadora."

"Is it true that you have a giant portal inside of Creonid Mountain that can allow an entire army to pass through at once?" Tedric asked.

Krete smiled and excitement at his companion's interest in his home prickled his skin. "Yes, it is, though I think it could only accommodate a gnome army if you tried to send that many people through at once."

Lorian chuckled. "That's incredible. You have to show it to me one day."

Hope bloomed in Krete's chest and he nodded. "Of course."

"It's time to move," Aeden said, interrupting the thief and the gnome.

A strange mixture of panic and anger flooded through Krete and he shrunk away from her. Aeden rolled her eyes as she and Tedric both stood and came toward him.

"You're going down first," Aeden said with a mischievous grin.

"No, I'm not," Krete retorted, the panic quickly overwhelming any anger he might have felt. "There is no way I am climbing down on my own."

Tedric reached down and offered a hand. "You aren't going to climb down on your own."

AFTER A CONSIDERABLE AMOUNT OF TIME SPENT SLIPPING, scrambling, and cursing, they made their way down from the tree and started on their way toward the rakshasa. They walked in tense silence, eyes and ears on full alert for any signs of the rakshasa or more elven scouts.

"It's coming toward us at a steady pace, so we need to keep our eyes open and ears alert for any sudden movements," Finriel announced after some time of silence. She rolled the map up and put it in its place before retrieving the page. Krete looked at her with a frown and she shrugged. "Just in case."

Krete took in a deep breath and lengthened his stride to keep up with the witch. "Now that we have been traveling together for nearly a moon, do you think you would feel any desire to tell me of your battle magic?"

Finriel stiffened and her ever-stony expression hardened even further. "I would not."

Krete's hopes fell, but after a moment, Finriel sighed and mumbled something under her breath, and he looked back up at her hopefully. Her caramel gaze was set upon the browned grass at their feet, and a dead leaf fluttered down to the ground beside her as she finally spoke.

"If I'm being honest, I don't know how I've never been discovered. My mother had battle magic and was banished from Keadora the day I was born."

"She was discovered?" Krete asked, and Finriel shrugged.

"Yes, though I've never gotten a very solid story about it

from anyone I have asked. It's part of the reason why I agreed to join this quest, so that I could go see her in the Witch Isles."

"I understand," Krete nodded, "but it's still strange to me that no one has ever found out about your abilities before now."

"Lorian has known of my abilities since we were children," Finriel replied, "but he and my ward were the only ones who ever found out."

Krete pondered what she said, surprise and compassion prickling his chest. "That is why you didn't want to speak of it," he said.

Finriel shot him a look. "What are you talking about?"

Krete looked up at her with new understanding and smiled. "You don't even know very much about your powers, therefore it's uncomfortable to speak of. I understand."

Finriel huffed, and to Krete's surprise, she nodded in agreement. "All I know is that I have a constant anger inside, and it takes nearly more effort to hold the fire back than it does to actually use it."

"It sounds like you need a teacher," Krete mused, and Finriel scoffed.

"That's another reason for me wanting to go to the Witch Isles. So that I can have at least some time where I don't need to live in fear everywhere I go."

Krete and Finriel fell into a comfortable silence, Finriel's story bringing Krete's curious mind to stillness. He had been expecting a large story about her powers, he realized, yet it was foolish. How could a twenty-year-old woman understand anything about her abilities when the whole world would hunt her for them?

The last of the large browning leaves were falling from the giant dark trees of the Farridian forest. The air was still around them, not even the slightest breeze grazed against Krete's cheeks. It was quiet, too quiet.

Krete turned and looked over his shoulder, catching a

glimpse of the long grey spires of Mitonir. The entire kingdom was quiet and lifeless, the feeling sending an uncomfortable shiver down Krete's spine. He'd traveled through Farrador the least in his many years of being a messenger, but it had always given him a sense of unease when he did have to pass through.

"Tedric!"

Krete's attention snapped forward at Aeden's warning, and he watched in horror as Tedric sank into the ground. He blinked his eyes a few times to make sure he had not been imagining it, but Tedric had indeed fallen into the ground up to his waist and was now thrashing his arms about and cursing.

"Stop moving, it's swallowing sand," Aeden hissed, and she lunged forward, moving slowly as she stepped carefully toward him. When she reached Tedric, she stretched forward and took each of his hands in her own and began to pull.

"Careful," Tedric grunted, and Aeden let go of his hands. "Not that careful!" he bellowed, and Aeden cursed, lunging and grabbing him once again.

Krete stilled in horror as he watched Aeden pull at Tedric, and within moments, the commander sprung out from the ground. The force of the movement made Aeden stumble and she fell to her back. With a grunt, Tedric reached forward and braced his hands on either side of her head to break his fall and avoid landing right on top of her. They looked at each other for a few seconds, panting and shaken from the fall.

Krete looked away, feeling like he was intruding on something he was not meant to see. A sour feeling filled his stomach and he shuffled away, concern for both of them and their potentially poor decisions filling his mind. They both needed to be careful, and Aeden had too many secrets; some that not even Krete, her oldest and closest friend, was aware of. He hoped for Tedric's sake that they would not do anything rash. Tedric scrambled up to his feet and offered a hand to Aeden. She ignored it and got smoothly to her feet, looking back down at the ground Tedric had just been sucked into.

"This is swallowing sand, it is used by the elves to capture any game or thieves that may enter their kingdom," Aeden said as she indicated the ground, and Krete noticed that her outstretched hand was trembling. "We must be very careful and make sure to watch every step we take."

"We need to keep going," Lorian replied. "I can keep a look out for the swallowing sand as we move, I know how to spot it easily."

"Why hadn't you said anything before?" Tedric roared angrily, and Lorian waggled his brows.

"I just enjoy watching you need the help of others some-times," Lorian replied. "It's good for the spirit."

Tedric humphed, and Krete sighed. "We should get a move on before we catch the attention of the elven scouts."

And with that, they were off again. Krete looked around the strange forest and found that his conversation and new under-standing of Finriel had helped raise his mood, if ever so slightly.

15

AEDEN

"I can't find the beast on the map," Finriel grumbled at Aeden's side.

Aeden nodded, her distracted brain not quite registering that Finriel's statement was not a very good one. Her mind was elsewhere, as it had been for the past few days. The forest had briefly opened into a large expanse of dried grass and rocky gorges in the early afternoon of that day, a sure sign that they were indeed getting farther north. Though now that they were back in a shroud of enormous gnarled trees and silence, Aeden found that her thoughts strayed back to the issue at hand.

Tedric.

Her heart stuttered at the thought of the commander, and she dared not glance behind her shoulder to where he walked with Lorian and Krete. Her hands felt clammy in an instant, and Aeden fought the urge to wipe them upon her pants. She didn't know how it had happened, yet a small corner of her heart had opened to the man. Yes, he was selfish and she hadn't even the slightest idea as to how he had become a successful commander, but she liked him all the same. And yes, she was sure that his good looks had helped in the matter of her feelings, but Lorian was not terrible on the eyes either and the thought of him in any other sense than a friend made Aeden feel sick.

Aeden huffed, and the tense conversation around her was muffled by her roaring pulse. She could not disclose how she felt to Tedric, not ever. Her father would truly kill her, she knew that. Anger surged through her veins at the thought of her father, and a distant memory flashed before her eyes. The boy she had loved, falling dead before her feet, his blood coating her hands. Aeden hated her father, and she hated all the terrible things he had done. She prayed that the plan would work, and that by the end of this quest, she would finally get the revenge she deserved.

A loud crack rang through the trees, making Aeden pause and scan their surroundings. She tensed and allowed for her senses to reach out toward what, or who, had caused the noise. To Aeden's surprise, she heard only the footfalls of a human, not a beast, and then a girl appeared from behind a gnarled tree. She was beautiful, her dark bronze skin soft and smooth, her deep brown eyes wide with innocent surprise as she looked at the five companions. Her flushed pink gown draped around her in intricate folds, her right arm exposed and bearing flourishes of red inked designs.

"Who are you?" Finriel demanded at once, eyeing the girl with the same look of mistrust Aeden was sure mirrored on her own face. The girl was clearly not an elf, but she did not seem to be a witch or fairy either. Perhaps she was a human. The girl licked her lips nervously and took a tentative step forward, her bare feet hardly making a sound on the soft earth.

"I am Rey," the girl began in a fluttery foreign lilt. "I was gathering herbs for my father, who is injured, but I appear to have gotten lost."

"What kind of creature are you?" Aeden asked.

Cold mistrust seeped through Aeden's bones, and her fingers twitched at her side. There was something not right about the girl, but she simply couldn't place what exactly.

Lorian sauntered forward with a lopsided grin and bowed low. The girl turned her attention toward the thief, allowing a shy smile as she examined his features. Aeden took a step back, not quite liking the tactic that the thief was using with the girl.

"Ignore my friends," Lorian said, his voice dripping with honey-coated seduction. "What they mean is, how can we help a lovely woman such as yourself?"

Aeden glanced over to find Finriel bristling slightly, her hands clenched into tight fists. The memory of flame erupting from those hands not so long ago sent another cold chill through her bones. Finriel met her gaze and rolled her eyes, and Aeden bit her tongue as she brought her attention back toward the scene unfolding before them. The girl smiled sweetly and took a small step toward Lorian. At this movement, Aeden felt herself stiffen. She angled her head slightly toward Tedric, who had moved to stand at her side, his sword drawn and held casually in his hand.

"Do *not* trust what she says," Aeden whispered. Tedric met her gaze with a soft frown, his lips opening as he started to speak, but Aeden simply shook her head. She quickly turned back to the girl before the knot in her chest at the sight of his parted lips caused her heart to burst.

"Why not? She's just a girl," Tedric whispered back, ignoring Aeden's silent effort to keep him from speaking.

She forced a deep breath through her lungs and shook her head again, narrowing her eyes toward the girl. "She's not just a girl, I can feel it."

Finriel had now stepped forward to stand next to Lorian. "Where is your father now?" she asked. "I have magic. I could heal him much faster than any of the herbs that you *don't have.*"

The girl took a step back, her eyes widening in fear. "I swear, I'm only passing through."

"In which kingdom were you born?" Finriel asked, and took another step forward, her hand drifting to her dagger.

"Farrador, of course," the girl squeaked, and Finriel shook

her head with a humorless smile.

"I don't believe you."

The girl's expression of innocent confusion fell away and was swiftly replaced with an evil grin. She took a step toward Finriel and opened her arms wide, as if welcoming her in for an embrace.

"You are smart, witch. I am glad that our paths have finally intertwined."

Finriel stood her ground and glared at Rey, who was now mere inches from her. Lorian frowned as he glanced between the two women and took a step toward the strange girl.

"Rey—"

"Lorian, don't," Finriel interrupted, but Lorian shook his head with a gaze of molten ice.

"I won't leave your side when it matters, not anymore," he vowed, and Aeden glanced at the girl who watched them with fury in her eyes.

Finriel opened and closed her mouth, clearly unsure how to respond. Lorian gave her a small smile and turned back to Rey, who transferred her glare onto him. Lorian stepped in front of Finriel and faced the girl, bringing the easy smile back to his lips and reaching out a hand.

"You must be tired from searching for herbs for such a long while, why don't you—"

"Lorian, stop!" It happened all too quick, and Aeden's call of warning was too late. The dark-skinned girl grabbed Lorian by his hand and yanked, sending the thief crashing against a nearby tree.

"Do not touch me," Rey hissed, and her beautiful features began melting away. Bronzed skin and soft black hair began to shed, dissipating into the air as the transformation took place.

The creature that stood before them now was something out of Aeden's darkest nightmares. What used to be the girl had now grown four feet into the air, towering even over Tedric's head.

The creature's scaly skin was a deep maroon and large yellowing tusks protruded from the sides of her wide mouth. Her eyes were no longer deep brown, but now bright yellow with thin catlike pupils. Long pointed claws had replaced the girl's fingers and her feet were now giant feline paws. The horrific creature cocked its head to the side and smiled, showing dirty teeth that pointed into razor sharp tips.

"What is it, never seen a rakshasa before?"

Aeden gaped as the rakshasa spoke, its voice still sugary sweet like the young woman that it had been only moments before. The creature laughed and sighed, shrugging in an unnaturally human way.

"I knew it," Aeden whispered, and Tedric stood frozen at her side.

The demon suddenly turned toward Lorian, who was still lying at the base of the tree. The thief wheezed, lines of agony stretched across his features as he tried to take a breath.

"You," the rakshasa spat as she prowled to him. Lorian groaned and scrambled into a half-sitting position, though the movement seemed to cause him enough pain to utter a gasping curse and double over.

"Open the map," Aeden hissed the order to Finriel, but she wasn't listening.

Krete darted from behind a tree and reached into Finriel's cloak pocket, retrieving the map. Finriel cursed and whirled toward Krete, but when she saw what was in his hand she simply growled and turned back toward the demon.

"The storyteller has a truly sick mind," Krete panted, unrolling the parchment and angling it toward Aeden and Tedric. They looked down at the map, and indeed, their location was supposedly right on the spot of the rakshasa. Aeden huffed and cursed under her breath.

"Rakshasas aren't described like this in legends," Tedric mumbled. "They're typically less ... leathery."

"Well, it's not a real rakshasa, is it?" Aeden snapped back. Krete and Tedric both tilted their heads in question, and Aeden clarified, "Do you really think that the three of us would be allowed to simply stand on the sidelines and watch this?" When the two of them looked at her blankly, she sighed. "Rakshasa demons, especially female ones, would have killed us all instantly. Besides, she was angry when Lorian tried to move in front of Finriel, and we've been discovering that each creature is partial to one of us."

"So, you're saying that the storyteller created them specifically for us?" Tedric asked.

Krete shook his head. "There is something far deeper to these beasts than we know. I have a feeling that neither King Sorren nor the Red King told us everything that we needed to know."

Aeden's stomach dropped, and she snapped, "Don't be rash, Krete. It's clearly—"

A sickening crack echoed through the forest, cutting Aeden short. She, Krete, and Tedric looked up and gaped at the sight before them.

"Drop him," Finriel ordered with clenched teeth, an orb of dark blue fire dancing across her fingers as she glared at the rakshasa.

Aeden's stomach dropped at the fire swirling around Finriel's hand, but the witch seemed to pay no mind to the blatant battle magic she was using. Aeden had overheard her quiet conversation with Krete, but was still unsure if she would ever get used to the sight of fire sprouting from Finriel's fingertips. Aeden shifted her gaze to the rakshasa to find that the terrifying creature was holding Lorian at eye level by an ankle, inspecting him with narrowed eyes.

"You have hurt her," the rakshasa snarled.

Lorian frowned, his face quickly reddening from his upturned position. "I never even touched her."

"Not all injuries are physical, you fool."

Lorian fell silent and shut his mouth at the demon's words, apparently understanding what she had meant.

"I said, *drop him*," Finriel demanded, her voice louder and angrier than before.

The rakshasa glanced down at her with what seemed like concern, and then back at the thief, who was turning an even darker shade of red.

"The page, Finriel," Tedric called, his voice wavering in what sounded like an attempt to keep his tone soft.

Aeden groaned as the rakshasa flicked her attention to the three of them, noticing their existence for the first time since her transformation.

"That was incredibly stupid," Aeden huffed.

"You!" the rakshasa shrieked and took a step toward them. "You all must die."

"Finriel!" Aeden called, but the witch seemed to get the message and was scrambling to unroll the blank page.

"Rey," Finriel ordered the rakshasa to look at her. The creature's feline eyes widened with fear as they landed on the page held in Finriel's hand. "If you don't let go of my friend, I will force you into this damn page."

"But the boy hurt you."

Finriel's eyes darted to Lorian, who stared at her with urgent, bloodshot eyes. Her furious expression softened slightly, and she looked back up at the rakshasa. "I know, but it doesn't change the fact that he is my friend, and I need you to let him go."

The rakshasa sighed and shrugged, then raised Lorian so that he was eye level with her grotesque face again. "If I ever find out that you have hurt her again, you will be killed."

"I will protect her with my life," Lorian wheezed, and the rakshasa curled her mouth into a grin.

"Good," the rakshasa spat, and flung Lorian behind her carelessly. He grunted as his midsection collided with the tree once again, and he fell to the ground in a heap.

"Thank you." Finriel inclined her head. "Now I need you to get back into this page."

The rakshasa placed a clawed hand upon her hip and cocked her head. "And why is that? I am a lot more useful to you right here than I would ever be in there."

Aeden's chest clenched at the scene unfolding before her. There was something not right about these creatures. They were too kind and too smart to simply have been created to cause trouble.

"What do you need from me in order to return to the page?" Finriel asked, and Aeden could tell that the witch's temper was beginning to fray.

The rakshasa shrugged again and picked at a sharp talon. "Only your promise to let me out again."

Aeden watched Finriel mull the idea over, a bad feeling crawling over her skin as resolution set on the witch's face.

"Fine."

"Fine?" Aeden blurted, unable to help herself.

Finriel shot her a look. "Do you want to get out of here or not?"

Aeden opened her mouth to argue, but a hand made contact with her shoulder and she jumped at the electric shock, instantly knowing who it was.

"Just let her do it," Tedric murmured. "She must have thought of something."

With a demonic sigh, the rakshasa walked leisurely toward the page and shimmered away, as if walking through the door of her home.

"Why did you promise to release her from the page?" Aeden demanded, the terrible sense of wrongness now clawing at her stomach.

Finriel rolled her eyes and made her way toward Lorian, who was still clutching at his abdomen and gasping for air.

"Promises can always be broken."

❦ 16 ❦

FINRIEL

F inriel tensed at Lorian's low groan of pain as he clutched at his midsection. His ribs were clearly bruised, if not broken, by the sound of the muffled curses he flung into the air.

Finriel looked down upon the parchment in her hand, a perfect illustration of the rakshasa now covering the once blank page. Finriel quickly rolled it up and shoved it back into her cloak. She turned to Krete, and found that he was already holding the rolled up map out to her.

"Thank you," she said curtly, and Krete gave her a smile, his grey eyes tired.

"We should go look around the perimeter to make sure no elven scouts are coming in this direction," Tedric suggested, and Finriel glanced toward her other companions

"Good idea," Aeden agreed. "We can try to find Nora in the meantime and make sure she hasn't accidentally walked into the city."

"Force her to come back with you even if she refuses," Finriel replied, and Aeden and Tedric turned away. Aeden waved a hand behind her shoulder to show that she had heard, and Krete jogged to catch up with them.

Finriel moved back toward Lorian, who was now lying on his back with his hands clutched around his sides, his pained gaze focused on her.

"You and Tedric need to stop playing the hero," Finriel grumbled, moving to kneel at his side. "Aeden and I are perfectly capable of handling ourselves."

Lorian didn't respond to her flippant comment, neither did he argue when she reached out and pulled his hands from his sides. Finriel cursed silently at her shaking fingers as she tentatively placed a hand over his shirt. *You don't really have to help him,* she thought as she gently felt around his midsection. He had left her to die so many years ago, and yet Finriel still couldn't leave him, no matter how tempting it may have been when they had first been reunited. It was different now. She didn't know how quite yet, but Finriel felt herself wanting to know what had happened to make him unable to come back for her. She wanted to know if what he had said to her all those weeks ago had been true.

"I'm going to have to touch your skin in order to feel for any proper damage," Finriel said, and Lorian nodded.

She forced her breath to remain even as she tentatively lifted his tunic and slid a hand over his already bruised ribs. Lorian sucked in a breath as she traced his side, his soft skin warm to the touch. Finriel dared not look into his eyes as she brushed her fingers over the swollen skin and reached out with her magic to confirm her suspicions of a cracked rib.

"You were an idiot protecting me like that," Finriel said, though her soft tone was not quite convincing.

Lorian simply watched as she continued to press gently against his ribs, likely in too much pain to give one of his insufferable responses. He had regained his health since the beginning of their journey, Finriel noticed, the skin under her fingers rippling with muscle instead of bone. She attempted to keep her hands steady, ignoring her racing heart. Part of her wanted to retract and move away from him, yet another part wanted to explore the planes of muscle on his stomach and chest. She growled and bit the inside of her cheek, snapping herself back to reality. Lorian looked at her with a raised brow, and she returned his stare with a glare.

"You're blushing," Lorian stated, and Finriel narrowed her eyes.

"I am not," she snapped, and in the blink of an eye, willed the cracked bone to mend, making Lorian double over with a pained gasp.

Finriel quickly retracted her hands from his sides, her fingers tingling from both her magic and his lingering warmth.

"You could have given me a warning," Lorian wheezed, slowly lying down again.

"You should be happy that I helped you at all," Finriel retorted, quickly looking down at the ground and sending a prayer to the goddesses that he would not say another word about her blushing. She had *not* been blushing.

"I am sorry." Lorian grimaced, forcing himself into a seated position. He groaned and leaned heavily against the tree, giving Finriel enough time to gather her spinning thoughts.

"You don't need to apologize to me," Finriel grumbled back.

"You're wrong," he countered, and Finriel looked up at him again in surprise.

"I've been a complete fool and I still blame myself every second of every day for leaving you there."

"Lorian, we were children—"

Lorian shook his head as Finriel spoke and cut her off, his expression desperate. "It doesn't matter. I see how much you hate me every time you look at me. I broke your trust because I was too much of a coward to face the boy myself."

Finriel's heart clenched and she wiped her sweating hands

upon her dirt-encrusted pants. "I don't hate you," she whispered. "I thought I did for a long time. I wanted to kill you the second I saw you again at the Crimson Castle. But I realize that maybe I need to try to push through that anger and pain. I'm not getting past anything by hating you."

Lorian's face opened and the touch of a smile played at his lips. "Does this mean that you forgive me?" he asked tentatively, straightening.

"No."

His face fell slightly. Finriel looked into his eyes and picked at a small fray on her cloak as she chose her next words carefully.

"I don't forgive you. I can't forgive you that easily. I still have memories of what happened, and I can't even touch cold water without getting a flashback or feeling like I am going to be sick, and in some corner of my mind I still blame you for all of it."

Lorian looked down at his hands. Silvery white scars lined against his fingers and palms, and Finriel found herself wanting to know how he had gotten each one of them.

"But," Finriel continued, "I can at least begin to try to forgive you."

He looked up and didn't hold back his smile this time. Finriel's entire chest constricted as his face lit up at her words. She had not expected that he was going to grow into such a beautiful man when they were children, but she supposed she had never thought about those sorts of things back then. She let herself linger on the curve of his lips before forcing her gaze back up to meet his bright eyes. Maybe she *had* been blushing, Nether damn her.

"That's all I needed to hear," Lorian said with a grin, and Finriel let the corner of her mouth quirk up in a half-smile. He held Finriel's gaze, and the world faded away from her slightly as she looked into his eyes. They had been her favorite part of him when she was younger, but now it was only one of the many parts of him she found alluring.

Stop it. He's still a terrible person if you haven't forgotten, she reprimanded herself.

The feeling of soft fur and the tickle of whiskers against Finriel's cheek made her jump and bring up her hand instinctively to stroke Nora's back as the mogwa sat next to her. Finriel's heart pounded heavily in her chest and pulsed in her ears. It felt so loud that she was sure Nora would be able to hear it, maybe even the whole forest.

"We spotted five elven scouts about two miles from here." Aeden's voice sounded from behind them. Finriel rose to her feet and turned to find Tedric, Aeden, and Krete approaching.

"Are they coming toward us?" Finriel asked.

"It's hard to tell." Tedric shook his head. "But they did appear to be on alert about something."

"Well, we weren't very quiet trying to put the rakshasa back into the page," Lorian snorted as he began to struggle to his feet.

"Don't," Finriel said, throwing her hand out. "Aeden, do you think you can put an enchantment on him to help with the pain of his bruises?" she asked, and Aeden nodded, moving toward Lorian.

The enchantment was quick work, and Aeden stepped back from the thief once it was over.

He sighed in relief and rubbed his sides. "Thank the goddesses for that. Aeden, I could kiss you for what you just did."

Aeden grimaced and shook her head, and Finriel swore that she saw Tedric place a hand upon the hilt of his sword in response.

Lorian smiled easily and got to his feet. "Some other time," he said with a wink, and Aeden shook her head again.

"All that matters is that the rakshasa is back in the page and we are all in one piece," Finriel said, steering them away from the uncomfortable conversation.

She couldn't deny the pang of bitterness that dropped into her chest at Lorian's proclamation, even if it was a joke. *Besides, you don't care about him in that way,* she scolded herself.

"None of it makes sense though, the way that the creatures seem to be expecting us when we get to them," Krete pondered.

"I agree. The only reason that this quest has been dangerous at all has been because of our own stupidity," Tedric said, giving Lorian a lopsided grin. Lorian rolled his eyes in return and hobbled over so that he was standing at Finriel's side. She forced her breath to come out in an even rhythm and focus on the conversation, even if her hands still burned with the memory of his skin.

"Things simply don't feel right," Krete replied. "The fire in the village, the beasts' behaviors, all of it."

"There seems to be something else going on, something bigger than what we know," Aeden agreed with an odd tension in her voice, though her expression remained impassive.

"Like what?" Finriel asked, idly scrubbing her hands against her pants.

Lorian glanced sidelong at her strange behavior before shrugging. "There isn't much we can do besides collect the other two beasts. We have no means of finding out if there's something more to this quest than what we already know."

"There is a way," Krete interjected. Finriel narrowed her eyes at him curiously, and he returned her glance with a kind smile and a shrug. "If we find the storyteller and ask him what he knows, we might gain some deeper understanding. I can try to contact the gnomes and find out if they have any knowledge of his whereabouts."

"Is this secretly a ploy to go back to Creonid?" Aeden asked cynically, and Krete shrugged again.

"We could use the rest, and besides, we need to find the storyteller."

"That's true." Aeden nodded in agreement. "But for now, we need to think more about getting out of this kingdom and away from the scouts."

❄ 17 ❄

MADNESS

I t was cold, so very cold. Pain lanced through his fingers, through his feet, all the way to his bones. Snow and wind lashed across his face, and he slipped with every other step he took. Hunger roiled inside his too thin body. It would be worth it, however. Only a few more days and he would be there. And he would be warm. They would welcome him. They were peaceful creatures, after all. They would not say no to a lonesome traveler who looked one breath away from crossing to the Nether. He had to admit that dying and going to the Nether sounded much better than this. At least then he could be welcomed by Nex instead of where he was headed to now.

A laugh bubbled out of his throat, sending a puff of frozen breath from his mouth. It would be worth it, all of it. The plan had been set into motion, and it was only a matter of time. Yes, it was approaching swiftly. The dead one had been kind to him, and he knew that she would show the path. Blood was coming, and it was coming soon. At least then he would get what he wanted.

❧ 18 ❧

LORIAN

M any days passed in a slow blur of walking, avoiding the countless groups of elven scouts and skirting around towns and villages. Since overhearing the scouts' opinions about their quest on their first day in Farrador, Lorian had suggested that it would be best to avoid making contact with any citizens of the kingdom. To his surprise, Finriel had agreed immediately and it took only a short while to convince the others. They stopped only for short rests of food and water, making camp amongst closely spaced trees in order to stay hidden from the elven scouts. They lit no fires for fear of being caught, which caused many damp and cold nights upon the hard earth.

Finriel had ordered that Nora stay close to them during their trek through the elf kingdom, and the mogwa walked at her master's side, her amber eyes hardened with frustration. They couldn't risk any more unexpected run-ins with anyone, let alone the elves. It was known by everyone that they would most likely be brought before the elven queen and sentenced to the Nether before they could even open their mouths to explain.

"We're almost at the edge of the forest." Aeden was the first one to break the silence in hours, causing Lorian to jump.

He was walking at Finriel's side, their shoulders bumping against each other occasionally, and he'd found her drawing closer to him since the rakshasa incident. They still never spoke of their childhood, however, and Lorian found himself growing more hesitant to talk about what had happened for fear of their fragile truce falling apart. He couldn't help but remember the way that her tan cheeks had flushed when she touched him. It was likely silly to think that she was beginning to fully trust him again, but a fool could dream. He'd been careful and kind, and they spent most of their time in a comfortable silence, both trying to catch a word or two of Aeden and Tedric's hushed conversations.

Lorian was growing suspicious of the energy around the warrior and the fairy, a sense of unease washing over him about their connection. There was something strange and otherworldly about the spark between them whenever they were near each other. He had tried to speak to Krete about the matter, but the gnome had grown quiet and grumpy since their night on the tree, resigning himself to walk at the back of the group alongside Nora.

"We must be careful about which direction we take when we exit the forest," Tedric said. "We don't want to end up—"

"You do not need to think about in which direction you are going to exit this kingdom," a rough and unfamiliar voice interjected.

Lorian tensed, and the companions stopped in unison.

"Who's speaking?" Tedric demanded, drawing his sword in a fluid motion.

The raspy voice chuckled, and a hooded figure emerged from thin air. A white fur-lined cloak covered the man's face, but he did not need to show his identity for the company to know what he was. Lorian's blood froze in his veins at the sight of the traveler standing before them.

Travelers were the beings native to Naebatis, the coldest

kingdom within Raymara. Lorian gulped and glanced around the surrounding bushes in search of his protector, the magical beings travelers could conjure whenever needed. He'd heard legends of travelers and the wrath they and their protectors caused during the War of Seven Kingdoms, and had prayed to never meet one as long as he lived. His singular meeting with a traveler on the outskirts of Naebatis when he was sixteen was proof enough that his prayers had never been answered.

The man lifted the white hood of his robe to show a surprisingly young face for such a voice. His features were plain, his grey eyes too high upon his face and his nose too large. Thin lips were peeled back to show a yellow-toothed grin as he looked upon the six of them.

"Traveler, you have no business in these woods," Tedric growled as he raised his sword slightly higher in defense.

The traveler's steely gaze slid to Tedric, and he examined the commander contemplatively.

"You are right, but none of you have any business in this forest either, especially not a human from Keadora. You could be sentenced to Queen Arbane's dungeons if anyone saw you."

"Why are you here and what do you want from us?" Aeden demanded, and she too stepped forward.

The traveler's eyes raked the fairy up and down, and his grin widened evilly. Tedric stepped forward, his expression one that promised bloodshed. The traveler turned his gaze to Tedric, and an understanding seemed to flash across his eyes.

"Ah, I see." He chuckled. "You two will have a very hard time figuring that one out."

"Answer the question," Finriel snapped.

Lorian angled his head to watch as she drew her dagger in one swift motion. Nora's grey fur rose and she bared her teeth at the stranger.

"Oh, I cannot tell you, the matter is of complete confidentiality." The traveler sighed. "Though it has to do with some little birds that informed me of a potential threat to the elves."

Lorian's stomach gave a flop, and his mind went straight of the flock of fisherbirds they had seen on their first day in Farrador. He glanced at his companions to see if they had noticed the traveler's words, but they seemed too on guard to realize what he had truly said.

"You do not have to pledge allegiance to the elves," Lorian replied, his tone sounding much calmer than he truly felt.

"Oh, but we do," the traveler replied with a cool smile. "Though I was still not very excited to have to meet with the stuffy elf queen, so I must admit that meeting you all has brightened my day dramatically."

"You will fail miserably if you try to even touch a single one of us," Aeden snarled.

Lorian groaned with growing fear. "You shouldn't have said that," he whispered to the fairy, who ignored him completely.

"I am aware of that," the traveler agreed. "That is why I am not going to touch you, my protector will do the dirty work. And he is not only going to touch you, but he is going to rip each one of you into ribbons. After his work is done, he will dissipate and I will remain free from the curse." The traveler then began to shimmer away, becoming more and more translucent by the second. "Have a wonderful time dying. Send my regards to Nex when you reach the Nether. She was the one who created my kind, after all." The raspy voice was the last thing that was left of the traveler, and then he was gone.

Krete exhaled with relief and wiped a hand over his brow. "Thank the goddesses that is over."

Tedric shook his head and began to walk forward slowly with his sword still raised, and Finriel conjured large tendrils of flame to envelop her free hand.

"It is not over yet, I am afraid," Lorian whispered.

The beast appeared out of nowhere and crashed toward them

with a roar. Lorian's mouth went dry as he watched the minotaur approaching at a surprising speed. The bull's head was covered in wiry black hair, two yellowing horns protruding from the sides of its forehead and curving inwards like a twisted halo. A large axe was held in the beast's human hands as it roared and raised the weapon above its head.

"Run, I'll hold him back!" Tedric yelled, and without a second glance, the companions shot in the opposite direction to the wild beast, which bounded through the bushes behind them with another ear-splitting roar.

"Now would be a great time to use that portal stone of yours!" Lorian yelled to Krete, who was attempting to keep his pace ahead of Finriel.

Branches sliced across Lorian's face and cut into his arms as they ran headlong into an unexpected thicket of brambles. He kept his eyes fixed on the ground as he wildly fought forward. The thicket thinned out soon enough and they were within the branches of shorter trees with dark bark and sun-kissed leaves.

"I'm working on it," Krete panted, and Lorian barely caught the movement of the gnome withdrawing a small blue stone from his vest pocket.

"Stop!" Aeden shrieked, shooting out her hand to hit against Lorian's chest. He stumbled back a few steps. He raised his brows at her, surprised at how quickly she had reached him. But she didn't turn to meet his gaze, instead, her eyes were trained on something before them. Lorian took another step back and looked down, his eyes widening at what she had just saved him from stepping upon.

Sand.

Dark *grey* sand.

Lorian exhaled and looked out toward the large expanses of red and grey sand that opened up before them. Krete and Finriel had stopped and lined up on Aeden's other side, gasping as their eyes met the shimmering wall of the new kingdom before them.

They all squinted as hot wind blew against their faces, sending small grains of sand pelting into their eyes even through the shimmering border.

"Crubia," Lorian breathed, curiosity still flickering through the terror that stiffened his bones.

The death kingdom was the most feared kingdom of all. No one spoke of it, as the name itself brought tears of fright to even the bravest man's eyes. Anyone who stepped upon the dark sand would never step into another kingdom again. Instead, they were locked within the barren desert forever with no food or water to keep them alive, and in time, madness took over until that poor creature died the most terrible death.

"It is said that before the curse was cast this kingdom was the nicest one of all," Krete offered quietly.

"It's also said that there is a secret colony that lives underground, and that people who are banished here don't actually die, they are simply found and brought below ground to live in the colony," Finriel replied, looking out upon the colored sand dunes with cautious interest.

"We don't have time for history lessons, we need to get out of here!" Tedric shouted from the tree line. "We have a minotaur on our heels and I refuse to just stand here and be killed simply because you're all trying to be smart asses!"

"There is no way in the Nether that I am taking one step into this kingdom." Finriel shook her head. "I would rather face the minotaur than risk being locked in a desert forever."

An earth shattering roar and the clash of weapons seemed to answer her, and Lorian looked around wildly. There needed to be some other way out, some place that they could go without retracing their steps back to where Tedric and the beast fought.

"Krete, the portal," Lorian said through gritted teeth, glancing over to the gnome.

"I know, I've got it," he replied enthusiastically. "Get Tedric. I am going to use the portal stone to get us out of here."

Aeden nodded without a word and spun on her heel, disappearing back into the brambles toward Tedric and the minotaur. Finriel looked down at Krete with a confused frown as he leaned forward and began to trace his fingers upon the grassy ground of the clearing. Lorian moved to where Aeden had once been standing so that he could get a better look at Krete's work.

"What are you doing?" Finriel asked as she peered down to look at Krete's quick movements with interest.

The ground below his fingers began to glow orange with a light that seemed to come from the ground itself. Krete didn't seem to notice that Finriel had spoken to him as he worked, and he stood up a few minutes later with a satisfied smile. The ground below him was a circle of intricate lines and symbols that were unfamiliar to Lorian, but he could only assume that it was some sort of gnomish scripture. Krete looked up at Finriel and Lorian, huffing.

"They still have not come back?"

Lorian shook his head, his hair falling into his eyes. He swept it back hastily and turned toward the sound of fighting not too far away.

"Aeden, Tedric! The portal will close soon. You need to come now!" Krete yelled toward the clang of swords and snapping branches, his eyes shrouded with worry.

Nora made a soft wailing noise as she looked toward the sound of the minotaur and the two companions fighting. Her body was taut, and it was clear she yearned to join them in the fight.

The sound of fighting stopped abruptly as a pained roar echoed through the forest. Tedric and Aeden crashed through the trees toward them, and Krete beckoned Finriel and Lorian closer. Finriel stepped forward with Nora at her side. The sound of Tedric and Aeden nearing grew louder, but Lorian tensed as another sound crashed behind them. The minotaur was coming too.

"Come on, or else we will have the minotaur coming through the portal with us."

Krete beckoned Finriel forward again, and Lorian tensed as she stepped toward the portal hesitantly. Nora was pressed against her master's side, the hair upon her hackles standing on edge.

"Now, step onto the portal with both feet at the same time. Keep your mind empty as it sucks you in and you should get through to where I want the portal to take us."

Both Lorian and Finriel shot Krete a look of alarm.

"What do you mean I *should* get to where you want it to take us?" Finriel challenged.

"No time now, just go!" Krete exclaimed, and he brought his hand up to shove Finriel forward. She stumbled into the portal and shimmered slightly as she was sucked into the ground, Nora leaping in behind her.

"Well, I liked her the least out of all of us, so if she does not make it, I must admit I won't cry as much," Krete grumbled to himself.

"What the Nether did you just say?" Lorian roared, anger briefly turning his vision red as he rounded on the gnome.

Krete pursed his lips together and looked up at Lorian with apprehension before he reached up and shoved Lorian forward into the portal. Lorian looked up, and the last thing he saw was Tedric, Aeden, and the minotaur crashing toward him before darkness swallowed him whole.

❦ 19 ❦

LORIAN

D ifferent shades of blue and grey swirled across Lorian's vision as he fell downwards for what felt like eternity. He waved his hands out, reaching for something, anything, to break his fall, but to no avail. Lorian screwed his eyes shut against the myriad of colors flashing around him, the terrible sensation of falling combined with the visual overwhelm making him feel close to being sick.

Lorian's back slammed against something solid, and he flung eyes open in shock. The impact sent dark blotches across his vision and he groaned in pain, the strength of the collision forcing the air out of his lungs. After a moment, the blotches disappeared and Lorian found himself in a sand clearing surrounded by sleek brown rock. A pained wheeze tore through his chest and he forced himself up onto his elbows to better examine his surroundings. The smooth stone rose up far above his head and the sand was not very deep. The course grains that flecked his pants were light brown, which contrasted with the sand he had almost stepped upon in Crubia. There was a faint smell of dew in the air, though he could sense no rain coming from the overcast sky. The place felt oddly familiar somehow, though Lorian could not remember traveling to this place in his entire life.

A yowl echoed through the clearing, and Lorian cursed at Nora's ear-grating greeting. The mogwa bounded over to him and sniffed his face curiously, and Lorian scrunched his nose against the featherlight tickles of her whiskers brushing his face.

"Lorian," Finriel gasped, and he angled his head in the direction of her voice. She approached in four long strides, appearing to be in one piece and barely shaken as she knelt by his side. "Are you all right?"

Lorian managed a nod, still quite unable to speak. Finriel exhaled with relief and helped him into a sitting position. Lorian winced against a new pain that bloomed at the back of his skull as he sat up.

"I've been waiting here forever," Finriel huffed, and the harsh mask of her usual glower returned. "I thought you had all been ripped to shreds by the minotaur."

"Krete shoved me into the portal not even two seconds after you," Lorian grunted in reply.

Gurgling in the sky made Lorian tilt his gaze upward to find the dark hole through which he had fallen still shimmering. The inside swirled with the colors of an angry sea during a storm, though the outer edges of the portal shimmered orange. The gurgling grew louder, and Lorian let out a yelp as Nora grabbed his cloak with her teeth and dragged him away from the spitting void.

Three bodies dropped from the swirling darkness like rocks, falling to the ground in a tangle of limbs and curses. Krete's head shot up and he quickly clambered over Tedric and Aeden's bodies. They groaned and cursed in muffled voices as he scrambled none too gently over them, his grey eyes trained up toward the portal.

He began chanting in gnomish, his face pulled into stony concentration as quick babbling words flew from his tongue.

Lorian glanced down to find Krete's left hand in a fist, and a faint shimmering light glowed around it, which was no doubt the portal stone. The shimmering orange light around the portal began to grow and pulse, appearing to swallow up the dark blue storm inside as the hole shrank.

An angry roar sounded from the mouth of the portal, and Lorian watched in horror as the minotaur's head emerged through the last of the blue swirling light. Krete began to yell the unfamiliar words, and with a loud sucking *pop*, the portal closed and the minotaur's now severed head fell to the ground.

Krete darted out of the way with surprising agility, and the beast's head landed on top of Tedric and Aeden with a heavy plunk. Aeden dodged out of the way as best she could, and only the nose of the beast brushed over her leg as she moved. The head rolled from Aeden's quick movement and tilted, falling directly on top of Tedric's muscled chest. Its slimy nose pressed against the commander's neck, and his face quickly changed from horror to disgust.

"For the love of— oh, dear Adustio."

"I don't think your witch goddess will help you now," Lorian croaked with a grin, his bruised ribs still throbbing from his fall through the portal.

Tedric reached up and grabbed the minotaur by its gnarled horns, groaning as he lifted it off his chest and shoved it to the side. The dead creature's grey tongue lolled out of its mouth and flopped against Tedric's face, making him roll to the other side and quickly scrub at the sheen of slobber with a loud curse.

"Oh come now, the minotaur was simply trying to give you some love and affection," Aeden offered with a playful grin.

"Enough with the jokes. They aren't helping the rest of us forget about the tension between you two." Krete waved his hand in the air, his face slightly red from exertion.

Aeden and Tedric's faces turned pink at Krete's comment, and Tedric scrambled to his feet and glanced at the fairy. She quickly looked away and turned in the opposite direction. What Krete had said was true, Lorian realized with some surprise. He had been so concentrated on mending his relationship with Finriel that he had not realized that there was perhaps a different sort of relationship blooming within the group.

"That sounded like something I would say," Lorian commented.

Krete threw his hands up into the air with a grunt and turned away from the minotaur's unfortunate remains. Lorian threw a wink at Tedric, who scowled and gave him a rude hand gesture before striding over to stand at his side. Lorian reached up and took the commander's outstretched hand, and Tedric hauled him up to his feet. Lorian took a steadying breath, the pain in his ribs slightly less than it had been minutes ago.

"What is this place?" Finriel asked, her change in subject almost immediately easing the tension in the air.

Lorian turned to face her, and his mouth fell open in awe at the sight of a black magnificent stone standing in the center of the clearing. It was the height of a fully grown dragon and as wide as a ship. The glossy black stone was as smooth as water, with not a single scratch or dent upon its surface.

"Oh, thank the goddesses. It's the naga," Krete sighed in relief, and he nearly ran to the sheer face of black rock with his arms outstretched.

"How is it that I don't remember that being here just a few moments ago?" Finriel asked, and Lorian shook his head in wonder.

"It's because it was not here just a few minutes ago," Krete answered, looking over his shoulder to throw the witch a broad smile. "And it is not just any stone. It is the naga, and it will get us out of here."

"What are you on about? There's no way in the Nether that we can scale that thing," Tedric said dubiously.

Krete turned back to the black stone and shook his head with a high-pitched laugh. Finriel and Lorian exchanged a furtive glance and Lorian raised his brows, suddenly convinced that the gnome had gone mad.

"We aren't supposed to scale it; that would be ridiculous," Krete replied after a moment.

"Excuse me?" Tedric frowned.

Krete took in a deep breath and sighed, gesturing toward the massive stone. "Some of the most powerful spells in the realm have been placed on the naga since the beginning of the thousand-year peace. It is a gateway that can take you across Crubia and transport you either to Creonid or Drolatis, whichever you choose."

Aeden took a step forward, examining the rock with curiosity. "And how is it that it only appeared now if it wasn't here when we first arrived?"

Krete shrugged. "No one truly knows. It appears when it wants to and cannot be summoned or forced to appear, not even by someone with the most powerful magic."

"Wait a moment," Tedric said at Lorian's side, "if we're not in Farrador or in either of the northern kingdoms, then where are we exactly?"

"We are in the In Between," Krete answered simply.

Confusion swam through Lorian's brain, and he thought hard to remember if he had ever heard of such a place, but he knew he hadn't. He glanced around at his other companions to find them staring at Krete as if he had completely lost his mind, and Krete returned their looks with one of his own.

"What? Don't you know of the In Between?"

Lorian pressed his lips closed and shook his head, and Krete huffed and pursed his lips with disappointment.

"Your rulers keep too much from you. The In Between is a place that doesn't exist in time."

"That sounds as though it doesn't exist at all," Lorian said, but Krete ignored him.

"It is a safe haven within the folds of the shimmering borders of each kingdom. No form of violence can occur here, and it is said that a fragment of this place lives within every creature of Raymara, which is why we've been able to live in peace for a millennia."

"So we are nowhere even though we are somewhere?" Tedric asked.

"We are in the folds between Farrador and the fork between Drolatis and Creonid. We all must go through the naga now though, before it disappears again."

Tedric blinked and nodded at Krete. "That was probably the most useful information I have ever heard you say since our first meeting."

Krete chuckled and gestured for them to come forward. "There isn't much time left. We must go."

Lorian took a tentative step toward the naga, finding his fingers trembling as he approached. There was a thrum of energy around the stone, something strange that sent his stomach lurching into his throat. Tedric walked at his side, his face impassive. Lorian wondered what feelings were being held behind the mask that Tedric wore, and he wondered if the facade had anything to do with Aeden.

Krete waved Lorian closer and gave him an excited nod. "Just picture in your mind that you are walking through the stone, and keep your eyes on me the entire time."

Finriel let out a small sigh and Lorian glanced at her, his already thumping heart skipping a beat. Excitement was written clearly on her face, and she looked as if she might leap into the stone. Lorian took in a calming breath before he pushed his hand against the smooth black surface. A grunt of surprise slipped from his mouth as his hand passed into the stone instead of pressing against it as he assumed it would. The air against Lorian's now invisible hand was cold and deathly still, and he clenched his fingers, fighting the urge to pull back.

"Let's go," Krete said, and he walked straight into the stone, a small ripple passing across the black expanse where he entered.

Lorian deepened his breath and exhaled as he stepped forward all the way into the naga. The world went black for a moment, and his stomach gave a flop as the ground tilted from under his feet. He took a blind step forward, blinking quickly to find Krete's faint outline in front of him. Two more shuffling steps and Lorian found himself out of the darkness, emerging onto hard stone surrounded by staggering cliffs. He instantly recognized it as Drolatis, the dragon kingdom, and his stomach gave a terrible flop.

The cliff he stood on was a place that still clung to his mind every day, even in his dreams. The ground was rocky and coated in a dusting of snow. Feet away, the wide surface gave way into a chasm, the darkness seeping upward from it like a bleeding wound. On the other side of the chasm lay a large meadow and the giant jagged expanse of the Steel Mountains. He had escaped to this very place on his first mission, the mission that had torn him from Finriel for so long.

Lorian shook the memories from his mind and took in a rattling breath of frigid air, which was an unwelcome change to the softer and warmer air in Farrador. Though he hated Farrador, he never had much of a taste for the thin, cold air of the mountainous regions.

A sound similar to rippling water upon a smooth lake made Lorian turn, and he watched as Tedric, Aeden, Finriel, and Nora shimmered into existence. The naga was nowhere in sight, and Lorian shook his head in wonder at the intricacies of the magical world. Lorian suddenly remembered Krete, and spun around to look for the gnome. He had followed straight behind him through the naga, after all. After a few moments, Lorian spotted him near the mouth of the chasm, the muted tones of his tunic and dusty red pants nearly camouflaging him completely.

"That was brilliant," Finriel breathed, gazing at their surroundings in wary awe.

Lorian tried his best to hide the smile that tugged at his lips as he watched her gaze at the stony alcove with growing excitement. As children, they'd frequently had long conversations about which kingdoms they wanted to visit, and Finriel had always said that she wanted to visit the mountains. Her eyes met Lorian's, and a true smile bloomed on her full lips.

"Do you remember?" she asked, and Lorian nodded, no longer caring to hide his own smile.

"You finally came to the mountains."

Tedric stepped forward and glanced between Lorian and Finriel, and then grinned at Aeden. "I don't know, the tension between these two might be worse."

Aeden pressed her lips into a grim line and started toward Krete without a word. Finriel seemed to notice what Tedric's comment had implied and quickly turned away, following the fairy, with Nora at her heels.

"You and Krete really must stop with the comments. There can only be room for one arrogant ass in this company," Lorian said, forcing his galloping heart to hide behind his dry tone.

Tedric lifted his arms in the air and raised his brows, grinning. "I am merely a messenger of the truth that so desperately wants to be told. I'm also finding how entertaining it is to watch people squirm with discomfort."

"I've taught you well." Lorian grinned. "Sometimes I now wonder how we are not brothers by blood."

"We don't have to share the same blood in order to be brothers, you know," Tedric answered, his face slowly becoming serious as he lowered his hands.

"How are we going to get across this chasm?" Finriel's voice rang out through the alcove, interrupting Lorian and Tedric's moment.

He looked over to where she and Nora stood with Aeden and

Krete, the witch's head tilted over to look into the darkness below. Aeden was a few healthy feet away from the cliff's edge, her angular features appearing more severe in the bleak grey light. Krete, however, seemed as nonplussed about the steep drop below as Finriel, and he peered over with a look of contentment.

"I thought you hated heights," Finriel muttered.

Krete shrugged. "It depends on the location."

Tedric and Lorian approached the group and Krete placed a hand on Finriel's elbow, gently pulling her a step back from the precarious ledge. Finriel let him lead her backwards, but her face turned slightly sour with obvious frustration.

"I know this place," Lorian said, breaking the silence. "The Guardian must come to us and reveal the bridge that crosses over the chasm."

"How do we summon this Guardian then?" Finriel asked, peering around as if expecting someone to appear out of thin air.

Krete shook his head and chuckled softly. "You do not summon the Guardian. She comes to you."

Finriel huffed and crossed her arms. Nora stood a few yards behind the witch, eyeing the rocky darkness below before letting out a tentative meow.

"So we simply wait?" Aeden asked, and Krete nodded.

Lorian shivered as a sudden cold breeze drifted through the alcove. The air grew thick and mist quickly began to flood upwards through the chasm and spread around the small clearing. Lorian's vision was completely obscured by mist now, and not even the dark rock at his feet was visible anymore.

"Ah, there she is." Krete's voice echoed through the air.

"Who comes to my bridge?" a soft, sad voice inquired.

Lorian turned his head blindly toward the familiar voice and took a step forward. The scrape of a sword being drawn from its sheath made him stop in his tracks and direct his hearing toward who had drawn their weapon. It had been Tedric, of course.

"Do not draw your weapons at my bridge or I shall not let you pass," the sorrowful voice echoed through the mist.

"Guardian, we only wish for safe passage across your bridge. We don't wish any harm upon you," Krete assured.

"Put your sword away," Lorian told Tedric in a low voice, and after a short pause, the slide and click of Tedric's sword being sheathed made Lorian release a small sigh of relief.

With a deafening *pop*, the mist sucked toward the darkness and began to swirl and fold in upon itself. Lorian blinked rapidly to watch in renewed amazement as the mist congregated at the beginning of the chasm. It began to swirl quickly, colors of brown and milky white flashing through the mist. And with another loud popping sound, the mist disappeared and a thin girl stood in its place, along with a rickety bridge that lay across the darkness below.

The girl looked young, perhaps only just past the age of what would be considered a child. Flame-colored hair lay in curls around her unnaturally pale face and traveled down to brush her waist. Her brown eyes were downcast as she scanned them with a sorrowful curiosity. A plain white dress hung over her skeletal frame, the frayed hem brushing against the snow-flecked ground. She looked as though the smallest gust of wind would be strong enough to knock her over and even the softest blow would have the power to kill her. But Lorian knew that she was already dead.

"I know of your passing." Her voice quailed. "I have seen it in the stars."

"Oh, no, not one of these prophesies again," Tedric grumbled as he removed his hand from his sword hilt.

"I am not one of the Sythril you met whilst traveling through Millris Forest. When you are someone like me, you have the power to ask the stars many questions."

Tedric's brow raised as he looked the girl up and down. Her gaze slid over him, and she nodded as if reading his thoughts.

"You are right, young commander. I am dead. I have been dead for more centuries than I could even try to remember."

"Why have you not traveled to the Nether yet?" Finriel's question to the Guardian was hushed.

The Guardian shrugged and looked behind to gaze almost lovingly at the aged bridge. "I will not travel until this bridge either collapses or is destroyed," she replied sadly. "I am tethered to it for all eternity. But the matters of myself are not important. I have seen that you five and the mogwa wish to travel across to the dragon kingdom, is this true?"

"I am afraid it is." Krete took a step toward the Guardian. "We're on a mission of utter importance that must be fulfilled."

The Guardian smiled, her troubled eyes looking down upon Krete with a twinkle in them. "The rules of this bridge have been the same since I was first placed as Guardian of it. You may not cross unless you pass the test."

It was Finriel's turn to step forward. "What kind of test?"

"It is very simple." The Guardian shrugged. "You must solve the riddle I give you before the time of one hour has been spent."

Lorian shoved down a rare surge of nerves and took a step toward the ghost. "Go on, then, what is it?"

The ghost swept her sorrowful gaze toward him, and Lorian wasn't sure if it was out of true emotion or perhaps the poor soul was just experiencing a very solemn and lonely afterlife.

"I remember you," she said, and Lorian smiled.

"You look just as lovely as before," he replied with a small bow, and the Guardian gave him a tired smile.

"Thank you," was all she said before she closed her eyes and took a breath, as if reciting the correct words in her head before speaking.

"There are four siblings in this world, all born together. The first runs and never wearies. The second eats and is never full. The third drinks and is always thirsty. The fourth sings a song forever."

Lorian opened his mouth, but then promptly closed it. He knew the riddle would not be easy to solve, even for his quick mind. Finriel bit her bottom lip in concentration as she mulled the riddle over, and Krete squinted as if the answer were somewhere in the horizon and all he had to do was spot it.

"Do we get any hints?" Lorian asked the Guardian hopefully.

She chuckled softly and floated closer. Nora sniffed suspiciously at the Guardian's translucent dress and took a step back.

"If you need one, I will allow a single hint."

"We will be able to solve it, thank you," Finriel replied with a narrowed look at the girl.

Tedric rolled his eyes and nodded to Lorian in a silent agreement for the hint. The Guardian seemed to notice Tedric's confirmation and spoke.

"Very well. The answer is close to your heart."

"That wasn't very helpful at all, but thank you for trying," Lorian replied with a tinge of frustration.

The Guardian inclined her head with a smile. "You may take the hint or choose to cast it away. I am far too dead to take offense."

"We are more likely solve this in time if we work together," Krete offered.

Everyone nodded and Lorian followed Krete and the others toward a large outcrop of layered brown stone. Finriel paused and turned back toward the Guardian, who was patiently floating near the opening of the bridge.

"What will happen if we don't solve the riddle in time?"

"I will disappear, as will the bridge. You will not be able or allowed to cross into Drolatis and will most likely be stuck on that ledge until you die of starvation."

Lorian turned to Krete and winked. "Or you can just use that little portal stone of yours to get us out of here."

Krete shook his head. "The stone needs to recharge. It could take a few weeks to be able to perform the way it did for us today."

Lorian's spirits sank, and he turned back toward the group. "Let's solve this riddle."

Krete moved to sit on a rock next to Nora, still squinting slightly. "Okay, so there are the four siblings, and each have problems in their lives that will never be solved."

"But it is not the problems that need to be solved. We know what the problems are," Tedric answered.

"What were the problems again? I've got too many of my own and seem to have forgotten," Lorian drawled, hoping that his quip would lighten the mood. It did not.

Aeden closed her eyes and took in a breath. She recited the section of the riddle to near perfection. "The first runs and never wearies. The second eats and is never full. The third drinks and is always thirsty. The fourth sings a song forever."

"There has to be a logical answer, especially if the answer is something close to our hearts," Tedric said, and Aeden nodded in agreement, her eyes fluttering open.

"I don't know how it can be close to any of our hearts," Lorian grunted. "Their problems sound terrible."

"The same way that listening to your ridiculous comments is terrible for the rest of us," Finriel snapped, and Lorian looked away, slightly stung by her sudden severity. He could never tell if she was truly beginning to forgive him or if she was simply putting on an act to make him feel better. He supposed the wound between them was too deep to heal so quickly.

Krete lifted his hands. "We'll waste too much time if we argue with each other."

Tedric nodded. "He's right. We need to use each of our skills together instead of against one another."

Finriel opened her mouth to respond but Aeden threw her a look that made her snap it closed. The company fell silent and Lorian muddled over the riddle in his mind. Something about the wording stuck with him, as though the people being spoken of truly were connected to one another. It was the only thing that made sense, but he wasn't sure how to put it together.

"Could it have something to do with the quest?" Tedric offered, his face set in a concentrated scowl.

"That would be too obvious, and besides, we're capturing beasts, not humans," Finriel replied in frustration.

Long minutes went by in silence, and Lorian found himself growing more impatient and pessimistic about their chances of ever solving the riddle. Finriel began gnawing at her bottom lip, which Lorian knew was never a good sign. She was likely getting frustrated like the rest of the companions by the dead end they faced.

"How much time has gone by?" Tedric asked the Guardian, who stared out toward the Steel Mountains, the pass through Drolatis they were to take. *Only if we can solve this damned riddle.*

The Guardian turned to face Tedric and glided toward the companions. "You have only half of your hour remaining."

Tedric thanked her and turned away, raking his fingers through his dust coated hair with a low curse. Lorian's spirits had sunk dramatically, and he found himself growing frustrated. How had he gone from being careless and arguably heartless to this worried shadow of a man? He sighed and crossed his arms, looking up at his companions. Then it struck him. It was because of them. He had never needed to worry about anyone other than himself, and at times didn't really care for his own safety during missions. But now he had others he had to take into consideration, and he realized that he truly did care about them.

Lorian shook the thoughts away and glanced toward Tedric, who was huddled close to Aeden and speaking in a low voice. A sense of unease washed over him at the sight of them together, especially now that he had realized their underlying attraction for each other. He could only guess what the outcome would be, but he wasn't certain if they realized how dangerous their dance of hearts truly was.

"Aeden, can you tell me the riddle one more time?" Krete asked, a sudden light in his eyes.

Aeden recited it, and Lorian grunted, tired of the serious silence that held thick in the air. "Well hell, I'm nearly always thinking about a nice pint."

"Shut it," Finriel snapped. "We'll never solve this riddle with your mindless chatter." The witch was obviously still angry with him, but Lorian was quickly losing his sense of caring over the matter.

"No, he has a point," Krete said, standing, his eyes widening. "Aeden, what is the one thing about being in Proveria that you miss the most?"

Aeden considered for a moment and then smiled softly. "My wings, though they never truly came in."

Lorian glanced at Aeden, her expression something of mingled sorrow and reminiscence. He had heard of fairies never truly growing wings, and that the occurrence of a fairy obtaining full wings was something of an anomaly.

"Do you know how many fairies with true wings are left in the realm?" Lorian asked, but Krete waved a dismissive hand in Lorian's face.

"No time for that," Krete said, and then turned and nodded at Tedric.

"I'm sorry, but I don't understand how reflecting on our past is going to help us solve a riddle," Finriel interrupted the gnome before he had a chance to speak.

Krete opened his mouth to speak when the Guardian's voice echoed softly around them.

"You have less than half of your time left. Use it wisely."

"We need to actually think and not—"

"Finriel, let me finish," Krete snapped angrily. Finriel closed her mouth with a scowl and the gnome turned to Tedric. "Now, Tedric, where are you from?"

Tedric snorted and shrugged. "Well, from Keadora, of course, you know that."

Krete turned toward Finriel and gave her an apologetic smile. "What form of magic comes easiest to you? Healing, tracking—"

"Fire," Finriel cut in automatically, glancing warily at the Guardian, though the ghost appeared not to hear.

Krete nodded with satisfaction gleaming in his eyes, seeming to have already known the answer.

"I myself was born out of the Mountains of Creonid, therefore I feel most at home when I am surrounded by thick stone." He then looked between the four of his companions expectantly. "Do you now see what I am getting at?" He was met by four equally blank stares. Everyone stiffened at the sad voice telling them that they had mere minutes remaining.

"Come on, think!" Krete said urgently. "Aeden, what do you like the most about even having the ghost of wings?"

Aeden stuttered, "I— the way it feels when I'm in the air."

"Using my magic feels liberating," Finriel offered, and Lorian watched her face change from one of confusion to one of realization. "Of course, I am an idiot."

"You have until the minute runs out," the Guardian called, her voice slightly urgent now.

"We are the four siblings," Finriel declared, and Lorian suddenly realized what she was saying.

"But there are five of us," Tedric countered.

"Doesn't matter. You and I are one sibling. We are from the same kingdom," Finriel replied with a wave of her hand.

"I see, and I suppose that we just tell her our names then?" Lorian asked.

Finriel shook her head and motioned for them to all come with her as she ran to the Guardian. The ghost and bridge were already beginning to shimmer away.

"Wait!" Finriel called.

The Guardian paused her departure and solidified once more. "Have you solved the riddle?"

Finriel nodded. "The answer is all of us— well, not really." She cursed under her breath and tried again. "It's the four elements. Water, fire, earth, and air."

As if her words were a spell, a sucking noise ricocheted through the chasm and the bridge popped back into reality. Finriel let out a breath and allowed a smile onto her face. The Guardian smiled back at the five of them, including Nora, who was eying her suspiciously.

"You have solved the riddle. You may pass," the ghost said, the sorrow returning to her voice. It seemed that perhaps she would be sad to be left alone again.

Lorian took a step onto the old bridge, and everyone began to follow suit.

"Wait a moment," the Guardian called. The companions paused and looked back at the lonely woman. "You are doing more harm to yourselves by keeping your creatures in those pages."

"I appreciate your care for our safety," Aeden replied. "Unfortunately, it's hard to believe that we would be doing ourselves any good by letting them out."

Lorian silently agreed. He didn't want to get tossed against a tree again.

The Guardian shrugged and sighed. "It is as you choose, but you would be wise to keep your pages very close. The creator of these beings passed by only a few days ago."

Lorian's pulse stuttered at the news. Krete clutched at his vest pocket instinctively, even though they had not yet found the creature that belonged to his page.

"Do you know in what direction he was headed?" Tedric asked, a nerve flickering in his jaw.

The Guardian nodded. "He is expecting to meet all of you

and told me to tell you all that he will meet you at a home underground."

Krete and Aeden exchanged a look and then turned back to the Guardian.

"Thank you very much, Guardian." Krete bowed. "It was good to see you again."

"Stay on your guard," the Guardian answered, "and be careful of who you trust."

TEDRIC

T edric cursed as he slipped yet again.

The rough gorges and steep mountain slopes they scaled were much different than the soft ground in Keadora, and Tedric found himself endlessly slipping on loose stones as they made their way through the Steel Mountains. Small creatures with inky black fur and six legs darted across their path, some pausing to watch the companions make their slow descent down the mountainside, others squeaking with alarm and scrambling between stones to get to safety as Nora stalked behind them hungrily.

Tedric's breath came out in short gasps with each step that he took, the cold, thin mountain air slicing through his lungs. Each breath felt like he was taking in ice, even though the air had been surprisingly mild during the day once they trekked far enough away from the Guardian's bridge, where the sky had opened up into a clear baby blue. A constant breeze rustled through the rocky, tree-barren land, sending his hair flying across his face, much to his agitation.

The ground under their feet was riddled with small holes and sharp stones, and the air was filled with whispering curses as Tedric's companions stepped carefully across the mountain pass. Tedric's feet slipped from underneath him again as he stepped on another loose stone, and he yelled out as he began to fall. Delicate yet strong hands grabbed him at the shoulder and waist with surprising speed, and Aeden chuckled as he took another unsteady step.

"How many times will I have to save your ass from dying or otherwise making a complete fool of yourself?" Her eyes twinkled with laughter, and her hands hesitated on Tedric's body as their eyes met.

"I wouldn't care for anyone else to save my ass." Tedric grinned back and brought his hand up, brushing a strand of violet hair from her face. She froze, and Tedric gave her a wink before turning and continuing to walk, this time watching his steps more carefully than before.

Tedric wouldn't admit that his body felt like hot embers where her hands had caught him, or that the insides of his stomach felt as if he had swallowed a live fish that was trying its hardest to leap out of his mouth. He couldn't admit it even if he wanted to.

"Stop," Finriel shouted through the shrieking wind that whipped around them. She had the map out and was looking down upon it with a concerned expression.

"What is it?" Lorian asked as he came up behind her to peer over her shoulder.

Tedric blinked in surprise as Finriel didn't shrink away from the thief, but instead brought the map further up so that it was easier for him to see. Astonished, he noticed the hint of what could only be a blush on her cheeks as Lorian leaned in and brushed against her shoulder. Perhaps those two were faring better than Tedric had realized.

"The mountains split here," Finriel said, pointing at the map, and Tedric took two long strides to Finriel's other side and looked. Her finger was pointing at a place not too far from their current location, and Tedric nodded, realizing what Finriel was getting at.

"We should keep more to the east," Tedric replied confidently. "It will keep us closer to the coast, so it should be warmer than there," he finished, pointing a dirt-encrusted fingernail toward the westerly portion of the Steel Mountains.

Lorian nodded. "I've gone both ways, the westerly mountain pass will be covered in feet of snow by this time. Besides, staying to the east here will give us a more direct line to Dragonkeep, which is where I am assuming we are headed."

"It's the only fathomable place to find the storyteller's dragon." Finriel shrugged. "That or the Clelac Crags."

Tedric watched Lorian curiously as the thief shuddered and shook his head.

"The crags can be our last resort." Lorian cringed. Tedric raised a brow in question and Lorian shook his head, answering quickly, "It's another long story."

"There's a large pond over there," Krete called, and Tedric turned slightly to look behind his shoulder.

Krete and Nora stood at the top of a small ridge a few feet from where Tedric and the others stood, and Krete waved them over.

"We stay east, then?" Finriel asked, and Tedric nodded in confirmation.

Finriel rolled up the map and the three of them followed Aeden to the top of the ridge. Tedric's tunic felt sticky with sweat, and he swore he could feel the endless dust they'd gone through now ingrained in his skin.

"There," Krete pointed, and Tedric looked.

A large meadow with sparse yet surprisingly still green grass stretched out beyond, and indeed a fairly large body of water glittered in the sun at the base of an enormous mountain. Large boulders were scattered throughout the meadow, casting long shadows across the ground.

"I say we stay here for the rest of the day and make camp by one of those boulders," Tedric said. "We'll be no good against a dragon if we don't take at least one day of rest."

No one argued against this, and the companions were soon making their way toward the large pond in the distance. Tedric's itching skin felt as if it too was anticipating getting to the water. He knew that the first thing he'd do was jump into the pond, no matter if there were large water snakes or other creatures inside. Tedric wanted nothing more than to feel clean for the first time in nearly two moons, and he'd go stark naked even in front of Aeden and Finriel to get a good bathing in.

"Here is good, don't you think?" Krete said, gesturing to a smattering of boulders spaced close to the edge of the pond.

Tedric nodded along with the others, his mind more on the prospect of a bath than where to set up camp. Being on the road had changed him, he realized with a jolt. Before, he wouldn't have even thought about his own comfort, ensuring that he followed protocol and created a home base before going off on his own. *Perhaps it's not such a bad thing to loosen up,* he thought as he walked over to the rocky shore of the pond.

"What do you think, any water snakes?" Lorian asked, making Tedric jump as the thief came to stand at his side and peer into the clear depths.

"I don't think so, the water is too clear," Tedric commented, finding that he could see the rock-and sand-covered bottom of the pond, which was not very deep at all.

"And too cold," Lorian agreed. "It might even be too cold for our snakes."

Tedric scowled, and the thief shrugged with raised brows. A resigned sigh fell from his lips and he began working at the clasp of his cloak.

"I'd rather risk that unfortunate event than be dirty at this point," he replied, pulling his tunic up over his head.

"Krete!" Lorian yelled over to the gnome, who was helping Finriel and Aeden search for kindling for the coming night. "Come join us for a swim."

Krete glanced at Finriel and Aeden, who gestured for him to go, and the gnome promptly dropped the few meager sticks in his hands and went to join the men.

"You could have invited the women over," Tedric grumbled under his breath to Lorian, who had also started to discard his grimy clothing upon the rocky ground.

Lorian snorted, though his eyes darkened. "I don't think Finriel would willingly come near me and a body of water any time soon."

A wave of guilt crashed over Tedric's good spirits as he set his pants atop his tunic and cloak. "I'm sorry, I had forgotten," he said apologetically, now standing in nothing but his undergarments.

Lorian stared at him for a moment, then burst into a fit of wild laughter. Tedric felt nothing but confusion at this, and he looked down at himself, trying to find something that may be of humor to the thief.

"I can't take you seriously with you baring your heart to me in nothing but your underthings," Lorian wheezed, nearly doubling over.

"Is everything okay?" Krete asked, already shrugging his vest from his shoulders as he approached.

"Lorian is just getting a good laugh out of me, that's all," Tedric growled, though he was finding it hard to remain serious himself.

"Ah, well, I can't seem to understand most things that come out of his mouth," Krete replied with a simple smile, and headed toward the water.

Tedric was surprised to find that nothing but muscle rippled underneath the gnome's tanned skin as he dove into the crystalline depths with barely a splash.

Lorian nodded toward Tedric's shoulder and said with a slightly more serious tone, "It suits you."

Tedric looked down at the scar that ran from the top of his shoulder and ended at the middle of his bicep, the raised red line a stark difference against his olive skin. Tedric flexed his arm, remembering how foolish he had been with the chimera. "It will be a constant reminder that I can do better," he said almost to himself.

"You're too harsh on yourself," Lorian sighed.

"Come on." Tedric motioned for Lorian to follow him into the water, and he trudged toward the shore. Perhaps Lorian was right and he was too hard on himself. A small ball formed at the pit of his stomach and Tedric shoved it down. Excellence was the only thing that had brought him and his father even the smallest bit of honor. Tedric wouldn't stop trying to be better, even if it killed him one day.

Tedric sucked in a breath at the sting of freezing water that lapped around his feet, the sensation of tiny pinpricks against his skin near painful. He looked over to Krete, who was standing a few feet off, scrubbing at his arms and head merrily as if the water were as warm as a regular bath. Tedric shook his head in wonder and forced himself a few steps further, cursing at the cold. He looked over his shoulder to get a glimpse at Aeden, and his stomach gave its familiar flop as his eyes landed upon her and Finriel lounging on a patch of grass, both of the women watching him and Lorian with looks of amusement. Tedric brought a hand up to wave at Aeden, but before he could, a hard body slammed against his back, sending him falling face first into freezing water. The cold was blinding, and Tedric pressed against the smooth rocks at the bottom of the pond to come back up for air.

"I hate you," Tedric spluttered, shaking his head and sending droplets scattering across the rippling water.

Lorian brought a hand to his bare chest in mock hurt. "Oh, now you've just hurt my feelings," he replied with a devilish grin.

A smile tugged at Tedric's lips and he lunged forward, bending slightly to aim his blow at Lorian's waist. His shoulder connected with Lorian's now filled out frame, and Lorian fell back into the water with a grunt of surprise. Aeden and Finriel's laughter rang through the air, but Tedric kept his focus on Lorian, waiting for the thief as he popped back up, spitting water from his mouth and wiping dark shoulder-length hair from his face.

Lorian was still grinning when their bodies collided again, and Tedric easily hooked his leg behind Lorian's knee, sending him back into the water in less than a second. Tedric couldn't help his smile from growing at Lorian's silly attempts of attack, though he knew that the thief wasn't trying very hard.

"I could beat you in a fight with my eyes closed," Tedric commented after he had thrown Lorian into the water yet again, and Lorian simply laughed.

"My apologies that I wasn't honed into a fighting machine at such a young age, but I also haven't been trying," Lorian replied easily.

"Oh?" Tedric said. "Please, do enlighten me."

"Come on, now," Krete interjected from where he stood a few paces away. "I'm just trying to get clean, and you two are making the water dirty."

"So sorry," Lorian panted. "We're nearly finished."

Krete sighed and quickly finished scrubbing at his mousy brown hair, grumbling under his breath about thieves and young men having as much sense as a brick. Tedric brought his attention back to Lorian, but found that the thief wasn't there anymore. A hand clasped around Tedric's ankle and he let out a yelp of surprise as it yanked his foot forward, and he fell into the icy depths once again.

"That's not proper fighting," Tedric finally said once he emerged from the water to find Lorian scrubbing at his now clean skin as if nothing had happened.

Lorian looked at Tedric and replied with a grin, "My line of work doesn't require proper fighting. It simply requires whatever moves will get you out of trouble quick enough."

"I could teach you a few things, you know," Tedric said, shivering against a sudden breeze.

"The commander of the Ten, train a wanted thief to fight?" Lorian said, and flung his hands into the air. "Next thing I know, the goddesses will return to Raymara, and I'll become a king."

Tedric laughed. "We should get out. We've already scared Krete away." He pointed at Krete, who was now crouched at the shore, dunking his clothes into the water.

Tedric and Lorian finished scrubbing the grime from their skin and hair, and Tedric relished in watching the lines of dirt fall from his skin.

"What's been the matter between you and Aeden?" Lorian asked, breaking up the silence.

Tedric paused his scrubbing, his heart skipping as he took a moment before answering, "There's nothing the matter between us."

"Oh, please." Lorian snorted. "Even Krete could see that there's something between you two."

"I couldn't say." Tedric sighed. "I still feel like I don't know her very well, and I would say more if I knew that she wasn't listening to our conversation."

Tedric glanced at their camp, and indeed Aeden had paused in leaning over something upon the ground. Lorian chuckled and patted Tedric on the shoulder with an understanding nod. Tedric and Lorian slowly made their way to the rocky shore. Tedric looked down at the ground to grab his dirty clothes, but frowned to find that they were nowhere to be seen.

"That's strange," he said.

"Maybe Finriel and Aeden took them," Lorian suggested, and the two of them set off shivering toward the women and Krete, who was now seated next to Aeden.

Nora was nowhere in sight, and Tedric could only guess that she was off hunting somewhere. He let his gaze travel over the wide meadow, though he knew that he wouldn't be able to spot the mogwa.

"Looking for your clothes?" Aeden asked as they approached, and Tedric nodded, his veins thrumming as their gazes met. Aeden quickly looked away and pointed to her right. Tedric followed her gesture to find his and Lorian's clothes on one of the large boulders close to them, dripping wet.

"You washed them?" Lorian asked, and Aeden nodded.

"It was more for us than anything. Finriel and I have barely been able to stand the smell of you two for the past few weeks."

Tedric padded over to the boulder and picked up a sleeve of his dripping tunic with another shiver. "Finriel, would you mind lending a hand? They won't be dry enough for hours on their own."

"I'm surprised," Finriel said with a raised brow. "I wouldn't have thought that a trusted warrior of the Red King would ask for me to break the law for him."

Tedric tensed and shot her a look of warning. She was right, however. He *was* asking her to break the law on his accord, even if it was just to dry his clothes.

"I have no problems with breaking a silly magic law." Lorian filled the silence. "You can dry both of our clothes on my behalf."

Finriel rolled her eyes but smiled in reply to Lorian's request, and Tedric dropped the sopping tunic sleeve as Finriel stood and came to stand at his side.

"It doesn't make you any less of a man, you know," Finriel said, and Tedric looked down at her in surprise.

He was speechless as Finriel gently closed her eyes and splayed her hands over his and Lorian's clothes. Heat began to radiate visibly from her fingertips. That had been the nicest thing she'd ever said to him, he realized, and he glanced down at the large red scar on his shoulder, which was just another reminder of what she had done to help him live.

"There," Finriel said with satisfaction, and she stepped away.

Tedric reached forward to find his clothes dry and warm to the touch, and he thanked her quickly before grabbing his tunic, pants, and cloak. Lorian came to stand at Tedric's side, and they began to dress.

"What is the matter between you and Finriel?" Tedric asked, his thoughts drifting to Finriel's sudden change in attitude toward Lorian.

"I suppose she's realizing that I'm not entirely the idiot that she thought I was," Lorian replied nonchalantly as he finished buckling his cloak, though Tedric found a note of tension in his voice.

"I see," Tedric nodded, and Lorian gave him a strained smile.

A FULL MOON BATHED THE OPEN MEADOW IN SOFT luminescence, and nothing but the sounds of even breathing and a whispering breeze filled the air. Tedric sat with his back against the cool stone of a boulder, watching his companions and the glittering pond beyond as he took the last watch of the night.

The companions had enjoyed a laughter-filled mealtime around a campfire, the remaining embers still glowing softly a few feet away. His heart had grown fond of his companions, even Nora, though she was rarely with them for very long periods of time. Tedric sighed through his nose, his thoughts drifting to what would happen after the quest. Would he be expected to simply return to his duties as commander of the Ten? Would he have to forget about the faces of the companions he'd grown to care for so deeply? He supposed that was the nature of any quest, but Tedric hadn't allowed himself to grow so attached to anyone but his men in his entire life.

His attention snapped back to the small camp, and his heart jumped as a familiar graceful body stood from among his sleeping companions and approached.

"Can't sleep?" Tedric asked as Aeden came to sit at his side, and he slid over so that she could rest comfortably against the smooth stone.

Tedric's skin prickled where their arms touched, and Aeden shivered as a cool breeze swept over them. He itched to bring her into his arms and shelter her from the growing cold, but he forced his hands to remain clasped in his lap.

"The moon is too bright," Aeden explained. "And I can never sleep on the full moon."

"I can't either," Tedric agreed.

"It's the last full moon before Clamidas," Aeden said again, and Tedric looked at her, finding that her expression was lined with worry.

"Is that a bad thing?" he asked.

"No." Aeden shook her head. "Though I've never enjoyed it as most fairies have. My father has never let me experience it in the forests."

"He sounds like a very controlling parent," Tedric mused, "though I could be wrong."

"You're far from wrong," Aeden said with a small smile. "He's a monster."

"What sort of things did he do?" Tedric asked, remembering that she had said something similar during one of their first conversations.

"After my mother died," Aeden began, "he was never the

same. He blamed my nan for her death, though her passing had clearly been nothing more than an accident."

"I'm sorry," Tedric whispered, and Aeden shook her head.

"Don't be. I did all I could to convince him, but my distaste for him had already grown thick when it happened."

Tedric wasn't sure if she was going to continue, but she opened her mouth again after a moment of pause. He watched her with a growing ache in his chest, wishing that he could look into her green eyes and hold her as she spoke with growing anger.

"I was sixteen when my father had him killed four years ago. He was my first and only love, but my father didn't agree with our desire for each other."

"How is that possible? He could have been cursed doing that," Tedric said, more of a question than anything.

"My father didn't kill him. He's too much of a coward to use his own hands, but he made me watch the man who was hired to do it," Aeden nearly spat, and Tedric shuddered.

"I'm sorry," she whispered, and Tedric found himself extending a hand to her. She took it tentatively, and Tedric squeezed her hand softly, reassuringly. She gave him a small smile, and his heart nearly stopped at the beauty of her.

"Why did he do it?" Tedric asked, and Aeden's smile faltered.

"My father has always been proud of his status, and the boy was a human servant," Aeden replied. "Because of this, he wanted to ensure that our house remained respectable and … clean."

Tedric nodded, though his stomach clenched at her words. He understood what it was like to hate someone of a different race, but he was beginning to find that he didn't feel the same about his hatred for fairies anymore.

"My father wanted to have the boy's death be an example of what would happen if I ever crossed him again."

"You have to stand up for what's right even if it means that it goes against your father," Tedric said, and Aeden's smile reappeared.

"You wouldn't say that if you met him." She sighed.

"I'd love to meet him, and kill him for you, if that's what you wanted." Tedric smiled and Aeden leaned into him.

"I'd like that very much," she giggled, but Tedric noted a tinge of sincerity there.

"My father is a complete fool himself, though it's not for a lack of trying," Tedric started. "He remarried when I began to train with the Ten, though I think it's because he wanted to try to start his life over now that I was beginning to do something good with mine.

"It didn't last long, unfortunately, and I still worry about him every day. I became a member of the Ten for him, to bring honor and security where he has none." Aeden was the one to squeeze his hand now, and Tedric looked down at their intertwined fingers. "I'm sorry, I didn't mean to speak of my father in such a way when you just spoke about how terrible yours is," Tedric mumbled, keeping his eyes trained on their fingers.

"No, it's okay," Aeden whispered, and Tedric looked up to meet her eyes.

Moonlight reflected in glistening tears as they rolled down her face, and Tedric brought up his free hand to brush them away. He longed to kiss her, to help ease her pain in any way that he could.

"I'm sorry," he whispered again, and Aeden blinked, another tear rolling down her cheek.

Tedric released Aeden's hand and brought his arms around her, enveloping her body in his. She settled against his chest perfectly, and he ignored the electric shocks that zipped through his skin as she wrapped an arm around his waist.

"Thank you for telling me about your father," Tedric whispered, and her grip around his waist tightened.

"Just hold me," she sniffled.

Tedric brushed a soft kiss against the top of her head, and nothing felt more perfect in that moment as Aeden's tears lessened and she eventually fell asleep against him. Tedric watched the final full moon of fall as it made its descent through the night sky, his mind perfectly empty as he held the girl who had taken his heart.

FINRIEL

"We're getting close to the nian," Finriel yelled over the screaming wind as the companions neared the end of their twentieth day crossing through the Steel Mountains.

It had been nothing but misery in Finriel's opinion, and she had officially renounced her desire to travel to the mountains ever again. Their day and night in the meadow had been the most enjoyable day in Drolatis as far as Finriel was concerned, and she was sure that her companions would agree, everyone besides Krete and Nora perhaps. Krete didn't appear to have any issues with the endless days of wind and scrambling through giant mountains with no apparent end, and she had barely seen Nora since they'd entered Drolatis, though she knew that the mogwa was hunting and keeping any potentially harmful animals off their path.

Every day had grown steadily colder and whatever vegetation that had pushed through the mountainous earth crunched under their feet. The company was making their way down yet another mountainside in silence when Tedric called for a break and Finriel opened the map.

"I might be a bit crazy in saying this, but the nian isn't my concern," Lorian said as he looked down at the map from over Finriel's shoulder.

"Is it the lake?" Tedric asked as he, too, came to inspect the map and pointed toward the large body of water near the edge of Dragonkeep, Drolatis's largest mountain and hopefully the location of their next beast. "That lake has been the only source of slaughter within this realm for one thousand years," Tedric said loudly in Finriel's ear so he could be heard over the wind, making her tilt her head away from him.

Lorian nodded. "It's a pretty awful lake."

Aeden snorted as she came around Lorian, leaving Tedric, who immediately slipped and cursed, barely catching a hold of Krete by his shoulder.

"I do hope you know we have to pass through the lake, right?" Aeden asked. Finriel paused and looked up at the fairy with a blank stare, even though her stomach threatened to launch out of her throat. Aeden stared back. "You did know that, right?"

Krete nodded confidently, although it was clear by the sickly pallor of his face that he wasn't looking forward to the endeavor.

"It's the only way to enter Dragonkeep. Well, that or flying in, which is why not many creatures besides dragons have been able to get into the mountain with all of their limbs still attached to their body."

"The lake isn't the only way to get to the Dragonkeep," Lorian interjected. "I reached it through the Clelac Crags."

Tedric barked a laugh at this, but Lorian's face remained impassive. The commander's smile died and he gave the thief an incredulous look.

"Wait, are you serious?"

"Unfortunately so." Lorian nodded. "I have been to the lake as well, I skirted around it when I was twelve. However, with the time constraint upon us, I think that it's best if we go through the passageway." He sighed as Finriel gave him the same look she'd directed toward Aeden mere moments ago. He shrugged and avoided her gaze, scuffing his boot against the hard ground. "Being a thief makes you do many stupid things. Including stealing a dragon's egg."

As if they had heard him, the distant guttural cry of a dragon sounded from somewhere beyond the next mountain ridge looming ahead. Lorian's jaw worked and he turned away abruptly, taking a few steps from his friends. Finriel felt a pang of sympathy as she watched the thief's hunched figure and the dark cloak that billowed around him.

"Just give him a moment," Finriel said softly to the others. They glanced at her and nodded, each still bearing an expression of curiosity. She watched him with an amount of concern that still surprised her, though she was getting used to the strange array of emotions that were beginning to follow along with her slow forgiveness for his betrayal.

"Come with me," Lorian finally called to his companions. "I know how to get to the lake."

Finriel followed Lorian as he started picking his way up the mountain. She lengthened her stride so that she was soon walking beside him, but he didn't look at her. His angular features were drawn into a grim expression, a black curl strewn over his clouded eyes.

Lorian's words still prickled in her mind, and she found herself growing more curious about his past with each day. She yearned to question him about why this place affected him so much. She wanted to stand with him and comfort him. The realization struck her in her bones, and yet she found that she didn't mind anymore. *Just another emotion to add to the list*, she supposed. She was beginning to realize that forgiveness was much easier than she had thought, and that holding a grudge since she was ten years old had been one of the most exhausting things in her life. Finriel still didn't know why he had left, and she had been too stubborn and hot headed to believe anything other than him not caring enough about her to stay. She didn't even have to ask the question that pushed at her tongue before Lorian spoke.

"Shortly after escaping my captures, a group of thieves employed me to steal a dragon's egg from a nesting pond at the base of Dragonkeep. I didn't want to go through the lake at all, because that would force me to go deep into the mountain. I skirted the lake and went through the entire expanse of the crags. It was a miracle that I even got ten feet through without getting burnt to a crisp by the dragons."

He paused for a moment, and Finriel stayed silent. It seemed a perilous mission for anyone, especially such a young boy. But she still didn't understand why it had affected him so badly. He opened his mouth to speak once more, but Finriel placed a hand on his shoulder and squeezed gently.

"You don't have to if it's too much," Finriel murmured. "When you're ready, I am here to listen."

Lorian looked up and suddenly they were children again, the baggage that had burdened Finriel for ten years fading away. She smiled and he returned it, bringing up his hand to gently brush her cheek. Finriel stiffened, but she didn't say a word as he seemed to realize what he had just done and quickly dropped his hand to his side.

Lorian and Finriel settled into a comfortable silence, only the sounds of boots crunching against stone and the soft murmurs of Aeden, Krete, and Tedric conversing behind them filling the air. It was much colder in the mountainous kingdoms than in the forest kingdoms, and Finriel shivered against the constant crisp breeze that blew against her face and down her neck. She placed a comforting hand on Nora's back, receiving an endearing purr from the mogwa in turn. Nora had returned from hunting some time ago, and had apparently decided to stay close to them for a few hours. The squeezing sensation in her heart persisted even after their conversation had faded for some time, and Finriel sagged against the extra weight as they started up another steep hill.

"STOP," LORIAN CALLED OUT AS THEY REACHED THE CREST OF one of the largest and most vexatious mountains, which they had begun to scale two sunrises before. Finriel took in a sharp breath at the landscape around them. The bottom of the mountainside they currently stood upon opened into a wide expanse of browning meadows and small pools. Animals of all types moved through the meadows and a flock of small birds set off into the sky in a dark cloud of feathers and wings. Finriel narrowed her eyes as she spotted the faint shimmering wall that lay in the center of the meadow, marking the kingdom line between Creonid and Drolatis. The large expanse of meadows and hills of Creonid was scorched black and a whiff of charred grass swam through her nose, sending a twinge of sorrow through Finriel's chest at the sight of the scarred earth. Krete had good reason to want to help get the beasts back into the pages and right the story-teller's misdoings. His kingdom had been depleted into ash and stone. She squinted, hoping to catch a glimpse of the fabled Creonid mountain, but the city of stone was still nowhere in sight.

Finriel took deep gulps of air as she watched Tedric and Aeden scramble the rest of the way to where she and Lorian stood. Nora bounded up to stand beside Finriel, the deep orange sun setting her thick grey pelt in an unearthly glow. Krete looked like he was taking a casual stroll through a flat forest as he climbed up the rock with a grace and nimbleness that surprised Finriel. He had not once complained during their time here, and it was clear that he felt truly at home in the mountains. He walked with a slight smile on his face as he reached the top of the mountain, where Finriel and Lorian waited.

Tedric sniffed and scrunched his nose. "Is that salt in the air?"

Lorian nodded dully and pointed to a glittering blue expanse at the far coast of Drolatis. "It's the Sandrial Waters."

Finriel gasped. She never thought that she would live to see the ocean. Yet here she was, laying her eyes upon the distant barrier that separated her from her mother for the first time.

A sharp cry shot through the air, and Finriel tore her gaze back to the meadow. She squinted to make out the change of terrain closer to the mountains, revealing dark rough ground and large caves. Farther to the east, the ground soon fell away to meet the ever-pounding crash of the Sandrial Waters below.

The ocean curved around the crag to disappear from sight behind an impressive mountain. Its surface looked blackened and dead, likely caused by frequent streams of dragon fire. Finriel eyed the mountain with growing trepidation. They would have to go inside of it, into the darkness and thick stone walls. But it wasn't the scenery that soon caused Finriel's blood to run cold. It was the dragons. So many dragons flew in the sky and prowled the ground. The beasts were still enormous even from so far away. Some dragons were so large that they seemed to swallow up the sky around them. Other dragons were so small that they were merely dark specks upon the ground.

"It's the Clelac Crags," Aeden breathed as she looked upon the dragons in awe.

Lorian nodded glumly and then pointed to a place slightly away from the Clelac Crags. "And that's Lake Lagdranule."

Finriel looked down upon the glittering blue water. The lake was enormous, taking up most of the space that was not open expanses of meadows and creatures. She gazed at the water as it sparkled and glinted in the lowering autumn sunlight, its color so vibrantly blue that it seemed as if it was a painting, not a real lake. It looked calm enough, but Finriel had heard of the terrors that lay beneath that cobalt disguise.

"There's a cave at the base of this mountain that should be safe to stay in for the night," Lorian said, breaking the tense silence. "From there, we can go to the lake."

"It's probably a good idea to have at least one good night out of the wind before we face the creatures of Lagdranule," Krete agreed, his attention still trained upon the Clelac Crags.

Dragons were beginning to settle in for the night, it seemed, the beasts that were still airborne began their descent to the dark stone crags.

"We should get moving unless we want to all turn into icicles or a crisp snack for the dragons," Aeden said, and gestured for Lorian to lead the way.

❧ 22 ❧

TEDRIC

The setting sun bathed the companions by the time they reached the wide dark opening of the cave. Tedric looked at the entrance, something like a gaping mouth, as he slid and picked his way down toward it. The cave appeared to be hand carved out of the mountain itself, and Tedric wondered just how many people and creatures alike had used it for shelter on previous occasions, or if it was perhaps already occupied at this very moment.

"Are you sure that it's safe?" Aeden asked from behind Tedric, apparently feeling the same unease about setting foot inside the cave.

"Of course it's safe," Lorian replied from a few feet ahead, where he, Finriel, and Krete were already nearly at the cave's entrance.

"The word 'safe' coming from your lips is not making me feel any better," Aeden grumbled, and Tedric grunted in agreement.

It had been many weeks since the companions had entered Drolatis, and Tedric had found a certain rhythm to each footstep and scramble through the loose stones and slippery mountain faces. He still hadn't decided which was worse, however, going up or down. Either way was exhausting, Tedric found, even though his body was honed for constant movement and strain. He would be glad when it was over and he could go back to trekking through fields and riding his horse. Tedric thought longingly of Dario, and hoped that the stable boys were caring for him adequately.

"Are you all right?" Aeden asked, coming up to Tedric's side.

His mind flashed to the night under the moon with her sleeping in his arms, and Tedric quickly hid his face. They hadn't spoken about it in the morning, as she'd simply risen at daybreak and, without another word, returned to her cloak by the other companions before any of them had woken up.

"Yes," Tedric replied finally, "I was just thinking about my horse."

Aeden smiled, and they finally stepped onto the more even ground that preceded the cave entrance. "He's in Keadora?" Aeden asked, and Tedric nodded.

"Perhaps I can take you to see him one day," he said with a smile of his own, but Aeden's expression tightened at his words.

At that moment, a soft swishing sound started from the darkness within the cave, making Tedric forget his sudden worry over Aeden's change of expression as he looked toward the sound. A deep sigh reverberated through the air, and Tedric watched petrified as an unfamiliar creature sauntered out of the darkness.

The creature's size was similar to that of a large bear, its muscled body seeming to be made out of a dark green shell, apart from the long sand-colored hair that covered its catlike face and back. Its small yellow eyes surveyed the companions one by one as it stalked toward them. Four long ivory horns grew from the top of the creature's head, dark designs and patterns swirling around them from base to tip.

"I have been waiting for you for some time, my master," the

nian said in a deep grumbling voice that reverberated through the air though its mouth did not move.

The nian's clawed feet dug into the hard earth as though it were nothing but sand, and in a few short moments, it was standing before them.

"To whom are you speaking?" Tedric demanded, his voice stronger than he had expected it to be.

"Why, to you, of course, my master," the nian answered calmly, inclining its feline face toward the commander.

Tedric choked on the curse that nearly flew from his lips as he eyed the beast before him. They had been told that the creatures were spreading death and fear among the lands, but now it was hard for him to believe. Tedric blinked in surprise at the nian's words, but quickly recollected his features before speaking again.

"I don't understand."

The nian swept his narrow gaze over the rest of Tedric's petrified companions with mild interest before saying, "I can kill these annoying creatures if their presence insults you."

"No, don't do that," Tedric barked, taking a step forward in defense.

The nian raised its hackles and let them fall as if shrugging. Tedric exchanged a glance with Lorian, who raised his brows, looking as nonplussed as Tedric felt.

"As you wish, they smell like pests to me though," the creature responded. "Now, I suspect that you are going to order me back inside of that page that you currently have in your left hand."

Tedric opened his mouth to speak, but then shut it again as he glanced down at the page he'd silently taken from his cloak. He simply nodded and stepped forward.

The nian took a step back and shook his head. "You must promise me one thing before I agree to go back inside of that page."

The five companions exchanged wary glances and then Tedric turned back to the beast, the page clutched in his hand as if it were a sword.

"Go on," Tedric answered tentatively.

"You must release me back into the realm on the night of the blood moon."

Lorian snorted and the nian turned its head slowly to give the thief an unimpressed look. Lorian's smile fell when his eyes met with the nian and he hastily cleared his throat, looking down and scuffing his boot against a loose stone.

"Why on that night specifically?" Aeden asked, and her left hand began to move restlessly at her side. "That is the night of Clamidas."

"The fairy festival?" Finriel asked, looking at Aeden, who nodded.

"It's celebrated every winter solstice during the blood moon as gratitude for our creation as a species."

"Why on this night in particular, may I ask?" Tedric now faced the nian, who was gazing at Aeden with a knowing expression.

The nian shifted its gaze lazily back to Tedric. "I am afraid I was created without the ability to tell you until that day comes to pass, but I can tell you that it will be a very dark night indeed."

"Fine," Aeden said hastily, "we promise upon our lives that we'll free you on the night of Clamidas."

The nian chuckled and shook his head. Aeden bristled and looked away, her hand still fidgeting at her side. There seemed to be something wrong with her reaction to this, something that brought an uneasy feeling into Tedric's stomach. Though he couldn't blame her for being ruffled about releasing a beast on the night of celebration for her kin's birth.

"I need the promise of my master, not the little girl."

"I am *not* a little girl," Aeden seethed.

"You have my promise that you will be released from your

page when the night of Clamidas is upon us," Tedric said hastily, glancing at Aeden with growing concern before he nodded to the nian.

"How do we release you?" Lorian interrupted. "We have only found out how to place you into the pages, not get you out again."

"It will come to you when the needed moment arrives," the nian replied simply before he turned back to Tedric.

The beast bowed his large hairy head in respect, and Tedric stepped forward. He stretched his hand out, the paged clutched tightly in his grip, and the nian pressed a gnarled horn against the thin parchment. The nian began to shimmer and quickly shrank into the page. With a final pop and tingle in Tedric's fingers, it was gone.

Lorian let out a breath of relief. "Well, that was certainly the most sophisticated beast we've met so far."

"He was still incredibly unhelpful," Finriel said with a shake of her head.

"I prefer the rakshasa," Aeden growled, and stalked away.

Tedric raised a brow with concern and watched her retreating form, squinting through the orange glow of the cresting sun. He turned toward his three companions and Nora, who was perched on a rock near the mouth of the cave. He could smell the stench of death rolling off the large cat and he scrunched his nose. Finriel would have some work to do with that.

"Why don't you three go in and get a fire going? I'll speak to her," Tedric told his companions, the momentary distraction of Nora's stench fading from his attention.

Lorian and Finriel nodded and started toward the mouth of the cave, but Krete paused for a moment and inclined his head toward Aeden.

"Be careful with her."

A wave of anger surged through Tedric's veins at his companion's words and he cut back a retort. Was he not being careful already? His control over his emotions was hanging by a thread, but Tedric had been nothing but respectful to her since they had met in Millris Forest nearly three moons ago.

"She's my dearest friend and something of a little sister to me. I care for her safety," Krete continued, and Tedric forced himself to nod in reply. Krete smiled softly and nodded as well before he turned back toward Nora's tail, which was disappearing into the darkness of the cave.

Tedric let out a shaky breath and turned to where Aeden stood, making his way across the sparse grass and rocks toward her.

"What's the matter?" Tedric asked as he stopped behind Aeden.

Her back was turned to him, her dark cloak billowing behind her in the cold breeze. She tensed at the sound of his voice and swiveled around to face him.

"You are the matter," Aeden snapped as she met his stare.

Tedric raised his brows in surprise. Even though her tone had been sharp, her conflicted expression betrayed such notions. He took a step closer, but she brought a hand up to stop him.

"Please, don't."

"What have I done?" Tedric asked. His chest constricted as he looked at her. The raw emotion in her gaze betrayed the defensive strength in her stance, and Tedric had to keep himself from looking away for fear of his own heart cracking. She rolled her eyes and glared at the warrior when she noticed his gaze soften.

"You haven't done anything," Aeden retorted, and then paused. "Just … forget about it."

She moved to stalk past him, but before he could think, Tedric shot his hand out and grabbed her wrist. Aeden turned to glare at him with molten anger as he found himself leaning forward to speak gently in her ear.

"You don't have to fear your heart anymore. Let it speak its truth."

Her gaze changed into one of resolve and they stood there, interlocked in a silent yet deafeningly loud battle as it pushed them together. The pressure in Tedric's chest spasmed and he let out a strangled breath. Their faces were close enough to touch now, and he could see the dark speckles of black within the mysterious green of her eyes, the soft curve of her lips as they opened in surprise.

Aeden gently pulled her wrist from his grasp and the moment was gone. Tedric let out a breath and looked down at his boots, cursing under his breath. Aeden was already walking back to the cave. He watched her disappear into the shadows without a second glance in his direction. Tedric sighed and turned back to watch as daylight dimmed and the first stars of night blinked to life. The darkness made its descent upon the sky, slowly swallowing the soft pink clouds that seemed to rest upon the top of Dragonkeep in the distance.

He wished very much to be at home now. It sounded better than where he was, halfway down a mountain and confused about a fairy girl. He cursed under his breath and kicked a stray pebble with his boot, not caring to see where it landed as he dragged his weary body to his companions and a warm fire.

❦ 23 ❦

KRETE

"No wonder the nian wanted to stay out of the page," Krete said cheerfully. "This cave is lovely."

Lorian snorted and wrapped his cloak tighter around his shivering body. Krete knew he'd never been more wrong in his life, but at least the cave was moderately dry.

"You live inside of a mountain. I'm sure that most caves are good enough to make you happy," Lorian replied, and Krete gave him a sheepish shrug.

Krete found that though Lorian was likely joking with him, the thief wasn't wrong. Krete had been in a foul temper ever since their time in Farrador, but now that they were closer to his home, it seemed that his spirits were lifting by the moment.

Finriel sat down a few feet away from Lorian and closed her eyes, small flames erupting across her fingers. The flames glowed orange and blue as they enveloped her hands, and she sighed with relief as she drew her hands around in a circle. The flame remained in a small ring of warmth upon the ground even as she removed her hands and let the fire die from her fingers. Krete shook his head in wonder and leaned back onto his elbows, relishing the warmth of the fire.

"You have more power than most of the witches I've met at the Witch Isles," Krete mused, his eyes still on the flames that now bathed the cave in a warm glow.

"What brought you to the isles?" Finriel asked, and Krete shrugged.

"Shipments of supplies mainly. The island is quite small and therefore very difficult for them to be completely self-sufficient with the amount of witches being there. They farm what they can, but king Drohan provides most of their other resources, mending and medical supplies, other foods, things like that."

Finriel frowned and reached forward with a finger to brush it through the flames. "I thought that Keadora brought them their supplies."

Krete shook his head. "Oh, not at all. I've never heard the witches say one kind thing about Keadora, nor the Red King for that matter. They all hate him, though they don't say why."

"Be careful that Tedric isn't nearby or he'll skin you for saying that," Lorian said, from where he was stretched out on his back, head resting on his rolled up cloak.

Aeden walked in at that moment, and Krete watched her with a pang of worry as she sat at his side with a short, frustrated exhale.

Tedric followed shortly after, his footsteps echoing slightly through the smooth walls. He was clearly flustered, Krete noticed, but the commander hid it well as he came to sit by the reclining thief, and a very healthy distance away from Aeden. Krete reached out and placed his hand on Aeden's knee, giving it a reassuring squeeze. She didn't do anything to acknowledge this, but Krete knew that silence was her way of dealing with negative emotions. He only wished that she would be more careful with them.

"The nian was quite strange, wasn't he?" Lorian spoke again, though his eyes remained closed.

"He was so adamant about being released from the page on

the blood moon," Finriel answered. "I don't even know why that day in particular was important to him."

Aeden snorted from her seat in the corner of the cave, and all eyes turned to her. She wasn't looking at any of her friends, instead, her gaze was boring into the flames of Finriel's fire. He knew that there was something off with his dear friend, something that likely had to do with the commander seated across from him.

"Care to elaborate on your noise, or did you just forget how to breathe for a moment?" Lorian asked.

Aeden's gaze flicked up to meet Lorian's, and she raised her hand in a rude gesture.

Lorian gasped and brought his hand to his chest as if he had been hurt. "For shame, young lady, you have wounded my pride."

Finriel laughed and shook her head. Now all eyes shifted to her, and she quickly closed her mouth. Krete sighed and brought his hands closer to the fire, rubbing them together. Aeden definitely wasn't acting right, though he wasn't quite sure what was right anymore.

"The blood moon was said to be the night that goddess Noctiluca birthed the fairies, and of course is the transition to the first day of winter, as you all know," Krete began. Everyone nodded, and he continued, "I am guessing that the nian wants to be set free during Clamidas, the fairy festival that honors their birth."

"What exactly happens during Clamidas?" Tedric asked curiously.

"Well, from my observations and readings, all fairies gather in the forests of Proveria and drink and dance from sunset until sunrise. There are rituals and ceremonies, as well as other certain group activities that I don't feel too inclined to say out loud."

Tedric raised his brows and grinned at Krete's last words, and the gnome's cheeks reddened at the thoughts that surely passed through each of his companion's minds.

"I'd like to participate in this Clamidas festival," Lorian said with a smile. "It sounds rather charming."

"It's far from charming," Aeden shot back, speaking for the first time since they had entered the cave. "There are things that I can't even describe that happen during the night. If you go up to the castle when everyone is gathered in the forest, it's as if the entire city has been abandoned."

"I stand by my word, it sounds absolutely dazzling." Lorian winked at Aeden, who scowled in reply.

"The question is if we should actually release these creatures," Tedric interjected.

"No, we shouldn't," Aeden replied coolly. "Clamidas is too important to my people for five beasts to run through the kingdom and ruin everything."

"Aeden's right," Finriel agreed. "I think we should respect the fairies, especially on Clamidas."

"Wait a moment," Krete said quickly, "don't you think that there might be a reason why we have been told to let them out of the pages? Something bigger than even our task?"

Aeden snorted. "Like what?"

Krete shrugged, his spirits dropping. "I'm not sure. But it must tie into everything else strange that we've encountered."

"We don't need to make any hasty decisions. We should get some rest for tomorrow and decide after we've captured the dragon," Tedric said with a yawn, and stretched out on his back, wrapping his cloak around his body.

Krete shook his head and turned toward Aeden, who kept her gaze trained upon the fire. Their companions were settling down and readying for sleep, but Aeden's muscles were taut, as if she were restraining herself from leaping to her feet and running away.

"You need to tell him," Krete whispered. Aeden retreated

further within her cloak, the material so dark that her light skin appeared starkly white against it.

"I know," she muttered, eyes flicking to the fair-haired warrior. Worry for Aeden nagged at Krete's insides. She had been growing more and more tense throughout these weeks, every moment closer to Tedric making her energy set off like a firework.

"How do I do it?" Her question was almost a whisper.

Krete squeezed her knee again and smiled, though an odd sense of sorrow made its way into his heart. He had known Aeden since she was a child, her dominant personality making her father worry about what kind of woman she would become. Krete had always liked that part of her, and watching it slowly fade away now worried him above anything else.

"You will know when the time comes, I'm sure of it."

Aeden's face fell, and Krete's heart nearly cracked as she looked at him with tear-filled eyes. "He will never forgive me."

❧ 24 ❧

LORIAN

Cool autumn sun beat down upon Lorian's head as he and his companions made their way down the mountain and toward the glittering trap they were about to face. No one spoke as they walked, as no one seemed to have the heart or stomach to try to distract themselves from the treacherous obstacle they were heading toward.

Lorian looked toward the glittering blue water that was coming ever closer, wishing to the goddesses that he could turn around and run back into the damp cave in which they had spent the night. It had been cold during the night, and Finriel's meager fire had burned out before dawn. Lorian snorted, the witch had been perfectly warm with that large feline fluff ball curled around her.

His heart clenched as his mind swam with thoughts of her. He was just glad that she would even speak to him now, let alone look at him. Their relationship had begun to feel civil again, almost normal. But he knew she would never fully forgive him, even if she wanted to. As if his thoughts had beckoned her, Finriel came to walk at his side, and he tilted his head to meet her caramel gaze.

"Have you met the creatures of the lake?" she asked.

Lorian quirked his mouth into a half-grin, trying his best to look as careless as he could, but was afraid that his act fell short. He felt like his past was swimming up to bite him in the ass, and he didn't like it. The mermaids had been kind to him when he encountered them so many years ago, but that had been after they had almost dragged him to the bottom of their lake. Twice.

"Oh yes, I certainly have," Lorian said. "They almost made me their noontime snack, and not in the way that you would think."

Finriel frowned but didn't reply, and he was glad of it. The memory of their hands on him still made his blood curdle, and he wasn't sure if he could say it out loud quite yet.

"We're close now," Aeden hissed, a few feet ahead as they stepped into a small thicket of trees just before the lake. Lorian could see the light grey and white pebbles scattered on the ground ahead of them, and a lump of fear settled in his throat.

Tedric pulled a branch back so that they could see the water clearly. "The mermaids haven't sensed our presence yet, we need to move quickly."

If Lorian hadn't met the mermaids before, he would have found their surroundings much too serene to believe that they were about to face such dangerous creatures. He wondered if any of his companions had ever seen a mermaid in their lives, or if he was the only one aware of what these creatures were capable of doing, as well as the beautiful masks they hid behind.

The companions made their way across the wide expanse of pebbles, and Lorian let his gaze wander around their beautiful yet treacherous surroundings. The salty scent of the Sandrial Waters wafted along the constant breeze and the blue waters of the lake lapped merrily upon the shore. Dragonkeep loomed ahead at the opposite end of the lake, its black stone face sending a sense of foreboding through him.

"Hand me your page," Finriel said suddenly, poking Lorian in the shoulder.

He whirled around and faced her. "Why?"

She held out her hand expectantly, and after a moment, he withdrew it from his cloak and handed it to her. She took it with a smile.

"Thank you. I need the other filled out pages as well," Finriel said, and Aeden tensed.

"Why?" the fairy repeated Lorian's question.

"Mogwas can't hold their breath for more than a minute at a time," Finriel began. "It's far too dangerous for Nora to join this part of the journey."

"And what does that have to do with the pages?" Tedric asked, though he took a step toward the witch with his page held in an outstretched hand.

Finriel took Tedric's page, and replied, "I'm sending Nora directly to Creonid Mountain with the filled out pages. She can wait for us there, ensuring both her safety as well as that of the pages."

"As long as she doesn't attempt to eat any of the gnomes, I'm sure that she will be welcome," Krete said with an approving nod, and Finriel gave him the ghost of a smile.

"I'll make sure that she stays on her best behavior." Finriel then looked at Aeden once more. "Your page, please."

Aeden paused for a moment, and Lorian narrowed his eyes as he noticed the faintest bit of tension around her shoulders. It was gone in a moment, however, and Aeden withdrew her folded page and handed it over.

With a whistle, Nora soon came leaping from the surrounding trees, and Finriel kneeled in front of her. Lorian watched Finriel speak softly to the mogwa, handing the stacked pages to her. The mogwa took up the pages in her large maw, and with a loving nudge against Finriel's chest, turned on her haunches and launched away from the companions toward the shimmering border of Creonid in the distance.

"I hope that the pages won't be ruined by her slobber by the time she arrives in Creonid," Lorian mused, and Finriel shot him a look as she straightened.

"Nora is careful, likely more careful than you are anyways."

Lorian shrugged but didn't respond, knowing that Finriel did have a good point. It was Nora who had been able to save her all those years ago, after all, not him.

"Now, how are we supposed to find the tunnel?" Tedric asked, taking a step toward the water's edge.

"Careful, warrior," Aeden warned, reaching her hand out to touch his shoulder in warning.

Lorian frowned as they touched and Aeden froze, her face going pale as she retracted her hand quickly. Tedric stiffened and stepped back.

"We have to find the mermaids and ask them to raise it for us," Aeden spoke again, looking at the sparkling blue lake as if expecting the creatures to surface any moment.

Lorian snorted and shook his head. "Oh, don't worry, they'll find us." He kicked a stone and ran a trembling hand through his hair. "They most likely already know that we're here."

"You are not wrong."

The companions spun around at once, looking around wildly for who had spoken. But Lorian didn't have to search long for their new company, he knew that the mermaids had arrived. He let his gaze slide down to the shore, where she was lying, half submerged in the eerie blue water.

Lorian felt his entire body freeze as shards of memory flashed through his mind. The feeling of water in his lungs, long finger-nails clawing through his skin and turning the blue water cloudy with red. He realized that this must have been what Finriel had felt before he had been taken from her: helpless, scared, and violated.

He shook the thoughts away and swallowed back his fears, then took a step toward the mermaid. She was beautiful, or as beautiful as any deadly water-dwelling monster could possibly be. Long silver hair cascaded down her back, a few loose strands framing her delicate face. And then there was the tail. Black and magnificent, the water droplets upon it glittering in the sunlight. She smiled at Lorian, and he shivered as he saw a row of razor sharp teeth exposed behind full red lips.

"I remember you, thief boy," the mermaid purred, "although you were much smaller back then."

"I can't say that I'm glad to see you again, for I'd be lying if I did," Lorian replied in the kindest voice he could muster.

The creature's grin widened, and her attention slid over to the rest of Lorian's friends. He did not like the way that her dark eyes watched his companions hungrily, or how she licked her lips when her gaze landed on Finriel. Mermaids could sense magic, and Lorian could only guess what the mermaid felt radiating from the witch.

"I see you have brought friends this time. Perhaps you think your chances of getting past my sisters and me will be easier than before with help?" The mermaid laughed, the sound similar to wind chimes blowing in a soft wind.

"We've come to ask your permission to enter Dragonkeep." Krete was the one to speak.

The mermaid tilted her head toward the gnome and considered. "That is kind of you to ask permission." The mermaid chuckled again. "But I'm afraid that it does not matter. I am not to let anyone through the tunnel."

"And who gave you those orders?" Tedric asked.

The four of them had now come to stand next to Lorian as the mermaid analyzed the companions.

"Why, Raymara itself; the water, the wind, the earth, and flames. Well, when fire still was allowed freely among this realm."

Lorian glanced over to Finriel, hoping that the mermaid hadn't noticed the flames coursing within the witch's magic, but he knew that his hope was likely useless. Another dawning realization hit him, and his fists clenched. The mermaid's words seemed awfully similar to the riddle they had solved upon their entry into Drolatis. Finriel met his gaze for the hair of a moment, and seemed to be thinking the same thing. She took a step forward and Lorian shot his hand out to hold her back.

"Don't step any closer."

"You would be wise to listen to your friend, witch," the mermaid warned. "You smell delicious."

Finriel took a step back with a grimace and softly pulled her wrist from Lorian's grasp, and he let his hand drop to his side.

"Is there any way that we can get through to the tunnel?" Aeden asked, taking a tentative step toward the mermaid.

The mermaid shook her head, as if sorry to tell them no. "I'm afraid that the only way you can get through is by sacrificing one member of your group to my sisters and me. Only then can we raise the portal to allow entry to the mountain."

Lorian groaned inwardly. He knew that it would come to this.

"That is not going to happen," Finriel snapped, and the mermaid's smile widened.

"I thought you might say that. However, the sacrifice of one of your friends would simply be a ransom. If you can get through the tunnel before it closes, then we will send the offered companion back to you."

Lorian glanced at Finriel and the others, resolve slowly setting in. The one thing he had tried to avoid for many years was finally upon him, but he found that he couldn't bear the idea of allowing his companions to sacrifice themselves.

"I'll do it," he said, and stepped toward the mermaid.

"No," Finriel countered, and now she was the one to hold him back. He looked down at her, breath catching as he smiled sadly and shook his head.

"I'm more expendable than any of you," he replied softly.

"You are not," Aeden said, and Lorian blinked in surprise at her worried expression.

"She's right," Tedric said. "I should do it."

"Oh, please, your heroics aren't welcome right now," Finriel snapped.

"I'm not trying to be a hero," Tedric retaliated. "I'm offering myself so that Lorian doesn't have to."

Aeden watched Tedric with a concerned frown, and Lorian noticed her fingers twitch toward him.

Finriel shook her head. "You can't do it either. This entire thing is ridiculous."

Krete ignored the argument before him and stepped forward tentatively, his eyes trained on the mermaid, who was watching Finriel and Tedric in amusement.

"You swear that whoever goes with you will be returned to us?" he asked, and the mermaid nodded.

"Only if you are all able to pass through the entrance before it closes. If you don't, then we will take whoever does not make it through and the sacrificed one to be our pets forever."

Lorian shivered, not liking the word "pet," especially not rolling off the mermaid's tongue. But he had to do it, he had to be the one to sacrifice himself. He had put their lives in danger countless times during the past few moons, but that would stop today.

Lorian looked down at Finriel again, and she met his gaze readily. He blinked in surprise. She truly didn't want him to die.

"I'm doing it," he made himself say, "and you won't stop me." He reached a hand up and brushed his fingertips against Finriel's, then pushed past her and walked toward the creature. "Take me," Lorian whispered as he approached the mermaid.

She smiled and motioned for him to come closer. He waded into the water until he was only a hand's breadth away from her and kneeled, his heart beating frantically against his chest.

The mermaid regarded his companions with a haughty look and spoke. "The tunnel will open, but only once your friend is with us and you enter my home to find it."

The mermaid turned back Lorian and pushed herself upwards, tilting her head closer. The last thing he remembered was the taste of blood and salt on his lips before the world swirled into darkness.

❦ 25 ❦

FINRIEL

"Well, that was bad," Tedric commented as Lorian's legs disappeared under the crystalline blue depths with a splash. Finriel cursed and stomped toward the water.

"Don't just stand there, this is part of the plan," Finriel snapped to the others. She peered into the water to find that it was clear, exposing a sandy bank beneath. The ground seemed to drop away and the water grew darker as she looked down into the bottomless depths. And then she spotted the flash of a tail and Lorian's dark figure as he was taken deeper into the lake.

"I see him," Finriel called to the others. At once, she tore off her cloak, folding it widthwise before tying it tightly around her waist. She turned to find the others watching her as if she had just gone mad. "What are you waiting for?" Finriel spat. "We need to get through the tunnel."

It's the only way to get Lorian back. She did not speak her thought out loud, for she wasn't quite ready to admit the worry that now gnawed hungrily inside of her.

Tedric and Aeden exchanged a look before they began removing their cloaks and folding them in the same fashion as Finriel had done.

"Krete, put your hat into Tedric's satchel," Finriel commanded as she handed Tedric their map. "And don't lose it again," she finished with a pointed look at Tedric.

The companions made quick work, and soon their cloaks were all tied around their waists and Krete's long hair was sticking up strangely where his hat once sat. Finriel gave them a nod, and they made their way into the water. It was warmer than Finriel expected and the sand was firm under her feet.

"Keep your eyes open for other mermaids, there will be more." Tedric's low voice rang in her ears.

The water was up to her chest now and Finriel's breath was beginning to quicken. She knew she would have to be submerged for longer than she was sure she could hold her breath, but she had to at least try. Her thoughts strayed, and Finriel silently prayed that Nora would make it to Creonid Mountain safely. Finriel knew how stubborn the mogwa was, and she knew the dangerous position she had put her companions into by separating them from the filled pages.

Finriel let the thoughts of Nora drift away as she sucked in one last breath of salty air before diving into the water, kicking her legs out to propel further into the depths. Finriel blinked as her eyes focused on her new surroundings. There was nothing but blue as far as the eye could see, and her heart lurched in trepidation as she looked down. There was no end to the lake, at least none that she could see. It seemed as if the lake was bottomless, the darkness below like a giant mouth threatening to snap shut.

Soon Aeden was gliding gracefully at Finriel's side. There seemed to be a current that moved toward the darkness, making it easier for Finriel to advance as she followed the fairy. Tedric and Krete were not so far behind, and she turned her head back toward the looming shadows.

The memories came far too soon. Rough hands were around her neck again, pushing her down into the icy water. She couldn't breathe. She was trapped. She was going to die. Finriel shook the memory from her head and blinked, trying to keep herself calm as she continued swimming deeper into the lake.

But then it came again. The hissing voice in her ear saying she was scum, a monster. Icy blue eyes watching from the tree line in terror. And he was supposed to rescue her. She shook her head again, but her body was beginning to betray her. Her lungs began to burn and blinding panic rose in her chest. Finriel stopped swimming, forcing herself not to open her mouth and take in air that was not there.

She was *not* going to drown. Not now. Not when she was the one in control of what she was doing. She put herself in this lake on purpose. And she was going to find that goddamned tunnel and go through it with Lorian. She *had* to find Lorian. A hand touched her arm and she flinched. It was Aeden, her green eyes full of concern as their gazes met. Finriel couldn't answer, but the fairy did not need words to know what was wrong. She nodded and closed her eyes. The hand on Finriel's arm began to glow, and a rush of calmness seeped into Finriel's bones.

Finriel cracked a close-mouthed smile in thanks, her entire body feeling more relaxed than she had ever felt in her life. Aeden nodded and the four companions began to swim again. The current had carried them down even when they had stopped swimming and Finriel kicked farther into the lake with a new sense of clarity.

Their surroundings were very dark now, yet Finriel couldn't spot any form of life. It was surprisingly calm, too calm for a mermaid-infested lake. Finriel looked around, and her heart leaped as the shimmering glow of something large and solid came into view. It was the tunnel that led to Dragonkeep. Would the mermaids truly return Lorian if they all made it through in time? Finriel kicked harder toward the tunnel, and as they drew closer to it, she realized the shimmering arches were made of scales. Mermaid scales. *These creatures aren't just deadly, but sick,* she thought with a grimace.

Moments later, a dark shape appeared before them. Finriel squinted, barely able to make out the small black opening in the center of the tunnel. Her heart sank as she examined it further and noticed that it was barely big enough for one person to pass through comfortably, if that.

A flash of something fast and dark shot past, and Finriel ground her teeth against the rising fear already speeding up her steady pulse. Tedric was beside her, and his head turned toward the movement. He must have seen it too. Seconds later, the flash came back, but this time she clearly saw what it was. Mermaids.

Finriel felt the pain before she saw who had inflicted it. Her side stung as the mermaid who had scratched her swam below the companions. There were more coming.

"Your friend will be on the other side of the tunnel," a sweet yet snakelike voice echoed through Finriel's ears. Her three companions looked around, and Finriel guessed that they had heard the voice as well. *"If we kill you before you make it through, it will not matter. We'd like for the shadow boy to remain as our strange little pet."*

Finriel tried her best to ignore the slithery voice inside her head, and she kicked hard toward the tunnel entrance. A shrill laugh rang through her ears and Finriel kicked forward. Just a bit closer …

A hand wrapped around Finriel's ankle, yanking her backwards. The shock made her mouth open, and warm water poured down her throat. She choked and stiffened as memories and fear gripped her. The mermaid that had her ankle was pulling her in the opposite direction from her friends, and Finriel frantically shook her head and waved her arms as they all turned toward her. They had to keep going. It was her life against all of theirs, and she needed for them to get to Lorian.

Black spots danced in her vision, and the pain in her ankle from the mermaid's death grip began to render her entire foot numb. She couldn't just float there like a dead fish, she needed to do something, anything. Finriel blinked, but the splotches in her vision continued to grow, as well as the panic that was slowly petrifying her body. Tedric, Aeden, and Krete appeared to be fighting their own battle as three mermaids began to circle in upon them.

Finriel needed to get this mermaid off her. She needed air. She knew she would black out from the lack of oxygen if she didn't get air soon. Her lungs were screaming as she turned and willed the last bits of her energy to form into fire—no. Fire wouldn't work underwater. Finriel had to think of something different. But she was so very cold. The idea struck her in an instant and Finriel forced herself to turn toward the mermaid at her ankle and brought her hands forward, willing the icicles to form from her hands and shoot toward the creature.

The mermaid shrieked and let go of Finriel's ankles as shards of ice slashed across the creature's arms and one struck into her outstretched hand. The mermaid thrashed and fell away into the darkness. Finriel forced her mouth to remain closed against the laugh that threatened to bubble out of her throat. She had never even thought to use this kind magic before, but now she had. Now she was in even more danger if she was caught.

Finriel blinked the growing darkness away as best as she could and turned back toward the entrance of the tunnel. Aeden, Tedric, and Krete were nearly at the narrow mouth, each fighting off a mermaid in what looked like slow motion. She was so close to them now, and Finriel used the last bit of her strength to propel herself forward and sidle next to Aeden. Her friends were blinking wildly, and Finriel could tell none of them were going to make it if they didn't go through the tunnel.

Finriel cursed herself silently and used any last magic she had. Ice shot out from her hands in rapid fire, striking their scaly attackers. The sound was awful, and Finriel clapped her hands over her ears as the mermaids' screams echoed through her head.

Aeden reached out a hand to grab a nearly unconscious Krete by the scruff of his tunic and kicked toward the looming tunnel, disappeared into it. Finriel did not wait for Tedric, but turned and dragged herself into the darkness.

AEDEN

Aeden choked and gagged as she burst through the tunnel, landing with a heavy thump against hard stone. Her chest burned from the elongated period without oxygen, and she forced back another gag as she willed herself to roll away from the mouth of the shimmering portal. Krete was splayed on his back not two feet from her, his breath coming out in quick ragged gasps.

"Are you all right?" Aeden croaked, her voice bouncing from the echoing walls of the small cavelike space.

Krete nodded, his face barely illuminated by a soft golden light that emanated from the stone walls. A loud swoosh sounded behind Aeden, and she turned to watch as Finriel emerged from the swirling blackness, shortly followed by Tedric. They landed in a heap of limbs, both coughing up lake water onto the dark ground.

Finriel dragged herself away from Tedric and lifted her head.

"Lorian?"

"He's not in here," Aeden coughed, and more lake water spewed from her lips.

"I ... Find him," Finriel wheezed, and pushed herself onto her hands and knees.

"No," Aeden gasped, but Finriel was already scrambling to her feet and moving around Tedric, who was relieving his stomach of lake water.

Finriel reached a hand out toward the swirling portal when another swooshing sound interrupted her and a body fell from it. Finriel barely leaped out of the way before the body crashed onto the ground, and Aeden blearily watched as the entrance to the lake shrank until it disappeared with a faint pop, revealing sleek black stone in its stead.

"He's not waking up," Finriel said, her voice now clear and thick with worry.

Aeden forced herself to her feet, ignoring the fact that her entire body felt heavy and her bones ached for rest. She pushed away the worry that called for Tedric, who was now seated and watching her through thick, wet lashes. Her heart clenched at the sight of him, and she yearned to push his hair back from where it was now plastered against his forehead, the tips brushing over his eyelids. She wanted to wipe the water from his cheeks and be held in his arms again. But Aeden could not do those things, no matter how much she wanted to. It would be too risky, too dangerous to even entertain the idea of them together.

She brought her attention back to Finriel, who was kneeling by Lorian's head and working at the clasp of his cloak. "Here, let me help," Aeden said, and came to kneel at the other side of Lorian's head. It felt all too similar to their time fixing Tedric's shoulder, and Aeden shuddered away the memory. The worry she had felt while she had held his head between her hands should have been the first sign to be careful with her heart.

Aeden focused back on Lorian, his light skin gaunt in the dim light. She reached forward and gently pushed Finriel's shaking fingers away, unbuckling the cloak in one simple movement. Finriel took up the soaking fabric and pulled it from Lorian, and his head lolled limply from the movement. Aeden took up his wrist in her hand with a prickle of worry, hoping that he was merely unconscious and nothing more. She pressed her index and middle fingers against the inside of his wrist and held her breath. A faint pulse moved against her fingers after a moment, and she let out a sigh of relief.

"He's alive?" Finriel asked, and Aeden nodded.

"I'll do my best to wake him up," she said.

"I can dry this," Finriel panted, and hunched over Lorian's sopping cloak.

Aeden ripped her attention away from Finriel's glowing hands and looked back down to Lorian, who hadn't stirred. With still shaking hands, Aeden gently pushed Lorian's shoulder so that he flopped onto his back. She brought her fingers under his nose, holding her breath until she felt his faint exhale upon her skin. With a silent prayer to Noctiluca, Aeden brought the heel of her palms against the center of his chest and pressed down, repeating the process quickly and with as much strength as she could manage. Aeden cursed at Lorian's immobility, and again brought her fingers under his nose to see if his breath had strengthened. It hadn't.

"Wake up," Aeden hissed, and Finriel turned to look at her with a questioning expression.

Aeden ignored this, and set her jaw as she reached forward and gently took up both sides of Lorian's face and tilted his head upwards. Her fingers still shook as she used her left hand to gently open his mouth slightly, the other hand pressing his nose closed. Aeden leaned forward and hid her grimace as she took in a deep breath and pressed her lips against his. She pushed her breath out into Lorian's mouth then pulled away, rubbing her mouth against her wet tunic before turning back to the thief. She returned her hands to his chest and pressed down in quick pulsing motions.

Lorian's eyes flew open, and Aeden barely had enough time

to fall onto her backside before the thief lurched onto his hands and knees and began to relieve his stomach of lake water. Aeden wiped her mouth again and silently thanked her late survival training master, who had taught her the simple trick of resuscitation many years ago.

"Are you all right?" Finriel asked as she came to his side and wrapped his now dry cloak around his shoulders.

Lorian nodded and took in a ragged breath, looking up to meet Aeden's gaze. "Thank you," he said. "I thought I was dead for a moment there."

Aeden smiled with a pang. "I'm thankful that it worked. I've never tried to revive someone like that before, only ever fake humans made of straw."

Lorian wheezed slightly. "I'm very thankful it worked then."

Aeden lifted herself to her feet and moved back to where Krete sat, again ignoring Tedric, who was now watching her with mingled curiosity and awe. She knew he likely hadn't expected her to be able to do what she had done, and it was just another reason why she couldn't allow her heart to grow any fonder. He couldn't know the extent of all the things she could do.

"I have just enough strength to either make a fire or dry all of our cloaks," Finriel said, and Aeden looked at the witch, who was now seated next to Lorian.

"Cloaks would be better," Tedric replied. "A fire would be too telling to the dragons that we are here."

"I would appreciate my shirt and vest to be dried perhaps, as I don't own a cloak," Krete said, and Finriel outstretched her hand, gesturing for her companions to hand her their cloaks, and Krete his shirt and vest.

After a few shivering moments, Aeden was wrapped in her now dry cloak once more, and she gave a relieved sigh as she leaned against the cave wall and let the warmth seep into her bones.

"We must travel straight to Creonid after we've gotten the

dragon," Krete said, speaking quiet enough so that only Aeden could hear.

"Yes," Aeden agreed, "but I need to return to Proveria."

"Did you tell him?" Krete asked, gesturing toward Tedric's hunched figure with a jut of his chin.

Aeden shook her head, and an awful combination of dread and butterflies swirled in her stomach. Krete didn't have to ask if she was going to tell Tedric, for she knew that he was aware that she wouldn't. How could she when it would ruin everything?

She let the dim light of the cave settle her nerves, and she looked at the two dark tunnel entrances directly ahead and slightly to the left of where she sat. She wondered which one of those tunnels they would take to find the dragon, and if one of those tunnels would possibly lead to their demise. She nibbled on a piece of bread Krete had handed her from Tedric's satchel, but she found that her stomach still felt too turbulent to manage much of anything. Krete fit his worn hat back onto his head with a satisfied smile and bit into an apple with a small grimace.

"Map," Tedric grunted, interrupting Aeden's thoughts with a jolt.

She watched as Tedric shuffled toward Finriel, who in turn cracked open an eye to watch the commander wave the map he had kept in his satchel in her direction. The parchment crinkled as she took it and rolled it out upon the ground. Aeden forced herself to stand up, and she and Krete shuffled over to look at their position within the mountain.

According to the map, they seemed to be fairly close to the next creature. Aeden gulped as the prospect of attempting to make a fire-breathing dragon go into a piece of paper went through her mind. That, as well as all of the things that could possibly go wrong along the way.

"It looks as if we need to take the passage straight ahead," Aeden said, trying to manage the shake in her voice.

Krete shook his head. "If we take the passage to the right, we'll get to the dragon faster."

"There's no way for you to know that, the map doesn't tell us the fastest route."

Krete sighed. "Aeden, I was born inside of a mountain, I think I would know how to navigate one a little better than a fairy."

"He's got a point, you know," Tedric commented. Aeden bristled and shot him a glare, but he only shrugged in return.

"Well, what do you two think?" Aeden asked Finriel and Lorian sharply. "Trust the mountain guru or the person who actually knows how to read a map?"

Finriel glanced at Lorian with a questioning look. He still looked pale and slightly sick, but attempted a smile.

"I like the ring of mountain guru better. I would probably choose his underground tour over, well, whatever you said," Lorian said.

Aeden huffed and tugged at her wet braid. "Fine, let's go your way, Krete."

Krete smiled with satisfaction and motioned for everyone to follow him.

"The mountain guru always wins."

"Oh, shut up."

✿ 27 ✿

LORIAN

Lorian wasn't sure how long they had been walking anymore, winding through the large mountain and meeting endless forks in their path as they went. Krete seemed sure of his way, and only hesitated for short moments before indicating the tunnels they were to take.

Their trek through the mountain had been very calm, almost too calm considering they were walking through the legendary dragon birthing grounds. But there was only silence. No growls, rumbles, squeaks, or otherwise. Lorian couldn't ignore the feeling of wary discomfort that tickled his skin, as if at any moment a dragon would burst through one of the many connecting tunnels and drown them all in a wave of fire. Granted, he had encountered many of the scaly creatures in his time, and he had to admit that he wasn't looking forward to meeting one again.

"I wonder if this dragon of ours will be embellished in any way," Lorian mused, his voice bouncing off the rounded walls.

"It's a black dragon, I would say that's embellished enough," Tedric said. "I'm not sure that it could get any worse than that."

"Maybe he's very nice," Krete offered, and Lorian snorted.

"The nicest dragon that I have met offered to turn my bones into toothpicks instead of just eating me whole." Finriel shot him a questioning look, and he shrugged. "Another long story on the list of many."

Tedric ignored their conversation and called to Krete, who was walking slightly ahead of Aeden at the head of the group. "How close do you think we are to the dragon?"

Krete stopped and pointed at the black stone before them. "Well, if the map was showing me correctly, the dragon should be just across this wall of stone."

"But it's so quiet," Tedric whispered. "Dragons are loud, violent, and ... Dragons."

Krete shrugged and returned to his inspection of the map. "Maybe the storyteller made it a mute."

"That would be a lot less annoying, yet also terrifying," Lorian answered.

Everyone muttered in agreement and continued to follow Krete as the gnome rounded the wall he had indicated. Seconds later, what sounded like a rain shower of thousands of small stones came from behind the wall, and Lorian paused mid-step.

"Is there someone there?" A menacing voice vibrated through the tunnel, and another small shower of stones sprinkled to the ground.

Lorian froze and watched as Tedric and Aeden stiffened in front of him, taking each other's hands in a seemingly unconscious movement. His stomach lurched as Krete came back into view, a look of horror plastered on his face as he ran as fast as his short legs could manage. He slashed a hand through the air, indicating for them to hide.

"I said, is there someone there?" the terrible voice asked again, a growl mixing at the end of its words. Soon came the loud stomping footfalls, making the entire mountain shake with each step the dragon took.

Lorian whirled around and frantically searched for somewhere, anywhere, that could be acceptable enough for them to hide. Krete zipped past him and Finriel, jabbing a stubby finger toward two outcroppings of rock on either side of the smooth passageway. Lorian cursed before grabbing Finriel's hand and dragging her behind one of the outcroppings. Aeden and Tedric ran and squeezed next to Krete behind the outcropping across from Lorian and Finriel.

"I smell flesh, but from beings who do not share the same blood," the voice continued, now right behind them. Seconds later, a long green scaled nose came to hover in between the two outcroppings of rock, blocking Lorian's view of Krete and the others. Lorian kept his gaze trained upon Finriel, who stood petrified as the nose inhaled and then exhaled slowly, hot breath sending her braid flying back against the wall. Their hands were still joined, and Lorian kept a firm hold on her cold skin as she inhaled sharply.

"It is young flesh, yes, and perhaps very tasty for my newborns to feast on for their first meal."

The dragon's nose slid forward and past them. A golden eye, the size of Finriel herself, came into view, and the cat-shaped iris pulsated as it adjusted to focus on her and Lorian. Another deep exhale from the dragon sent hot stinking air against them, and he fought against both a gag and a terrified shiver.

"Oh, how disappointing your sizes are," the dragon growled. "I guess I will just have to scare you. I know that most differ, but I find that adrenaline always makes the meat taste better." With a reptilian blink, the eye retracted once more until not even the snout was in view.

One word was all the companions needed.

"Run."

Lorian didn't have time to even blink before Finriel wrenched her hand from his and flung out her arms toward the dark rock above the dragon's head. With a grunt, she made a sharp downwards movement, and large shards of rock cracked and fell, landing upon the dragon's head with sickening thunks. The emerald green dragon let out a pained roar and reared its head upward, momentarily dazed by the rocks that had fallen atop its body.

"Move, now!" Finriel roared, and dashed from behind the outcropping of rocks and ran between the dragon's legs and out of sight.

Lorian shoved himself away from the outcropping with a curse and slipped underneath the dragon's enormous clawed feet and dodged around its wildly thrashing tail. *At least it doesn't have spikes*, he thought. Krete, Aeden, and Tedric appeared behind him a few short seconds later, and Finriel yelled at them from the bend that Krete and the dragon had appeared from moments before, "Let's go!"

"Go through the tunnel to the left!" Krete yelled at Finriel, and Lorian forced his legs to go faster and catch up to her as she ran through the mouth of the leftmost tunnel that loomed ahead.

Lorian's tired lungs burned as he and his companions ran blindly through the winding tunnels of Dragonkeep with the enormous green dragon at their heels. The natural light pulsing from the stone seemed to be dimming as they wound deeper into the mountain, and soon he was squinting in order to be able to see even one step in front of himself. The ground shook beneath them with each footfall the dragon took, and he could tell from the stinking heat on his neck that it wasn't too far behind. They wouldn't be able to run forever.

"What do we do?" Finriel yelled breathlessly at Lorian's side, their shoulders bumping against each other as they felt their way through the darkness.

"Over there; I see daylight!" Krete yelled from behind them.

Lorian looked around wildly, and soon enough, spotted warm light spilling onto the dark stone floor only a few hundred feet ahead. Going back out into the open could prove perilous, but at least they would have more space to run. Lorian pushed his legs to go faster, his breath coming out in ragged gasps.

"Fire!" Tedric's voice rang out behind them, and Lorian didn't think as he grabbed Finriel around the waist and pushed her to the ground with his own body, pain shooting through his knees as they cracked against the stone. A loud burst sounded behind them, followed by singeing heat over Lorian's entire back and head. He smelled burning clothing and hair, and Finriel cursed as the fire licked across her neck. Lorian roared in pain, and Finriel ripped her hands free and pushed them outward. A thin shimmering light surrounded them, and the heat decreased moderately until it completely went away.

Lorian rolled off her, groaning in more shock than pain. Finriel scrambled up and examined his body, and he forced himself to sit up as she looked at him wildly. Aside from his cloak and the ends of his hair being singed, he felt okay.

"Lorian, why in the Nether—"

"There's more of that coming, get up!" Tedric bellowed as he, Aeden, and Krete sprinted past them and rounded into the brightly lit room ahead.

Lorian felt Finriel's hand grasp around his as she hauled him up to his feet. Indeed, the dragon was coming closer, orange heat rising up through the transparent membrane between its scales. They got to their feet and leaned into each other as they ran the rest of the way into the bright opening of the passageway. They were so close to getting out into the open, and Lorian's legs pumped faster as they crossed the last few steps into the light.

The sight that met Lorian's eyes made his gasping breath leave him completely. He stood in shock next to Finriel and their other companions, who also appeared to be paralyzed by the room in which they now stood. Lorian did have to give a blink of appreciation at the hoards of crystals and enormous uncut gemstones that littered the room, for it was a thief's dream. Yet it was not the brilliant kaleidoscope of gemstones and crystals that glowed vibrantly and sent rainbows of color bouncing across the high cave ceiling. It was the large black dragon that gazed at itself through what appeared to be a giant hand mirror made of white crystal. Lorian allowed for his gaze to travel upwards, and found a large opening in the center of the cave that gave way to a sunset orange sky. That would have to be their only way out.

"Oh, dear, being stuck in this dark mountain has made me so pale," the dragon said in a low, grumbling voice.

"Did the dragon just say that he was pale?" Tedric asked, but Lorian found that he for once had no words of reply.

An earsplitting roar sounded behind them, the vibration sending a few large gemstones tumbling from an especially large mound, cracking as they hit the hard stone floor. Lorian cringed and turned to face the menacing green dragon that scrutinized him and his companions hungrily.

"You cannot run now," it hissed. "How I am looking forward to discovering how you little two-legged creatures taste."

"I thought you were going to feed us to your children," Lorian replied, managing to grasp the last strand of fearlessness he still had.

The green dragon cocked its head to the side with apparent confusion, and Lorian offered it a grin. Movement behind Lorian made him angle his head to find that the black dragon had swiveled its head toward the commotion, and the crystal mirror dropped to the ground with a loud thump.

The black dragon slid its feline golden eyes across the companions and then up toward its kin. The black beast roared and flared its giant membranous wings at the green dragon. The noise pressed painfully into Lorian's ears, and the entire cave around them shook.

The green dragon cowered and scrambled back into the passage they had just come from, and soon its heavy steps slowly faded away as it retreated. Lorian remained as still as possible as he watched the black dragon slowly fold its enormous wings against its scaled sides. Large pearly white spikes lined the creature's back, each one getting smaller until they reached the tip of its tail.

The black dragon snorted once in irritation at the interruption and slowly swung its long neck around to face them. Lorian gulped in trepidation as the dragon's golden eyes inspected each of them.

"H-hello," Krete said in a shaky voice. The gnome looked like nothing more than a small babe in comparison to the size of the dragon before them, but Lorian silently thanked him for speaking, as he seemed to only be able to make one cocky comment to one dragon at a time before losing his voice.

"Who are you?" the dragon asked. "I have not seen any of your kind in this mountain before." He chuckled and attempted what looked like an unnatural shrug. "I've not lived in this mountain long though, so who am I to know?"

"Did you live on the crag?" Krete asked, his tone slightly hopeful.

The dragon shook his head. "No, I haven't lived anywhere before this. I was created nearly three moons ago. I do still regret what I did to that poor village of strange pointy eared folk."

Krete nodded enthusiastically and glanced over to his friends. The dragon noticed this action and cocked his head to the side.

"Do you know where I came from?"

Krete looked up and stiffened at the slight growl in the dragon's voice. He then nodded, but this time slower. "Yes, we have come to put you back into the page from which you were created."

The dragon took a step back as Krete withdrew his page from his satchel, mistrust glinting in the creature's eyes.

"And why would I go back into that page?"

"Because we must get back to my home in Creonid before the blood moon. After that, I must deliver you to King Sorren."

Lorian raised his brows, impressed at Krete's sudden ability to speak to the beast as if it were an old friend.

Aeden's face turned stony and she poked Krete in his side. "Don't go telling him our entire plan."

Krete shrugged. "Honesty won't hurt us."

"Wait a moment," the dragon said, "you are planning to go to Creonid on foot and hope to arrive back to your king before the blood moon? That is only three days away, and traveling to Creonid will take much longer than that."

"Well, we don't have any other way of getting there, do we?" Aeden snapped, and Lorian transferred his impressed look to the fairy, as she seemed to have forgotten that she was speaking to a fire-breathing beast that could kill her in the blink of an eye.

The dragon scoffed at Aeden, "Well, I would offer to fly you all to the mountain."

The dragon's words quickly snapped any fatigue from Lorian's body, and he blinked at the beast in disbelief.

"But why?" asked Krete.

"Because I hate this mountain, well, aside from all of the pretty jewels." The dragon looked back lovingly at the heaps of shimmering gemstones behind them. "I have been forced to use fire to protect myself against the other dragons many times, and it has unfortunately cost the beautiful landscape a few scars. But I suppose it's better for the land to be scarred instead of my scales."

Lorian glanced at Krete with a raised brow, and there was indeed sadness in the gnome's stormy eyes. He supposed that the gnome hadn't expected his kingdom to have been destroyed due to a dragon simply trying to protect himself against a few sour souls.

"So, you will take us?" Krete asked, and the dragon narrowed its gaze.

"Well, of course I will," the dragon replied. "Besides, I need some sunlight on my wings."

They all exchanged looks, considering. It made some sense to Lorian, even though he didn't completely trust that the dragon would stay true to his word.

"What if you fly off after you deliver us to Creonid and we can't put you back in the page?" Aeden asked.

"Darling, I hate every single one of the mother dragons in this cave, who would definitely eat you all before you even got close to getting out of here on your own." The dragon paused before speaking again. "Besides, where else do I have to go?"

They fell silent at that. Krete stepped forward and tucked the paper back into one of the many pockets on his vest.

"Very well, dragon, take us to Creonid Mountain."

The beast nodded and knelt down so that they could climb up and sit between the large spikes on his back.

"Careful, the scales are very sensitive around my spikes," the dragon warned as they settled onto his back.

Lorian sat behind Finriel and tentatively grabbed one of the spikes. It felt like old worn bone, and yet also as if it had been glossed over somehow. Krete sat in the very front, and Aeden and Tedric made themselves comfortable in front of Finriel. Lorian gulped away a new wave of fear that leaped into his throat, and he kept his gaze locked upon Finriel's dark braid. He had never flown before and never thought that he would ever do so until now.

"We're ready," Krete called.

In response, the dragon unfurled his large wings and tensed in preparation to fly.

"And by the way," the dragon said, "my name is Suzunne."

❧ 28 ❧

LORIAN

There was one thing that Lorian knew for a fact, and that was that he hated flying. He hated it very much.

He gripped the large milky white spike with all his strength as the dragon, Suzunne, as he had called himself, flapped his wings and sailed through the clear dusk skies. Lorian let his gaze travel downwards, and couldn't help the breath of awe that escaped his lips. The wide expanse of mountains that stretched across Drolatis were an array of different shades of brown, each color seamlessly blending into the next. Small patches of snow blanketed areas of the mountains, and he could see the exact places where the barren rock of the mountains met the grassy earth of the meadows beneath them.

The grass was beginning to die and fade, leaving a yellowish earth behind, a sure sign that winter would arrive soon. Lorian gulped as his eye caught the glittering greenish blue waters of Lake Lagdranule. *Now that place is a pretty mask uncovering a terrible secret,* Lorian thought with a shiver as he watched small waves crashed into white foam against the base of Dragonkeep.

Suzunne suddenly dove, causing Lorian's stomach to lurch up into his throat and his hands to tighten even harder around the spike. The dragon banked sharply to the right, and Lorian felt the small shiver down his back that indicated they had just passed through the kingdom border into Creonid.

The kingdom looked exactly the same as Drolatis, which was likely why they were called the twin kingdoms. The only noticeable difference between the two was the fact that Creonid had only a single enormous mountain in the realm, surrounded by many small hills and enormous patches of blackened, burnt earth. Krete had been right about the destruction his kingdom's lands. Lorian looked back at the large mountain, which was an understatement in itself. It spread out for miles, its peak so tall that it seemed to swallow the sky itself.

Krete let go with one arm and Lorian watched him point excitedly toward the mountain. It loomed before them like a wall, the mix of light and dark browns and reds swirling together in a similar way as the mountains of Drolatis.

Lorian groaned and pressed himself against the spike yet again as Suzunne dropped even lower and flapped his wings, sending them closer toward the mountain. Lorian gulped as a wide crack in the stone face came into view. As they got closer, the dark opening grew larger, and Suzunne pulled his wings slightly closer to his sides so as not to scrape them against the stone.

"Damn bleeding Nether, no—" Lorian yelled as the walls swallowed them and they sped into a small alcove in the mountain. They landed with a hard thump, and Lorian was sure that he had gotten a concussion. Suzunne's claws scraped on the stone, sending dust flying behind them.

"I cannot say I am too proud of that landing, my apologies," Suzunne said, panting slightly.

A high-pitched scream began to ricochet through the small alcove they had landed in. Lorian clapped his hands against his ears and looked around in confusion. He peered over Finriel's shoulder to watch Krete, who waved and cursed angrily at the walls around them.

Suddenly, an onslaught of what appeared to be a herd of armored children poured out of the darkness, and Lorian had to keep himself from laughing as the small army of gnomes raised their bows and shouted in their native gnomish tongue. It sounded to Lorian like they were simply babbling the way babies did when first learning how to speak.

"Stop, it's Krete!" Krete shouted from atop Suzunne, who was simply staring at the gnomes in a fashion similar to what Lorian was sure he himself was doing.

The gnomes quieted slightly, but kept their weapons raised. A gnome in particularly well-made armor pushed to the front of the crowd. He looked similar to Krete, aside from the very blonde mop of hair that covered his small grey eyes ever so slightly. He looked younger than Krete as well, though not by much. Finriel turned to give Lorian a curious glance, and he shrugged and winked at her. She looked away quickly, but he was sure that a soft shade of pink flushed across her cheeks. That was twice that she had done that now, Lorian noticed with a small spark of satisfaction.

"Krete?" the gnome asked in a shrill voice, curiosity and fear showing openly on his face as he peered up at them. Krete scrambled up to his feet and waved at the small man.

"Mott, it's me!" he exclaimed, and began to crawl his way down Suzunne's front leg at a snail's pace.

"Watch my scales, Krete, I told you how sensitive they are," Suzunne warned as Krete finished making his way to the ground.

"Sorry, Suzunne," Krete apologized, and then turned to the small man.

The gnome was slightly taller than Krete, and he kept his small sword raised as he examined Lorian's companion. Lorian held his breath, almost concerned that the gnome wouldn't believe Krete and have the army of small men attack them and

Suzunne. He wasn't so sure how successful gnomes had once been in battle, but going up against a dragon for their first time in one thousand years would likely end very badly for them.

Suddenly, the gnome exclaimed and broke out in laughter, and he and Krete embraced, clapping each other on their backs. They babbled in their gnomish language, and every few moments, Krete pointed at his companions and Suzunne in exclamation, waving his hands around as they conversed excitedly.

Suzunne sighed, making Lorian vibrate slightly, and he forced himself not to grab for the spike to keep from falling off.

"Do gnomes typically talk so much?" Suzunne asked in exasperation. "I really need to groom my wings after all of that flying."

"Come down, it is safe," Krete called up to them.

Lorian hauled himself up to his feet, his legs screaming from both lack of use and soreness. Tedric let out a muffled curse, and Lorian watched as both Tedric and Aeden shimmied their way around Suzunne's spikes, grumbling as they went. Once the four of them had scrambled onto the ground, Lorian groaned in relief. His legs felt like they were about to fall off, but at least he was back on solid ground.

"Let's see what we have gotten ourselves into," Tedric whispered, surveying the cave in disappointment.

"Why, were you expecting a lavish castle when you pictured this place? It's a mountain, you idiot," Aeden retorted with a grin.

Tedric gave her a surprised smile, and Lorian looked away. Whatever was going on between them, he wasn't sure if even they knew the extent of it. He jumped as Finriel came to stand at his side, her expression distant as she seemed to be looking around for something, or someone. Goddesses save him, he needed to figure out whatever was going on between the two of them as well.

"I've spoken to Mott, and he has allowed for you to stay in here if that suits you," Krete said, turning to Suzunne.

The dragon huffed and looked out at the sickening drop below, then angled his head back to Lorian's companion after a moment.

"Will there be food?"

Krete nodded. "Whatever you would like."

"I will stay then," Suzunne replied nonchalantly, and moved toward a sandy area of the cave and sat down with a dull thump that shuddered through Lorian's feet.

"Wonderful, it will be brought to you soon," Krete said, and clapped his hands together. "Shall we?"

Lorian walked a few paces behind the rest of his companions and Krete's gnome friend as they made their way through the twisting and turning tunnels of the mountain. Lit torches lined either side of the passage, setting it in a cheerful glow.

The tunnels were much narrower than the ones they had encountered in Dragonkeep, and Lorian was beginning to feel anxious about the confined space. He sent a silent prayer to the goddesses that this wasn't the way that the entire mountain would be like. Krete and his friend were babbling to each other excitedly in gnomish, and their high-pitched voices bouncing off the walls did not help Lorian's feeling of being closed in.

As if the mountain had heard his prayers, their path suddenly opened up and Lorian found himself blinking away the brightness that greeted his eyes. Finriel took in a surprised breath at his side, and Lorian looked around with wide-eyed amazement.

They were at the opening of what looked like a city square, with gnomes and other furry creatures milling about. Beautiful gardens of vegetables and fruits spread out all around them, the outer edges lined with trees budding with colorful fruits. The ground was of cobbled stone, and paths wound around the different garden beds and toward an enormous tree that stood proudly in the center of the square. Lorian didn't even have to ask what this tree was. It was one of legend, and he had to admit that until now he didn't truly believe in its existence.

"The Viure," Finriel said softly, her face lighting up in awe as she drank in the sights around.

The tree was magnificent, soaring higher than Lorian's eyes could see. Smooth white bark encapsulated the enormous trunk, and black knots dappled across its almost flawless skin. Emerald green leaves the size of Lorian's palm filled the branches, nearly hiding them completely. Legend told that Tellas had created the Viure, and the gnomes had been birthed from the tree not long after that. The Viure was their mother, and one of the oldest living things in the realm.

Lorian let his gaze wander up the towering branches, and noticed that they were indeed in the center of the mountain. He found himself regretting his disrespect of the gnomes as he took everything in.

Rows of raised walkways staggered hundreds of feet above them, each lined by carved stone rails. Lorian could make out doors and passageways branching away from the main square that likely led to other parts of the mountain. The branches of the Viure blocked Lorian's view of exactly how high the mountain went up, but he could only guess. He noticed the same moss from the forest in Proveria spread out at the base of the tree, bathing its trunk in warm light. Lorian spun around, confused by the amount of light around them that seemingly had no source. Gnomes were geniuses.

A loud meow that sounded on the edge of a yowl broke the silence, and many gnomes jumped in fright, cursing under their breaths. A large grey cat jumped from the tree branches and loped toward them. At once Lorian knew that it was Nora, and he smiled as the mogwa bounded up to greet them. So she *had* listened to Finriel and come directly to the mountain. Now it was only a matter of finding out where she had hidden the pages.

"Thank the goddesses," Finriel laughed, and crouched down as Nora slid to a stop before her.

Lorian looked away as they greeted each other. The sense of familial intimacy around the exchange made his heart squeeze with the faint memories of a long forgotten home. Moments later, something wet pressed against his hand, and he looked down in surprise to find Nora's amber eyes trained on him.

"Hello again," he murmured, and reached out a hand to stroke her soft grey fur. Lorian looked up and his gaze met with Finriel's. The world stilled for a moment, and Lorian cursed her silently for having such an unreadable expression. After a moment, Finriel offered him a weak smile, and Lorian's heart threatened to beat out of his chest.

"Welcome to Creonid," a voice boomed through the air. Lorian turned at the voice and found an abnormally tall gnome standing before them. He was dressed in simple brown pants and a red tunic, yet the bronze band atop his dark brown hair made Lorian think that perhaps he was not just any ordinary citizen of the mountain.

"Hello, King Drohan, it is good to be home," Krete answered at once, and he bowed low.

Lorian and the rest of his companions hurriedly offered a bow as well. The king smiled warmly and nodded at them. A female gnome stood at his side, and Lorian had to admit she was pretty, well, for gnomish standards. Long waves of mouse brown hair tumbled down her back, and her wide hazel eyes twinkled as she looked between Krete and Mott.

"It's so good to see the two of you together again, little brothers," the woman that Lorian assumed was the queen said.

"It's good to see you too, Brinna," Krete laughed. He clapped Mott on the back before striding up to the queen and giving her a tight hug. The queen giggled and returned it, saying something in gnomish that Lorian did not understand.

"Wait, you're the queen's brother?" Tedric spluttered.

The gnomes separated and Krete turned to nod at Tedric. He gestured toward Mott and the queen.

"These are my siblings."

"Well," Lorian said, "I'm glad that I only just found out. I don't know how long I could have lived being forced to call you *Your Highness* during our quest. I suppose *Your Heinie* could have been a good compromise."

Mott shook his head with a smile. "Neither Krete nor I are of royalty. It is only our sweet sister who has become queen through matrimony with the king."

"Yes, yes, I know how that all works, thank you," Lorian answered dismissively.

"You must all be hungry and tired from your long journey," King Drohan said. "Come, let us eat."

Lorian settled into step next to Krete, who looked around at his home with an expression of glee that warmed even Lorian's worn soul. He had to admit that the combination of being held hostage by a colony of mermaids, then nearly getting eaten by a dragon, had fatigued him. Not to mention the fact that he had flown atop a dragon for nearly an entire evening, which just might have been worse than being close to death twice within a few short hours.

"You promised to show me your giant portal," Lorian said, nudging his friend on the shoulder.

Krete nodded. "Of course, perhaps tomorrow, once we're rested and finished speaking with the king."

Lorian made himself content with Krete's promise, promptly deciding to ignore his comment about speaking to the king. He didn't wish to speak. In fact, he didn't feel like doing anything other than eat his weight in something other than bread and apples, then fall sleep on a soft bed.

Brinna and Mott departed, Brinna giving the king a feathery kiss upon the cheek before she and her brother moved away. Lorian tracked their descent down a flight of steps before he shrugged and followed the king and his companions toward a light red door.

"Here we are," King Drohan announced and opened the door, revealing a room that made Lorian stagger to a halt.

A large table laden with every sort of food and dessert that Lorian could imagine was set before them, with six plates lined in front of their respective chairs. Steam from the food carried an array of tantalizing smells through the air, and Lorian's mouth began to water at the prospect of a proper feast. The room was made out of smooth glowing stone, much like the rest of the mountain, and a small fire crackled merrily from a hearth at the far end of the room.

"Please, sit," King Drohan said, extending a hand out toward the companions as he sat.

Lorian didn't need to be told twice, and he quickly pulled out a chair next to Krete before shoveling food onto his plate, hardly seeing it. Drohan was most reserved out of the lot with his food, as he clearly hadn't lived off the equivalent rations for a peasant for nearly three moons.

They ate in silence, save for soft hums of delight from everyone in the room. Lorian eyed a creamy orange dish and scooped it over a mound of dark grains, the taste exploding with spices as it hit his tongue. He delighted himself with thick stew, fresh vegetables cooked in lemon and basil, along with many dishes that he'd never seen in his life.

Lorian gently pushed away the last few spoonfuls of cherry tart left on his plate a good while later, having eaten more than he had in a very long time. His spirits had lifted significantly and he found that the thought of using his brain to speak to the king didn't sound so bad after all. Lorian glanced around at his companions who each looked quite satisfied as they leaned away from empty plates.

"Now," King Drohan said, an important tone coating his voice, "Krete has told me very little as to why you have all come here, as well as why the storyteller desires to meet you all."

"The storyteller is here?" Aeden asked, and the king nodded.

"Yes, he arrived not two weeks before you. He is currently detained in our dungeons, but he has requested to see the five of you since his coming here."

Lorian glanced at Finriel and Tedric from across the table with raised brows. Tedric met Lorian's look of confusion with one of his own, and the commander turned to King Drohan.

"We were not aware that he wanted to see us, nor do we know how he got the information that we would be coming here."

Lorian nodded in agreement, having thought the exact same thing. Perhaps the storyteller had some sort of secret clairvoyant ability.

King Drohan shook his head. "I'm not sure either, but the man is half mad. I wouldn't be surprised if his proclamations and your coming here was simple luck. However, he did insist on the meeting if it would suit you."

"Yes, we would like that." Finriel spoke for the first time since greeting Nora by the Viure. "He might be able to answer a few of the questions we have."

"What might those questions be?" King Drohan asked, and Krete leaned his elbows on the table, which even Lorian found surprising as they were in the presence of a king.

"As I have told you, the storyteller's beasts acted very strange when we came into contact with them," Krete said, ignoring the casual slump in his posture. "We also spotted a flock of birds only native to Keadora while we were in Farrador, and passed a traveler who said some strange things about the birds sending a message about a threat to the elves."

"We also came across a village that appeared to have been damaged by one of the storyteller's creation, yet when we asked the villagers, they said that shadows had caused the destruction,"

Tedric added, and Lorian noticed Aeden tense at the recalling of the Proverian village.

"Damaged how?" Drohan asked.

"Fire," Finriel replied stonily. "Three of the buildings were burned to the ground, and unfortunately two villagers fell victim as well."

King Drohan shivered. "I was not aware of such happenings, though I have to admit that I've never been involved much in the politics of the other kingdoms."

"Why is that?" Lorian asked, and King Drohan smiled at him.

"Because we gnomes are frequently overlooked as inferior, even though we are one of the most prosperous kingdoms in the realm."

Lorian saw Tedric tighten his grip around his fork at the king's words, but the commander said nothing.

"So you don't know anything deeper to what has been happening?" Krete asked. "Has the storyteller not said anything to you about why he created the beasts?"

"I'm afraid not." King Drohan shook his head. "As I said, the storyteller is not right in the head, though he has been nothing but polite when he's not babbling to himself about keys and locks."

Lorian exchanged a wary glance with his companions, the keys and locks sounding far too similar to the prophecy they had been given by the Sythril. He didn't say anything, however, finding that his friends too were keeping their mouths shut.

"I did overhear a conversation between King Sorren and Queen Arbane of the elves," King Drohan said, breaking the silence. "It was during a private meeting following the release of the beasts and the first rampage upon the Proverian village."

"Do you remember what they were talking about?" Lorian asked, but the king shook his head.

"I couldn't get close enough to hear everything, as we

gnomes do not have any special hearing abilities and they were nearly whispering. I heard the Red King mentioned once or twice in moments where their voices rose, but nothing more."

Curiosity flooded through Lorian at this, and he leaned forward excitedly. He was about to open his mouth to ask more when Aeden cut him off, her voice polite but cold.

"When can we meet with the storyteller? It's likely we can get more answers from him."

The king's eyes flashed with what Lorian could only guess was concern as he looked at Aeden, but he nodded, the smile gone from his face.

"Yes, I can make an arrangement for you to meet with him in a few hours."

Tedric nodded. "Good, we should clean ourselves up and rest before then."

"Good idea," Lorian agreed, looking down at his dirty cloak and pants with a shake of his head. *The best thing about being freed from this bounty will be baths whenever I please,* Lorian thought as they all stood up and followed the king out of the room.

Three serving girls stood by the door when they stepped out of the dining chamber, and King Drohan told them to show the companions to their rooms. Lorian offered the king a short bow as they bid farewell, and he found the curiosity of meeting the storyteller wash away as the feeling of a full stomach and prospect of a warm bed lifted his spirits.

❦ 29 ❧

AEDEN

Aeden scrubbed at her dirty skin with a wet cloth in silence, the drip of water turning her once clean basin a murky grey. She glanced down at the page Finriel had given her upon finding their rooms; Nora had apparently hidden the pages within a fold of branches on the Viure. The faces of the brownies stared up at her from the page, their intricately drawn features nearly identical to how they had appeared in physical reality.

The ghost of a shiver ran down Aeden's arms at the memory of being surrounded by the dozens of furry creatures, completely unaware at first that the brownies had been trying to protect her from her companions. *This does change things*, she thought, *damn the goddesses*. She did not wish it to be so, but perhaps Krete was right about a deeper meaning behind the beasts and the reason for their creation. This had the potential to change everything that had brought Aeden on the quest, along with everything she had been offered as a reward in exchange for her return.

The flash of a memory appeared behind her eyes, and Aeden stiffened at the image of a young man, her love, falling to the floor as blood poured from the fatal slash across his throat.

"This is what happens when you defy me," her father had said calmly as she watched the life drain from the boy's eyes.

She had tried to save him, to staunch the flow of blood even as it coated her hands in a warm crimson blanket. She'd looked up into the eyes of the guard who had done the deed in place of her father, finding a shadow of sorrow across the older man's face.

"Stand up," her father had snapped. *"Another lesson for you, my dear daughter, is to never get your own hands dirty. For if you let others do the killing for you, you shall be free from the curse and your conscience will remain clean forevermore."*

Aeden gritted her teeth and forced the memory away, knowing that if she lingered in her thoughts, only more would come. She quickly thought of Krete, who had consoled her after discovering her crumpled upon the floor of her chambers, hands coated in the drying blood of the only one she had ever truly loved. Krete had cleaned her hands without questions and stayed with her the entire night, telling stories of the ancient goddesses until the sun had risen, if only to keep her mind from her father's destruction.

Aeden's heart thumped almost painfully and she wiped a stray tear that fell onto her cheek. Krete was the only one who had always been there for her, the only one that she could trust. Tedric's face floated into her mind, and Aeden groaned in frustration, clenching her fists, warm water seeping around her fingers from the rag still clutched in her left hand. *You cannot love him, no matter how much you want to.*

She jumped at a soft knock on the door, and she dropped the dirty washcloth into the water basin.

"One moment," she called.

She knew that she had taken too much time. They were supposed to be on their way to meet with the storyteller. Aeden fought the shiver seeping into her bones as she shrugged on the simple blue dress that had been provided by the gnomes. It was a little short, falling slightly above her ankles. Aeden did't care though, and she strapped her belt on before putting on her cloak. She grabbed her sword from the doorway and sheathed it at her hip, just in case she had to fight any rogue storytellers.

Tedric stood waiting outside the door, and she nearly gasped from his sudden nearness. It was times like this when she hated her heightened fairy senses. Even the sight of him felt like a shower of small electric shocks all over her body.

"You look cleaner," Tedric said with a smile as she closed the heavy door behind her.

"As do you," she replied. Tedric was indeed a lot cleaner, his once dirt-smeared hair now soft and shining. It had grown since she had met him, now tucked behind his ears and brushing against his neck. He was clad in a plain white tunic and dark pants, his sword strapped to his belt. Aeden tried to ignore the fact that the tunic was slightly too small for him and exposed toned muscle beneath.

Aeden made herself walk past him and down the door-lined hallway. She would be leaving him soon anyway, and there was no point in yearning for something she couldn't have. She glanced over the stone railing and down into the main square. The Viure was still impressive from this grand height, its emerald green leaves swaying in a nonexistent wind. Everything seemed connected and peaceful, the gnomes milling about as they cared for the gardens or watched their children climb about the roots and play in the shimmering grass. Aeden even spotted Nora splayed out on one of the lower branches, her eyes half-lidded as she gazed down at the scene below with mild interest.

"You seem to know where you're going," Tedric commented, and she glanced behind her shoulder to nod at him.

"I came here many times as a child to visit Krete," Aeden said. "I know where nearly every door leads to, as well as a fair majority of even the most hidden places."

"Impressive," Tedric murmured, and he was soon striding in step with her.

A warm hand slid into her own, making Aeden jump from the electric shock. She looked over to find Tedric gazing down at her with a mischievous grin and she narrowed her eyes in return, but she didn't pull away. They walked for a few moments before he broke the silence. He pulled her around to face him, and she yet again noticed how close they were.

"Aeden, you can't keep pushing me away," Tedric said softly, his eyes searching hers.

She gulped and glanced at his exposed collarbone, trying to choose her next words carefully. Aeden's heart began pulsing in her chest, blood thrumming through her veins.

"I don't want to push you away," she replied, willing her expression to remain blank.

Aeden saw the half-smile tugging at Tedric's full lips, and she found herself trying to keep herself from smiling as well. He brought his free arm around to hold her waist and pull her closer to him. Aeden hadn't realized how much shorter than the commander she truly was, and she tilted her head up slightly to hold his gaze.

"So then why is this so hard?" he breathed.

Before Aeden could stop herself, she had entwined her fingers around his neck and pushed up on her toes, closing the space between them. The world around them faded away as their lips brushed together, and her entire body felt as if it was melting and yet becoming more present than ever at the same time. She brought one hand into the waves of his hair and leaned into the kiss. His lips were rough but sure as they pressed their bodies close. His hands gripped tightly against her body, and she breathed in surprise, smiling against his lips. A chuckle vibrated through his body, sending warm shivers down her spine.

A strange sensation hit her in the stomach, and they both gasped and choked, stumbling away from each other in pained surprise. She took a wheezing breath and looked up to find Tedric staring at her as if the same thing had happened to him. She groaned. This had been what she was trying to make *not* happen. But she was too weak to pull away from what had been so clearly there. The solution was clear, but the thought of carrying it out pained Aeden more than she could bear.

"What was that?" Tedric gasped, his hair falling over his brow as he raked his fingers through his blonde locks. Aeden closed her eyes for a second before calling upon any remaining strength she had to compose herself. She introduced the most nonchalant look she could muster and opened her eyes.

"Don't touch me," Aeden demanded as he reached out a hand. It felt like the words were being ripped out of her body as she pushed past him and began to walk. She heard his hand fall limply against his leg before he started after her, though his footsteps remained slow and cadenced a healthy distance behind.

"It would be best if we kept our presence to each other as sparing as possible," Aeden said, fighting to keep her voice stern.

"Aeden, stop," Tedric said, and Aeden gasped as another painful shock ran through her body at the brush of his fingers against her wrist. He seemed to feel the shock as well and pulled away almost immediately. Aeden forced herself onward, massaging the place where he had touched her wrist with her other hand.

"Tedric, don't. Please." Aeden's words sounded more like a plea than a demand, but Tedric seemed to understand.

A moment of silence enveloped them like a suffocating glove before Tedric replied, "I understand. I won't bother you again."

Spoken like a true commander. Aeden turned and continued down a separate hall. She glanced back down to the main square, and was almost surprised to see that nothing had changed. Gnomes were still milling about and the tree was still standing in all of its ancient glory.

Aeden blinked back threatening tears and quickened her

steps, forcing herself not to look back at Tedric. The feeling in her chest was slowly turning into a strong stinging sensation, and she knew it would be there for days. No matter how much she wanted to turn around and explain everything, she knew she couldn't. It was simple. It wouldn't end the way fate wanted it to end. She had committed and would *not* change her mind. She wouldn't let herself even think of the endless possibilities that had just revealed themselves.

30

KRETE

"Here we are," Krete announced as he, Finriel, and Lorian stopped in front of an iron door near the bottom levels of the mountain.

Their descent to the dungeons had been mostly silent, apart from Krete occasionally offering a fact about an old artifact on display or where a certain corridor led. It seemed that both Finriel and Lorian were as fatigued as he felt. The desire to sleep for days and days seeped into Krete's bones. He had a feeling that he wouldn't get that luxury anytime soon, however.

He had been able to catch a quick nap and lovely bath in his chambers, which Krete had to admit he had missed greatly. He now wore a pair of comfortable grey cotton pants and a loose-fitting mustard yellow tunic, though he hadn't forgotten his hat, which was now clean atop his head. Lorian and Finriel were both refreshed as well. Lorian's clothing was much the same as Krete's, if only slightly too small, and his tunic was the color of a brilliant sunset.

"Aeden and Tedric aren't here yet," Finriel noticed, turning her head back toward the torchlit stairway from which they had just come, her hand picking idly at the hem of the dark brown sleeve of her new dress.

"Maybe they've forgotten," Lorian suggested. "They might be busy doing other more fun activities."

Finriel rolled her eyes at Lorian, who was waggling his brows, and Krete shook his head with a forced smile, partially because he knew that what Lorian said was possible. He could only hope that they weren't so foolish. Krete was about to turn toward the two guards stationed by the iron door when footsteps sounded from the stone stairway and a very flustered Aeden came to stand next to Finriel. She didn't smile at any of them, and Krete ran a worried glance over her wild violet hair, now free of its usual braid, along with the wrinkled sky blue dress she wore. She looked wearier now than at any point in their journey.

"Let's get this over with," Aeden huffed, slightly out of breath and looking murderous.

Even Finriel looked at her with some worry, and the witch asked, "Where's Tedric?"

Aeden scoffed and threw her hands in the air, and Krete was worried she might actually yell. Yet she didn't, and Tedric's form came into view not ten seconds after Finriel asked. He too looked disgruntled, but Krete found that he was hiding his emotions much better than Aeden was currently managing.

"Are you two all right?" Krete asked, his worry for Aeden ruling over his previous decision to remain silent about the matter.

Aeden bit her lip and Tedric merely gave Krete a stony-faced nod.

"Just fine," Aeden bit out, and Krete sighed.

"Okay, then. Let's meet this storyteller," Krete said, and motioned for the guards at the door.

As they walked in, Krete wasn't surprised to see that the cell was not much of a cell at all, rather only a very small chamber. He had never been allowed near the lower tier of the mountain, as he was still a part of the royal family in name, and any guard was forced to turn him back to the upward levels as a matter of safety. Yet, as he inspected the cell, Krete found himself all the more proud to call himself a gnome. They were not creatures of ill wishing, and still offered the most evil trespasser a comfortable place to rest their head as they awaited their fate.

The room was very plain in comparison to his own, however that too did not surprise him in the least. A simple cot was pushed to the far corner of the room, adjacent to a small basin and cloths for cleaning. Against the other wall was a small desk, where the storyteller sat balanced upon a very old looking chair that seemed as if it might collapse at any moment. The room smelled of a mingling of earth and human sweat, though not to the point where it was truly bothersome.

The storyteller himself appeared quite clean, aside from the soot and hole-ridden robe that draped over his thin body. A shock of short white hair had initially indicated to Krete that the man was old, but as he turned his head, Krete's eyes widened in surprise as he was met with the face of a barely middle-aged man. And it was a man that he had seen before.

The storyteller's features were soft and human, and Krete guessed that he seemed to be perhaps five years younger than Krete's forty years of age. The storyteller's strange silver eyes flashed as he regarded the companions, seeming to recognize them all at once. Krete had definitely seen this man before, and a sudden realization struck him in the chest.

"You were the villager who was brought to king Sorren with the pages," Krete blurted, and the storyteller paused his observation of the companions to look at Krete.

"Not quite a villager, but yes." The storyteller spoke softly, a shy smile blooming across his ruggedly handsome face. "Please, call me Egharis."

Krete and Aeden exchanged a glance, and he bit his cheek at the obvious rage that flickered behind her green eyes. He let out a shaky breath to calm his nerves before turning back toward the man. Their quest could have been avoided entirely if they'd only known it had been the storyteller that night. And yet a small part of Krete was grateful that they hadn't known, for he wouldn't be standing in this cell, surrounded by friends that felt more like family now.

"Thank you for meeting with us, storyteller—I mean, Egharis," Krete stuttered, stepping forward. None of his companions seemed to be very inclined to speak, and Krete had to admit neither was he. The storyteller's gaze lingered on Krete, and to Krete's surprise, his smile widened.

"Krete, isn't it?" the storyteller said. "How do you like your dragon?"

The ground tilted slightly under Krete's feet and he sputtered in surprise, the storyteller waited with a smile for Krete to regain his composure.

"M-my dragon? Do you mean Suzunne?"

"Ah, so he did end up giving himself a name. How quaint."

"Well," Krete began, "he is quite strange. One of the only reasons that he agreed to bring us here was because he needed to sun his scales apparently."

Egharis's expression turned into one of fondness and he chuckled. "Yes, I would say I am most proud of his creation." Egharis slid his gaze across the five of them, his attention now seeming to rest on all of them at once. "However, I sense that you have put the beasts back into their pages. All but Suzunne, of course."

They all shifted uncomfortably under his knowing stare, all but Finriel, who replied, "It was the task we were given, and I didn't feel too inclined to keep piecing my friends back together."

"Ah, but you are not the kind to take orders," the storyteller countered. "I think you are all scared of the beasts."

At this, Finriel closed her mouth and shot a glare of daggers at the floor. Egharis opened his arms as if to welcome them all into a warm embrace.

"It is nothing to worry about. I understand that I may have created you five rather questionable creatures. Besides, the time is still just far enough that you can release them before they are needed."

"I'm sorry," Aeden countered. "I don't think any of us are quite sure what you mean when you say you created the creatures *for* us. We hardly know you."

"Ah, well, that is where you are wrong, young fairy. One who weaves stories does not simply do that one thing. We can see into the future if the goddesses truly believe that we are needed to help it change for the better in some way."

When no one answered him, Egharis continued more seriously, "I have seen visions of blood and terror. The realm of Raymara laden thick with shadow and bloodshed, the thousand-year peace wiped away in the blink of an eye."

"The prophecy," Finriel breathed, and Egharis smiled.

"Yes, my dear witch. It is the prophecy I speak of, and a future I would like more than ever to be stopped."

"But we thought that was your entire motive," Krete countered. "To create these terrible creatures in order to bring Raymara back into a state of violence. That's why we were sent to capture them, and you, to be destroyed."

The storyteller looked between them, and his calm expression nearly cracked. The room suddenly felt colder and Krete found himself shivering, from discomfort or actual cold, he was not sure.

"That is the story that has been twisted around my creations to distract you from the real problem. You five are the keys to Raymara's survival. I created these beasts as a loophole in the formidable acts I have been employed to commit."

"What terrible acts?" Tedric asked. "And who is your employer?"

The storyteller paused, looking at Tedric with a strange expression that Krete could not quite place. The storyteller opened his mouth, but no sound came out. Instead, a pained groan escaped from Egharis's throat, and the man doubled over, clutching at his abdomen. Tedric rushed forward and helped righten the storyteller before he fell to the ground, and Krete simply watched in confusion. It would be terrible if the story-teller simply fell over dead before telling them anything useful. Krete cursed himself inwardly. Those sorts of heartless thoughts belonged to Lorian, or other men of his sort.

"Thank you," Egharis wheezed after a moment, and pulled away from Tedric's supporting grip.

"Are you all right?" Krete asked, and the storyteller nodded.

"It is a curse I was put under by my employer. I cannot say his name, or anything even close to who he is or where he comes from. I am also not to speak of my exact task, though I would love to help you all very much."

"And if you do try?" Finriel asked.

"What you just witnessed happens, my dear," Egharis replied with a weak smile. "Blinding pain in my entire body, though I was warned of bones breaking or organs failing if I fight against the curse for too long."

"That's terrible," Tedric growled. "Can the curse be broken?"

Egharis shook his head. "I'm afraid not, at least not until I have completed my task."

"What's in it for you?" Lorian asked from where he leaned against the far wall by the cot. "I mean, unless you were forced into working with the man."

"My wife and son were taken from me," Egharis said bitterly. "I do not know where they are, but my employer ensured me their safety, as well as a reunion with them once I have completed my task."

"And if you fail?" Lorian asked.

"He'll kill them," Aeden breathed at Krete's side, answering for the storyteller, who nodded at her sadly.

Krete reached up and squeezed Aeden's hand, knowing how close the storyteller's words must be hitting her. Aeden's cold fingers squeezed back, though she looked quite ready to run from the room.

"So you must complete this task, whatever it may be," Lorian said. "Which I am assuming based upon your abilities has something to do with creating more beasts."

"You are smart," Egharis replied with a more genuine smile at Lorian, who grinned back.

"It's my job to be smart," he replied. "I'm also guessing that this employer of yours is a person with power, or at least has a considerable amount of it."

Egharis shook his head. "For fear of my liver or any other organ failing, I cannot confirm or deny what you are saying."

Krete bit the inside of his lip, mulling over everything that had just been said. The storyteller was not half bad after all. But who was he working for? And how could they help stop this mysterious employer if they hadn't the slightest idea as to who they were?

"Could you simply try to find your family and not complete your task?" Krete asked.

The storyteller barked a laugh. "Oh, no, I'm afraid not. Even if I wanted to, I could not find them, and I am sure that my employer has found some measure of knowing my whereabouts at all times."

"He sounds like an ass," Lorian said, and the storyteller laughed again.

"I pray he never hears you say that." Egharis then turned serious again. "But I am begging you to keep your pages close and never lose them. You must use them when the time is right, for when it seems like all is lost, they can help you."

"How do we know you aren't lying?" Finriel asked. "How

can we know you aren't just trying to trick us into releasing your beasts again so they can go off to destroy more lives?"

Egharis shot his head up and glared at the witch. "When you found my beasts, were any of them rampaging a village, killing anyone, or even laying a breath of violence against anything around you?"

"Well, the chimera did try to kill me," Tedric interjected. "And Lorian was slammed into a tree by the rakshasa."

"That was because both of you were being idiots," Finriel replied under her breath.

"He has a point," Lorian interrupted. "We never heard or saw them causing any trouble before we found them. The only thing that could have been their doing was the fire."

Egharis inclined his head toward Lorian as if in thanks for his defense. "I can assure you that whatever fire you speak of was not caused by any of my creations," Egharis said. "They were not created to destroy, but to protect."

"What about the first night they were released?" Aeden asked. "Every home was burned to the ground and four citizens died. Even you claimed it was the five beasts who did it."

"That was my fault." Egharis's silver gaze dipped to his hands. "I was angry when I made them, and creations retain whatever emotion is used as fuel to conjure them, though only for a few hours."

Krete looked at his companions, who were all wearing mingled expressions of confusion and interest. Aeden was still pale, and her fingers had gone limp in Krete's hand. He looked up at her to find her looking between Tedric and the storyteller, her expression mostly blank though he knew that pain lashed her heart.

"Look," Egharis said, "I will not attempt to convince you to let your beasts out, just know that you would be wise to keep your respective pages close in the coming days."

The gnome guard outside the cell cleared his throat and indicated that their time had passed and they had to leave.

"Thank you for speaking with us," Krete said truthfully to the storyteller. Egharis nodded to the five of them, an unreadable expression on his face. They all turned and filed out of the cell, but just as the gnome guard was about to close the door, Krete turned around and looked at the storyteller.

"Can you truly not tell us what your employer wants?" he asked.

Egharis met his gaze and took in a deep breath before replying, "The most I can say is that he wishes to change the realm in completion. I fear that if he succeeds, Raymara will return to its prior state of death and darkness."

An involuntary shiver went through Krete, but he forced himself to incline his head in thanks and be ushered from the room by the guard. He walked up the steps behind Finriel, his mind whirling from their discussion. Could they even believe a word that Egharis had told them?

"That was certainly interesting," Lorian said once they reached the top of the steps and found themselves in another torchlit hall that led to Krete's chambers.

"We can't trust him," Aeden replied. "He's clearly lost it, and weaving ludicrous stories is in his nature."

"He didn't seem mad to me," Lorian remarked. "And he didn't say anything much about keys, though he did talk about the prophecy."

"Which is my exact point," Aeden snapped. "We simply cannot be the people spoken of in the prophecy, that would be ridiculous."

"What if it is us?" Tedric asked, and Aeden failed to meet his gaze.

"You would love to have a ballad written after you, wouldn't you?" Lorian said, though Krete noticed that Tedric's returning smile didn't quite meet his eyes.

"It's too late to talk about this now," Finriel sighed. "Can we discuss it over breakfast tomorrow? I feel as though I could fall asleep on my feet, however dangerous the storyteller made our future sound."

"I agree." Krete nodded, noticing the dull ache of fatigue beginning to seep back into his joints. "Let's meet in the morning in the same room where we dined with King Drohan. I can arrange it with the servants."

Everyone murmured their agreement, and soon were all heading to their quarters. Krete was more than happy when he fell into his bed minutes later, but found his dreams were accompanied by fire-breathing dragons and images of Creonid Mountain bathed in a waterfall of blood.

❧ 31 ❧

TEDRIC

Tedric felt as if he might be sick.

He wiped his clammy hands upon his pants as he stood before the closed door of Aeden's chambers, wondering if he should go through with his plan. He was going to talk to her one last time, he *had* to after what had happened between them. His body felt like a constant electric current was running through it ever since their kiss, and he didn't think that it was merely the memory of her touch that made him feel this way.

Tedric needed to know what that shock had been, and why she had pulled away so quickly. He cursed himself inwardly at his selfishness, knowing very well that his mind needed to be focused upon what the storyteller had told them and the future of the realm, but he simply couldn't.

"Come on, do it, you coward," Tedric growled to himself under his breath, and with a lurch of his stomach, he brought his hand up and knocked against the old wooden door three times.

The seconds it took for Aeden to reach the door felt like torture. Tedric had half a mind to believe that she could be sleeping, and let out a muffled curse at his lack of foresight. Yet soon enough, the door handle turned, and Aeden's head peaked out from the other side of the room. Electric shocks ran through Tedric's body as their eyes met. Her hair was wild and she looked like she had just gotten out of a fight with some gnomes. Maybe she *had* just gotten out of a fight with some gnomes.

"I need to talk to you," Tedric said. "Can I come in?"

"I don't think there is anything to talk about," Aeden replied coolly, and Tedric's heart felt as though it had just been stung by a thousand hornets.

"Please, if only so that I can understand," Tedric pleaded, and Aeden's cold expression molded into surprise.

Aeden didn't reply as she stepped aside, allowing just enough space for him to enter the room. His breath caught as his hand brushed against hers, but he ignored it and moved to stand by the bed. The room looked nearly identical to his, with a thick grey rug that took up most of the floor and a large bed pushed against the far wall. The light sea green bedding was rumpled, a clear sign that she had been lying there before he had entered. He immediately regretted his decision to come to her at such a late hour, and he cursed again.

"I'm sorry. I shouldn't have come."

Aeden turned in confusion as Tedric started toward the door again. Aeden took a step toward the warrior and brought her hand up inches away from his chest. His breath caught as her hand came close enough to touch.

"Tedric, I thought you understood—"

"Yes," Tedric cut her off, "but it doesn't feel right." He let himself look down upon her agonizingly beautiful face. His muscles felt taut with strain, his jaw working as he carefully thought of his next words. "Ever since I laid eyes on you in Millris Forest, it was like something lodged itself into my chest."

Aeden opened her mouth, but now Tedric raised a hand to stop her and let his gaze fall to the rug at his feet. He wasn't sure if he could bear looking into her eyes with what he was about to say.

"I can't get you out of my head, and I need you to know that what I feel for you is stronger than anything I've ever felt in my life. You slipped under my skin and somehow made me feel … more. It's maddening," Tedric said and looked back into her green gaze, which was locked upon him.

"Damn the Nether, I've never been so soft," he growled, and grabbed his shaggy hair with rising frustration. "I've never been one to express tender emotions. I'm not very good at this," he said, and gestured between him and Aeden.

Tedric let out a small breath and held her gaze, and his entire body ached at the pain so clearly written on her face. He stood there in silence as Aeden's jaw worked. He shouldn't have come, but his chest felt so close to bursting that he couldn't think of anything else. Tedric sighed as Aeden shook her head and looked to the ground.

"Right, sorry. I'll go." Tedric turned away from Aeden and started toward the door without another word.

"Tedric, wait."

Surprise shook through his body and Tedric lowered his hand from the door handle, stilling. He turned back to find Aeden walking toward him slowly.

"I know what you've been feeling, because I've been feeling it, too."

Tedric's eyes widened, and the feeling in his chest leavened every so slightly. Aeden looked down and shook her head again. Tedric took a step closer, placing a hand gently on her shoulder. He stifled a gasp from the shock, and Aeden jumped under his touch. She opened her mouth to speak, but couldn't seem to find the words.

"Tell me," Tedric whispered, easing his grip and letting his hands slide down her arms to envelop her delicate hands in his own. The touch made Aeden quickly withdraw with a shuddering breath and cross her arms across her chest.

"I closed myself away from anything close to love ever since my father—" Aeden broke off, and Tedric nodded, suddenly understanding.

"Since he killed the boy you loved," Tedric finished for her, and Aeden looked away, blinking quickly.

"Yes," she managed to say after a few moments. "I've only known numbness since then, and anger."

"You don't seem angry," Tedric frowned, and Aeden chuckled.

"I don't need to lash out like Finriel in order to prove that I'm angry. But that's beside the point." She sighed. "What I'm saying is that I didn't expect to feel anything remotely close to love for anyone again, and especially not another human."

Tedric's heart leaped into his throat, and he closed his mouth. She was beginning to love him?

"And then there's—well, never mind." Aeden shook her head and hugged herself.

Tedric took a step forward. "What is it?"

"It's nothing, just a stupid thing." Aeden faltered, and Tedric felt more confused than ever at her vagueness. "I never believed in it," she continued almost to herself, and Tedric took another step toward her with rising confusion. "Ever since I was a child, I thought it was just a fairy tale."

"What?" Tedric asked.

"I thought it was merely a nan's fable to keep the older fairies hopeful for something other than living the rest of their lives without sharing their bed with another."

"Aeden," Tedric interrupted. "What are you talking about?"

She stopped and turned back to face him, her expression grave as she spoke. The word tumbled from her mouth, and Tedric's mind began to spin.

"It's the vinculum."

"Excuse me?"

Aeden sighed and looked up at him. He glanced at her hand twitching at her side. Tedric reached for it, squeezing her fingers gently with reassurance. Worry, guilt, and horror knotted in his stomach, and for a moment he thought he was going to be sick.

"Whatever it is, I can help."

Aeden barked a laugh at this, shaking her head. "You can't help, I can't—" She broke off and removed her hand from his grasp. She wasn't making any sense. The temperature in the room seemed to drop as the deepening night washed over the mountain and cooled the citadel. Aeden shivered, the sheer nightdress she was wearing most likely not protecting her skin from the cold. Tedric noticed her dress and his eyes glanced down at her figure. The lines of her curves under the thin cloth made his body tense, and he trained his eyes back up. He then took a step forward, frustration pulsing through his body.

"For Nether's sake, Aeden," Tedric cut through the silence. "Just tell me what this damn vinculum is."

"It's the mating bond," Aeden blurted, her arms rising and then falling back down at her sides.

Confusion flashed across Tedric's mind, and the sensation in his chest pulsed again as if in answer.

"Mating bond? I thought that only existed among fairies."

She nodded and tugged on her loose side braid. "The shock from the kiss, but I don't understand why. I didn't know that it could be shared with others besides fairies. I didn't think …"

Aeden took a step toward him, and Tedric stepped toward her, closing the space between them as he wrapped his arms around her. He felt Aeden's body crumple against his, her lithe frame heavily leaning into him. Thousands of emotions swirled inside Tedric's body at once, making his brain and heart feel thick.

After a moment, Aeden let out a shaky sigh and pushed away, but only enough so that she could look up at him comfortably. She opened her mouth to speak again, but he leaned forward and softly pressed his lips against hers. This time the small shock was almost pleasurable, and she returned the kiss at once, pressing her body into his. The kiss was soft and gentle, the strangeness of her touch making Tedric feel almost unsure of himself. He silently scoffed. *Tedric Drazak, a man notorious for his* many *skills in life, caught off guard by a fairy girl.*

Aeden broke away at once, and their panting breaths sang in tandem. Everything felt so right as a shy smile played at her lips, and she gently placed her hands on his chest. Tedric couldn't help his own smile, and his body ached for her even though they were already touching.

"Great goddesses, woman, I thought you were going to say something like the storyteller had escaped or Suzunne roasted all of the gnomes in the mountain for dinner." Aeden let out a laugh as he spoke. "I can deal with a mating bond."

She snorted at this, and Tedric chuckled as her eyes widened with embarrassment. But then she shook her head, trying to fight the grin on her face. "It's not only that, though."

Tedric didn't wait to hear what she was about to say, but instead tilted his head down and kissed her. The world disappeared as their bodies molded against each other, every touch sending electric shocks down Tedric's spine. She inhaled sharply as he trailed his lips down her jaw to her neck. He paused, but she brought her hands up to his waist, indicating for him not to stop.

"Tedric," Aeden gasped as he brought his face back up to hers. He paused, and her green eyes were like a shock of lightning through his bones. She reached up and kissed him again, his lips burning hot as they moved against each other.

His hands explored her body, and every feathering touch felt like it was heightened to a thousand times that. She arched against him, her mouth opening against his as his fingers trailed and discovered her skin. His mind shattered into a kaleidoscope of colors, any thoughts that might have betrayed him now being swept away in a current of longing.

She brought her hands under his shirt, feeling the hard planes of muscle that had come from years of training. She brought her hand to his chest, and he was sure she could feel his heart thundering against her touch. It was her heart now.

They moved toward the bed, still in each other's embrace. Tedric felt clumsy, his trained warrior instincts betraying him as his foot caught against the corner of the rug. They both tumbled to the floor, and he landed on top of Aeden with a wince.

"Shit," Tedric gasped, and quickly brought each hand to rest at either side of her head. He propped himself up and let his gaze trail freely down her body, sending his self-restraint to the wind.

"Are you okay?" Tedric asked, slightly out of breath.

Aeden smirked and pulled him down so that their bodies were flush against each other. She reached up and kissed the place where his neck and shoulder met, and a rush of electric pleasure lit across his skin. He let out a strangled breath as his body came alive, and Aeden leaned her head back onto the ground with fire in her eyes.

"As long as you're with me."

❧ 32 ❧

AEDEN

The faint song of wind chimes echoed through Aeden's dreams, bringing her back to the waking world and into her room in Creonid Mountain. Warmth spread through her body when she realized that her head was lying upon Tedric's olive-skinned chest, his even breath causing her head to rise and fall slightly. Their legs were intertwined beneath the blanket of the bed they had eventually migrated to during their long night.

Aeden couldn't keep the smile from blooming on her lips as she stretched, bathing in the memories of the night. Tedric stirred at her movement, and she looked up to find his half-lidded gaze upon her. Aeden lifted her hand, which had been slung over his hard stomach, and brought it up to brush a lock of golden hair from his brow.

"Good morning," Tedric murmured in a raspy voice that sent tingles through Aeden's toes.

"Good morning," Aeden replied almost shyly, and Tedric caught her hand, which was now gently playing with the lock of hair, and kissed her fingers.

She simply smiled, allowing for the warmth of his gaze to fill her completely. The worries that had previously filled her mind about the matter now felt slightly less important, and she bit back the small tendril of worry in her stomach. She only focused on the sensation of her skin on his, the way that their bodies seemed to mold perfectly together, as if they had been made to be this way.

Aeden pushed herself up so that she was resting upon her elbow, and Tedric released her hand. She leaned forward and placed a feathery kiss upon his lips before she leaned back again and began to trace small patterns against his smooth skin and along the stark red scar on his right shoulder and bicep. Aeden received a hum of relaxed pleasure from the commander, and she could feel his eyes upon her.

"Does it still hurt?" she asked as she let her finger run along the scar, and Tedric shook his head in reply and closed his eyes. "We need to get ready for breakfast with the others," Aeden said, and brushed her lips against his chest before pushing up and moving to step off the bed.

A strong hand wrapped around her stomach, and she let out a surprised yelp as Tedric groaned and pulled her back against him.

"Too tired," Tedric yawned before he nuzzled his nose against her neck.

Aeden fought against the desire to lean into the touch, and instead pulled away once more, darting from the bed before he could wrangle her back. She wasn't sure if she would be able to say no to him a second time.

"Come on," Aeden laughed, and padded over to the small water basin to freshen up.

Soft footsteps padded up behind her and she smiled as warm lips pressed against her shoulder. She wiped the water from her eyes before turning to him, still smiling as she stood up onto her toes and pressed another kiss on his lips.

"Careful now," Tedric growled as she pulled away, and she could still feel his brown eyes on her as she grabbed the blue dress she had worn the night before. "Your kisses are making it difficult to want to go back out there."

Aeden rolled her eyes and turned to face him, her breath nearly leaving her at the sight of his beautiful body. Planes of muscle rippled beneath bronzed skin, and Aeden let her eyes dip lower to his hips, her cheeks burning as memories of the night intruded her thoughts. Even the long scar along his shoulder and bicep suited him. A shadow of stubble now ran along his chiseled jaw, and locks of thick hair fell in waves over his brow.

"Do you think we should keep what happened between us from the others?" Aeden asked as she threw him the pants that she found by her feet.

Tedric caught them with one hand and pulled them on. "There's no point. I don't want to hide how I feel anymore, if that's all right with you."

Worry reared its head once more, and Aeden bit her lip. "I don't mind."

"Besides, Lorian will probably be able to sense what happened with that strange intuition of his," Tedric half-joked, and Aeden forced herself to smile as she watched him shrug on the slightly too small tunic.

Tedric frowned, clearly noticing her discomfort. He padded over, and she forced the smile on her face to grow as he wrapped his arms around her waist.

"What is it?" Tedric asked, searching her face. "Do you not want this?"

"No, it's not that," Aeden shook her head. "I'm just not used to someone loving me anymore."

Her words weren't entirely a lie, as she genuinely hadn't felt the swell of fluttering warmth inside of her heart for nearly four years. But she didn't feel quite ready to tell the entire truth— not yet.

AEDEN'S CHEEKS HEATED AT THE SOUND OF LORIAN'S WHOOP and applause upon her and Tedric's arrival in the dining room some time later. The table was again laden with an array of food, and their three companions had already tucked in before they'd arrived. Finriel looked cheerful enough as she gave them a nod before returning to a steaming bowl of porridge and fresh fruit, her dark hair now gleaming and clean in its usual braid. Krete glanced up from his eggs and gave Aeden a strained smile, but she found that she could not return it. He knew what she had done, and they both knew the consequences.

"Good morning, lovebirds," Lorian greeted through a mouthful of eggs, throwing them a wink from where he sat next to Krete.

"I told you he would know," Tedric murmured quietly into Aeden's ear as they settled down next to each other, and Aeden busied herself with shoveling fresh strawberries and porridge into the aged yet skillfully made wooden bowl in front of her.

"Finriel, can you pass me the honey?" Aeden asked, completely ignoring all of her male companions and smiling in thanks as Finriel handed her a large glass pot of amber syrup.

"You two must have had so much fun you're too tired to talk then, eh?" Lorian said, and raised his brows at the two of them.

"Stop it, Lorian." Finriel gave the thief a meaningful look, and Aeden shoveled a large spoonful of porridge into her mouth.

Tedric squeezed her free hand underneath the table, and she squeezed back lightly. Their hands remained together as they ate, and soon enough, Lorian shut his mouth after realizing that neither she nor Tedric were going to take his bait.

"So," Tedric spoke after a few minutes of silent eating, "do we listen to the storyteller or not?"

Aeden's chest tightened, but she kept her voice steady. "I don't think that we should. What if we release the beasts and they begin to truly destroy things this time? And we can't release them on Clamidas, I refuse it."

"The storyteller only said to release the beasts when the time comes. He didn't say a word about the blood moon," Lorian replied, and Aeden huffed as she scooped more porridge into her bowl.

"It's not only the question of releasing the beasts," Finriel said. "It's whether we should trust his word at all. I don't know how good of an idea it would be to keep the pages for ourselves."

"It would be a dishonor to both of our kings," Tedric said, and Aeden grimaced as his fingers tightened around hers.

"He has a point." Krete spoke for the first time since their arrival. "Perhaps if we return the pages and explain what Egharis told us, King Sorren and the Red King could help."

Tedric nodded in agreement, but Lorian shook his head. "I have a feeling that neither king would do much good."

"You're wrong," Tedric bristled.

"Am I?" Lorian shot back. "It's clear that King Sorren is widely disliked by everyone in this room, including someone who lives in his kingdom. Am I wrong in thinking that he's not to be trusted with the pages?"

Aeden met Lorian's querying gaze and shrugged, her heart beginning to pound in her chest. "I don't know."

"The Red King is the oldest ruler in the realm, and he was the one who helped end the War of Seven Kingdoms. Do you truly think that he'd willingly place the realm into another war?" Tedric asked, his voice blistering with anger.

Lorian used his teeth to rip apart a flaky pastry and chewed thoughtfully before he replied, "I don't trust anyone who has enough power to have lived for over a thousand years."

Tedric snorted. "You are ridiculous."

"I'm careful with where I put my trust." Lorian narrowed his eyes upon Tedric, and Aeden was surprised by the steely power that radiated from the thief.

"Look," Aeden said quickly, "I don't trust King Sorren, nor do I like him. But I'm more scared of the consequences that would come with hiding the pages from him than the ones of letting him handle the situation."

"So, you think that we should give the pages back, then," Finriel said, her words more of a statement than a question.

Aeden realized that there was no anger behind Finriel's words, in fact, the witch's expression was blank, if only slightly thoughtful. Aeden shrugged, and she knew that whatever she said wouldn't change anything. The outcome of their current situation was far out of their power, Aeden knew that. She was bound to her original quest, and she could not break it.

"Krete, couldn't you ask King Drohan what he thinks about this?" Tedric asked. "We all trust him well enough."

Lorian shoved the rest of the flaky pastry in his mouth and rolled his eyes. Aeden felt a sudden desire to hit the thief, but she pushed away the urge. It wasn't worth her energy to beat him when it clearly wouldn't make him any more in favor of returning the pages to the kings.

"I can certainly speak to King Drohan," Krete replied with a nod. "I will ask if we can share our afternoon meal with him, but for now we should try to relax and rest a bit more. There's no use in figuring out what to do with the pages if we're all too tired to actually do something about it."

Lorian's face lit up. "You did promise to take me to the portal."

Krete gave Lorian a tired smile. "Of course. I can take you there once I've met with King Drohan."

❀ 33 ❀

LORIAN

"It's bigger than I expected." Lorian circled the enormous swirling and gurgling blue portal with interest, and then looked over to Krete, who gazed at it proudly. Lorian glanced around the room, which was a black stone cave the size of a large manor. Hundreds of steel chests lined the torchlit walls, and the glow from the cobalt blue portal reflected upon the high stone ceiling.

"I did say that a gnome army could go through it," Krete replied, and Lorian snorted as he went to inspect the chests.

"Suzunne could go through it *with* the army," Lorian chuckled, glancing at the enormous portal once more.

It was at least the size of the large pond that he, Krete, and Tedric had bathed in during their day of rest in Drolatis, perhaps bigger. Lorian wasn't sure how big of a portal stone or how many had been needed to create such a thing, but he didn't ask Krete for fear of a droning monologue.

"What are these?" Lorian asked once he reached the nearest chest and ran a finger over the cold lid.

Krete was at Lorian's side in an instant and shooed him aside with a wave of his hand. Lorian obliged and watched as Krete lifted the lid with a small grunt of effort, and Lorian cursed as he was nearly blinded by the glow of hundreds of small blue stones glittering merrily within the chest.

"Are all the chests filled with these?" Lorian asked, running his hand over the smooth stones in awe.

"Yes, iron helps charge them, which is why they are glowing," Krete said with an obvious note of pride in his voice.

"So why is that one glowing?" Lorian asked, pointing toward the swirling mass of light feet away.

"This part of the mountain is almost completely made of iron. It's the only way for us to be able to have a portal of this dimension and for it to stay charged for more than half a second."

"Interesting," Lorian mused, continuing to feel the small portal stones between his fingers.

"Be careful," Krete said, eyeing a stone that was now held between Lorian's fingers.

Lorian noticed small veins of pulsing light running throughout the stone, though its light had dimmed drastically the moment he took it from the chest.

He looked down at Krete and raised his brows. "I am the master of being careful, don't you worry."

Krete snorted and turned away. "Put it back and close the chest. We've got to go meet the others and King Drohan."

Lorian tucked the stone into his cloak pocket with a smirk and closed the lid of the chest with a dull thud. He turned on his heel and followed Krete out of the iron door, and a small pulse from the stone emanated from his pocket as if it were a second heartbeat. Lorian knew that he would have done better to listen to Krete and put the stone back, but he couldn't help himself. And besides, perhaps it would come in handy for them all in the near future.

Krete and Lorian made their way through winding halls and cavernous rooms, and Lorian allowed his mind to wander as

Krete led them back toward the center of the mountain. He wasn't quite sure how good an idea it was to share the information that Egharis had given them the night before, but Lorian didn't want to tell that to anyone, especially not Krete. He knew how much the gnome loved his king, and Lorian's distaste of most rulers was likely not a very good argument against keeping the new information a secret.

"What do you think about Aeden and Tedric's newfound love?" Lorian asked instead as he and Krete turned a corner.

Krete shook his head. "I'm not so sure how I feel if I'm being quite honest. They are very different from each other."

Lorian noted a hint of hesitation in Krete's voice, but he ignored it and nodded in agreement. He hadn't fully trusted Aeden since the night of capturing the nian, mostly due to her sudden change of mood surrounding Clamidas and her manner of speaking to the beast. There was something else though, something that Lorian could not quite place. He had always noted the energy and connection between her and Tedric, but it made him feel strange, as if there were a greater force involved.

"I just hope that they don't hurt each other." Krete sighed.

"I hope so too," Lorian muttered. "Our situation is already messy as it is. We don't need heartbreak to muddle it up even more."

Krete shot Lorian a look he knew was likely related to his own relationship with Finriel, but he merely smiled. For the first time in ten years, he finally felt like there was hope for their friendship, though he couldn't deny that at times he wondered what it would be like to have more. As the sounds of voices neared, Lorian hastily shoved down thoughts of Finriel blushing and the warm brush of her fingers against his stomach. Krete motioned for him to round one last corner, and Lorian plastered an easy smile on his face as they came to the familiar walkway overlooking the Viure and courtyard below.

King Drohan and their remaining companions were waiting

for them in front of the dining room door, and Lorian blinked in surprise to find that Finriel was engaged in polite conversation with the king as Aeden and Tedric stood close, each looking slightly disheveled and almost too happy in Lorian's opinion. He allowed his attention back to Finriel for a split moment, and his heart gave a quickened thump as he noted that her dark hair was now free from its braid and tumbling in waves down her back. Her forest green dress complemented her caramel skin in a way that nearly made Lorian speechless, though he wouldn't tell her for fear of losing one of his fingers, or any other favored appendages.

"There they are. Krete, mister Grey." King Drohan welcomed them each with a nod, and Lorian smiled and gave the king a small bow in greeting.

"Shall we?" Krete asked, and King Drohan nodded, gesturing toward the dining room with a flourish of his hand.

The companions began to follow the king and Krete, but Lorian stepped forward and grabbed Aeden's wrist before she could slip past. Aeden whirled and shot him a look of confusion, but Lorian ignored it and led her back out of the room so that they were alone.

"What is it?" Aeden asked, crossing her arms over her chest after Lorian let go of her wrist.

"I know that you don't want to release the beasts from the pages, but I think that you have a reason aside from just keeping your little fairy festival safe from harm," Lorian said in a low voice.

"What—"

Lorian held up a hand and cut her off. "I only thought of that just now, so don't ask me why I think so. But if there's one thing I pride myself on, it's knowing when someone is lying."

Aeden's face paled slightly but her expression remained impassive. "I haven't been lying."

"Oh please," Lorian scoffed. "We are all liars in some way."

"Of course you would say that," Aeden snapped. "Your job is to lie and cheat."

Lorian sighed and crossed his arms. "Look, I know that you're hiding something. I don't know what it is, and I'm not asking you to tell me. There are many things that I know and have done that I'll never tell to another living soul."

"Then why are you saying all of this? Are you just trying to make me agree with you to let the beasts out of their pages?" Aeden hissed.

"No, I'm telling you this because I want to make sure that whatever you are hiding doesn't negatively affect Tedric." Aeden fell silent at Lorian's reply, and he swore that her already pale skin turned even more ashen at his words. Lorian continued, "He is like a brother to me at this point. It is my duty to make sure he doesn't get hurt."

"I don't want to hurt him," Aeden whispered, and Lorian noted a hint of sincerity in her meaningless words.

"Then don't." With that, Lorian turned on his heel and left Aeden as he walked into the dining room with a smile. Tedric looked up expectantly, and scowled slightly at Lorian as he sat down across from the commander, next to Finriel.

"Is everything all right?" Finriel asked.

"Oh yes," Lorian replied easily, "just had to discuss Aeden's choice of color for her dress today."

Aeden entered moments later, and Lorian nearly applauded her outstanding performance in attempting to look like absolutely nothing had happened. Her dazed smile was back, if only slightly strained now, and she gave Tedric a small nod as she sat at his side and he murmured something into her ear. Aeden's green eyes met Lorian's for a split second, and she nodded again before quickly looking down at the spread of mouthwatering dishes set in front of them.

"So," King Drohan began, "what did you want to discuss?"

Krete recounted their meeting with the storyteller, not

leaving a single detail out. King Drohan's brow furrowed slightly when Krete mentioned the storyteller's employer and the curse that had been set upon him in order to maintain secrecy, but he listened intently during Krete's tale. Lorian busied himself with eating the mound of potatoes fried in butter and rosemary along with an assortment of other root vegetables cooked in a delicious dark sauce as Krete told the king of the meeting.

"I cannot say that I have heard any news of someone attempting to create an army of beasts, but it is certainly concerning to hear that someone is trying to introduce violence to Raymara once more," King Drohan said, his fingers steepled together as he gazed off at the gleaming red door.

Lorian scooped a large serving of rhubarb and strawberry crumble onto his now empty plate and tucked in, briefly glancing up at Aeden, who had barely eaten anything from her plate. He bit into the mouthwatering crumble with some frustration at her blank expression, which was much like that of his other companions as they waited for the king to continue.

"Are you sure that the storyteller did not give you any information as to who this employer is?" King Drohan asked, and Krete shook his head.

"No, he was taken over by the curse before he could say anything."

"He did say that the employer wished for darkness to return to Raymara, and that he had power," Lorian said through a mouthful of crumble.

Aeden shot him a look. "You said that the employer had immense power, not the storyteller."

"But he didn't say that I was wrong either," Lorian replied, pointing his fork at her.

"Stop, you two," Finriel snapped, and Aeden transferred her glower to her potatoes and stabbed one with her fork.

"With the lack of information, it is hard to say exactly what I would do," King Drohan sighed, ignoring Aeden and Lorian's brief spat.

"Would you recommend that we release the beasts as Egharis told us to do?" Tedric asked, and Aeden visibly stiffened.

King Drohan tapped his fingers together in thought for a moment while Lorian served himself another helping of crumble. His stomach was near bursting, but he didn't care. He wasn't sure if this would be their last meal before having to transport Egharis and the pages back to Keadora, but if so, he wanted to eat as much as he could before going back to dark bread and apples.

"I think that releasing the beasts might be your best chance of safety," King Drohan replied finally. "We can't be sure if or when the storyteller might be called to create the army, but it is better to be prepared when the time comes."

"Once we return him to the Red King, we won't have to worry about him creating the army," Tedric said confidently. "We have the highest level of security in the realm, and I can assure you that the Red King wouldn't allow him to do such a thing."

"We could give King Sorren and the Red King our pages as well then," Finriel offered. "It would be better to let them take care of the situation should anything arise."

"I wouldn't be so sure of that." King Drohan shook his head. "The Red King and King Sorren have been known to act behind the backs of the grand council in order to get what they want. I do not know if I would trust them with the pages."

Lorian pursed his lips and readied himself for Tedric's outburst of defense against his king, and it came within seconds.

"The Red King always makes decisions that are for Keadora's highest good. I would trust him with the pages more than I would trust the five of us."

"Do you actually mean that?" Lorian snorted, but Tedric merely glared at him in reply.

"You five bear more responsibility for the safety of this realm than you may realize, and though I do not know you very well, I trust you more than I do either king," King Drohan replied evenly. "You have Creonid's full support and assurance of safe haven should you wish to keep the pages."

With that, King Drohan stood, and Lorian and his companions stood as well, each bowing low as the king made his way to the door. King Drohan turned toward them once more and gave a small nod.

"I wish upon the goddesses that you will make the right decision. You may stay here as long as you wish."

The king turned away and exited, and Lorian sat back down with a small sigh. He felt more confused than ever, finding personally that King Drohan hadn't been very much help at all. It seemed as if they were alone in this once again.

❦ 34 ❦

FINRIEL

F inriel padded silently down the dark corridor, cold shooting up through her bare feet with every step she took. She'd been walking aimlessly through dimly lit halls for some time now after deciding that sleep would not be greeting her tonight. She thought of Nora, who had been snoring loudly when she left, deciding it best not to wake the mogwa for a simple stroll. She hadn't been sleeping well for the past few nights, as her mind was too busy with thoughts of the prophecy and everything that had happened in the past three moons of her life.

The companions had argued for some time after their meal with King Drohan, and still hadn't come to a compromise. Finriel wasn't sure where she stood, though it seemed that only Tedric and Lorian had very set opinions on the matter. Tedric of course had said that they needed to return to the Red King immediately, and Lorian had insisted that they stay and keep the pages for a little longer. They ended up leaving in a muddle of yells and frustrated curses, and Finriel hadn't seen any of her companions for the rest of the day. Thoughts of keeping the pages filtered through her mind, but she quickly fought them back as her muscles tensed with an all too familiar sense of hopelessness.

Finriel turned to peer through the mouth of a corridor to her left, finding the large branches of the Viure a few meters away. She turned in the opposite direction and headed toward a door to her right, where soft light spilled over the sleek stone floor. She walked for some time down the plain hallway when a sudden draft of cold air blew against her skin, causing her to wrap her cloak closer around her body. The hall curved and she soon found herself in a hall that was lined with enormous carved out spaces in the mountain, much like the opening that Suzunne had flown through two days before. Finriel walked closer and paused as a dark figure caught her attention. But it was only Lorian. Finriel's shoulders relaxed, and she walked to where he was seated.

He was slouched at the very edge of the windowsill, his feet dangling out from the inside of the mountain to float in the air. His dark hair was messy, as if he had just gotten out of bed. His simple clothing was also crumpled, the cream white tunic slightly askew on his filled out frame. Finriel hadn't noticed how much healthier he looked compared to the way he had been at the beginning of their journey, and she forced her gaze away from the bare skin of his collarbone.

"Are you waiting for someone?" Finriel asked softly, stopping a few feet away to look over the scene below. The scarred meadow glittered under a blanket of soft dew, and the sun was starting to peak over the ridge ahead. The warm pink glow of the rising sun gave everything a feeling of tranquility that seeped into Finriel's bones. No wonder Krete was proud to call this place his home.

Lorian lifted his head to look at her, a soft smile on his lips. "Only for you."

Shivers rushed up Finriel's spine at the tone of his voice, but she ignored the feeling and sat down next to him. The white stone pillar felt cool and comforting against her back as she leaned against it, and she watched Lorian as he turned to look back down at the the scorched earth and rocks.

"I now understand why Krete was so homesick all of the time," Lorian mused as he gazed down at the world below. Finriel nodded in agreement and tilted her head back, letting the calmness soak into her bones. The magic in Finriel's veins sung here, pulsating as if a second being lived inside her body.

"How are you feeling?" Finriel asked, and Lorian turned his head to meet her gaze.

"Tired, but I can't sleep. It appears that I can be worried about something other than you for more than a day," Lorian said with a smile, but his expression molded into something of surprise at his own words.

Finriel bit the inside of her cheek in order to stop herself from gasping at his forwardness. Her body hummed with energy, and she hastily squashed the small bit of warmth that bloomed inside of her stomach.

"Let's talk about something other than our quest," Finriel said. "The storyteller and the pages have been keeping me from sleep too."

Lorian nodded in understanding, and looked down. "I missed you."

"I missed you too," Finriel answered, feeling shocked at her own words as they tumbled from her mouth. But it was true. She had missed him terribly, even if she had hated him at the same time. It was now Lorian's turn to look surprised as he rose to his feet. Finriel rolled her eyes and stood up as well, knowing exactly what he was going to do.

Lorian began to pace back and forth with long strides, his arms crossed tightly over his chest. Lines of taut muscles rippled against his shirt sleeves, and Finriel had to drag her gaze away and up as he clenched and unclenched his jaw.

"Stop it," she ordered, throwing her hand out to grab his

shoulder. She hated it when he paced, a habit that he had as a child whenever he was afraid to do something.

Lorian stopped abruptly and turned toward her. In a moment, his arms were wrapped around her, squeezing tightly as he held her against his chest. Finriel wrapped her arms around his waist instinctively and closed her eyes. He felt strong against her, like an anchor holding her down against even the strongest of tides. But then the memories came rushing into her brain like a tidal wave, and the anchor flew from the ground.

"I can't," Finriel gasped, pushing him away with a thrust of her hands. He stumbled backwards with a look of confusion and pain that made her heart ache more than she cared to admit.

"You can't what?" he asked, his voice quiet, as if to trying to keep her calm.

Finriel clenched her fists and stared down at the polished stone under their feet. "It's like my heart and my mind are in a continuous battle and I can't seem to figure out what the best decision is," she started. He took a step closer, but Finriel brought a hand up for him to stop.

"You left me to die. The one person who I thought would be there for me no matter what. I thought you were going to stay and stop Barrin, but you didn't. And now every time I think about you, I feel like my heart wants to burst with joy, yet I also feel like I want to make you burn in the Nether for what you did."

Lorian looked down, and Finriel could tell her words had struck a chord. She kept deathly still, waiting for a reply. Moments passed as he kept his gaze down, clenching and unclenching his fists. Finally, he dragged his eyes of ice upward, and a different kind of shiver crept down her spine. It caressed the pain and eased it to mend, but she wouldn't let it. Not until he simply explained *why*.

"Finriel." Lorian took another step closer and placed his cold, calloused hands upon her cheeks. The anguish marring his features almost made her look away, but their gazes were locked together as he spoke. "I hate myself for what I did to you. I was a coward and I was too scared to save you myself. I thought ordering Nora to save you would be enough, and I'd be able to go with her, but when I got captured, that possibility was wiped away."

Finriel gasped, and Lorian wiped his thumb across her cheek. Only then did she realize that she was crying.

"I want you so bad," he whispered, "and I don't care what I have to keep doing in order to gain your trust or even just your forgiveness. I want my best friend back."

Finriel didn't realize what she was doing until her arms were around his neck and she was crying silently against his chest. His arms immediately wrapped around her waist and squeezed gently, his strong frame tense against hers. He bent his head to rest in the crook of Finriel's neck and released a strangled sigh.

"I tried to come back for you every single day. When I was ordered to steal the dragon's egg from Dragonkeep, I almost didn't and went to look for you instead. But I knew that if I recovered the egg, the thieves would give me enough gold to afford a horse. That way, I would be able to cover more ground." His voice was muffled against Finriel's shoulder as he spoke. "I tried so hard to find you, but as the years passed, I slowly lost hope and fell further into thievery. I hate myself for leaving you."

Finriel's heart clenched inside her chest as she listened to Lorian speak. She had wanted to know what it felt like to be in his embrace for a long while now. It felt liberating and yet strangulating to be this close. Finriel pushed against him slightly, just enough to look into his icy blue eyes that caused so many to shudder.

"I didn't know that you sent Nora to help me," Finriel answered in barely a whisper. Guilt crushed her heart for assuming that Lorian had abandoned her when he had simply been trying to save her.

"I should have gone myself," Lorian growled.

Finriel could feel the self-loathing that was beginning to pulsate through his body. She placed a hand on his chest and shook her head.

"No, you could have gotten killed. The boy was mad, I think he would have stayed true to his word about ending your life."

"That was to be your fate if Nora hadn't come. And then it would have been my fault."

"It's not your fault," Finriel answered with an attempt at a soft smile. Smiling had never something she was good at doing. Lorian shook his head again and looked down. Finriel didn't know how to make him feel better, but she understood now. *She* had been the terrible and foolish one. She'd been so stuck on believing that he'd left her for dead that the thought of anything otherwise had felt implausible

"I'm sorry," Finriel whispered.

Lorian's head shot up at this, his eyes wide with surprise. "Why would you be sorry?"

Finriel let herself gaze at the smooth planes of his neck and collarbone for a moment as she pulled her thoughts together. The open drop and meadow below made Finriel almost dizzy, the light winter breeze ruffling her hair and making her squint. Her blood began to pump faster as she realized just how close they were. Their bodies pressed together, his arms around her waist. Her hands on his chest. He seemed to notice her body tense and began to take a step back, his grip on her loosening.

"I'm sorry because I was too stubborn and pig-headed to realize that you *did* care and hadn't left me on purpose," Finriel began. "I'm sorry because I didn't know that you had been captured trying to come back. I'm sorry that after that day, I hated you so much, until now. I'm sorry because I thought about you every day, thinking about every method I could use to kill you the next time I saw you."

Lorian watched her blankly. Finriel knew that was his expression of not knowing what to say in response, so she pushed on. "I'm sorry that I was so terrible to you ever since we met again in the castle and given this damned quest. I fought against every fiber in my body not to simply send you into flames then and there just so that I could make you go away. But the truth is, I was terrified. I was terrified because I hadn't expected to see you, and I was also terrified because I realized that deep down, I didn't truly hate you."

"Stop," Lorian interjected. "Please, stop."

Finriel closed her mouth, suddenly feeling both empty and yet so full of emotions that she couldn't breathe.

"I don't need your forgiveness," he murmured.

They stared at each other, and Finriel wasn't sure if she was still crying. His heart thumped wildly against her hand, singing in tandem with her own frantic pulse. Lorian's gaze drifted to her lips, and Finriel couldn't help parting them slightly. Her body suddenly felt hot, and his arms tightened slightly as she inched closer.

"Lorian—"

With a deafening crack, the entire mountain shuddered. The floor beneath them wobbled and loose pebbles fell from the high arched stone above their heads. Lorian and Finriel stumbled back and looked at each other in trepidation, glancing around wildly as if they would be able to spot what was causing the mountain to cry. And as abruptly as the rumbling started, it stopped. Lorian was still panting as he looked at Finriel and then toward the hall behind her.

"We need to find the others and see what in the Nether that was."

FINRIEL'S LUNGS WERE BURNING BY THE TIME THEY REACHED THE courtyard, which was now in chaos. Gnomes rushed around them frantically, calling and babbling to each other in their common tongue. Lorian took hold of Finriel's hand to stop her from being barreled over by a group of gnomes. She hated the fire that still curled deliciously in her stomach at the thought of their touching skin, and she shoved away the mortification of how close they had been. *You wanted to get closer.* She silently cursed herself and shook her head. Now was not the time to be caught up her feelings, no matter how overwhelming or confusing they were.

"We need to find Krete," Finriel yelled over the din.

Lorian nodded and they began to search the crowd for a sign of the gnome, or any of their companions for that matter. It didn't take long, and Finriel pointed at Krete before waving him over.

"What happened?" Finriel called.

"Someone used the portal without permission," Krete panted as he approached, his eyes wide with worry.

"Well, that isn't too bad, then, is it?" Lorian offered with a shrug.

Krete shook his head and looked between the witch and the thief. "It's just that, though," he gulped. "Egharis has disappeared."

All color drained from Lorian's face and Finriel's stomach gave an uncomfortable flop. That was not a good sign.

"What do you mean?" she asked. "Is he not in the dungeons?"

Krete shook his head again in reply and Lorian cursed.

Just at that moment, a shout from the tier above them made the three companions look up to find Tedric walking briskly toward the stairs that led down to the square. His blonde hair was disheveled and tangled, and his face was set into a hard mask. As Tedric approached them, he roughly ran his fingers through his hair and met all of his friends' worried glances with one to match.

"Aeden is gone, and I think she took both of our pages."

Krete looked down and sighed, his face falling. "Oh, no."

"Do you know something that we don't?" Tedric asked, his voice a razor sharp edge.

The gnome opened his mouth to respond but then closed it again, his shoulders hunched with discomfort. Lorian took a step forward with a raised brow.

"Krete, what is it?" Finriel urged.

"It's Aeden," Krete replied sheepishly. "She must have taken Egharis through the portal."

Tedric took Krete by the collar of his shirt and lifted him off the ground so that he was at eye level. Krete gasped and thrashed his legs as the warrior growled, "You're lying."

Krete shook his head urgently, his stormy eyes widening.

Finriel put a hand on Tedric's arm. "Let him go, Tedric. Aeden's actions are not his fault."

"Besides, if you let him live, he could actually tell us where she went," Lorian added.

Tedric held the gnome for a moment longer before letting out a huff and dropping him. Krete stumbled as he landed on the cobbled ground and sucked in a deep breath.

"Where did she go?" Tedric demanded.

"She's most likely halfway back to Proveria by now," Krete stammered. "King Sorren gave her a deadline of returning with the pages by Clamidas."

Tedric cursed colorfully and grabbed at his already wild hair. "She didn't tell me that."

Finriel shrugged. "Well, the quest is over, and we were all going our separate ways."

"But *we* were supposed to be the ones to take the storyteller to *our* king," Tedric snapped. "That was not her duty."

"I'm not sure that we can do anything about that now," Krete sighed, and Tedric shook his head.

"No, I can't accept that," Tedric growled. "We were in charge of the storyteller, no matter what our decision about the pages was going to be. We need to go after her and get Egharis before she reaches the fairy king."

"I agree," Finriel replied. "Aeden has potentially caused an even larger disagreement between Proveria and Keadora than we can afford."

The thought of seeing her mother sent another flop through Finriel's stomach, and her resolve set in. They needed to get Egharis back. She would not allow herself to have spent three moons of her life trekking through the realm just to have failed at her mission, and especially to have failed at finally being able to meet her mother for the first time.

"We need to go after her then," Tedric replied at once. "If we leave now, we could get a good head start."

Krete shook his head. "The portal needs time to rejuvenate, it could take days."

"We do have a dragon at our disposal, if you haven't forgotten," Lorian chimed in.

"We would be too visible, and besides, what do you think the sight of a black dragon flying through the sky would bring to anyone who happened to look up as we pass by?" Finriel replied, and Lorian gave her an exasperated look that popped the happy bubble still managing to hang onto her heart.

"It's the only option that we have that will get us there fast enough," Lorian said. "If we travel through Naebatis, the mist cover will hide us from any travelers or other residents of the kingdom."

"He's right," Tedric agreed. "It's the only way. We can skirt around any villages once we enter Proveria and have Suzunne land somewhere far enough away from Anemoi Citadel in order not to cause any attention."

"But it's Clamidas," Krete interjected. "There will barely be any part of the forest that won't be swarming with fairies."

"We're going to have to try," Tedric growled, and it was clear to Finriel that his patience was wearing thin.

"Okay, but I'm going with you," Krete replied. "I've known Aeden since she was a child. It's my duty as her friend to make sure that she is okay."

"You can ask her why she broke our agreement as well," Lorian muttered, and Finriel felt a flicker of anger as she silently agreed with the thief.

"Let's get changed and gather our things," Tedric said. "We can meet in Suzunne's alcove in ten minutes."

"What about Nora? She can't travel on Suzunne," Finriel said, and bit her lip with worry.

"She will have to stay here," Krete said. "I will arrange for Mott to care for her until we return. If you don't come back here in time, I will bring her to Keadora myself once this is over."

Finriel fought back a sudden burning sensation behind her eyes and forced herself to nod. She had never been separated from Nora for more than a few days since the mogwa had been gifted to her by the elf, but she knew that it needed to be done. She took a deep settling breath and nodded to Krete.

"Okay. Let's go."

❦ 35 ❦

TEDRIC

"Hello there," Suzunne greeted cheerfully as Tedric entered the large chamber that had been sectioned off for the dragon.

Finriel, Krete, and Lorian made their way into the clearing behind him, and Suzunne gazed down upon the four companions with calm golden eyes and sighed.

"I see you are all in your power outfits once again, what's the occasion?"

"We need you to fly us to Proveria," Krete answered.

Suzunne chuckled and looked upon his master with amusement. When no one else laughed, the dragon quieted.

"You can't tell me you are serious."

The four companions nodded in unison.

"We need to get there before sundown preferably," Tedric said with a stiff edge to his voice.

Suzunne angled his head down to inspect the warrior closer. "Your aura has changed," he murmured. "It's a lovely color. It reminds me of—"

"Can we stop speaking of auras and get a move on?" Tedric interrupted sharply.

"As you wish," Suzunne huffed. "Get on."

They climbed onto the dragon one by one, being careful to mind the more sensitive scales as they settled between the large spikes on his back.

"Is everyone ready?"

"Yes, just go," Tedric demanded from his seat before the frontmost spikes.

They flew over the vast expanses of meadows that spread away from Creonid Mountain, wind rushing through their ears as Suzunne's giant membranous wings pushed them through the sky. Tedric's face was set into a grim stare as they flew over the edge of Creonid and he felt a shiver of them getting closer to Naebatis, the coldest and second cursed kingdom in Raymara.

Tedric's thoughts drifted to Aeden and a shaky sigh tore from his mouth as pain squeezed at his heart. He simply didn't understand why she had gone without warning. She had probably left in hopes of saving him from her father, both of them really. She could use what little magic she had to hide her feelings, and Tedric would have to forget. But he couldn't. His body still thrummed with the memory of her smile and the whisper of her touch. Tedric may very well have been putting himself in a trap, but it was worth the risk. Anger then replaced whatever feelings he had. Aeden had betrayed him, she had betrayed all of them. It had never been the deal that she take Tedric's page and Egharis when the time came for them to go their separate ways. Tedric needed to find his page, and that was what he was going to do. He was the Commander of the Ten before anything else, and it was about time he began to act like it again.

Tedric could see the edge of Naebatis clearly through the shimmering white wall of swirling mist and snow. Tedric had never been to Naebatis, and the stories he had heard as a child never made him too keen on going. Everyone knew the ice kingdom had once been a place of warmth and bounty, but the curse had turned the land into a harsh and eternal winter. Travelers were the holders of the kingdom, and legend had it that they were some of the only beings who thrived in the frigid climate.

Cold air suddenly stung Tedric's face, and he squinted as they passed through the shimmering border into Naebatis. *The kingdom of eternal winter was clearly an understatement,* Tedric thought as he wrapped his thick cloak tighter around his body.

The land was covered in snow as far as his eyes could see, aside from jagged black rocks that protruded through the ground like daggers and thick pine trees that dusted areas of the small rolling hills. As Tedric looked around, he noticed that everything was shrouded in a thin layer of mist and small white speckles of snow dusted Suzunne's dark back like a blanket of stars.

But the air was so still.

Too still.

Even as they pushed through the sky, there had been wind rushing through Tedric's ears as they had flown through Creonid. Now, the beating of Suzunne's wings caused nothing but a light breeze. The lack of life sent a chill down Tedric's back. There wasn't even a cloud in the sky, only the overwhelming mist and relentless snow. And the cold. Movement below caught Tedric's eye, and he held the dragon's spike a little bit tighter as he peered down.

It was hard to tell exactly what he was seeing, and he squinted as he watched a white mass bound through the snow. It was large, probably half the size of Suzunne if they had been on the ground. Its long fur was white, and the creature nearly blended completely into the snow as it made its way toward a dark cave a little ways off. Tedric gulped as spatters of red fell onto the snow behind the beast as it ran, and he realized that there was something dead in its mouth. *Likely a deer*, Tedric grimaced, and looked forward once more as the creature disappeared into the cave.

"Legend has it that there are yetis in Naebatis," Lorian offered from behind Tedric.

"Your stupid jokes are not helping, Lorian," Tedric grumbled. Maybe yesterday he would have laughed at the jest. But not now, not when his chest stung like an angry beehive and confused thoughts swam around his brain like scared fish. The only joke that he needed right now was that Aeden's actions were not out of betrayal and she hadn't truly meant to rip his heart from his chest.

"It's not a joke if it's true," Lorian grumbled, and Tedric gave him a foul hand gesture in reply.

"What's our plan when we arrive?" Finriel asked, cutting off the slew of profanities Tedric was about to aim at the thief.

"The fairies have some of the highest security in the realm, so I doubt that all four of us will be able to do anything sneaky," Lorian said with a definite note of disappointment in his voice, and Tedric looked down at Suzunne's back in angry contemplation.

"What do you think, Krete?" Tedric asked, turning his head slightly so that he could see his friend.

Krete looked up at him and shrugged, though Tedric saw a note of worry on the gnome's face before he looked down again. "I say that we go to the king directly and speak honestly," Krete said after a few moments of silence. "His say is higher than that of anyone in Proveria, including Aeden."

"What are you saying? We just waltz in and ask for the storyteller to be returned to us?" Lorian asked, and Krete shrugged again.

"It's the only thing that would work that I can think of. It would be a bad idea for King Sorren to make a move against the Red King if he's aware that the Red King made a claim upon Egharis first."

"Krete's right," Tedric agreed, feeling an inkling of strength return. "King Sorren would be a fool not to listen to us. Even if we fail in getting Egharis back ourselves, we can at least ensure that King Sorren delivers him directly to the Red King."

Finriel nodded in agreement and Lorian cursed colorfully as Suzunne banked to the left, sending Tedric's stomach lurching slightly. He just hoped that he would be able to find Aeden after this was all over. He needed to ask why she had kept her deadline of returning to Proveria by the blood moon from him, and why she had taken the storyteller and both of their pages. Perhaps he didn't know her as well as he thought.

SUZUNNE'S WINGS BROKE THROUGH THE MIST BARRIER AFTER what felt like ages, and they found themselves flying within the fork between Proveria and Keadora. There was a slight shimmer in the air, and Tedric looked to the right, toward the wide open fields of Keadora in the distance. A pang of longing shot through his chest at the sight, and at that moment, Tedric realized just how much he truly missed his homeland. He missed his life as a commander, where the only thing he had to worry about was how many of his men had gotten drunk in the tavern and the names of the countless women he had slept with. But that life was far gone now, no matter how badly he wanted it back.

Suzunne banked away from Keadora, and they pushed through the border into Proveria. A shiver crawled its way down Tedric's spine, a feeling of unease washing over him. There was something not right in the air, as if the entire kingdom was holding its breath in preparation for the blood moon and Clamidas.

"There's something wrong," Tedric muttered. The observation was not toward anyone in particular, and the overwhelming silence turned his shivers into ice.

"What do you mean? I thought all festivals were held in complete silence," Lorian joked.

"I will throw you off this dragon if you don't shut up," Finriel replied. Though her tone still dripped with sarcasm,

Tedric was sure that there was a certain amount of truth to what she said. He felt a surge of gratitude toward Finriel, Krete, and even Lorian. For the first time in a long time, Tedric felt like he had a family that was not only bound by duty.

"We're approaching the castle," Suzunne said after some time in silence. Indeed they were, and Tedric's body tensed as he spotted the crystal spires of Anemoi Citadel peaking through the trees.

"Land in the clearing below," Krete said. "It should be far enough from the festival circles for the fairies not to notice our arrival."

Suzunne began his descent into the small clearing that Krete had indicated, and soon they were sliding off the dragon and standing amongst the meridiem and towering trees. Wisps of clouds were tinged with soft pinks and oranges, and the sky was beginning to come aflame with the sunset. The blood moon would be upon them shortly.

"I think that it would be best for you to go back into the page," Krete told Suzunne once the companions had climbed down to the soft mossy ground.

Tedric's legs felt slightly like jelly from being seated for so long, and he found that he felt much better now that he was on the ground. He looked between Krete and Suzunne, noting Suzunne's enormous body beginning to stiffen with surprise.

"And why is that?" Suzunne asked. "Do you not trust me after I have helped you twice now?"

"Of course we trust you," Krete said. "It's just that fairies are very territorial and it could be dangerous for you to be alone in the forest when you have already caused damage to their land once."

"It's also the blood moon, and I don't think that finding a black dragon in the midst of their celebrations tonight is a very good idea," Tedric added, and Suzunne gave a loud harrumph.

"I suppose you're right. Promise me that you will let me out as soon as you can though. I hate how stuffy it is in there," Suzunne sighed, and Krete gave him a relieved smile.

"Thank you. Yes, of course."

Moments later, Suzunne touched the page outstretched in Krete's hand and disappeared into it with the same bright light as the other beasts. Krete quickly rolled the parchment up and tucked it into one of the many pockets in his vest before looking up at Tedric and the others.

"You do realize that you might have lied to him," Finriel said. "He'll likely be destroyed if you give the page back to the king."

Krete gave her a strained smile and nodded. "I know."

A lump of sadness formed in Tedric's throat, and for once he actually felt a twinge of regret about returning the pages. But they had to give them back. It was their duty, his duty. Tedric took a step away and gestured toward Krete.

"Lead the way."

Krete gave Tedric a tight-lipped smile and started past him, leading them toward the thicket of forest that loomed ahead. Tedric was certainly not expecting to be back in Millris Forest so soon, if at all. He wasn't quite sure how they were going to get back home before Aeden had left so unexpectedly, but Tedric had to admit that his thoughts hadn't gone that far forward after their night together. Tedric's chest clenched, and he barely took in the strange sounds and flowery scented air that ruffled his hair as he walked behind Krete in silence. He could only think of Aeden and how happy he had felt during the short time they'd spent together, *truly* together. He was not sure why she had left, but he needed to find out, if only to save his own heart.

Some time passed, and the meridiem moss now lit their way through the forest. Tedric angled his head upwards to look at the small amount of sky that was visible through the enormous pines to find that it had deepened into purples and darkening blue.

"It's nearly nightfall," Krete said, breaking up the silence.

"That means that the festival will begin soon, doesn't it?" Finriel asked from behind Tedric, and Krete nodded.

"Yes, as soon as the moon begins to rise, we should be able to hear music and the festival will begin. Make sure not to focus on the music, it has magical properties that can cause some to be lured into the celebration circles."

"That doesn't sound so bad," Lorian said easily.

"Fairies change during Clamidas in a way that is not always good. Typically those who are lured into the circles are toyed with in ways that I don't want to repeat," Krete said sternly, and Lorian fell silent.

Tedric briefly wondered if Aeden would be in one of those circles tonight, but quickly forced away the thought with a surge of anger. He would find her even if she was in one of those circles. He just needed to speak to her. He needed to understand.

Krete suddenly stopped mid-step, and Tedric had to jump to the side in order not to slam into his companion.

"What is it?" Tedric asked as he came to stand next to Krete, who was looking down upon the ground at a path made of gleaming silver stones.

"It has to be the path to the castle," Lorian said. "Only fairies would use such unnecessarily precious stones to lead to their capital."

Tedric forced down the defensive growl in his throat, aware that Lorian did have a point.

"We should follow it then," Finriel said easily, but Lorian came up next to Tedric and shook his head.

"I can go find an alternate route to the castle. It would be rude to just waltz in, especially on such a special day for the fairies," Lorian said.

"Entering a king's home without an invitation is rude on any occasion," Finriel pointed out.

"I've been welcomed into more high class places entering through an alternate route than I have being caught and brought in through the front doors like a common criminal," Lorian retorted.

"We can start on the path and you can look for an alternate route. If you find one, then find us and we can go your way," Tedric cut in, not much in the mood to watch another argument between the two.

Lorian seemed satisfied with this, and took a step toward Finriel. The ground tilted under Tedric's feet and he nearly fell over with surprise as Lorian squeezed Finriel's hand and winked before setting off through the meridiem-lit forest without a sound.

"What was that?" Tedric spluttered, and Finriel's faint smile quickly disappeared as she looked away from the direction in which Lorian had just gone.

"Nothing," Finriel snapped.

"Let's keep going," Krete said urgently. "We need to reach the castle before the festivities begin."

Finriel shrugged and started up the path, Tedric following soon after. Each step felt like both an eternity and no time at all as they walked in single file. Tedric's thoughts quarreled with each other as he walked in silence, moving between surprise at Finriel and Lorian's sudden demonstration of warmth toward one another and his own pained heart.

He was hurt, yet he was slowly beginning to understand. She had left without saying goodbye in hopes of saving him, but taking the page that did not belong to her was wrong, and the pull of responsibility to the Red King would have to be greater than the pull of his heart.

Not even two minutes after they had begun to follow the path, a faint rustling in the trees that was different than that of the birds and rodents caught Tedric's attention.

"What is that sound?" he asked.

"Maybe it's Lorian coming back," Finriel said hopefully, but

Tedric doubted that Lorian had found a way to the castle from the tops of the trees.

"Oh no," Krete groaned, and Tedric followed the gnome's gaze upwards toward the rustling sounds.

Tedric's stomach gave a flop and he drew his sword as six fairies in golden armor descended upon them from the highest branches. Their descent seemed to be controlled, and after a moment, Tedric was able to make out the faint shimmering ghost of wings flapping behind each of the guard's backs. They each drew a long, thin blade once their golden boots touched the ground, and headed toward the companions with stony expressions.

"You have been found trespassing upon the silver path, and are required to be escorted to the castle." The fairy who spoke looked similar to Aeden, but his bone structure was even more pronounced. His light brown hair was long and straight, the front of his hair braided and held together at the back of his head. His pointed ears were long and seemed to move slightly, as if constantly listening to his surroundings. The other guards looked similar, but their hair was cropped.

"Tedric, put down your sword," Krete whispered desperately. "I know these folk. We have a better chance of getting Egharis and your page back if we cooperate."

Tedric spared a glance at Krete, who was frozen in place with his hands plastered to his sides. Tedric sighed and shoved his blade back into its scabbard, going against all of his training. *Commander Eldron would be ashamed of your actions if he were still alive,* Tedric thought bitterly. He had been careless and insensitive toward his late commander to have even entertained the idea of allowing a fairy into their company at the beginning of the quest, yet he had, and now their hearts were entangled. He forced down another wave of anger as the fairy guards took up position around Tedric and his companions, two on either side and one behind them, while the apparent head guard went to stand in front of Krete.

"Why didn't you take our weapons?" Tedric asked in a near growl as the guards began to lead them up the path.

The lead guard did not look back as he replied, "Raymara is a peaceful realm, and besides, it would be more entertaining if you actually had a weapon, should you decide to cause any trouble."

The path inclined slightly as they walked the final distance to the castle, and Tedric was half glad that Lorian had disappeared before they'd been caught. Perhaps he would be able to save them if things went south. It was still unnervingly quiet, but the moon hadn't risen yet. He wondered if any music would be heard from this far up and away from the heart of the forest.

They were led through a large birch wood gate woven with silver, and they entered a covered walkway that wrapped around the outside of the castle, which Tedric could now see was shaped in a crescent moon. Tedric had assumed that there would be parties and dancing, but then he remembered what Aeden had said about the castle being deserted and ghostlike during their conversation in the cave. He gave a slight shiver as they continued. She had been understating how strange it felt to enter through the deserted, dimly lit crystal walls.

A large courtyard sat before them, and rich emerald grasses and yellow flowers filled the open area. A silver fountain depicting a woman with a crescent moon crown trickled with sparkling clear water in the center of the courtyard, and a shaded path made from silver stone circled it. The very air around them seemed to be holding its breath, and Tedric fought down a shudder. Apart from servants and a few courtiers milling about, the place was practically deserted.

Tedric let his gaze travel upward toward the rest of the castle. Large clear windows overlooked the forest beyond, and the walls of the tall castle were made entirely of crystal. Veins of silver and gold ran through it, and the crystal itself seemed to change color with each second of the setting sun. The fairy guards nudged them forward, and they were led through the giant white wood doors of the castle. The inside was mostly barren, and only a few fairy servants walked here and there as they carried on with their tasks. They were led down the crystal halls and up a silver set of stairs. They rounded another corner, toward a set of white doors flanked by fairy guards on either side.

"Where are you taking us?" Krete asked.

"To the king, of course."

Tedric tensed at the words, cold sweat beginning to run down his back. The guards at the door stepped forward and opened it, and the companions were led into the throne room. Like the rest of the castle, the room was mostly barren, apart from a large white tapestry at the far end of the room bearing a blood red moon encircled by silver leaves. Two crystal thrones were set upon a raised dais that looked upon the rest of the room.

But it was who was seated upon the thrones that made Tedric stop in his tracks and his blood run cold. King Sorren sat on one throne, enrobed in white silk. His long hair was done in a similar fashion as the head fairy guard, the darkness of his tresses contrasting with his white skin. But it was not the king that made Tedric's muscles and chest spasm in pain. It was the woman sitting on the throne next to the king.

Aeden.

36

TEDRIC

"Aeden?"

The world tilted dangerously below Tedric's feet as she met his gaze with an impassive stare. She was dressed in a similar fashion as the king, but instead of thick robes, her white outfit consisted of hard leather pants and a bodice with gold trimming along the sleeves. Her violet hair was loose, and it tumbled down her shoulders like a waterfall. Aeden's green eyes pierced into his, no emotion showing through her beautiful face as she looked down upon the companions.

"You will refer to my daughter as Your Highness, human," King Sorren replied smoothly, his voice almost musical as he examined Tedric and his companions.

Tedric stumbled back a step, receiving a hard nudge from the fairy guard behind him. Of course she was a princess. The way she carried herself, the way she spoke to others. It was so painfully obvious.

"Why didn't you tell me?" Tedric whispered, and he could have sworn her expression fell for a split second.

Her throat bobbed, and she blinked at him before a devilish grin grew on her red lips. "I didn't think it was necessary to make you even more in love with me. We all know how much you just fall to your knees for royalty."

Tedric pressed his lips together and forced back a groan of pain. His vision blurred at the sting of her words, but he blinked back his tears and forced his gaze up once more. The king turned to Aeden, and Tedric could see the similarities between the two of them. How could he have been so blind to not have realized it? The fairy king had visited Keadora on many occasions in recent moons, and Tedric had escorted him to and from the throne room almost every time.

The fairy king clapped his hands in satisfaction and smiled down upon them, but Tedric could not possibly understand the smug look on his face. Krete stepped forward to stand next to Tedric, and he could see sadness clearly written across the gnome's face.

"Ah," the king said, "Krete of Creonid Mountain. I must say, you have looked better on past occasions."

Krete bowed his head slightly. "I am in good health nonetheless, Your Majesty."

"I am glad to hear it," King Sorren replied. "However, you and your two companions here have been captured for trespassing on the silver path without invitation, and for that there must be consequences."

Finriel stepped forward with a small curtsy. "Forgive us, King Sorren, but we have good reason to have come to you."

"Oh?" King Sorren replied with mild interest as he looked down his nose at the witch.

Finriel glanced at Tedric questioningly, but all he could manage was a small gesture for her to continue. He wasn't sure if he was currently able to speak or if only a loud string of curses and perhaps a roar of pain would come out instead. Finriel gave him a look of sympathy that made him almost as surprised as he was by Aeden sitting upon the throne before them.

"We were sent on a quest by the Red King to recover three

beasts released by the storyteller, who is, to our understanding, in your kingdom now." Finriel shot Aeden a glare as she spoke the last words, and Aeden simply returned the look with a haughty stare.

"My daughter has told me of your success in recovering the three beasts." King Sorren nodded. "But that does not explain what you are doing in my kingdom."

"I was about to get to that," Finriel snapped, and Tedric watched as King Sorren tensed at her casual tone. "The thing is, we were also told to—" Finriel paused and furrowed her brow as if confused, then continued, "we were told—"

Finriel groaned suddenly and clutched at her head, and Tedric barely had time to rush to her side and take her by her shoulders to stop her from falling upon the silver floor. Finriel sagged against Tedric and groaned again. Concern filled his gut as he helped her sit on the floor, completely disregarding the etiquette he knew they were breaking.

"Are you okay?" Tedric asked, and Finriel began to rock back and forth, her hands clutching at her temples.

"There's someone inside my head."

"What?" Tedric blanked, and on impulse looked up at Aeden.

His heart gave a painful spasm as he found both Aeden and King Sorren gazing down upon Finriel's crumpled form with mild interest but nothing more. Tedric tore his gaze away from Aeden, who was plainly refusing to meet his hard stare, and brought his attention back down to Finriel.

"Who's in your head?" Tedric asked, but Finriel shook her head.

"I can't … it hurts," she whimpered.

Krete rushed over to Finriel and knelt by her side, taking Tedric's place in supporting her by the shoulders. The gnome bore an expression of agony, but Tedric found himself angry at him too. He'd kept Aeden's secrets from them until it was too late. Krete gave him a pleading look, but Tedric merely shook his head and shoved down his anger toward the gnome. He would have a talk with him later.

"Is King Sorren doing this?" Tedric growled, attempting to keep his voice as low as possible.

"Your whispering will not stop me from being able to hear you," King Sorren replied for Krete, who had started to respond. "But I am afraid I am not the one who has caused your friend to fall unceremoniously upon the ground."

Tedric clenched his fists, fighting down the roiling anger that swelled inside of him. He knew that he could not lay a hand upon the king, but he was beginning to find it quite difficult to keep himself from running onto the dais and running the man through where he sat.

Finriel let out another scream, and a pained sob tore through her body. "Get out of my head," she croaked, slapping a shaking hand against the crystal floor.

The sound of commotion outside the grand white doors made Tedric jump to his feet and grip the hilt of his sword. The doors burst open, and Tedric nearly fell to his knees again as the Red King swept into the room.

The Red King was dressed in his usual blood-red robes and his long white hair was braided back. His black eyes glittered as he surveyed the room with mild interest. The remaining members of the Ten flanked him on either side, and their faces flashed with recognition as they looked at him. Tedric's gaze met Bordin's, the archer of the Ten. The man clenched his jaw and gave Tedric a curt nod.

The Red King took a step closer, and Tedric forced his body into a low bow.

"My Lord."

"Ah," the Red King said coolly. "My favorite commander has returned. Yet I see that you have returned to the wrong kingdom."

Tedric swallowed the lump in his throat as he rose, not meeting the king's dark eyes.

"My Lord, I—"

Tedric was cut off by Finriel, who let out a rattling breath that echoed through the crystal walls. Tedric tilted his head to find her staring at the Red King with hatred in her caramel eyes.

"Get. *Out.*"

The Red King gave her a humorless smile before he looked back up to the fairy king, confusion muddling Tedric's nerves at their exchange. *Does Finriel mean that the king is inside her head?* Tedric shook the ridiculous thought from his mind. The Red King was a good man, and there was no reason for him to do such a terrible thing to the witch.

"My Lord, we were not expecting you," the fairy king said coolly.

"I have to admit that I was not planning on gracing your kingdom with a visit, yet I decided it was the perfect day to retrieve my storyteller," the Red King replied. "Where is he? I know that he is within these walls."

Tedric frowned at the Red King's words, unsure if he misheard the king referring to the storyteller as *his*. The walls seemed to close in slightly and he took a steadying breath, resting his hand upon the pummel of his sword for support. He kept his eyes upon the Red King, not daring to look up at Aeden or Finriel, who was still being held up by Krete.

King Sorren's smile faltered, and he cleared his throat before speaking. "How did you know of the storyteller's whereabouts? Last time we had been informed of anything, he had been seen crossing through the Farridian forest."

The Red King chuckled and took another step toward the dais. "Oh, come now, Sorren. Did you really think that I would allow for my storyteller to be brought into your kingdom without my knowledge?"

King Sorren blinked. "I am afraid that I do not follow what you are saying."

The Red King gave a booming laugh that startled Tedric. He had never heard the Red King do more than let out a small sigh of amusement from time to time.

"It is your daughter, of course, King Sorren. She has been the greatest help in keeping me informed about tonight."

"What?" King Sorren roared, and Tedric did stumble backwards a step now.

Tedric forced himself to look at Aeden, who didn't appear surprised at all by the Red King's outrageous comment. In fact, she looked almost pleased with herself as she turned to regard her father with a cold smile.

"Aeden, no," Krete whispered, and Tedric looked down to find the gnome shaking with tears shimmering in his eyes.

Finriel was still clutching at her head and seemed too occupied with the pain to realize what had just happened, though Tedric's mind was still reeling at what the Red King meant by all of this.

"Explain. Now," King Sorren growled, and Aeden opened her mouth to speak. "Not you, foolish girl," King Sorren snapped, and Aeden's pale cheeks flushed with anger.

"This quest was meant to clean up the mess that my storyteller created, but I decided to turn it into a little game in order for us all to gather here tonight," the Red King began, ignoring King Sorren's outburst. "It has worked excellently, and now in order for the game to be finished, I must ask for you to return the storyteller and pages that are in your possession to me."

Tedric didn't know what to do. He wasn't even quite sure he was still standing, as he seemed to have lost feeling in his entire body. Was the Red King saying that *he* was Egharis' deadly employer? Had he truly planned their quest out of some sick desire to make war return to Raymara? Tedric tightened his grip on his sword until his knuckles turned white, the cool feeling of

metal and leather biting his skin the only thing keeping him tethered to reality. He didn't know how to feel or what to think.
Perhaps the Red King was just bluffing in order to get out of this
mess.

"Now," the Red King said, breaking the deafening silence,
"where is my storyteller?"

"I will not bring him to you, especially not on the night of
our sacred festival," King Sorren spat.

The Red King's black eyes glimmered with amusement. "I
have no care for your holidays. Bring him to me now."

"I will not," King Sorren snarled. "The pages will be safer in
Proveria, locked up in a vault that no one can find."

"You will surely be able to find them," the Red King replied
calmly, yet Tedric noted an edge to his tone.

King Sorren continued, ignoring the Red King, "The storyteller will also remain in my custody until further decisions are
made about his future."

"I have the two pages," Aeden announced, ignoring her
father's look of disgust in her direction.

The Red King smiled up at her and nodded, indicating for her
to continue with a flourish of his hand. Bile rose in Tedric's
throat as she opened her perfect mouth and spoke words of
poison.

"I also know where Egharis is. I will give him to you if you
wish it, and those three have the remaining pages," Aeden
finished, pointing her finger in Tedric's direction without looking
at him.

Tedric barely held back the rage that threatened to boil over
inside as she spoke, now standing before her throne in all of her
despicable glory. He did not know if he hated or was in awe of
her strength as she stepped forward and off the dais, ignoring her
father's barked order to return to his side.

Krete and Finriel scrambled out of the way as she walked
toward the king, and Tedric thought he saw Krete whisper some-

thing to Finriel before he slipped to the far end of the room, where an impressive open window overlooked Millris Forest. The blood moon was beginning to rise, and the dimly lit room was slowly being bathed in red.

"There's nothing you can do, dear old father." Aeden reached into her coat and began to withdraw something. "In fact, I'll give the pages to you right now."

"No," the fairy king snapped. "Guards, detain her."

But the guards were too late. Aeden withdrew the pages and handed them to the Red King, who nodded at her with a small smile. She took a step back and curtsied, and a sense of unease washed over Tedric at the exchange. There was something very wrong going on.

"Bordin, take these," the Red King said, and Bordin stepped from the line of men and took the pages from the king.

Tedric tried to catch Bordin's attention, but his old friend ignored his small hiss and fell back into line, his hard gaze focused upon the floor with trained blankness. Tedric cursed internally and whipped his head back toward King Sorren as the fairy king stood in a whirl of white fabric.

"Aeden, how dare you!" King Sorren bellowed. "Guards, now."

The fairy guards moved at once, seizing both of her arms. She yelled and struggled against them, but they were like stone. With another gesture from the fairy king, the remaining guards began to surround the Red King, and the Ten closed in behind him.

The Red King chuckled and shook his head. "I am afraid that you have made the wrong choice, my friend."

With a snap of his fingers, the Ten sprung into action. Tedric froze, unsure where to go or who to protect as the clash of metal upon metal rang through his ears and more fairy guards spilled into the throne room. The Red King was walking calmly away from the carnage, and a jolt of surprising fury ran through

Tedric's limbs at the sight of his king. Aeden continued to fight against the guards, who were now leading her away from the fighting men and back up toward the dais, where King Sorren stood with anger blazing in his eyes.

Tedric turned and ran toward Finriel by the back wall. She was slowly rising to her feet, looking as though she might be sick. He offered her a steadying hand as she took large gulps of air that was now thick with the coppery scent of blood.

"Are you all right?"

Finriel nodded. "The pain is gone."

"What did you mean when you said that the Red King needed to get out?" Tedric asked, and Finriel's expression turned stony.

"He was the one using my brain as a playground," she growled, and Tedric's mouth went dry.

"I don't understand it," Tedric breathed, and was about to ask Finriel if she could walk when she cursed and pointed at something behind him.

Tedric whirled around and drew his blade as a stray fairy guard made her way toward them, her thin blade raised in a dangerous arc over her head. Tedric sidestepped away from her attack and disarmed her with ease before knocking her cold to the ground with his fist. He would not kill if he could avoid it. He couldn't risk the potential of his misery getting any worse than it already was.

"Let's go," Finriel said, coming to stand at Tedric's side.

He nodded and they set off into the heart of the fight. The world became a blur as the clashing of swords rang through his ears. A fairy guard ran toward him with his weapon outstretched, and Tedric swirled to the side, blocking the blow and slashing a shallow wound in the fairy's side from behind. The guard groaned and fell to the floor. The thousand-year peace had undoubtedly made all races in Raymara unused to battle, but the Ten were always prepared, as they trained with each other and used the few unlucky bastards who broke the law as target practice, though never killing them. Tedric knew how to fight, and now the taste of it was swimming through his veins like a drug.

Tedric glanced upwards at a movement below the dais, finding Krete attempting to make his way back into the throng. Tedric clenched his jaw and fought off another fairy guard, careful to avoid any members of the Ten, who looked at him warily, clearly unsure whether to consider him friend or foe. A yelp of pain sounded from behind, and Tedric whirled around with another curse of surprise to find Lorian wielding a bloodied sword as he fought off a rather small yet skilled fairy guard. The thief bore his same easy smile as he slashed at the fairy's free hand, causing a large pool of blood to well up and spatter to the ground, along with the fairy's index finger. The fairy screeched in pain and fell to the ground, clutching at his missing finger with a roar.

"Looks like you've dropped something," Lorian said easily, and turned toward Tedric.

"How in the Nether did you get in here?" Tedric bellowed, barely blocking a stray sword that slashed by his ear.

Lorian gave Tedric nothing but a wink in response before he set off again, and was soon lost in the mass of fairy guards that had entered and now barred the front doors of the throne room.

"Damn thief," Tedric muttered to himself, though he couldn't help a small smile from blooming on his lips as he entered the fight with a new sense of vigor.

A strange sense of calm settled into Tedric's troubled mind as he fought, blocking, parrying, and slashing whatever blade, human or fairy, came at him. He didn't know who he was fighting for anymore, nor for what cause. He only knew that if the Red King was not lying, and he was the storyteller's employer, Tedric couldn't allow him to leave with Egharis or the pages.

A harsh laugh pierced through Tedric's ears and he turned in the direction of the sound, finding the Red King looking at Finriel with amusement as she fought off a fairy with her dagger.

"Please, child, I know of your powers. You are just like your mother."

Tedric gulped and looked at Finriel, knowing that she would not be happy with the Red King's proclamation. Tedric cursed and ducked under a slashing blade, but looked up again as Finriel promptly shoved her dagger into its sheath and stalked toward the Red King.

"Finriel, don't!" Tedric yelled, but it was too late.

Finriel shot her hands out, and hot hair blew against Tedric's face as an enormous jet of fire exploded from her hands and headed straight toward the Red King. The Red King's smile vanished, and he raised his hands above his head before sweeping them downwards to the floor. The flame split in two a hair before it touched the king, and arced toward Tedric and the mass of fighting bodies behind him. Finriel cursed and flung her hands out toward the flame. Tedric gasped and stumbled backwards as a tendril of flame licked at his face before frigid cold air swept over the room.

"You fight well, witchling," the Red King said calmly, "but not well enough. I will get those pages from you and your little friends."

The Red King made another casual flicking motion with his hand, and Finriel flew backwards with a yelp of pained surprise before she landed on her back and skidded against the far wall. She sat up with a groan, and a faint trickle of blood ran from the corner of her mouth. The world staggered to a stop. Tedric hadn't known that the Red King possessed battle magic. He, like everyone else in the realm, had been led to believe that Adustio's dormancy spell had been cast upon the Red King before anyone else.

How many other lies am I going to face tonight? Tedric thought as he began to make his way toward Finriel, but Lorian shot past him before he took more than two steps. Tedric pivoted and swept back into the fight, deciding it best to stay hidden from the Red King for as long as possible. He knew he should be feeling angry at the betrayal of his king, the man who had helped him achieve something close to greatness. But he felt nothing, nothing except for the burning necessity to get his companions and the pages out of the castle and far away from Proveria. The blood moon shone ominously into the room, and Tedric shivered as a faint echo of song filtered through the window.

"Tedric!" Krete's voice made Tedric turn to find him dodging and darting his way past fighting fairies and humans as the gnome made his way toward him.

"We need to get out of here," Tedric snapped as soon as Krete approached, and the gnome cursed, wiping at a large droplet of blood that had sprayed onto his cheek.

"There's no way that I can let Suzunne out now," Krete said through gasps. "We can't risk someone taking the page."

"What about your portal stone?" Tedric bellowed, and Krete shook his head.

"I didn't have time to exchange it for a new one," he replied in despair. "It's got as much magic as a common pebble now."

"Krete, catch!"

Krete turned and reached out his hands just in time to catch a small blue stone that Lorian flung to him from across the wide room. Krete paled, and a strange mixture of both relief and anger crossed over his face before he whirled and charged toward Lorian.

"I told you to put the stone back before we left the portal room!" Krete yelled at Lorian, and Tedric glanced over his shoulder to find bodies, fairy and Ten alike, all quite occupied in the fight. He cursed under his breath and jogged over to his companions, finding Krete and Lorian engaged in a heated argument. He shot a glance toward Finriel, who aside from a few bruises on her right cheek and drying blood on her chin, looked in one piece.

"You stole from the portal chest," Krete yelled, and Lorian shrugged.

"You shouldn't have expected any less from me," Lorian replied, "and besides, now we have a way out of this place."

Krete opened his mouth to shout once more, but Tedric cut him off.

"Listen to me!" Tedric panted, and Krete took a step forward, ducking as an arrow flew over his head and bounced off the wide window. "Get Finriel and Lorian out of here, *now.*"

Krete paled and pointed behind Tedric's shoulder. "Fairy."

Tedric spun and ducked at the exact moment the head fairy guard slashed at the spot where his head had been a second ago. Tedric growled and shoved his sword into the guard's stomach, twisting and pushing it upwards into him. The fairy guard's eyes grew wide in pained surprise and he gaped down upon the blooming wound in his stomach.

"Don't *ever* touch me or my friends, understood?" Tedric growled to the fairy, and twisted the sword one last time before he wrenched it out and the fairy fell to the floor.

A pool of dark blood spread onto the floor around the beautiful fairy guard, and the air suddenly shifted, their surroundings now bathed in deep crimson light as the blood moon crested in the sky. Tedric gulped down the shock and adrenaline that pulsed through his veins and tore his gaze away from the fallen fairy. It was too late to think of what he had just done, and the repercussions that might follow.

Laughter and music filtered from the forest, and Tedric fought down a shaky laugh. The thought of fairies drinking and dancing as they celebrated their birth at the same moment bloodshed and death graced their capital was almost unfathomable.

"Make that portal," Tedric growled, and Krete gulped before nodding. "Make sure that he isn't disturbed," Tedric said to

Finriel, who, to his relief, also nodded and headed toward Krete, who was now huddled in a corner parallel to the window.

"What are you going to do?" Lorian roared.

A scream rang through Tedric's ears and, without thinking, he turned back toward the throne and Aeden. He took another step, but then remembered that Lorian had spoken. He spun toward the thief, resolve settling over him as he spoke. "I will find my own way out."

Lorian nodded, a sad smile growing on his face as he clapped Tedric on the shoulder. "Be safe, brother."

Tedric gulped and nodded, unable to reply. He glanced over at Finriel, who was standing in front of Krete, blocking his quick moving body from the rest of the room. She gave him a curt nod and a grimace that he knew was as close to a smile as he would get from her.

Tedric clenched his jaw and glanced back toward the fight behind him before looking back at Lorian. "Go, now."

Tedric didn't wait another moment, but instead made his way toward Aeden, blocking and slashing his way through the ever-growing number of fairy guards that continued to pour into the room. The Red King strode toward the back stairs of the dais, casually bringing up a hand and using his magic to send any unfortunate guards slamming against the ground. Tedric reached the dais, and he spared a glance down at the mayhem before them. There was blood everywhere, the once silver floor now covered in a blanket of crimson. The fallen were mostly fairy, but Tedric felt a stab of sadness at the sight of two fallen warriors of his own.

But Tedric could not save his men now. They knew how to fight, and they would do it well. The only thing on his mind was Aeden. He whirled back upon the scene before him. He strode toward her, the fear in her eyes pushing him forward. The guards held her tightly, their grip unrelenting no matter how much she resisted and thrashed against them.

"Let me go!" she yelled. "I am your princess!"

"Aeden, you are a shame to our kind. You have grown weak," the fairy king said as he slowly strode toward her. "For this, you must receive the worst punishment."

Aeden's scream was almost animalistic now as she thrashed and kicked against the guards holding her. King Sorren shook his head, though his face showed no sadness. "I did not wish to do this to you, but I can smell your weakness toward these companions of yours. I cannot have that weakness upon my throne."

All thoughts of portals flew from Tedric's mind, and he broke into a determined run as the fairy king's hands began to glow an icy blue and Aeden screamed in both fury and fear as her father reached for her. Tedric did not think as he lunged, striking his blade forward and up.

Metal drove into flesh, breaking bone and tissue. A surprised gurgle escaped from the fairy king's mouth as Tedric drove his blade through his stomach with a sickening sound. Warm blood pooled over Tedric's hand and he wrenched his sword out of the fairy king with a grunt of effort.

Aeden gasped, but Tedric wasn't able to tell if the sound was from horror or surprise before the guards detaining Aeden rushed toward Tedric. He easily disarmed and knocked them down as if they were nothing but weeds.

With her hands now free, Aeden ripped her sword from its sheath and took two long strides toward her father, who swayed upon his feet as he looked down upon the blooming wound in his abdomen. Aeden's blade connected with the king's already wounded stomach, and King Sorren's eyes widened as green eyes met their mirror.

"Why are you doing this?" King Sorren coughed, and his blood spattered across Aeden's cheeks.

Aeden pursed her lips and drove her blade upward into her father's chest. King Sorren let out a terrible wheezing sound and sagged against Aeden, who stepped back. The king fell to his knees with a loud crack, and Tedric could only watch in frozen horror as Aeden leaned down so that she was eye level with her dying father.

"I hate you," Aeden spat. "I hate you for never being a true father. I hate you for never listening to me." Aeden twisted the blade slightly, and foaming blood spattered against Sorren's lips, yet she continued to speak. "I hate you for blaming Kittia for my mother's death and sentencing her to die even though I begged you against it."

Confusion swam through Tedric at this. She had never spoken of someone named Kittia before. His thoughts were quickly disrupted, however, as another gurgling splatter of blood poured from the fairy king's mouth.

"Aeden, I—" Sorren gasped, and Aeden twisted the blade again, making him stop speaking abruptly.

There was no beauty left on Aeden's blood-spattered face as she spoke again. "I hate you for killing my dear Warren, and for making me watch your guard slit his throat because you didn't wish to get your hands dirty. Well, I suppose I never learned your lesson, Father, because my hands are dirty with *your* blood.

"I have been forced to betray and lie to every single person that I have ever loved because of you," Aeden continued bitterly, "and now, in order to defeat you, I have had no choice but to become you."

King Sorren took in one last rattling breath, and Tedric was able to catch his final words as he slumped against Aeden's blade.

"Forgive me."

Tedric opened his mouth, but was cut off as the ground began to shake. The walls rumbled around them, and Tedric lunged for Aeden, covering her body with his own as rubble fell around them. A faint pop sounded behind Tedric, and he let out a small breath of relief as he clutched Aeden's shaking body and looked around to find that Lorian, Krete, and Finriel had disappeared.

The rumbling strengthened and soon the ground felt like it might crack open. Tedric watched numbly as the wall facing the forest fell away into nothingness, revealing the blood-colored sky, bathing the room in its unearthly glow.

At once, Aeden shoved him away. Tedric gasped in surprise. He fell at the sight of her glowing eyes as she rose to stand while the castle crumbled around them. She began to shake, and Tedric watched as faint glowing veins begin to trace up her arms and neck, framing the corners of her cheeks and lips. Aeden tilted her head upwards and groaned, in pain or in pleasure, Tedric couldn't tell. As soon as the glowing began, it stopped.

The shaking slowed, and a blinding pain shot through the top of Tedric's head as a large chunk of crystal fell from the roof and crashed on top of him. He gasped as his vision blurred, and he had the faint sensation of falling before his cheek met the warm, wet floor. He blinked quickly and looked up at Aeden's blurred form as she came to stand over him. Tedric blinked again, but her face remained blurry no matter how hard he tried. Black splotches began to dance around his vision and he attempted to open his mouth to speak. Only a strangled groan escaped his lips, and Aeden crouched down before him. He could barely make out the sharp lines of her face now, the face of the woman he hated to love.

"You were right," Aeden said softly through the sudden silence, and Tedric heard faint footsteps approaching through his fading consciousness.

"I never break a promise," the Red King's calm voice rang out through the walls, and Tedric closed his eyes as the splotches in his vision finally gave way to complete darkness.

37

FINRIEL

F inriel's mind felt oddly blank as she, Lorian, and Krete sat huddled in the corner of a small pub that went by the name of The Horsehead Inn. Dim candlelight filled the wide room, and the roars of laughter and conversation coming from drunken men and women rang dully in Finriel's ears as she gazed down at the dented and scratched oak table before her. The pub smelled slightly of vinegar and sweat, but she supposed that it was better than the overwhelming tang of blood that had filled King Sorren's throne room.

Lorian had suggested the idea of teleporting to Fortula, the only human-ruled region of Keadora, before they had escaped the castle. His reasoning had been simple, Creonid was no longer safe for all three of them, and Fortula was close to many major traveling roads and ports, which led to a higher concentration of thieves and bandits passing through for easy jobs with good access in and out of the city. Therefore no one would question why they appeared to have just gone through battle.

And now, as she sat by Lorian's side with a mug of steaming apple cider in her blood-smeared hands, she could only think of Tedric and Aeden. Three bowls of stew had gone cold on the table, as none of them seemed to have much of an appetite. Lorian took a swig of ale, but Krete simply stared down at the dented and scratched table.

"I hope Tedric is all right," Finriel said quietly, speaking for the first time since teleporting from the castle.

Lorian nodded glumly. "He was too proud to leave the fight so soon."

Krete looked up at this, and Finriel noticed that his eyes were glassy with unshed tears. "He was trying to protect Aeden from the rubble as we left."

"I hope he ran her through, too. He's likely cursed from killing the fairy guard anyways," Finriel growled, and an ember of fire sputtered feebly in her stomach even through her exhaustion.

Krete shook his head sadly. "I had a feeling that she was hiding something, but I never expected her to do what she did." Finriel and Lorian remained silent as Krete took a fitful gulp of cider before speaking once more. "I knew that her father was a monster ever since I met him. It was part of the reason I grew so close to Aeden. I wanted her to have someone she could rely on other than her nan, though King Sorren killed the poor woman on Aeden's thirteenth birthday."

"What?" Finriel hissed, and Krete shook his head.

"She was sentenced to death for the murder of fairy queen Maidre, though both Aeden and I had come forth to Sorren with solid evidence of Kittia's innocence. Aeden watched her execution, as well as the private execution of her lover, also by her father's hand."

"I heard her say that name before we escaped," Lorian muttered, and Krete took another sip of cider.

"The murders of two people she loved were the last things that broke her relationship with King Sorren. It also broke the last bit of true happiness that I ever saw from her, but I didn't realize that the darkness had consumed her entirely," Krete sniffled.

"Why didn't you tell us that she was a princess?" Lorian asked, and Krete shrugged.

"Aeden made everyone attending the emergency council meeting swear an oath of secrecy to keep her true identity secret upon our acceptance of the quest, which I suppose should have been my first indication that she had ulterior motives."

"She was working with the Red King the entire time in order to control our quest," Finriel growled. "She knew who Egharis's employer was and she didn't tell us."

"We can only assume that the Red King is the mysterious employer," Lorian reminded Finriel with a tilt of his head.

"It's the only thing that makes sense!" Finriel hissed, attempting to keep her voice down through her sudden surge of anger. "Why else would he have come to Proveria? And the way he spoke as if Egharis was his property, it's the only logical answer."

Krete sniffled again, and Finriel's heart gave a feeble thump of sadness as she watched a single tear streak down his dust- and blood-smeared face. Silence enveloped them again for a few minutes, and Finriel took a small sip of cider with her left hand while Lorian clutched her other hand in his. She wasn't sure if it had been a conscious decision on his part when they had first sat down and his hand found its way to hers, but she hadn't pulled away. She was grateful that he had left the path before they'd been caught by the fairy guards, and she was happy to have him by her side.

"So, what do we do now?" Lorian asked through the silence.

"I need to return to Creonid and inform King Drohan of what has happened." Krete sighed. "Hopefully he can send a messenger to the elves before the Red King and Aeden decide on their next course of action."

A sudden idea sparked through Finriel, and she leaned toward

Krete. "You said that you have been to the Witch Isles before, right?" Krete nodded, and a spark of hope shot through the shadow of exhaustion and pain that shrouded Finriel's spirit. "Do you think they would have any information on the Red King that would be helpful to us?"

Krete tapped a finger on the rim of his clay mug and pondered for a moment. "They certainly might. I know that they don't like him much, which could help your cause."

"Excellent." Finriel smiled. "Maybe they could teach me as well. It would be helpful to actually know how to control my battle magic if I will be needing it in the future."

"Do you think that you will need to use it in the future?" Krete asked, and Finriel shrugged with uncertainty.

"I don't know. But it's clear from what Egharis said that the Red King isn't simply trying to play a sick joke on the realm."

A strange mixture of excitement and dread filled Finriel, and the thought of meeting her mother sent tired excitement thrumming through her veins. But she did truly need to learn how to fight properly after her dreadful performance tonight. The Red King had blocked her attack and blasted her onto her backside with nothing more than a flick of his hand. She took another swig of cider, feeling the steaming alcohol warm her up inside as she settled with resolve.

"You know that we're talking about war here," Lorian said quietly, and Finriel's excitement withered.

"Yes," she whispered.

"It's something that Raymara hasn't experienced for one thousand years," Lorian continued. "The people of this realm are not prepared for such a thing. I mean, I'm quite skilled with a blade, but it's only because I've been forced to use one. There are many in the realm who have never even seen a real sword."

"Then we must be prepared to protect those people," Krete replied with a new strength in his voice. "King Drohan was right.

We do have a lot more responsibility for the future of the realm than we thought."

Finriel swallowed the last bit of her cider, allowing for Lorian and Krete's words to settle into her skin. Krete was right. She was responsible for more lives than just her own now, and yet the thought did not bother her. It filled her with a strange sense of calm that she hadn't experienced before, as if she had been waiting for this to happen her entire life. Finriel glanced out of the dust-smeared window to the moonlit streets beyond. It was likely the first hours of the morning by now.

"We should get going then," Finriel said finally. "You can release Suzunne and get to Creonid before the town wakes."

The companions stepped out of the musty booth and flipped the hoods of their cloaks over their heads in a meager attempt hide their bloodied and bruised appearances. Lorian retrieved a gold coin from his pocket and placed it on their table, giving Finriel a wink as she frowned up at him. She had forgotten about him stealing from the old woman in Proveria. To Finriel's great surprise, she found herself feeling grateful for his misdeed, if only for the fact that they wouldn't get in trouble for being unable to pay for their meal. She had dealt with enough fighting for one night.

They filed out of the pub, and Finriel's nose was finally rid of the smell of old cider and sweat as fresh winter air brushed across her face. Lorian remained at her side as the three of them walked silently out of the pub and came to stand in the shadow of a neighboring building. Krete turned to face them with a shiver as a gust of cold wind blew through the street.

"You would do well to release your beasts once you get to the Witch Isles if what Egharis said is true," Krete said through chattering teeth.

Finriel couldn't blame him for being cold, as he had only his vest and bloodstained tunic to protect him. She dared to press herself closer to Lorian's side, and his warmth radiated into her shivering bones.

"We will," Lorian reassured the gnome with a tired smile.

"Good," Krete said, and gave them a sad smile. "I will portal to meet you two so that we can make further plans once I've given King Drohan the news."

"And please make sure that Nora stays safe and out of trouble," Finriel added, unable to ignore the pang in her chest.

"Of course," Krete replied. "I can bring her with me when I come to the Witch Isles, if you'd like."

Finriel gave him a nod. "Yes, I would like that."

"I will miss you two," Krete said after a moment with a small sniffle.

"Don't cry for me," Lorian chuckled jokingly. "We'll see each other again soon."

"Yes, well, I should get going and release Suzunne before people begin to wake up," Krete said with another sniff. "I look forward to our next meeting."

And with that, Krete turned on his heel and began down the street toward a rocky hill beyond. Finriel and Lorian stood in silence for a few minutes as they watched Krete's form grow smaller and smaller until he was nothing more than a speck at the crest of the hill.

"You've been quiet about what you are going to do now," Finriel said finally, turning to face Lorian. She couldn't fight the small jolt of nervousness that ran through her as his icy blue eyes met hers.

"What do you mean?" he murmured, and Finriel shrugged.

"You haven't said where you'll go next."

Lorian frowned. "I'm going with you, of course."

She shoved down a smile and her stomach gave a nervous flop. She couldn't deny that she was hoping for him to say those words, but it felt so much better to hear them come directly from his lips.

"I won't leave your side again, not even if someone tries to tear me from you by force," Lorian promised, and Finriel knew that he meant every single word.

He wouldn't leave her, not anymore. She could trust him, or at least continue to mend their once broken friendship. The ghost of his embrace rushed against her skin, and Finriel offered him a shaky smile. He returned it and stretched out a bloodstained hand toward her. She took it without thinking, and stepped forward to close the space between them. She let go of his hand and wrapped her arms around his waist, leaning her head against his chest. She didn't care that it was caked in dried fairy blood and crystal dust, she only cared about the warmth that radiated from him and the steady yet slightly quickened beat of his heart against her ear. He stiffened for a split second before his arms wrapped around her back in a comforting embrace.

They were a team once again, and in a way that was more than Finriel had ever dreamed of. She would never leave his side either, not even if someone tried to separate them. Lorian planted a soft kiss on top of her head and then spat, making Finriel look up at him with a frown.

"What?"

"You need to bathe," Lorian said, rubbing his lips together in disgust.

Finriel's smile widened, but Lorian's expression suddenly turned serious.

"As lovely as this is, I think we'd better find our way out. The Red King will likely have set the Ten on our trail by now."

The smile died from her lips, and Finriel let out a small sigh. That also likely meant that the Red King would eventually think of looking for her at the Witch Isles, if he hadn't already somehow blocked the the sea pass.

"Okay," Finriel said.

Lorian took a step back and smiled once more, though his half-shrouded gaze sent a shiver down her spine.

"Are you ready?" he asked, and Finriel nodded.

She took in a steadying breath and brushed a hand against the pocket of her cloak, knowing that her page was safely tucked away within the folds. She looked up at the now cloudless sky, taking in the beauty of the changing shades of purples and oranges as the sun began to rise. Though a heavy responsibility now rested upon her shoulders, Finriel found that she felt more confident and content than she had in her entire life. She would reunite with Krete again, and they would rescue Tedric. Together, she knew that they would find a way to save the realm from the Red King.

Finriel took a steadying breath, and to her own surprise, gave Lorian a true smile.

"I'm ready."

ACKNOWLEDGMENTS

It is an absolute dream come true that this book is a reality and out in the world.

I first want to thank Lorian, Finriel, Tedric, Krete, and Aeden for growing and evolving with me throughout these years. Thank you for allowing yourselves to change and be part of my healing, as well as the intense transition from teenager to adult.

Now, onto thanking non-fictitious people.

Mama, Papa, and Doug: thank you so much for raising me in a way that made following my chosen path a possibility. Thank you for your endless support and belief in my dreams. I feel forever grateful to be your daughter, and I know that none of this would have been possible without you guys.

Max Regan, writing mentor and friend. Thank you so much for your passion for this craft, and for helping me develop and turn this story into what it is today. I have learned so much from your bootcamps and our discussions, and I look forward to learning so much more!

Lisa Birman: Thank you for your eagle-eyed editing skills! I am so grateful to have been able to work with you.

To Travis Hasenour, who created the BEAUTIFUL map of

Raymara. You are so talented and this map is an absolute dream come true. It was truly a delight to work with you!

Thank you Damonza for the amazing cover. I was blown away by how quickly each change was made and the ease of working with you.

Thank you to the amazingly talented Gabrielle Ragusi, who illustrated Lorian at a time where my confidence in this story was at an all-time low. You truly captured the essence of my favorite thief, and it was so much fun to work with you and experience the process of your art!

To Raven, my adorable, silly, loud, and awkward dog. I know you will never read this because the only thing you know about books is that they make excellent chew toys, but just know that your presence was so important during the process of writing the last two drafts of this book. Your doe eyes and silly noises truly helped me feel loved and excited to keep going at times where it felt impossible to do so. I love you.

To Maggie Stancu: You seriously are the most supportive human being in the entire world, and I'm so glad that I stumbled across your Instagram writing challenge during NaNoWriMo 2020. You have been such a steady shoulder to lean on during the publication stage of this process, and I'm forever grateful for you. Your excitement and openness about how much you loved this world when I shared it with you truly means so much to me, so thank you.

To Madison and Connor: Thank you both for being so willing to talk about possible plot lines, plot twists, and strange names. I'm so grateful for your support and love throughout this entire process. I'm so grateful to be friends with two giant fantasy nerds who keep me feeling inspired and excited about being part of the writing world.

To my beautiful, amazing sister Iohanna, who pushed me to keep going and do what was right for me, not for anyone else. Thank you so much for sitting with me through countless mental breakdowns, and for helping me stand back up every time I fell. This book would not have been published without your guidance and endless words of affirmation. I am forever grateful for you and our ravishing conversations about new book ideas and grumpy fae men.

PRONUNCIATION GUIDE

Characters and Goddesses

Lorian Grey: LOR-ee-in Grey

Finriel Caligari: FEN-ree-el Ca-lee-GAR-ee

Tedric Drazak: Ted-rick DRAH-zah-ck

Aeden Siltra: Ay-den Sill-Trah

Krete: Creet

Egharis: Eg-GAR-iss

Agonur: Ah-GO-noor

Sorren: Soh-ren

Naret: Nah-ret

King Drohan: Droh-han

Kittia: Kit-ee-ah

Adustio: Ah-DOO-stee-oh

Anima: Ah-NEE-mah

Tellas: Tell-ah-s

Noctiluca: Noc-tee-loo-cah

Places

Keadora: Key-AH-dora

Proveria: Pro-very-ah

Farrador: Fair-AH-door

Crubia: Crew-BEE-ah

Drolatis: Drow-LAH-tis

Creonid: Crey-OH-nid

Lake Lagdranule: Lag-drah-nool

Naebatis: Nay-bah-tees

Anemoi: Anne-emm-mwah

Mitonir: Mee-THO-neer

Clelac Crags: Clay-lack Crag

Nivalis: Nee-vah-lis

Xeles: Sell-iss

Tiltha: Till-tha

Fortula: Fort-ooh-la

Things/creatures

Mogwa: Mow-gwah

Chimera: Kai-mare-ah

Sythril: See-thrill

Nian: Nee-on

Youl: Yool

Rakshasa: Rack-SHAH-sah

Veloria: Vel-oh-ree-ah

Meridiem: Mer-id-ee-am

Viure: Vee-oor-ay